G. Hamer

COMPLICIT

Acknowledgements

I've thoroughly enjoyed the journey of writing Complicit and all the research and local history and legend I've learned along the way. This story was originally inspired by the find of a gold treasure hoard near my home in Staffordshire but of course had to be adapted to fit the location and a period in history that has long fascinated me.

Again, I owe a huge thanks to my mum and dad for introducing me to North Wales and for all the opportunities. To Adrian for his constant support, loyalty and thoughtfulness. As ever, I owe a debt of thanks to my loyal bunch of writerly friends whom I rely on so much: Sheila Bugler, Amanda Hodgkinson, Jill Marsh, Liza Perrat, Kat Troth and a special mention for the many and varied talents of Jane Dixon Smith. Thank you all for sharing your skills with me and making this whole experience so great. And thanks also to various members of the Writing Asylum for their support over the years.

"The Druids held the symbols of the serpent and the dragon in the highest esteem and considered them insignias of royalty. These Servants of Truth held greater power than the kings who took advice from them."
—Michael Tsarion: The Irish Origins of Civilization.

Chapter I

MONA INSULIS, BRITAIN - AD 60

*C*rimson *eddies swirl around my legs, splashing sparkling tears of garnet across my thighs. Storm clouds join forces above me, darkening the already leaden sky. I am close. I know I am close. I push forward against the surging current, holding my cloak high, screaming my father's name.*

Cadadius ... Cadadius ... Cadadius!

My head pounds in time with a distant drumbeat. A tide of scarlet marches towards me, row after row of men far into the distance, swarming over our beloved land like ants. Rolling like a sea stained by a flaming sunset. Flashes of gold and white turn into rivers of blood, pouring down into the icy water.

Eyes closed, I pause, summoning all the powers of nature to aid me. I slip my hand into my pocket and grip the amber eagle amulet that was my mother's. I hold my wand of willow above my head, praying for the return of the sunlight, to show me the chosen path.

But there is nothing but murky greyness, swirling like smoke, and the choking smell of burning. I hear the screams of men. Hundreds, no, thousands of men. I smell fear and death, shit and blood.

'Awen ...'
The voice is distant and weak.
'Cadadius! Where are you?'
'Awen, help. Help me ...'
'Father! Show yourself ...'
Fronds of weed curl around my ankles as the water recedes. The smoke is thicker, clogging my lungs. The screams are louder. Metal clashing on metal and the terrified snorts of horses fill my ears. Shrieks of men, women and children cut the air.

I look down and the fronds are fingers. I recognise the amber ring on the forefinger, identical to my own. I grab my father's hand, hold it to my heart, willing my strength, every heartbeat, into him.

He lies on his back, eyes wide open. I fall to my knees and scream to Hu the Mighty. A gaping red wound across his throat leaks blood down the front of my father's white and gold robe. He opens his mouth, but only a gurgling noise rattles across the deserted shoreline.

His grip weakens. His fingers slip from mine. His eyes close.
'Father ... No!'
'Awen ...'
'Awen ...'

"Awen!"

She sat bolt upright, trickles of sweat soaked her back, sticking the thin cotton robe to her body. Her heart banged and her head drummed with the heavy thud of imaginary horse's hooves. Gasping, Awen grabbed her throat, holding back the scream that threatened to escape.

"My lady! Another vision?"

Gentle hands touched her brow, smoothed back long, blonde hair. A cool cloth, heavy with lavender, pressed against her face. She dropped back onto her pillows, licking her lips as the grip of the moment passed.

She looked up into the scared and watchful eyes of her servant, Ked.

"More powerful than usual," Awen replied. "But nothing to fear."

To her own ears, her voice was shaky, but Ked's frown dissolved as she lifted a cup of elder wine to Awen's lips. It was sweet and cold, soothing her burning throat, and she realised she must have been screaming in her sleep. No wonder Ked looked more like a frightened roe deer than usual.

"Would you like to break fast now?" asked Ked.

Awen shook her head. "I need to speak to my father, but I must first bathe. See to my things then send a messenger to ensure he is free. Tell him it is an urgent matter and I shall be visiting him before midday meal."

Ked nodded and retreated.

As the door closed, the strained smile slid from Awen's face. Although they had few secrets, she could never discuss her fears with Ked. This kind of news would shatter Ked's gentle and superstitious soul. Awen slumped back against the pillows, frowning as she pulled tangled thoughts from the back of her mind, wincing as she relived the most gruesome images. Sorting them into some kind of order, some kind of purpose, seeking the message she knew must be hidden there.

Awen carried her mother's gift as a seer, the most reputed of the priestess line. A 'seer derwydd' or oak seer they called her kind; the name from where all Druids originated. She was proud of her gift, and it had never once caused her to fear it since coming of age. But these past weeks, the gift had become her greatest torment, with prophecies visiting her every night, each more terrifying than the last. She had no doubt the battle she saw was real and already made its way towards Mona. It was time to confide in her father.

Awen turned onto her side, laid her face on her hands, and studied the world outside her small window. Through thick branches of budding lime oak leaves, the sun was already high in a clear, blue sky. The copse was full of the sound of woodland birds; the air heavy with the buzz of insects. Her stomach rumbled as the smell of cooking carried on the warm breeze – something meaty like boar, mixed with the fragrance of honeysuckle that filled the air. Although her body craved sustenance, she could not face food, not until she talked to her father.

It was a shame her mind was in such turmoil. This fifth month, Saille, was her favourite of the twelve stages. Long days and cool nights with all of nature displaying its charms. How could this beauty be tarnished by such fear?

She clutched her woollen blanket tighter. The cooling sweat made her shiver as she forced herself to recall the pinnacle of the vision.

The red scar and blank eyes.

Hard to admit, but if she believed with such certainty the battle to be real, then by association she believed the death of her father to be real too. She couldn't afford to put it off any longer.

Today she must tell her father, their leader, Chief Druid Cadadius of his forthcoming death. And today, he must listen.

Chapter One

"**B**loody hell, talk about the back of beyond."

Detective Sergeant Chris Coleman winced as he climbed out of the Volvo's passenger seat, hands on hips, bending back and forth with a pained expression.

"You're going to have to get used to these aches and pains now you've reached the big four-o, buddy." DS Gareth Parry slammed the driver's door and joined his partner. "Nice spot though," he added, nodding at the spread of blue in the distance, beyond the swaying grass, where the rolling waters of the Menai Straits led the eye into the shadow of Puffin Island beyond.

"Yeah, crackin' … if you want to be murdered in your bed, that is. I could've stayed in Liverpool for that." Coleman scowled. "What's the story?"

"Local farmer called in a 999 this morning. His wife had been down to the cottage with the weekly milk and eggs order. Found the occupant, an Iris Mahoney, dead. Drove back home in a panic and raised the alarm. Suspicious circumstances. That's all I know. First attending officer was Miss Eager-Beaver so all should become clear very soon …"

Coleman raised his eyebrows and rolled his neck. "Ah. Eager-

Beaver. No need for us then, mate. She'll have solved the crime and made an arrest by now."

Gareth smiled. "Ease off her, Chris, you were young once. A long time ago, granted, but still." He ducked as Coleman aimed a slap at his head. "Come on, let's go detecting."

They picked their way down the narrow path, around half a dozen meowing cats, all of which were doing their best to avoid capture by a uniformed WPC who was muttering obscenities under her breath as she chased, red-cheeked, around the garden.

"I'll do a quick once-over round the back, meet you inside," said Coleman, before disappearing under a gateway trellis, heavy with hanging blooms of roses.

Gareth ducked into the shadows of the hallway and followed the Common Approach Path already in place, leading through a door on his right. There was a stink in the air, one that no one could fail to recognise once smelt. The smell of death.

DC Megan Jones stepped forward, cleared her throat. "Morning, sir. It's a nasty one."

As Gareth's eyes adjusted to the dimness inside the room, he made out the figure of an elderly woman, arranged – not sitting, the angles were too awkward to be a natural pose – on an upright chair in the centre of the room. She wore fluffy pink slippers, with a rabbit's face on each toe, pitifully out of place in the horror of the room. Both arms were twisted awkwardly, restrained at each wrist to the arm of the chair, and her head was slumped forward, chin on the chest of a once white blouse now stained a vivid crimson down to her waist.

"A Mrs Morgan found the body; she's waiting in the squad car, but needs to make a move and is getting a bit tetchy. And Dr Connolly is taking calls in her car," added Megan as Gareth carefully picked his way full circle around the corpse. "I asked her to wait till you arrived before moving the body, but from initial examination she says the neck wound is the cause of death."

Gareth nodded, dropping to his haunches. "And murder weapon, what does she think we're looking for …?"

"She thinks you're looking for a kitchen knife, serrated edge, like a bread knife, around nine inches in length. And I'd say she died from blood loss, so the death wouldn't have been instant. She'd have suffered, the poor old thing."

Gareth looked up, feeling his cheeks begin to blush, noticing the pathologist in the doorway. "Susan. Hi. I didn't hear you come in."

"It's fine." She dropped her medical case on the sofa. Her eyes looked dark with worry. "Couple of points of interest I wanted to show you."

Gareth moved aside as Susan passed. He caught the briefest hint of her perfume; a fragrance he remembered. What had it been called? Lillies. No. Orchids. Something about orchids. Wild Orchid. Her favourite flower.

She pulled a pair of latex gloves from her pocket, and prodded the right wrist of the corpse. Gareth noticed a tremor in her hands. Something about this corpse seemed to affect the usually cool pathologist. Perhaps the elderly woman reminded her of someone in her own family, maybe someone she'd lost. Gareth made a mental note to enquire at a more appropriate moment.

Susan exhaled. "Handcuffs. Rudimentary. Bog-standard industrial cables ties, but she was definitely restrained. Same around the ankles."

Gareth nodded.

"And these … pretty gruesome." Susan held up a small plastic bag. "I picked them out of the carpet under the chair."

Gareth frowned. "What are they?"

Megan Jones leaned in close. "They look like fingernails. God, are they?"

Susan nodded. "A nice shade of pearlised pink nail varnish." She lifted the left hand; Gareth noticed a thin gold wedding band buried in the age-blemished skin of the third finger, before his eyes rested on purple shredded skin. "Left behind a hell of mess."

Gareth leaned closer. "They were pulled out while she was restrained?"

"Looks that way. No wonder there are tear streaks on her face, the poor love, it would have been so painful." Susan turned away. "God knows what she'd done to deserve that."

Megan Jones continued to make notes, the scratching of her pen loud in the silence. The steady tick of a carriage clock on the mantelpiece was the only other noise in the room, adding an ominous, yet strangely fitting, backdrop to the scene.

Megan voiced what everyone was probably thinking.

"Almost like she was interrogated under torture, don't you think, sir?"

"Perhaps." Gareth nodded. "Positive ID?"

"The cottage belongs to a Mrs Iris Mahoney. Seems quite likely she's the vic but it's not definite as yet."

"Anyone else living here?"

Megan shook her head. "I spoke to the postman by chance, took the mail off him." She gestured to a couple of brown envelopes on the window sill. "He was fairly sure she lived alone, no other post comes here anyway. Couldn't help with anything much, only been on the round a few months."

"So, can I get her moved now?" said Susan, slipping the evidence bag containing the fingernails into the side pocket of her case.

"Sooner the better. I was just waiting on Chris; he's gone off round the back somewhere."

"Someone using my name in vain?" The room seemed smaller as Chris appeared from the kitchen. "I've found a young lass hovering in the garden but she's clammed up on me. Can you go work your magic, pet?"

"Me?" Megan raised her eyebrows. "What do I know about kids?"

"More than me and you don't look half as scary. Well, most of the time." Chris winked. "She's with WPC Hewines. Seems she knows the old woman, seemed surprised I'd never heard of her actually."

Chris stopped beside the corpse, observing as Susan began snipping off each of the cable ties and bagging and tagging them in individual sheaths of plastic.

Gareth gave him a puzzled glance. "Why?"

Susan snorted. "Men. You mean you've never heard of Iris Mahoney?"

Gareth shook his head. "Should I?"

"*Y Ditectif Seicig*," said Susan.

"I know you try to impress folk with your bilingual skills, but it's lost on me."

"*The Psychic Detective?* It's a television programme that investigates old, unsolved crimes using witnesses from beyond the grave. She talks to the dead, contacts loved ones. Does live séances and all sorts. My mum went to see her on tour in Bangor. *The Psychic Detective* is the most popular programme on S4C. Iris Mahoney is ... was ... a world-renowned expert in psychic phenomena."

Chris raised his eyebrows. "Not that much of an expert. Clearly she didn't foresee her own death. Utter bullshit."

Susan shrugged, a flash of anger passing across her face. "Some don't think so."

"I'm afraid I agree with Chris," said Gareth, still studying the pathologist's flushed features. "But let's go and see what this girl knows. Chris, the farmer's wife who found the body is in the car, can you go and speak to her, she's keen to get off apparently."

Chris mock-saluted, ducking his head as he left through the front door.

"You want this one ASAP I take it?"

Susan began to unfold a plastic sheet, laying it in front of the chair, ready to begin the delicate process of removing the corpse, while disturbing as little trace evidence as possible.

"Please. It's going to be twice as messy if she's a celebrity, it's all we need. Call me if you find anything as I doubt I'll have time to attend the PM. Megan might want to be there though, if that's okay?"

"Sure. No problem."

Gareth paused as he headed towards the kitchen. "You okay, Sue? Long time, no speak. I keep meaning to catch up but you know how it is, time just runs away."

"Okay as in ...?"

Gareth shrugged. "Happy ... I guess? You seem ... distracted?"

Susan turned to face him. "What have you heard?"

"I ... Nothing. I mean ... what's to hear?"

Susan looked away. A little too quickly.

"I'm fine," she muttered. "And how about you? Are you ... okay? That seems such a trite thing to say. But are you getting over it, you know?"

He swallowed. Yes, he knew ... but best he lie.

"Getting there, time's a healer, you know the clichés."

"I know. And your family?"

"Pulling together, that's the important thing. My aunt is speaking to me now. Finally. Like I say, life goes on, one day at a time. You have to get on with it, don't you?"

Susan sighed, looked up, her eyes roamed across the corpse and then met his own, unusually bright as if tears were close. "We should go for a coffee. Catch up properly."

Gareth nodded; a shot of adrenaline fired through him. "I'd like that. Really. I'll text you, okay, but I'd better ... you know." He gestured towards the garden. "I'll be in touch."

Gareth's breathing quickened as he made his way through the dimly lit kitchen out into the brightness of the morning. He'd ached to talk to Susan Connolly almost every day since his cousin's murder; many nights he'd had one-sided conversations with her whilst alone in his flat. She always knew the right things to say, always had the best advice. He could talk to her like he'd never opened up to anyone else. She'd understand that he still woke most mornings in a cold sweat, haunted by the image of

Edwina, face down on the mudflats at Gallows' Point, with that slimy piece of lime green seaweed looped across her ear. He couldn't free himself of the vision ... or the guilt. And over the past year, he'd tried everything from alcohol to fitness regimes to one-night-stands.

Avoidance tactics, he knew that. He needed professional help but kept delaying the inevitable. If anyone could help him, it would be Susan Connolly. But every time he'd thought of calling her ... imagined her voice, her face, the exasperated look she'd given him so many times ... he also remembered the diamond engagement ring she'd been so proudly showing off when they last met.

In the garden, Megan Jones was deep in conversation with a teenage girl, both sitting on a low stone wall that bordered a compact, well-tended, vegetable patch.

Gareth approached, shielding the sun from his eyes with his hand, and fixed a smile. She looked about fourteen – going on twenty. Minimal make-up, but she didn't need it with her perfect skin and blue eyes, and blonde curls twisted into a knot on top of her head. She wore the shortest denim shorts he'd ever seen, showing off tanned thighs a supermodel would have died for. On top, a torn white jumper that slipped from one shoulder, revealing more nut-brown skin and the lack of bra strap. There was something of a rebel about her appearance, but there was no hiding the grief in her eyes.

Megan looked up. "This is Anna. Anna Brown. She was a friend of Iris."

"Hello, Anna. I'm sure this is a shock. I'm so sorry."

Anna nodded, sniffed, looked round for a tissue. Gareth was pretty sure there was nowhere she could have hidden them. Megan came to the rescue and offered across a small plastic pack.

"When did you last see Iris, Anna?" said Gareth.

The girl blew her nose. "Yesterday morning, first thing."

"And did she seem okay? Nothing worrying her you knew

about?"

"She was fine. She was going to make up a picnic and we were going to go out exploring on Saturday. She loved walking. We both did. We went miles together all over the island." She stopped and wiped away fresh tears. "I'll miss her so much."

Megan stroked her arm, offered a fresh tissue. "I know it's hard to talk about now. If you prefer we could come and see you at home, get a statement later –"

Anna scrambled to her feet, eyes bright with unshed tears. "No, please. My dad would … no, I don't want to make a statement. I can't. I mean. This is my fault. I told Iris what I saw and now she's dead!"

Sensing her intent, Gareth got to his feet a fraction of a second too late.

Anna backed away. "No … I-I don't know anything. Sorry."

The door of the cottage opened with a creak, men's voices and a roar of laughter reached them. Anger tightened Gareth's chest. Had they never heard of bloody respect? Two white-suited pathologists' assistants appeared from the gloom carrying a stretcher covered with the black plastic shape of a human being. Talk about timing, he thought, moving to one side to try and block the scene from the girl.

Susan Connolly appeared on the door step, fury on her face, sharp words hissed to the men whose demeanour changed in an instant. Susan looked across the lawn, raised a hand as a parting gesture. Her eyes locked onto something and widened; an unreadable expression on her face.

"No!"

Megan's voice shattered his thoughts.

In one quick movement Anna was gone; sprinting across the lawn, she cleared the garden boundary and disappeared into the swaying grass of the sand dunes.

Gareth made it as far as the wall. "Anna!"

Megan appeared beside him, panting. "Well, so much for my child-friendly skills. What was all that about?"

Gareth shrugged. "Search me."

He glanced back to the cottage, the door step empty.

"Sod it." Megan kicked out at a rhododendron bush, scattering cerise petals across the grass. "I'm sorry. I thought we were getting somewhere too."

Gareth squeezed her shoulder. "It's okay. No biggie. We'll find her."

"But what did she mean about her father? And what did she see?"

"No idea. But we'll ask her, don't worry. Come on, we've got a hundred and one things to be getting on with. Including a post-mortem I thought you might like to attend?"

Megan's face brightened and she quickened her step. "Absolutely."

Chapter Two

The sun breached the tip of the mountains of Snowdonia away to her right as DC Megan Jones negotiated her Nissan down the coast road to Penmon – but the splendour was lost on her. She loved Anglesey, it was her home, but she couldn't ooh and aah about the fantastic views and stunning coastline. She'd been born and bred in Holyhead; a family of four generations of fishermen, until the stocks dropped so low her father had been forced to sell the boat and take work on the railways. The beauty of the islands was part of her life but not something she admired on a daily basis; it was just there.

And while she'd never lose touch with her roots, she craved a chance to taste city life. One day she planned to get a transfer to London – the Met or even a specialist unit at Scotland Yard. That was her ambition. Not that she'd had the courage to tell her parents or her colleagues yet. She just had to keep chipping away, making her way up the ladder, one careful step at a time. CID already and only twenty-four; uniform had only ever been a stop-gap for her. She was not born to tread the beat. She knew what the men called her behind her back, but she didn't give a damn. They'd be laughing on the other side of their faces when she waved goodbye to Bangor and they were still grafting away in the same office as they approached retirement.

The same focused dedication drove her out of bed at 5.30am every morning. That was why she was now on her way back to the previous day's crime scene before the sun had fully risen. Megan needed to see the place again, one final time, as it would have been on a regular day – without the mask of horror and death. It was something she often did; revisiting the scene of crime once it had been cleared of the initial assault of professionals.

She parked outside Iris Mahoney's cottage and climbed out. The first thing she noted was the solitude, which pleased her. She'd had a worry the place would be crawling with press this morning. So far it looked as if they'd been lucky. Either the psychic's home address was a close-kept secret, or news had yet failed to reach the media hounds.

She stood at the gate, taking in the white-painted cottage, nestled in a dip in the sand dunes. Without the crowds of police and white-suited SOCO agents, the house looked quaint and homely, no echo of the previous day's horror. Yellow roses followed a green-painted trellis above the front door and across the side entrance; two small window boxes bloomed with multi-coloured pansies, and although the garden was basically a square patch of sandy grass, that too had been attended with care.

Megan turned at the sound of an approaching vehicle. A battered silver pick-up slowed to a halt and the window lowered. Pat Morgan. The farmer's wife.

"Morning. Back again? How's things going?"

Megan shrugged. "Hard to say, early days."

"But it *was* murder, so they're saying, word's all-round the village. And it ain't me that's been spreading gossip." Pat shook her head. "Though it had to be murder, I know, I saw the blood, didn't I? But it don't seem real, that's the thing, not real at all."

"I know. It's shock. If you need to talk to anyone, we have specialists –"

Pat shook her head. "No, no. That's not a worry. You see a fair amount of life and death on a farm. It's just evil. That's what's so shocking. Round here, you don't expect it. I said to Ted last night, I said, I dunno how we'll sleep in our beds until this bastard is caught and locked up for life ... excuse my French."

"Well, we'll be doing all we can, I assure you, and I don't think you've anything to worry about –"

"No? Burglary gone wrong was what I heard –"

"That's one line of enquiry; obviously I can't really discuss the case at the moment." Megan took a card from her jacket pocket. "I know you spoke to DS Coleman, but if you think of anything, or need to talk, give me a call, okay?"

The woman took the card with chapped fingers, and slipped it behind an elastic band that appeared to be holding the sun visor together. "He said I'd need to attend the inquest. Said I'd be called to give evidence."

"Probably. Not for a while yet. The inquest will be opened and adjourned. Besides, there's nothing to worry about, it's all standard procedure. You just have to repeat what you've already said in your witness statement and answer any questions the coroner may put to you."

Pat ran a hand through her cropped grey hair. "I know it sounds selfish, but I ain't looking forward to standing up in no court, being on show, it's not our way, see. We don't mix with them kind of folk. But then … poor Iris. She was a good woman. It's not like she asked to be butchered in her own home, is it? It's only right I do my bit to see the bloke pay for his crime, I suppose."

"Exactly."

"I still can't believe it. I mean who'd want to kill Iris Mahoney?"

"That's probably the hardest thing we have to discover, Mrs Morgan."

"Call me Pat, please, love. I said to Ted last night, I said, I wonder if she got her comeuppance for meddling in the occult. And he laughed, said I was daft, but I don't know as much. Besides, bet there's a fair few scroats would have had issues with some of the things she brought up on that television show. Bet there were a few arrests on cases re-opened after Iris Mahoney went meddling. Be interesting to know, eh?"

Megan nodded but stayed silent, not surprised the woman's train of thought was following their initial line of enquiry. Pat Morgan was no fool.

"Mrs Mahoney lived here alone, didn't she?" Megan asked, deliberately changing the subject.

"Yeah, Ted says she was one of them recluses. All alone except for her cats."

"What made you think she lived a reclusive life?"

"This little place." Pat nodded towards the cottage. "I mean it's quaint enough, but it's hardly luxurious is it? I'd have thought a famous TV psychic could afford something a lot grander, even have something built to her own tastes, you know. Like I say, it's a lifestyle choice she made, ain't it? And to my mind, to move to a remote spot like this is an odd choice for someone in the public eye who must be worth a bob or two. And then spend a small fortune on security. That alarm system can't have been cheap."

Megan looked up at the alarm as she mulled over the comment; there was something in the woman's words.

"How long had Mrs Mahoney lived in Penmon?"

"Not long. 'Bout three years, might be a bit longer. A newcomer by our standards."

"You don't know where she lived previously?"

Pat shook her head. "If I did, I've forgot. Sorry."

Megan nodded. "Did you ever see any visitors? Did Iris mention any family?"

"I never met anyone here, never saw her with anyone either. I did hear she was widowed young so perhaps there were no children? There were a few fancy cars parked in the lane from time to time. I supposed it was them television folk. I did see Iris driven away once in this huge black Mercedes with them tinted windows."

"Mrs Mahoney didn't drive herself?"

"Not so far as I know. I saw her on a bike once or twice; think she got a bus down to Beaumaris once a week."

"I met a teenage girl here yesterday, said she was a friend of Iris'. Anna Brown?"

Pat's eyes darted to her rear-view mirror. "Oh, Anna, aye, I know her. The lass from the Hall."

"Hall?"

She raised her hand, pointed away to the left. "Derwydd Hall. We're tenant farmers on its estate. It owns all this land, used to own this cottage too, till Iris came. Anna's dad owns the place, Matthew Barrington-Brown." Pat wrinkled her nose, checked her mirror again, eyes narrowed. "Anyway, I best be off. It's Farmer's Market in Beaumaris today."

Megan leaned against the gate, watching until the truck disappeared around the bend. Another reason for her early visit back to Penmon was to track down the elusive girl, Anna, and she'd succeeded. She'd felt guilty yesterday; the girl racing off like that as if the question about her home-life had pierced a nerve. Was it her imagination or had Pat Morgan given the impression she really didn't wanted to talk about Matthew Barrington-Brown and Derwydd Hall either?

In which case, that was double the reason for Megan to do so. However, she had to call it in. It would be a black mark against her name if she took on something like that alone and it backfired on her. And the wrath of DI Macrae was something seriously worth avoiding.

Still, she thought with a smile, she was looking forward to breaking news of her fresh line of enquiry to the rest of CID.

"Excellent work."

DI Macrae smiled and jotted Anna's name to the board in the incident room next to a photograph of Iris Mahoney taken from her official website. The intelligent-looking, bright-eyed face of an elderly lady smiled back at them. Her grey hair was coiffured, the make-up minimal yet perfect. It was hard to imagine the bloodied corpse from the cottage.

"An excellent lead, so I'd like you and Parry to get out to this Derwydd Hall as soon as we're finished here. Speak to Anna. Speak to her father ... if he sold her the cottage, he must have known Iris too. And there may be other people there who knew her. Ask around, see what you can find out. Seriously, good going, Megan."

She smiled and felt warmth travel from her cheeks down her neck as she consciously ignored the stares of her male colleagues.

"Thank you, sir."

There was something about DI Ian Macrae that demanded respect. Not just his soft-spoken Scottish accent or how he never raised his voice. Not the way he held himself or his impeccable dress sense and attention to detail. And not just his clear-up rates which were the envy of most forces across the country. No, there was something about the man himself that made you feel you were honoured to be in his presence, even more honoured to be selected as part of his team. Hers was only on a temporary basis, but she was determined to make it permanent. This was a big case. A murder enquiry. A perfect opportunity to get her name recognised. If it meant treading on a few toes ... well, so be it.

"Sir, I've looked up this Matthew Barrington-Brown fella." Chris Coleman's voice intruded into her daydream. "He has a fair bit of form. Couple of counts of Class B possession in the early nineties. Twelve months inside for identity theft in 1996. And, listen to this, two allegations of sexual assault that were subsequently dropped – by two different women."

Megan opened her notebook and began taking down the details, silently scolding herself for not doing a records check before making her big announcement.

"Quite a character, then," said Macrae. "Interesting."

"Looks like he's a bit of a conman, too," said Coleman. "Used several aliases. There's some cracking photographs, not camera shy, for sure that one. I reckon he's a right player."

"He might be all of those things and more," said Macrae. "But don't let it cloud your judgement. We have absolutely nothing to connect him to this murder, not a scrap of evidence, so don't get carried away."

"Other than Anna, sir. She did react pretty violently," said Megan. "And she mentioned her father totally unprompted."

"Yes. I read your notes. I'm just saying go in with an open mind. There are thousands of scallys out there, very few are murderers. It takes a very different mind-set to kill."

Megan nodded, remained silent.

Gareth Parry looked up from his computer screen. "Sir? There's something else. I thought that Derwydd Hall name rang a few bells too."

Macrae pulled out a chair, hitched his trousers and took a seat next to Megan. The subtle aroma of expensive aftershave drifted across, filling her nostrils. He rested his right ankle on his left knee and adjusted the hem of his trousers.

"Spill," said Macrae.

"Derwydd Hall is a commune, or retreat – some might actually say cult – that's run by Barrington-Brown. It's very hush-hush, not for the likes of us if you know what I mean. You need a fair few zeros on your bank balance to get a place at Derwydd Hall. That's always been the rumour anyway ... but I can't say I've ever looked into the place before. It's got one hell of a fancy website. Most of it members only and password protected ... but it boasts that Derwydd is the only guarantee to 'achieving one's precise path and understanding one's true spiritual nature.'"

Coleman hid a cough behind his hand. "Bollocks."

Macrae smiled. "Open minds, gentlemen. And besides, I'm not too sure I understand even now I know what the website blurb says. Seems like you two may be in for an interesting afternoon; this Mr Barrington-Brown sounds a delightful individual. Make sure you know enough about this cult, religion, whatever, not to be floored by it when you get there." The DI got to his feet and returned to the white board. "The other item we touched on briefly yesterday. Chris, I want you to follow up this psychic detective thing. Contact S4C and get some recordings of this programme, and at the same time find out if she has an agent or management company. And dig around, see if there are any high-profile cases she may have been involved in. Get your contacts to talk, find out if she made any local enemies."

Coleman nodded as he made a list. "Sir."

Macrae looked up as he finished ticking off the items on his fingers. "I think that's everything covered. Anyone else have any thoughts?"

Megan held up a hand. "Are we sure this isn't a random robbery that went wrong? You seem quite certain this was premeditated, sir."

"Not certain, not at all. My instinct is this was premeditated. The handcuffs more than anything ... and the nails ... almost like she was being interrogated under torture." Macrae shrugged. "I don't know, but just now all options stay open. That's why I hope Chris might dig up something useful. If it was a burglary that went wrong, she's high profile, so let's hope someone knows about it." He paused, looked around the room. "Any more questions?"

Three heads shook in unison.

"Okay then, let's get cracking."

Chapter II

MONA INSULIS, BRITAIN - AD 60

"On your feet, you lazy bastards!"

Centurion Marcus Sextus grimaced as a masked soldier strode into the makeshift arena, leading two shackled slaves. Heckles echoed around the campsite; whistles and jeers rose like heat haze. Despite the bronze faceplate, Marcus knew the master of ceremonies was Centurion Sabinus, not one of his most favoured comrades.

Sabinus took his job far too seriously, playing to the braying crowd like Rome's greatest gladiator instead of the snivelling hypocrite he was. Marcus sighed, looked away in distaste, putting up with the event for the sake of his men, knowing it was well-needed entertainment.

After three full days guarding the narrow stretch of water across to Mona without a single break, Legate Lucius Bestia had named a day of relaxation for the returning men. Rested, well-breakfasted, the first event was a bout of mock-gladiatorial combat. They may not have any of the real super-star Gladiators to hand in this small northern outpost, but they had plenty of noxiis and slaves eager to grab the slightest chance of freedom.

Sabinus dragged the two unwilling men to the centre of the

circle.

"On my right," he bellowed, lifting the man's limp arm as high as his shackles would allow, "we have a trained swordsman, the best of the Britons, so they say. And on my left, a wild Celt warrior who fancies himself handy with an axe. Gentlemen, if you would like to place your bets, the fight shall commence shortly!"

Both men slumped to the ground. Naked, apart from small leather loin guards, they were weighed down by heavy chains joining wrist to ankle. Sabinus marched from the circle to the shouts and jeers of the hundred or so men now scurrying to place bets with the camp prefect.

"Are you not placing a wager, Marcus?" asked Titus, his optio.

Marcus shook his head. "I still live by my father's rules, and he forbids any form of gambling in our family. Besides, I have better things to waste a week's pay on than the life of some poor bastard."

Titus nodded, his eyes flashing to the jostling line of legionnaires.

Marcus smiled. "But ... if I were a betting man, I'd put my money on the Briton. He is fit and agile, well-trained and has that killer instinct, I suspect."

"Really? But the Celt is twice as big, built like a bathhouse!"

"And slow and clumsy as one too. No, the Briton would get my money. *If* I were a gambling man."

Marcus sat back, crossed his legs at the ankles, and waited. Titus watched the line dwindle as men retook their seats ready for the fight to begin. A nervous energy ran through the crowd; the hum of voices and laughter a welcome relief from the tension of the past days.

Titus sighed and rubbed his hands down the front of his tunic. But he stayed in his seat.

Marcus leaned forward, close to Titus's ear. "You best hurry, lad. It will be starting soon."

Titus jumped, turned with a grateful grin. He was on his feet and gone before Marcus could respond. He raised his leather canteen and took a long pull of water, lifting his tired face to the bright sunshine. A strong north-westerly breeze blew salty air through the camp, and it helped clear the fog of his mind. The past weeks had been gruelling; the mountainous journey to get to camp among the worst conditions he'd experienced. On top of that, the fear of the battle to come weighed heavy on his mind. These local tribes had reputations no sane man would ignore, and rumours were they amassed many hundreds of men. Yet, he knew they had no choice but to take them on. Defeat was not an option. No one stood in the way of the progression of the Roman Empire.

Today, the mountain landscape looked magnificent against the blue sky, so different to the fog-draped, rain-lashed nightmare of the journey. For the first time since they'd crossed this hostile land, Marcus saw the country in all its pride. And for the first time, he realised its potential and saw why the local tribe guarded their small island with such fierce resilience.

Titus took his seat as Sabinus re-entered the arena. Handing each man a weapon, he freed them from their chains. For a second, Marcus saw a flash of fear in the Celt's eyes and knew he'd been right. The Celt scanned the crowd, seeking any escape through the barrier of men. Then his shoulders slumped as he weighed up his options, knowing he had none but to stay and fight for his life.

The Briton was blond-haired, lithe, and quick on his feet. The Celt was taller, stockier as Titus remarked, like a juvenile bull – but not yet fully formed. His head and body were covered with short dark curls, and his beard made him look older. But neither was much older than Titus. Early twenties, if that.

Knees bent, they circled each other slowly like two wild beasts as Sabinus backed away from the centre of the arena, one arm aloft.

As he reached the perimeter, his arm fell. "Begin!"

At the cry, the Celt lunged forward, the blade of his axe glinting in the sun as he swung it round his head. The swordsman held his ground, parried the shots effectively. The ring of clashing metal loud in the air. Men were soon on their feet, whistles and cries circled Marcus as the excitement mounted. The Celt thrashed forward again; this time the axe found its target, catching the Briton on his shoulder-blade. Stunned for a second, he fell to his knees, head lowered. As the Celt charged in for the kill, the Briton sprang to his feet, burying the hilt of his sword into the other man's thigh. The Celt spun in a slow circle and crashed to the ground in a cloud of dust.

"Ha!" Marcus clapped his hands. "A good actor. Bravo! This is a good match."

"Get to your feet, you lazy bastard, before he guts you!" cried Titus, his face blood- red and his fists clenched as he punched the air. "Get up and fight like a man!"

Marcus grinned at his optio's intensity. Truth was, Marcus too was a good actor. He did not have the stomach for such games. His honour as a soldier differed from his fellow men; differed in fact, from most of the men of Rome. He had long understood and accepted that. Killing was a necessity of his job, yet Marcus found it distasteful to see it used as sport. But in this environment it was a secret he kept close to his heart.

A shadow passed across the dusty ground as a man appeared at Marcus's side; he recognised him as a camp messenger.

"Request from the legate, sir. He'd like to see you in the staff tent."

Marcus checked behind him, then looked up into the man's dark eyes. "Me?"

The messenger nodded. "At your earliest convenience, sir."

Marcus jumped to his feet, knowing the politeness to be a veiled order meaning 'now' and also glad of the excuse to get away from the arena.

As he crossed the camp, the slave's cries reached a crescendo of blood lust. He looked back in time to see the Briton raise his sword above his head, before plunging it into the heart of the prone Celt. He turned away and wiped his brow.

The messenger held back the tent flaps and announced his arrival. Marcus stooped to enter the cool dim space. As he straightened, he saw the legate at his desk. Another taller man turned, stepping forward from the shadows.

"Uncle!" Marcus cried, heading towards the man. He stopped in his tracks as he read the other's facial expression. Marcus glanced at the legate's frown. "Forgive me, I mean, Commander Suetonius Paullinus, a pleasure to see you, sir."

The man nodded and hid a brief grin behind his hand. "And you, Centurion Marcus Sextus. You are well?"

Marcus nodded. "Yes, sir."

Legate Bestia cleared his throat. "Your uncle has arrived to take charge of the invasion of Mona, Marcus. It has been agreed your century is to be involved in the initial assault. It will be tomorrow morning at first light. Make sure your men are well rested and fed. We leave one hour before dawn; it is a thirty-minute march to the crossing point. Horses and boats will be waiting for you there; we are working under the cover of darkness to gain the greatest advantage."

"We are not crossing here?" Marcus asked.

"No, this is a ploy to confuse the Celts," said Paullinus. "And you have done a good job holding their attention while supplies and equipment have been put in place down water. Tomorrow, I will lead the men and then I must take my leave. Matters in the south are becoming more pressing with each passing day. I know under Legate Bestia's eye you will see my work is carried through. I put my trust in you, Marcus Sextus."

Marcus bowed his head. "Thank you, sir."

"Now, see to your men. I hear there is disquiet among the camp, fear and dread about a clash with the Druids. Stamp on those who spread such gossip, Marcus. Make it clear this assault is vital and they shall be honoured for their part." He paused, adjusted his tunic, adopting a softer tone. "And be ready to march before dawn. There will be no trumpet call; we shall leave quietly by the mountain side of camp, away from the Celt spies. Do you understand?"

"Yes, sir. My men will be ready."

"Good." The commander stepped forward, held out a hand. "Until tomorrow, nephew."

When Marcus reached his tent, he found Titus slumped in the shade of the awning, spooning food from his mess tin, a scowl heavy across his brow.

"What's with the long face, Optio?" he asked, dropping down beside Titus and inhaling the delicious aroma of food.

"I should have listened to you. Two weeks' wages it cost me."

"You bet on the Celt?" Marcus shook his head. "You bloody fool. You have a lot to learn about the art of fighting *and* the art of reading men, young Titus."

"Yes, sir."

"Something smells good," Marcus said, nodding to the mess tin.

"Hare stew. It's delicious," said Titus, greasy juice dripping from his chin.

"Good. Then get me some. We need to fill our bellies tonight. I'm not sure when we shall see our next meal."

Titus stopped chewing and stared, his eyes questioning.

Marcus nodded. "We leave before dawn."

Chapter Three

Tall wrought-iron electric gates blocked the driveway to Derwydd Hall. The centrepiece of each gate was a gold and green circular crest, with the name Derwydd encircling what looked like an oak tree, bordered by an intricate knot design.

Gareth leaned out of the driver's window of the Volvo and looked for a button or microphone ... or anything. "What are we supposed to do here, then?"

Megan Jones tugged her seatbelt and leaned forward, forehead almost touching the windscreen. "There's a camera up there." She pointed to the far side of the gates; a small black lens concealed in a clipped hedgerow. "It moved from left to right, like it's reading the number plate or scanning the car or something."

Gareth opened the door and leaned out. "Hello." He waved at the hedge. There was a discreet buzz and the lens twisted in his direction. He dug his ID from his pocket and held it up in front of his face. "Police. We'd like to speak to Mr Barrington-Brown."

Another buzz, the camera shifted. Then, from the heavens, a male voice. "Good afternoon. Welcome to Derwydd. Can we assist you?"

Gareth dropped back into the car, slammed the door. "Police. We'd like to speak to Mr Barrington-Brown."

"I see. Could I take your names please? Do you have an appointment?"

Gareth sighed. "No, we don't have an appointment. We're police. Could you open up please?"

A pause. "I'm sorry, I didn't catch your names?"

"That's because I didn't give them." He clenched the steering wheel. "Look, I could tell you our names were Holmes and Watson or Poirot and Marple, what difference would it make? Your boss will never have heard of us. You've seen my ID and have probably done a DVLA check on the car by now. It's clear who we are. So, this is my final polite attempt at gaining entry. Do you understand?"

There was more static, a mumble, and the gates slid silently open.

Megan chuckled. "That was a good start. Not exactly welcoming. Hope we don't have more trouble getting out of the place. I've heard about these cults ..."

Gareth smiled as they drove along an immaculate gravelled driveway, bordered by flat lawns and endless concentric rows of high yew hedgerows – both trimmed to within an inch of their lives. A few minutes later, the drive made a left turn, and the hedgerows disappeared.

"Wowsers," said Megan, her eyes wide and face animated.

Gareth thought, not for the first time, that Megan Jones could be one hell of a looker if she tried. A bit more make-up, maybe let her hair down once in a while, literally, and wore something different to the unflattering trouser suits she favoured. She hadn't the thighs or ass to pull them off with any degree of success – but that was an opinion no doubt best kept to himself.

"Wowsers, indeed." He nodded. "What a stunning building. Tudor, you reckon?"

Megan shrugged. "Not a clue, but it's certainly beautiful."

Gareth gave a low whistle as Derwydd Hall gradually appeared through the late afternoon heat haze like a fairytale castle rising from the ground. To his untrained eye, it looked as if the hall had been built in stages; the wings on each end were a darker reddish brick in comparison to the more rounded central section. The drive took them over a bridge, where crystal clear water bubbled over moss-covered stones, and ended in a circular car park, the centre point of which was a white marble fountain.

As they climbed out, a figure appeared at the top of the steps leading to the front door. A thin man, mid-forties, salt and pepper hair and beard, with a deep tan and sharp, intelligent eyes. He was dressed all in white, cotton trousers and long shirt, edged on the collars and cuffs with a gold-coloured design.

He smiled and held out a hand as they met on the bottom step, squeezing Gareth's hand with both of his in a way that made Gareth think of his local priest back home.

"Hello. I'm Matthew. I believe you wanted to speak to me."

Gareth nodded, waited while Megan showed her ID. "DS Parry and DC Jones, we have a few questions. Is there somewhere a bit more private we could go, Mr Barrington-Brown?"

The man lowered his chin in an apparent gesture of humility and clasped his hands in front of his chest. "Here, I am simply Matthew. Out there –" He raised a hand in a sweeping gesture. "I am a Barrington-Brown. Alas, today is an important day at Derwydd. A meeting of the elders. It is with regret that I cannot allow you access to any part of the Hall until after the meeting. Which ..." He tugged up a gold cuff to reveal the face of a diamond-encrusted salmon-coloured Rolex. "... will be starting very soon. The guests are imminent and I'm afraid it is part of our protocol that I be here to meet them. If you'd care to call and make an appointment, I will be more than happy –"

Gareth took a step forward. "And it's part of our protocol to ask questions as and when we need. Especially in the middle of a murder enquiry. I'm sure you understand. Now, if we aren't allowed inside, how about we have a stroll through your lovely gardens and chat as we go?"

Another glance at the Rolex. "My guests –"

Gareth turned his back and headed towards an archway in the long wall at the side of the house. "This way, is it? Sooner we get going, sooner you can be back to greet them."

Gareth saw Megan hide a smile as she hurried to keep up with his pace. Seconds later, as they followed a path that hugged the high wall, Barrington-Brown caught them up. Voices, laughter and the clink of glasses travelled across the lawns. On the rear terrace, beside a huge set of double French windows, two men and two women dressed in uniform lilac-coloured shirts and trousers, were busily arranging glasses in regimented lines on a pristine white table cloth. Gareth recognised a row of Krug champagne bottles. No expense spared on today's elders it seemed.

"Quite a party," said Gareth, nodding to the terrace. "Almost tempted to stay and join in the fun."

"Much as I would love you to experience our hospitality here at Derwydd, I'm afraid that wouldn't be possible. Today's meeting –"

"I know. The elders. You said. I'm pulling your chain, don't worry. We'll try not to inconvenience you too much; we'd like a quick chat about Iris Mahoney. And then we'd like to speak with Anna please."

The man's expression changed. Not at the mention of the murder victim, but at his daughter's name. Gareth looked at Megan. From her face, she'd seen the change too.

"I'm afraid that won't be possible," said Barrington-Brown. "Speaking to Anna, I mean. She's not here at the moment. Please, come through, there are benches in the kitchen garden."

A narrow archway led down stone steps, out of the sunlight, into a shaded vegetable garden. Twisted vines of fruit bushes lined one wall, still in direct sunlight away to their right, budding raspberry and strawberry plants. Bees buzzed from one to another, and the air was heavy with the scent of lilac from the row of purple-blossomed trees dotted along the path.

Megan frowned. "We spoke to her yesterday."

"Yes, she left this morning. A week with a school friend at the family villa in the South of France. I try to break up the summer holidays for her. I'm aware it must be tiresome being stuck with me all the time; she needs to mix with people of her own age more. Believe it or not, it's a battle to get Anna to make friends."

"I believe she had a friend in Iris Mahoney?" said Gareth.

Barrington-Brown frowned as they reached the first green-painted bench. He sighed as he lowered himself onto the seat. Megan sat beside him while Gareth observed from a spot on a low wall opposite.

"Yes. And I have to admit it didn't really meet with my approval, but Anna said she was happy. Besides, she's such a headstrong child; she would have ignored me even if I'd forbidden them to meet."

"What was your problem with their friendship?"

The man raised his eyebrows. "I'd have thought that was obvious."

Gareth shrugged. "Not to me. I can't see how Mrs Mahoney would have been a bad influence."

"No? You knew Iris Mahoney, did you?"

Gareth looked up at the sharp tone, determined to match it. "No, sir, clearly I didn't. She was dead when I first met her. Why don't you tell me?"

Barrington-Brown seemed to make a deliberate point of relaxing his shoulders. "It wasn't just the age thing. I think I'd been aware for a while Anna craved female company, so I should have been glad she'd found a role model. She seemed to go out of her way to detest every nanny and au-pair I employed." He sighed, ran a hand through his hair, focused on a point in the far distance. "Anna is a difficult child, yes, but it's not her fault, not really, and I try to recognise that. She lost her mother at an early age. Five. I don't think either of us ever really got over it. For every step I take forward in our relationship, I seem to slip a half dozen back." He paused. "I think I was jealous of the bond she seemed to find with Iris. But my concerns about their friendship go much deeper than just that or the age difference. I assume you know about her reputation as a psychic?"

Gareth nodded, trying to fight the urge to dismiss all this soul searching as melodrama. For a man surrounded by intrigue and secrecy, this unprompted admission of the breakdown of his family life seemed too painfully honest to be appropriate.

"It's something I oppose very deeply on a personal level and also through our teachings here at Derwydd. And because of that, and Anna's need for rebellion I suppose, she went out of her way to spend every available moment with Iris. Because she was aware how much it would irritate me, I suppose."

"I see." Gareth waited while Megan caught up with her note-taking. "How did you hear about Mrs Mahoney's death?"

"Anna came home in a state yesterday. Borderline hysterical. I was shocked of course, although I don't know the facts. I didn't know it was murder though …?"

"We're keeping an open mind at the moment." Gareth looked around the neat rows of cabbage, leeks and carrots; round silver-skinned onions that reflected the sunlight. "When did you last see the victim?"

Barrington-Brown exhaled, opened his palms. "Sorry, I have no idea. Weeks ago probably. I saw her occasionally in Beaumaris. We'd exchange pleasantries, we could manage politeness, but we weren't friends. I think she probably had a low opinion of me and vice versa."

"Why?" asked Megan, looking up from her notes.

"I thought I said, I didn't approve –"

"No, sorry, I mean, you said you thought Mrs Mahoney had a low opinion of you. What made you think that?"

He shrugged. "I don't know. Maybe things Anna had said about me? She often threw that at me in arguments … that Iris had said such-and-such. Like I said, I was jealous and angry, things always seemed so awkward." He looked up, fixing his gaze on Gareth. "Jealous, angry, worried. All those things. But I didn't kill her."

"She bought her cottage from you?" said Gareth.

"Yes. It used to be part of the estate; we rented it out to guests, but then the recession hit and I decided to sell off some of the assets to raise capital needed for repairs on the big house. Iris paid the asking price. We met once back then I think; mostly it was dealt with by our respective solicitors." He made a show of checking his watch again. "I understand how important your enquiries are, believe me, but I really must go and greet my guests. Is there anything else I can help you with? I assure you I've seen or heard nothing at all about Iris's death, other than via Anna. If I could help, I would, I'm sure that goes without saying. It's awful to think of that poor woman, out there, alone. I would wish her no ill-will."

Gareth got to his feet. "I have to ask where you were the night before last, sir, between the hours of nine pm and midnight? It's purely procedural."

Barrington-Brown frowned as he stood and brushed the seat of his trousers. "I was here. I suppose your next question will be if there were any witnesses? Well, yes, in fact I had a staff meeting, running through the arrangements for today with my PA and the house-keeper and security. That ended about 8pm, then I had dinner with Anna, and then spent the rest of my evening alone in my study. I can assure you I was nowhere near Iris Mahoney's cottage and I have no motive or inclination for murdering the woman either. Is that all?"

He held out his hand in a determined manner.

Gareth shook it. "For now. Thank you. When do you think we will be able to talk to Anna?"

"She flies home a week tomorrow. I'll ask her to contact you."

"Okay. Here's my details."

He took the card with a curt nod and began to walk away, across the lawn towards the French windows.

"Sir?" Megan called after him. "This trip of Anna's. Was it

very last minute?"

He stopped, turned, focused on Megan as if seeing her for the first time. "No. Why?"

"I spoke to Anna yesterday. She said the last time she spoke to Mrs Mahoney, they'd made plans to go on a picnic together ... tomorrow. This Saturday, she said. Why would she say that if she knew she'd be in France?"

Barrington-Brown licked his lips, showed his teeth in an attempt at humour. "Teenagers. I'm assuming, detective, you're far too young to have children of your own. One day maybe you'll understand the complexities of the teenage brain." He turned away, dismissing them again.

"Er, sir ..." Megan called. "That doesn't really answer the question, does it?"

There was no hint of the smile when he turned back. "Doesn't it?"

Megan stood her ground. "No, sir."

"Well, I'll try and make it a little simpler. Anna was a scatterbrain. She most likely forgot. Some days I don't think she knows if it's Tuesday or Christmas."

"Really? She didn't come across that way to me."

"Then you really didn't get to know my daughter at all in the *very* short time you spoke to her, did you?"

With that, he strode away, increasing the distance between them, preventing any further attempt at communication.

"Well ..." said Gareth.

"Yes, that's one word. Knob is probably a better one."

Gareth smiled. "Very astute, DC Jones."

Megan shoved her notebook in her bag, hard. "If that kid is screwed up, then you don't have to look far to find the source. No wonder she spent time with Iris Mahoney, probably the only bit of normality she got in her life. Her father's so far up his own backside, he most likely wouldn't recognise his daughter if she walked past him in the street."

"You can't say that, it could be a front. Why the dislike, it's not like you?"

Megan shook her head and buttoned her jacket. "I don't know. He rubbed me up the wrong way. He's all show, isn't he? Especially about Anna. For all his fancy words, all his 'call me Matthew', I get the feeling this place and what goes on here is far more important to him than his daughter's happiness. Clearly he thinks employing a string of au-pairs will cure all his problems, and then he's shocked when it doesn't. The poor kid probably just wants to be loved."

Gareth glanced sideways, both in admiration and concern. There was a passion in Megan's voice he'd never heard before, but her summing up of the situation was almost an identical interpretation of his own. For such a newbie, and a *young* newbie at that, she had all the right instincts and was beginning to show excellent people skills.

"You're very cynical for someone so young, you know."

"Cynicism has nothing to do with age. I hate false people and hypocrites. And I'm always extra critical when people divulge personal information like that straight off. I mean, it's not normal behaviour, is it? People tend to paint the best picture possible in general – that kind of deep, personal stuff you keep for close friends and family. It's more likely, talking to us, they'd make it sound like it was the least acrimonious divorce, or having your heart broken was a great learning curve. See? It's human nature to gloss over the cracks."

Gareth nodded. "So, you're thinking if that's his best attempt at glossing over the cracks … what is the real story?"

"Exactly."

"I'm impressed, Megan. I never knew you were so good at reading people … or kept such strong opinions to yourself. You should let go more often, it could be the making of you."

Megan shrugged. "It's not a deliberate thing, it's who I am." They passed a small gardener's hut, the door ajar. She gestured inside. "See that spade? It looks like a spade, works like a spade. So, why call it a hose pipe? That's me. The world would be a lot simpler if everyone were the same."

Gareth grinned as they stepped out of the shadows of the vegetable garden and into the sunlight. "Well, for the record, I'm not going to argue. I think you're right about Anna too."

"Did you notice she called herself Anna Brown, not Barrington-Brown? Another deliberate attempt to distance herself from her father. Having met him, I can see why. I understand her reaction to our questions too; she must have known what her father's response would be. Poor kid."

"What I don't see is why her father would have such a knee-jerk reaction to sending his daughter away," said Gareth. "And if he did ... I don't know ... have a sudden feeling he needed to protect her or whatever ... why lie about it? I can't say Anna came across as a scatterbrain who didn't know what day it was."

"No, me neither. I think she was unhappy, and not just about Iris's death. But if they were close, surely she would have wanted to be around for the funeral, not whisked away to some friends' villa. What happened to her being headstrong?"

"Trouble is, we only have his word, and it could be the truth. The holiday could have been arranged and she might have forgotten. Oh." Gareth paused as he reached the Volvo. "I think we need to beat a hasty retreat, it looks as if *the elders* are arriving."

As they climbed into the car, a steady stream of vehicles rolled across the bridge, parking in synchronised rows around the car park. It was a car enthusiast's paradise. Bentleys. Aston Martins. Maseratis. And a good assortment of cars he didn't recognise.

"I think this deserves another wowsers," he muttered.

"You think? Makes me itch to run a load of vehicle checks to be honest."

Gareth grinned, liking this ballsy side of DC Jones. "Well, withhold your temper. They aren't suspects, unfortunately, and we don't want to rattle unnecessary cages. I am, however, going to spend an evening doing research on Barrington-Brown and his merry band of elders. I'm intrigued now if I wasn't before."

A red Porsche Boxster waited for them to cross the bridge first. Gareth acknowledged the driver as the cars passed, caught a glimpse of platinum blonde hair and large dark glasses. Megan swung round in her seat.

"Isn't that that opera singer? The one from Llandudno who sings at the rugby and stuff. The blonde, goes out with a footballer, what's her name?"

"Katie Tennant? Really?" He braked and studied his interior mirror.

The Porsche had disappeared, but Barrington-Brown was in full view, posing at the top of the steps, smile fixed, arms wide. Gareth was sure he had half an eye on the retreating Volvo.

"If she's an elder, she's a young one. She's only a year older than me," said Megan as Gareth accelerated and changed gear. "I wonder what really goes on here?"

Gareth shrugged. "I'm curious, I'll admit. Trouble is, we could be in danger of taking our eye off the ball. There's no connection between this place and Iris Mahoney's murder, don't forget that."

Megan folded her arms and pursed her lips. "Hmmm. Not yet."

Chapter Four

Megan set the treadmill for thirty minutes on varied incline, popped on her headphones and closed her eyes as the machine began to move. Slowly at first, feeling the muscles start to work in her calves. Within minutes she'd reached her optimum pace. She tuned out the noise and bustle of the gym around her, and settled into the welcoming security of running, against the backdrop of the music of Muse.

She let her mind roam. She'd spent a good few hours the previous evening researching Derwydd Hall and the Barrington-Brown Empire. An empire apparently founded in the grey area of 'financial services' and the family wealth of his late wife. Megan lost count of the numerous mentions of L Ron Hubbard in the same sentence as B-B – as she'd begun to call him – associations made, it seemed, by B-B himself as well as interviewers and journalists. Although she knew the term, Scientology was a word she associated with Hollywood and Tom Cruise. It was nothing she had any degree of knowledge about. But now, after several hours solid reading, if B-B really did see himself as the next Ron L Hubbard – she was so pleased she'd taken an instinctive, violent dislike to him.

She'd drifted to sleep, eventually, and her dreams had all been sweaty, uncomfortable interludes of memories from Iris Mahoney's post-mortem, intermingled with Anna Brown's scared face and her father's patronising, nasal voice proclaiming himself as a visionary of the future, the key to true meaning of life.

What utter bollocks.

Megan opened one eye, groped for her water bottle and took a long swallow. It had taken every fibre of will-power to drag herself out of bed when her mobile beeped at 5.30am. But she was glad she had. Twenty minutes on the rower already, a good run, and then she'd allow herself thirty minutes in the pool, including ten in the steam room. It was part of her life to have routine and consistency. She found she couldn't cope with her line of work, which could be spontaneous and haphazard, if she didn't organise her free time into manageable pockets she could divide up as needed.

She took another sip of water and settled the bottle back in its holder. Today, after debrief, she had to focus on motive and witnesses. Yesterday had all been about the post-mortem, making sure Iris's death was murder, today was when the interesting work began. She hoped D I Macrae would continue to let her play an active role in the investigation and not return her back to desk duties. In truth, she felt a degree of responsibility that she'd missed her chance to question Anna Brown before she disappeared; that it may even have been her fault the girl had taken flight in that bizarre way. She needed another chance to show her worth.

The machine changed down a gear and slowed her pace to a speedy walk. She'd come to the middle of her routine, five minutes of walking before the final push. She opened her eyes, grabbed her towel from the sidebar, and dabbed her forehead, chest and back of her neck. Muse continued to swirl away around her brain as she mouthed along with the words of one of her favourite tracks.

Megan jumped as someone touched her arm. Glancing to her right, she smiled at the gesticulations the man on the treadmill beside her was making – clearly telling her to remove her headphones, he looked like he was doing some geeky kind of dance. He dropped his hands as she pulled off the headphones and resumed a normal jogging position.

"That's better. I've been talking to you for the last five minutes. Convinced you were blanking me till I finally spotted the iPod. You okay, Meg?"

"Fine, thanks. Bit breathless. Not sure I can chat."

Adrian made an okay gesture with his thumb and forefinger. "Speak in a bit then. Don't go dashing off this time though."

Megan frowned but let the comment go. A tiny flutter of pleasure tickled her ribcage. Adrian Bolton was a friend of her elder brother, Gregory. They'd played rugby together at university and for a few years, Adrian had been a regular visitor at Megan's home. Greg stopped playing years ago, but Adrian was now on a post-graduate course and still had an active role in the rugby team. He was certainly fit and had all the physical attributes Megan looked for in a guy. Plus, he was funny, charming and intelligent – and, according to Greg, recently single.

They'd spoken a few times here at the gym, and, on the last occasion, Adrian had chucked out a passing remark about going for a coffee later. But after hanging around in the reception for as long as she dared without attracting attention, he hadn't appeared. She'd gone home cross and embarrassed, hoping her brother never got to hear how she'd misread the signals. And at this time in the morning, she really wasn't in the mood for a reminder of the incident.

They continued to run in silence until Megan's routine dropped to a steady walking pace for her two-minute warm down. Adrian glanced across at her display, and adjusted his own speed accordingly. Megan noted he'd hardly broken sweat, and couldn't help but admire the muscular sheen on his upper arms, shoulders and neck. She felt his eyes on her, and embarrassed, pulled her gaze away and reached for her water.

"Better?" he asked. "I've never seen anyone run with their eyes closed before."

"I do it to stop myself checking the time. If I open my eyes before the fifteen-minute mark, I'm always convinced I'll never finish as the time seems to go so slow. Over the fifteen minute, it's a breeze."

Adrian nodded. "Psychological willpower. I like it."

"I'll take any willpower I can get at this time of the morning, thank you very much."

He laughed and grabbed for his towel as the treadmill creaked to a halt. "Are you done? How about letting me buy you breakfast as you so rudely stood me up last time?"

Megan stretched her hamstrings as she stepped down from the machine. She checked the time on the bank of television screens on the far wall. Six forty-five. She had plenty of time. Why not?

"I didn't stand you up. I waited in reception for ages."

Adrian snapped his towel at her backside. "Ah, that explains it. I was in the café, you loon, staring moodily into two extra-shot lattes. Where did you think I meant when we agreed to meet for coffee?"

Megan's cheeks tingled at his natural intimacy. "Ah. Yes. I never thought."

"And I thought you were some fancy detective now?" Adrian tutted. "And they reckon blokes are thick? Well, to avoid doubt." He checked his sports watch. "I'll meet you in the café in twenty minutes, okay?"

Megan nodded. She could fit in a session in the pool after work with luck.

"Okay."

"Cool. Something I wanted to ask actually. See you in a bit."

With that he turned and headed towards the men's showers. There was a confidence in his loping walk; the way he raised his hand in acknowledgment as he passed the gym instructors and a group of guys on the fixed-weight machines. Adrian carried his six-foot-plus frame like a graceful dancer, but she knew from her brother, he worked hard to maintain his fitness and place on the rugby team.

She shivered as she urged herself to get a move on – and not just from the after-work-out chills.

Megan twisted her freshly blow-dried hair into a ponytail, looped a band around and pulled the ends apart to tighten the hold. It would have to do. She checked her watch. Almost half-seven. She'd have to make a move if Adrian didn't show soon. She stirred a single sugar into her extra-shot latte, and glanced, for the umpteenth time, at the stairs that led down from the changing rooms.

"Hiya." She jumped as Adrian's voice came from behind her. "Sorry, I went to dump my bag in the car and found a couple of missed calls I needed to deal with. Ah, you've got them in, thank you."

Megan leaned her elbows on the table. "Figured I owed you from last time. Do you want any food?"

Adrian took a quick sip of coffee. "I do fancy a bacon roll. I'll go. Can I get you anything?"

"I wouldn't mind one of those fresh muesli and yoghurt pots. Cranberry please."

Adrian made a face as he backed away. "Yum."

Megan checked her phone, noting a text from Gareth Parry. The debrief had been put back till 9.30am, which was good news for her. In the meantime, he wanted Megan to locate Iris Mahoney's solicitors and try to find out the contents of her will. Megan frowned. That would be no easy task. Chris Coleman hadn't mentioned finding a will among Iris's personal paperwork, but then, he may not have thought she needed to know. She scrolled through to his number and sent a text asking the same question.

She thought, as she hit send, that he might not even be up yet, and hoped her text didn't wake him. No, on second thoughts, she hoped it did. He'd been late a few times recently, and she knew unofficially – because he'd told her himself – that he'd had a verbal warning from Macrae about his time-keeping. Although punctuality was a massive thing to Megan, she could sympathise. She knew Chris had gone through a traumatic marriage breakdown, and if the rumours about his drinking and gambling were only been partially exaggerated, Coleman was on a seriously slippery slope. And it was a shame. She liked Chris. He was a guy who called a spade a spade like herself ...

"Penny for them?"

Megan realised Adrian had retaken his seat unnoticed. She shook her head. "Just work. Nothing important."

He took a sip of latte and wiped his upper lip. Dressed in a white short-sleeved shirt and black trousers, Adrian looked effortlessly handsome. His biceps strained the white cotton sleeves, and when he leaned back in his chair, she caught a glimpse of a thick, gold chain nestling among delicate curls of hair at the base of his throat.

"I was going to ask, actually," said Adrian, raising his voice above the hiss of the espresso machine. "I heard about that murder. Iris Mahoney. Are you working on the case?"

Megan sipped her coffee and nodded. "Yes. Why?"

They paused as a waitress arrived with Megan's yoghurt and muesli, and a large, floured roll bursting with crispy rashers of bacon and brown sauce. Megan sighed and reached for a spoon from the cutlery jar, barely able to tear her eyes away from Adrian's plate.

"Want a bite?" he asked, smiling.

Megan shook her head. "Willpower. I never give into temptation."

"That's a shame."

Their eyes met. Megan pulled away first.

"So, why the interest in Iris Mahoney?" she asked, dipping her spoon into the creamy mixture.

"It's not an interest really. It's just a name I recognise. She did some work with my dad a while ago. I met her once." He bit into his roll, chewed in silence for a moment, then dabbed his lips with a napkin. "Hmmm. That's good. Sure you don't want a bite?"

Megan shook her head. "What was she like?"

Adrian chewed and swallowed. "Really nice. *Really* Irish. But after all the hype I'd read about her and that crappy TV show, I was surprised what a down-to-earth woman she seemed. Hard to imagine why anyone would want to kill her. I was shocked, I tell you."

Megan put down her spoon, took another sip of her latte. "Why would a uni professor work with a psychic?"

"Actually, he's recently got a promotion. He's the new Head of the School of History, Welsh history and Archaeology. He engaged Iris as guest speaker at one of his meetings. I can't remember the details now. You should ask him. He was horrified about her murder."

"I probably will, yeah. Thanks." She scooped up the last of the muesli. "Have you heard of a guy called Matthew Barrington-Brown?"

Adrian chewed as he considered. A little dab of brown sauce was lodged at the corner of his mouth. Megan resisted the urge to reach across and wipe it away. She diverted her attention by wiping her own mouth with her napkin. Adrian's tongue darted out, licked the sauce, as he shook his head.

"I thought maybe the name rang a bell, but no, I don't think so. Again, you should ask my dad, especially if it's anything to do with uni, he has contacts everywhere." He pushed his plate away. "Why ... is the guy a suspect?"

Megan smiled. "You know I can't say. But I'm grateful for the tip off. We're trying to build a background profile on Iris, so I'd love to speak to your father. Could I have his number?"

"Sure." Adrian dug his mobile from his trouser pocket, pressed a few buttons, then laid it on the table between them. "Office and mobile. I'll let him know you'll be in touch. I know he'd want to help."

"Cheers." Megan glanced at her watch. "Look, thanks for

breakfast, it's been nice to catch up, but I have to make a move." She got to her feet, slid her gym bag out from under the table with her foot. "Would you – would you like my mobile number?"

Adrian looked up with a vacant stare. "What for?"

She pulled on her suit jacket. "Nothing. Sorry, I just –"

Adrian reached out. Megan trembled as his fingers circled her wrist and squeezed.

"I was having you on. I'd love your mobile number … if I hadn't got it already that is."

Her mouth dropped open.

Adrian held up his hands in surrender. "Sorry. Don't be mad. I bullied Gregory until he gave it me on Saturday night. Boozy night at the club. I'd made my mind up if I didn't see you here this week, I was going to call you next weekend. Seems fate played a hand, could've saved myself a whole load of embarrassment. Your brother is a heartless bastard, I'll say that for him, he enjoyed seeing me squirm."

Megan's cheeks warmed. "I spoke to Greg this week. He never said."

"He wouldn't. I threatened him with castration. I wasn't totally sure I wouldn't bottle it."

Megan gripped the back of the plastic chair, trying to ignore the thump of her pulse. "Bottle it, why?"

"Well, you're CID now. Important. Going places." Adrian drew his thumb nail across the table.

A surge of adrenaline shot through her body. She felt taller and empowered, not to mention excited.

She picked up her gym bag and slung her handbag over her shoulder.

"Then don't leave it too long to call me, okay?"

Megan slipped her mobile from her handbag and held it in her lap under the edge of her desk. Checking no one was looking, she accessed her Inbox.

'*How long is too long? Is now too short or too long? Please advise. A x*'

Megan smirked, tapped reply, noting the kiss.

'*Now is just about perfect, alas, am at work. How about this eve?*'

Seconds later, the phone buzzed in her palm.

'*Sounds a plan. Drink? The Antelope? 8pm?*'

She paused, tapped her nail against the screen. What was stopping her?

'*I should have told you, I'm teetotal.*'

Another buzz.

'*Shit. Really. I mean ... really?*"

She clicked reply.

'*Yes, really. But you can buy me a cranberry juice. See you @ 8.*'

"... when you're ready, DC Jones."

Megan looked up, cheeks ablaze. DI Macrae stood in front of her desk. She slipped her phone back into her bag. "Sorry, sir, I was following up a promising lead."

"Hmmm. A lead that makes you blush like that must be *very* promising."

She kept her head down as she heard a wave of chuckles.

"Sorry, sir."

"I was asking how you'd got on tracing Mrs Mahoney's solicitor?"

Megan cleared her throat. "Chris came up trumps, sir. He found the details in a locked writing desk at her cottage. No will, just a name and contact number. I'm waiting on a call back. He's in London and all I've had so far is the client confidentiality line from his secretary. He's back in the office on Monday and I've made an appointment to see him at 9am. I'm hoping to clear up the question of family too. No one has come forward yet, I take it, sir?"

Macrae shook his head. "No. But good work."

Megan sighed in relief as Macrae turned his attention

elsewhere.

"Chris, how about house-to-house enquiries, how are they going?"

"Bloody slow, sir. Most places around the cottage are summer lets, either empty at the moment or strangers who know nothing – and see and hear about the same. It's hard work and I can't see it leading anywhere. I'd be tempted to knock it on the head after today and use the resources elsewhere. I've just received telephone data from BT so with respect, I'd like to spend the day combing through that."

"Sure thing. And how did you get on with your local contacts?"

"Drawn another blank, sir. If Iris Mahoney ever upset any of the local low-life it was kept very quiet. No one I spoke to had ever heard of her – clearly not fans of the paranormal, our local criminals."

Gareth cleared his throat. "That may have been more by design than accident though."

Macrae walked back to his chair. "What's that?"

"I spoke to the production company, Trentwise Productions, who make *The Psychic Detective*. One of their criteria was that none of the crimes Mrs Mahoney investigated are local. They wanted to ensure she couldn't be accused of any insider knowledge for one thing, but also I think they were aware of possible reprisals."

"I think that's something to stick with, Gareth," said Macrae. "It screams motive. So, go back as far as you can and find out any old cases that were reopened by Mahoney's team. Check if there were any actual convictions. Any grudges we should know about." Macrae paused. "You know, call me naïve, but I didn't think she investigated real crimes."

"Yes, apparently so." Gareth nodded. "Quite a few famous names too. A lot of old cases though, sometimes from requests from victims' families who felt the original investigations weren't good enough. I've seen a lot of praise on Iris's website, run by Trentwise. I've not been able to find out the statistics on her success rate, but I'm guessing there'd be a fair few people out there who would have issues with this famous psychic."

Megan nodded. "Good thing they didn't investigate any local crimes, then. We know how to carry a grudge round here."

"Trait of the Welsh, eh?" said Coleman with a smile. "I can't say you've ever made this little *Liverpoolian* fella feel at home."

Gareth grinned. "Folk on Anglesey look at people from the other side of the water as outsiders."

"You mean Ireland?" asked Coleman.

"No. I mean Bangor. And go so far as Penmaenmawr or Caernarfon and they're as good as illegal aliens. We're not known for mixing round these parts."

Macrae frowned. "You're not intimating this is down to Iris being an outsider?"

Gareth shook his head. "No, sir, I can't see any extremists going that far. It's not the way of things now. Twenty or thirty years ago they might have burnt down your holiday home, but I've never heard of any case involving murder."

"What else did you learn, Gareth?" asked Megan, reaching into her bag for her notebook. Her mobile buzzed against her fingertips, but she resisted the urge to read it.

"I spoke to her agent. Emily Roy. The agency is based in Manchester. From what I can make out, they communicated mostly via email and telephone. They only met up once or twice a year. The last time was just before Christmas. Iris signed a two-book deal and a new contract with S4C. Large sums involved. The last time they spoke was two weeks ago and Ms Roy said she sounded fine, was enjoying working on her current book. She was due to start filming the next series of the television programme in September, two weeks filming in Cardiff, and Ms Roy was planning to meet up with Iris then. I asked her the usual questions about enemies and grudges, but she clearly wasn't close to Iris on a personal level. She said she has over a hundred clients, I guess she can't spread herself too thin."

"So, that's another dead end. How about S4C? Did you speak to them?"

"I did. They have couriered over tapes of the last series, but they had no dealings with Iris at all."

Gareth held up a pack of DVDs. "Shall we?"

Macrae nodded. "Why not."

Megan tensed. There was always something chilling about seeing a dead person on television, or even hearing the voice of someone who had died. During her time in uniform, she'd spent countless hours scouring CCTV images, observing the disturbing sight of victims involved in their normal day to day routines, heading with unstoppable force towards their death. Many times she wished she had the power to press the pause button, stop the events unfolding. One case seemed to stick with her; a nurse stabbed in the hospital car park in view of the cameras. The scenes had been shocking. But what affected Megan more was seeing the images of the same girl, smiling and flirting with her work colleagues, moments before leaving the brightness of the hospital reception, and heading to the gloom of the underground car park where she was raped and murdered.

Megan took a deep breath, crossed her legs and settled back into her chair, concentrating on the haunting panpipes that heralded the opening to *The Psychic Detective*.

"Well, what a load of bloody shite," said Chris Coleman half an hour later when Gareth ejected the DVD and switched on the lights. "I'll give you the fact the ridiculous bloody sub-titles didn't help, but you can't tell me those poor buggers in the audience actually believed she was connecting with some ex-con who wanted to pass onto his family who was really responsible for his death, and who had stolen the family treasure? It has to be a setup, right?" Chris looked around the room, expectant and incredulous. "Give me strength. You lot can't be serious. You believe in that utter shite?"

Megan smothered a smile. "It doesn't matter what *we* believe or don't believe. Enough people did believe in Iris Mahoney. Enough to make her a rich woman. That alone is enough of a motive."

Macrae spoke up. "And it's clear from the reaction of the people in the studio she had a lot of followers, a lot of people believed every word she said. What if it got round she was going for a big reveal in the next series? Would someone want to get in first to shut her up?" He turned to Gareth. "Can you get back on to Trentwise? They must have researchers working on this programme if the next series is due to be filmed in a couple of months. Can you get a list of all the stories they have planned and check them out?"

Gareth nodded and made hurried notes. "With permission, I'd like to take a trip down to Cardiff, sir."

"Granted. I think this is a serious lead. Keep me up to speed." Macrae looked around the room. "So, if there are no further questions, I think we all have plenty to be getting on with today. I'll allow you a bit of free time tomorrow as it's Sunday, but –"

Megan coughed. "Could I discuss a potential lead, sir?"

Macrae turned towards her. "Of course. Go on …"

Megan quickly recapped her conversation with Adrian Bolton.

As she finished, Chris held up a hand. "Interestingly, as I said, I've had a list of incoming and outgoing calls from Iris's phone sent over this morning. I'd only run one trace so far to a number she rang on a regular basis … and it's a direct line at Bangor Uni."

Megan pulled her handbag onto her lap. "Here, I have the professor's contact numbers."

She carried her phone across to Chris's desk, and heads together, they studied his computer.

Chris tapped the end of his pen against the screen. "Yup, here we go. Here, here, here. At a quick tally at least half a dozen calls in the past month to his office number and the same to his mobile."

Macrae rubbed his chin as he added Professor Bolton's name to the whiteboard. "Okay, there's some serious connection here, the first we've come across so far. And I'm wondering why the radio silence from this professor? He clearly knew Iris was dead … and the circumstances. So, why not come forward to help? Can you two take a trip over to the uni and speak to Bolton as a priority?"

Macrae met Megan's eyes. "I seem to make a habit of saying this just now, but good work, Megan. Bloody good work."

Chapter III

MONA INSULIS, BRITAIN - AD 60

"Amusing you always pleases me, Father. But at the moment I see no reason to jest."

Cadadius leaned towards her, and, with a tender gesture, brushed a lock of hair behind her ear.

"Do not worry, I know this matter is no joke, far from it – but at times you are so like your mother, I confess it amuses me."

He tweaked the end of Awen's nose, chuckling as she pulled away in disgust, before settling back in his chair.

"I come to you with a matter that is more weighty, more serious than anything I've faced before," said Awen, her face glowing, "and all you do is ridicule me. I think you fail to appreciate the seriousness of this –"

Cadadius lifted a finger. "Ah, you see. There. Serious. That's the word. The scowl and the down-turned lips. The image of your mother's face. Like you, my darling Awen, she took her gift far too seriously and took much weight on her shoulders. I do not want to see you carry the same burden. Not for me."

"How can you say that? How can you be so frivolous? I have been so worried, scared to tell you what I've been seeing these past weeks –"

"Awen, my fawn, you shouldn't be afraid to tell me anything."

"Not even a vision of your own death?"

She watched a cloud pass over her father's face, the smile faltered. He reached across the low table and took a small amount of chopped hazelnut from a wooden bowl, chewing for several moments before speaking.

"Awen, I knew your mother when she was your age, younger even; we were brought up within the same family. She went through similar periods in her early years as a seer, *tests of will* she liked to call them. She saw so many things when her gift was still in its very early stages. Had we believed every single one of her visions, she would have run mad – and so would I."

Awen's heart drummed as it did whenever her father spoke of her mother. It happened so rarely there was always a flurry of excitement to learn something new. Leaning forward, she fingered her mother's eagle amulet in the pocket of her tunic.

"What manner of things?"

Her father waved her question away with his hand. "Too ridiculous for words – but the point is, even the most gifted of seers are not always right; your visions can be affected by all sorts of things."

"But Mother foresaw her own death. You told me she had all of the details –"

"Ah, but that was many years later. After you were born. Your mother was one of the most gifted women on Mona by then. She'd learned to use her gift – as you will in time."

"Then if she saw her death, why do you doubt I may have seen a genuine portent –"

"Awen, enough." He held up a hand, then propped his hands on his knees and got to his feet. "There is much talk of an invading army at present, much talk of the end of Mona as we know it. I know you hear the same news as I do. It is obvious such speculation will play on your emotions, affect the development of your mind and your intuition. It may be time to make a gift to

Hu, ask him to help ease your torment."

"And that, I assume, is an end to the matter? You're dismissing me. Just like that. What will it take for you to take me seriously?"

"That word again, my fawn. Do you see?" Cadadius straightened his robe as he opened the door, sunlight flooding the room. "Never believe that I have anything less than every faith in you ... and your gift. All I ask is you trust my judgment and experience on this occasion."

Awen swallowed a bubble of indignation, and answered her father with a curt nod.

Cadadius paused, casting shimmering shadows across the small central hearth.

"Look Awen, I meet with Fathan, and leaders of the Deceangli and Silures tribes, this eve to discuss the advance of the Romans. Come with me. You can air your concerns in front of the assembly. Will that prove my faith in you?"

Awen frowned. "I don't understand, Father. If you believe in what I see, why refute what I see for you?"

Cadadius shrugged. "I still believe too many emotions are involved at your age." He rubbed his long white beard. "And perhaps a part of me wishes only to believe what I choose."

With a swish of white silk, Cadadius slipped out of the door leaving Awen alone with her thoughts.

Swirling smoke drifted across the small clearing, meandering its way through the swaying branches of the giant oaks and dissipating into a sky touched with the first hint of a golden sunset. Eventually the ritual was complete; the clay pipe returned to the Ordovice Chief, Fathan. He rapped it three times on the upended log in front of him. The mutters ceased in an instant.

Fathan lifted himself to his knees. No man stood. No man would be higher in stature or status than his neighbour in these gatherings. All were equal here, regardless of gender, riches, title or age. So said the old laws of the tribal assembly.

"Men ... and lady ... of honour," he said, flashing a smile at Awen. "Thank you for attending. I know some of you have had to leave perilous situations to be here. But today a speaker joins us who faced the Romans and defeated them; someone who has turned to the Ordovices for shelter over the past dozen years. And now, we turn to him, Caratacus the Junior of the Catuvellauni."

A tide of hushed whispers filled the small grove, followed by a ripple of applause. Awen watched in interest as a tall, middle-aged man with silver hair and beard knelt.

"For those who are not so well informed of what happens on the mainland, I have many reports from my spies. An army has set up camp, a whole temporary garrison on the far bank. Hundreds of tents, thousands of men, but no sign of imminent attack. There is talk they are planning to build a fort there." He looked from one man to the next. "This is a decoy. A half hour march down water, there is a creek, a natural harbour. Here, there is much movement. I have men stationed at both places. But your reserves are much smaller than my father's were, and pitiful compared to what is reported on the far bank."

"Surely that is obvious, Caratacus," said Fathan. "We are not an army. We're a tribe who, for the best part of a hundred years, has known a peaceful existence. How are we expected to have the same resources as the army of the biggest empire in the world?"

Caratacus raised himself on one elbow and smiled with little amusement. "Then you must build an army, Fathan. And quick. Or your lands will be pillaged and your people slaughtered. It is as simple as that."

Murmurs of fear rippled between the men.

Cadadius raised his hand, waited for silence. "Let us keep our emotions under control. We are all tense. Rightly so. This is a serious matter. Our very existence is in question. We must work together to succeed, divided we can only fall. Please, do me the honour of listening to my daughter, Awen. She joins us here today as a renowned seer. Her gift is at our disposal, and it may prove to be a valuable asset."

Awen got to her knees, aware of a few mutters of discontent. Caratacus was among the most vocal. Having had no prior dealings with Druids in his battles in the south of Briton, she knew he held little interest in their ways. She'd been taught that men from other lands often had strange opinions on women. In some regions, women had no more say than a dog. Awen felt blessed to be born into civilisation.

Awen cleared her throat. "I agree with Caratacus." She saw the flash of interest in his eyes. "There is a battle approaching, unlike anything any man here has ever experienced. You will require men in many numbers, well-trained and well-equipped. You will need men to be braver than they have ever been in their lives. And it will require the assistance of every single inhabitant of Mona, be that man, woman or child, to stand firm against this enemy."

She paused, licked her lips. "The visions have become stronger in recent weeks. Last night, I saw further armies marching towards our land, reinforcements for those already here. They will arrive within days and the invasion will be immediate."

"When?" A large bearded man, Nudd of the Gangani, rose to one knee. "Be specific, girl, you can be no use to us with vagueness. You tell us nothing we do not already know."

Caratacus replied. "That is not true. My spies tell me only in recent days have there been rumours of another battalion on its way from Viroconium, under the leadership of Paullinus, the best general in the country. Listen to this child, gentlemen. I have no knowledge of her gift, as you call it, but you would be foolish to dismiss her words."

Nudd lifted himself again. "Then, tell us, Awen, if your sight is so useful. Is this a battle we will win?"

Awen closed her eyes, seeing again the breaking waves of crimson, smelling the burning, hearing the screams of injured, the heavy tang of death. She shuddered and pulled her tunic cuffs low over her hands, dropped her gaze to the mossy floor. She swallowed. "That I cannot say."

Chapter Five

Gareth pushed open the door of the pathology lab and as ever recoiled at the unusual stench; a heady mixture of chemicals and deodorants and decay. It was a smell that seemed to cling to you for days after a visit to what he still called 'the morgue' and it never failed to surprise him that Susan was always so fragrant. If he worked here all day, he'd spend most of his time in the shower trying to scrub away the after-effects of formaldehyde and the like.

The message from the pathologist had been waiting for him when he arrived at the office. She needed to see him urgently. Fifteen minutes later, he headed towards her desk. Susan Connolly was examining something under the microscope, and turned as he approached. She pushed her hair away from her eyes and smiled, instantly taking a decade off her face. He'd never known anyone, male or female, whose appearance could change so much simply by manipulating a few facial muscles.

"That was quick," she commented. "No doubt you abided by the speed limit all the way?"

"Of course. Besides, you got me all excited." He winked. "I didn't want to keep you waiting."

Sue wrinkled her nose. "As chat-up lines go you were never up there with the best, were you?"

"It's a waste of time flirting with you, Susan Connolly; I worked that one out a long time ago. So, what have you got for me? Have to admit I get a frisson of anticipation when you come up with one of your theories."

Sue got to her feet. "Hmmm. Flattery doesn't work on me either. But I do think I'm onto something, and I'm a bit cross I missed it at post-mortem."

"Go on."

"The analysis of a small deposit under the nails of the first two fingers of her right hand has come back showing traces of Iris's own DNA. Tiny amounts of blood and flesh were recorded."

Gareth raised his eyebrows. "Her *own* blood and flesh?"

Sue nodded. "It's actually not as unusual as it sounds. Even in natural deaths, there can be reasons like … I don't know, they picked their nose a bit too hard, or scratched themselves during a fall. See what I mean?"

"Yeah, gross, but I get it. So, what's different?"

"You'd better come and have a look. See if you're seeing what I see."

Gareth grimaced as he followed Sue into the next room, affectionately known as the 'holding pen'. Rows of numbered stainless steel doors lined one wall, like lockers in the gym. But Gareth knew what was behind each door, and it wasn't pairs of sweaty socks or badminton racquets.

Sue pulled on a pair of latex gloves and tossed a pair across to Gareth. She unlocked number fourteen door, and slid out a gurney, containing a human shape concealed by a pale green sheet.

Sue looked up and asked the question with her eyes. *Ready?* Gareth nodded.

Beneath the sheet, the lifeless shell of Iris Mahoney stared back up at him. Even ignoring the labyrinth of post-mortem scars, the corpse looked worse today than it had back in her cottage. More dead, if that were possible.

"So, I got to thinking about how we found her. If the blood and traces of skin found under her nails were connected with her death, how could that be possible?"

Gareth frowned. "Sorry, I'm not with you."

Sue walked round to the right-hand side of the gurney. "Remember how she was tied? Wrists and ankles both secured with cable ties. How could she scratch herself?"

"Yeah, okay, I get that. So, maybe it was done prior to her death."

"A possibility. But she seemed a very clean woman, and it wouldn't have been there if she'd washed her hands. So, I re-examined her wrists, and the bruising on this wrist – the right – is a lot more pronounced than the left. See?"

Sue leaned across the corpse and lifted both hands towards Gareth. He took a step back. It was almost like a parody of his being offered the back of her hands to kiss. But he could see what the pathologist was getting at. Even to his untrained eye, the colours of the skin on the right wrist were much darker purple and black bruises, rather than the lilac and green shading on the left.

"Also, on the underside of the arm, the tie on the right wrist has broken the flesh."

"What does that tell us?"

"It shows that she pulled against the restraints to such an extent that the tie cut into her skin."

"But surely that's normal? That she would tug and tug to try and break free?"

Sue nodded. "Sure. But with one hand? That's what I found odd. Well, odd enough for me to explore a bit further." She smiled. "You know what I'm like."

He did. A Jack Russell terrier had nothing on Susan Connolly when she got her teeth into something.

"And from the smug expression, I take it you found something?"

"I think so. But you tell me, I'm the first to admit I have an over-active imagination at times."

She slid the sheet upwards, from the feet, exposing pale, thin legs, scattered with a network of dark blue veins.

"Come round here. What do you see?"

Gareth moved in beside Sue and bent to study a pattern of bruising on the upper right thigh, bordering her hip. There were definite scratch marks on a small area of skin that looked pink and raw in comparison to the grey shade of the surrounding area.

"Here." Sue handed him a magnifying glass. "Ignore the lividity, concentrate on the scratches. What do you see?"

"Nothing. I mean, there's something there, but ..."

"It's clearer if you stretch the skin. Let me."

Gareth stepped away; he had no desire to touch the waxen flesh. Sue laid a hand either side of the bruising and eased the skin taut, flattening the wrinkled surface. He bent lower and studied the marks. The random shapes began to form a pattern, and from the pattern, he began to make out a letter.

"Christ." He exhaled.

"You do see it then?"

He nodded, lost for words.

"I just wasn't sure –"

"But how ...?"

"Here, let me demonstrate." Sue pulled the sheet back over the corpse and crossed to a chair in the corner of the room. She sat in a position that was a rough resemblance of the position of the corpse when the body was found. "Iris was wearing a white shirt and loose cotton trousers with an elasticated waist. Remember how her wrists were secured to the chair? Well, I reckon she could – with persistence – have managed to twist her hand into a position where she could expose her upper leg or maybe slide her hand inside the waist band of her trousers."

Gareth watched as Sue demonstrated with her own jeans, sucking in her tummy as she twisted her hand down inside the material.

"My jeans are tighter obviously, but it wouldn't have been easy," said Sue. "And it would indicate she was probably tied up for a fair length of time, and that she was left alone during that period. But that's what I am going to record in the report. That she manipulated her right hand into a position where she could deliberately mark her upper thigh. Can you read what it is?"

Gareth nodded, still struggling to put his thoughts into words. He had to look again at the marks; he had to be sure. Had to convince himself that this poor woman really had gone to the monumental effort of scarring herself in an attempt to leave behind a clue. What sort of mental strength did that take? The same human mind-set that gave people the ability to cut off their own limbs if it proved to be the only way to escape. He already felt a quiet admiration about what he'd learned about Iris Mahoney so far. Now he was almost choked by her courage. He lifted the sheet, traced a finger around the markings, almost like a tattoo.

"Any idea what it means?" asked Sue from over his shoulder. "B.B?"

Gareth swallowed and nodded. Christ, yes, he had a bloody good idea.

Before he could answer, the silence of the room was broken by a cacophony of noise. His mobile vibrated against his thigh, and at the same time, Sue dug her own phone from the pocket of her lab coat and wandered out into the main laboratory.

Number Withheld flashed on the display.

"Parry."

"Hello, Gareth. It's control. We have an elderly IC1 female found dead in the kitchen of a farmhouse at Tal-y-bont. Possible suspicious circumstances. WPC Hewines is first attending officer, she called it in, said to tell you the MO looks identical to the Mahoney case. That makes sense to you, I hope? Are you in the area and able to respond?"

Gareth acknowledged the call and asked for the address to be text through to his phone.

Sue appeared at the doorway. "You got the same call? Tal-y-bont?"

He sighed. "Did you get any information?"

Sue nodded. "Sounds like we've got a copy-cat killing or …?"

"Or worse. A serial killer. Christ." He ran a hand through his hair. "I need to call in the rest of the team. Meet you there, okay?"

He took one last look back at the shrouded corpse.

B.B.

Chapter Six

"Last time I sat outside an office on a naughty chair, I was about to get a week's suspension for locking Darren McCallum in the girls' loos overnight, resulting in a police search across the whole of Merseyside. Oh, and making him eat a whole toilet roll."

Megan rolled her eyes. "Any particular reason?"

Chris Coleman nodded. "He asked Tricia Wagstaff to the Christmas disco."

"And that was bad because …?"

"He knew I was plucking up the courage and got in first. Little bastard."

"And Tricia? Was she worth the grief?"

Chris finished biting his thumb nail and spat out the excess. "Nah. She went with David Cross in the end."

Megan nodded, deciding it was probably better to let the rest of the tale go before it got far too complicated to be interesting. Coleman was certainly a character, someone she never fully got to grips with. A living embodiment of total opposites. His attention to detail in terms of his appearance left a lot to be desired. With black, spiky hair and heavy stubble, he always made her think of a traveller, someone who worked on the fairground, did a lot of manual labour and had a permanently tanned, slightly soiled appearance. His shirts were never ironed, his jeans needed a belt, and the brown wax jacket he favoured had seen better days before WWII.

And yet, Megan knew that privately Chris was borderline OCD about cleanliness. He disappeared to the loo to wash his hands and face every hour, and one day, while searching for a case file, she found a toiletry bag in his desk, bulging with deodorants and moisturisers and cleansing wipes. Chris always smelled gorgeous. Today, there was an aroma of mint mixed with a tangy lime-scented aftershave.

Yes, he was one complex character, and he was the instigator of a lot of the teasing that went on behind her back. Eager-beaver. She knew that's what he called her, but in fairness, she'd been called worse. She still respected the guy, and although he had his demons, Megan rated him as a detective.

Chris blew out his cheeks and shuffled on the hard plastic seat. "What time did they say the prof would be free? I'll be getting piles if I sit here much longer."

"That's an image I didn't need." Megan glanced at her watch. "Anytime now. His class should just have finished."

"So, what's the story with his son? Bit out of the blue ... you just meeting up like that?"

Megan shrugged. "Not really. We've seen each other at the gym a few times recently, and he went out drinking with my brother last weekend. I suppose he knows I'm CID and put two and two together. He didn't know Iris Mahoney himself."

Chris nodded. "And this prof, what is he again?"

"He's head of the School of History, Welsh history and Archaeology. He's been at the uni since the dark ages. He taught Gregory, my brother."

"And what's his son into?"

"He's at uni too. He took a couple of years out to travel after his BA. And now he's post-graduate, just starting his MA."

"I got to say, I don't understand all these BA, MA, post-grad, under-grad bollocks. I just about passed my GCSEs. Does he study history like his pa?"

"No. He got a first class honours in psychology; I remember

Gregory saying he was way too clever for his own good. Typical bloke's jealousy, I suppose."

"And he's good looking and rich and hung like a horse, I suppose?"

"Chris!" Megan glanced along the empty corridor. "I've no idea to the latter, and no opinion on the former."

"Yeah, right." Chris started up on his other thumb nail. "Tell that to your face."

"Get lost."

Before the argument could escalate, voices made their way along the corridor. Two figures appeared, one male, one female, heads bent close together, talking animatedly. What looked like a typical student-professor conversation. Megan almost didn't want to break them up, but she had no choice. She got to her feet and coughed. The man looked up, his expression open and curious. Despite his silver hair, his face was smooth and his eyes bright and intelligent.

"Sorry to interrupt." Megan stepped forward, held out her ID. "Professor Bolton? I'm DC Jones and this is DS Coleman. I wonder if we could have a few minutes of your time?"

The professor studied her ID. "Is there a problem? Is it Adrian?"

Megan shook her head, surprised at the professor's reaction. "Everything's fine. Sorry, I should have said, nothing to be alarmed about. We need assistance on a current enquiry, and your name came up. We hoped you may be able to help? We have a few questions."

The professor took a few moments to respond, then nodded towards the door at the end of the corridor. "Okay, sorry, I shouldn't panic. Paranoid single parent reaction, excuse me." He turned to his companion. "Can we discuss this later, Ellie? I'll see you at the tutorial."

The girl blushed, and stepped away, almost curtsying before retracing her steps.

"Go on through to my office. I'll grab some tea, I'm gasping.

Can I offer either of you a drink?"

After declining, Megan followed Chris into a book-lined office, dominated by a chestnut-veneered desk that took up a good portion of the room. The smell of furniture polish and old books invaded the space. She settled into a leather chair and waited for the professor to arrive. Chris did a circuit of the room, pausing to examine book titles and a row of photographs on the windowsill. Megan recognised Adrian as a toddler, pink-cheeked and screaming; next as a poker-faced, spotty teenager in a maroon school jumper; and finally as a proud graduate with a mortar-board perched at a jaunty angle. Megan's pulse quickened as she studied the photographs. She rubbed her palms together and did her best to appear disinterested as she saw Chris sneak a glance in her direction.

The door opened and the professor appeared, balancing a mug of tea as if he had a full tray of crystal champagne glasses to contend with. He took small, careful steps across to his desk and breathed a sigh of relief as he deposited the mug successfully.

"I would never make a waiter. I get into dreadful trouble for slopping tea on the carpet. And the cleaners here …" He shook his head and shuddered.

Megan smiled. It was hard not to take an instant liking to Professor Bolton. There was a lot of Adrian in him, both in physical terms and also his deep voice and quirky mannerisms, although the professor seemed more vulnerable than his confident son. It was both interesting and endearing. He made her think of the archetypal bumbling professor whose knowledge failed to extend far outside his chosen field. Megan would take a guess this man had no idea what was top of the charts or even how much a pint of milk was nowadays. But ask him about the decline of medieval villages in mid-Wales and he could probably keep you entertained for hours. He'd certainly do an interesting father-in-law's wedding speech. Megan shook her head, wondering where on earth that thought came from. She blinked and tried to concentrate on the exchange between Chris and the professor.

The professor took a sip of his tea and nodded. "Poor, poor Iris. I heard. Such a tragedy."

Chris settled into the seat beside Megan. "When did you last see Mrs Mahoney?"

"Let me see. About two weeks ago, at the last meeting, here at the uni. But I spoke to her on the phone only a few days ago." He shook his head. "I'm so glad none of us has any inkling what's around the corner. She sounded fine, full of her usual vigour."

Megan pulled her notebook from her bag. She was bursting to interrupt but she understood the importance of protocol. Chris was her superior. She had to keep quiet until he gave her an opportunity to contribute.

"Vigour?" Chris said, with a puzzled frown. "I'm not sure I understand the relationship you had with the deceased. You mentioned a meeting?"

Professor Bolton steepled his fingers in front of him and rested his chin on his thumbs, so he looked almost to be praying. "Iris Mahoney was quite a formidable opponent when she got her teeth into something. I was glad to have her on my side of the fence." He seemed to almost be talking to himself rather than anyone else in the room.

Chris leaned forward. "Sorry, sir, I'm not clear who she had her teeth into?"

The professor blinked, focused on the detective. "Sorry. My mind wanders. I shall make more effort to control it. I should start somewhat closer to the beginning for any of this to make sense."

Chris relaxed back into the chair. "Yes, please, sir."

Bolton took a long swallow of his tea, wiped his lips on the back of his hand. "Do either of you know much about the history of Anglesey? It's importance two thousand years ago as the centre of Druidic teachings?"

Chris frowned. Megan shook her head.

The professor nodded. "You see … that is where the story

really begins."

Chris sighed. "Perhaps we could get a potted version then, sir?"

Bolton smiled. "Point taken. Salient information only. Okay. So, for as long as I've been teaching at Bangor there have been rumours about hidden treasure somewhere along this coast. A few historical documents detail it, but are vague to say the least. Gold, the spoils of war, what we call a trophy hoard. I'm not sure if you know there were huge battles along the Menai Straits in the period in question?"

Both shook their heads.

"Romans fought the Celts for Anglesey – or *Mona Insulis* as it was then – twice. 60AD they had their first shot, then 77AD they came back and were more successful, set up a huge military fort at Caernarfon. Called Segontium?"

Chris shrugged but Megan nodded. "I went there on a school trip."

The professor beamed. "The original battle in 60AD was fierce, and a lot of Roman gold was stolen by the Celts and given to the Druids, who ruled the island at the time, as payment for the magic powers the Celts believed were used to protect them. The story is that a hoard was buried by Cadadius, the great Druid leader, somewhere along the Menai Straits, ready to collect once things settled. But it was never recovered and the gold was lost to time.

"There has been study after survey done to find it. Geo-physics is a modern-day miracle, but where to survey? All the way from Bangor to Caernarfon, from Penmon to Malltreath? Miles and miles of coastline on Anglesey *and* the mainland. Impossible. As for research, there's virtually no documentary evidence from the Celts, and while we have a few lines here and there from the Roman writer, Tacitus, there's no mention of a hoard. The two documents we have are much later, and mention some kind of memorial stone which has never been found, but that's the sum total of our evidence. The Druid tradition was very much an oral one –"

The professor paused. "I can see your eyes clouding over, but stick with me, these are salient points you need to know in order to understand what fired up Iris Mahoney. Trust me."

Chris nodded. "I'm listening."

"So, as I said, Anglesey was the seat of the Druids. Romans feared the Druid cult and that was one of the major reasons for capturing and defeating the island and its inhabitants." Bolton paused. "This Druidic history was also the reason Iris came to the island. Her family come from a long line of Druidic ... royalty, I suppose you'd call them ... that stretched across the Irish Sea. One of her direct ancestors was the leader, Cadadius, and she carried many gifts associated with her lineage –"

"The Psychic Detective?" Megan blurted, lost in the professors' story.

He smiled. "Some would say that. I prefer to call it 'second sight' – a gift strongly associated with Druid powers. Another reason for Iris returning to Anglesey was the stories of this possible hoard. The teachings connected the treasure with her family and she was desperate to find it, establish it in a museum, before anyone else got their hands on it for less worthy reasons."

"What kind of reasons?"

The professor took a sip of tea. "I wonder if you've come across an individual named Matthew Barrington-Brown in the course of your investigation?"

Megan's eyes widened as she nodded.

"He has become somewhat of a thorn in the side of historians and people like Iris who want to maintain the true legend of the Druids. Derwydd, the name of Barrington-Brown's home is the old Celtic word for Druid. He's even included the most potent Druidic symbol, that of a sacred oak, into a tacky family crest." Megan saw anger in the academic's face. "He is trading on the history and associated power of the area to make money from our heritage. I've no idea what mumbo-jumbo goes on behind closed doors at that place, and I've no desire to know, but I do know he's earning a fortune in investments, mainly on the premise of discovering this treasure hoard by claiming he has incontrovertible proof the gold is on his estate."

Chris cleared his throat. "And does he?"

"Not at all. It's poppy-cock. It's not even known if the treasure, if it exists, is on the island or the mainland. Whatever 'proof' he has must be forged. The man is a charlatan, trading on the reputation of Iris Mahoney and the like to make himself a multimillionaire before vanishing to some private Caribbean isle no doubt. Men like him make my blood absolutely boil."

"And Mrs Mahoney felt the same?"

"Oh, yes. Very much the same. She clashed with Barrington-Brown on numerous occasions. So, last year, we set up a campaign group to get Brown investigated and Derwydd Hall closed down."

"I'm a little confused about how you and Mrs Mahoney got together?"

"I led an archaeological dig last summer at Moel-y-don. Another failed attempt to discover the hoard. Iris read about it in the local press and contacted me with her concerns about Derwydd Hall. And things escalated from there."

Chris cleared his throat. "And forgive me, professor, but when you heard about Mrs Mahoney's death, did you not to think to contact us? Or suspect it might be connected with your campaign?"

The professor sat back, stunned, as if the thought had seriously never once occurred to him. "Well ... no. Not at all. I mean, why would it? Barrington-Brown might be every kind of con artist, but he wasn't violent. Never so much as a threat against our name. I always saw him as something of a coward. I honestly can't imagine this has anything to do with him." He frowned, shook his head. "No. It would make no sense. Why would he want to kill Iris?"

"Well, I can see a motive if I'm honest, sir. If Mrs Mahoney was as tenacious as you make out, and she was seen as a serious threat to his business empire, then surely this would be one way to shut her up and eradicate the problem." Chris shrugged. "Maybe an argument went too far this time, someone snapped. It seems logical to me."

Bolton swallowed, studied the back of his hands. "I don't know why it never seemed logical to me. I can see now I should have come forward and it was remiss of me. I actually considered contacting someone to try and find out about the funeral arrangements. But honestly, detective, I never once connected Barrington-Brown with her death. I suppose I must be naïve."

"Not necessarily. I think as police we're probably programmed a little differently. It helps to see things from an outsider's point of view too." Chris got to his feet and slid a card from his pocket. "It's been really useful speaking to you today. If you think of anything else – however tenuous you may think it is – give me a call. And I'll contact you myself once I know about the funeral, don't worry."

The professor got to his feet and shook Chris's hand across the desk. "And it goes without saying, whatever assistance I can be, in whatever capacity, I'm more than willing to help. I'll do anything to see whoever murdered Iris behind bars for the rest of their worthless life."

Professor Bolton turned to Megan, shook her hand. "I realise who you are now, your connection to Adrian. He mentioned you'd met up by chance. He seems keen to see you again too. I think you could be very good for him. I hope to see you again soon." He winked, looked at Chris, then back to her. "And I apologise if I've embarrassed you in front of your colleague, but I have to say my son seems well and truly smitten."

Megan's cheeks began to flood with heat and she mumbled an awkward thank you before bolting for the door. She was half-way down the corridor before Chris's footsteps caught up with her.

"K.I.S.S.I.N.G. Megan and Adrian –"

"Get stuffed, Coleman. Drop it. That was mortifying, not to mention creepy. I've not even been out on a date with the guy and I have his father's blessing."

"Don't knock it. He's a decent enough fella. And he's given us a ton of new leads to work on. Who'd have thought old Iris Mahoney came from Druid stock? No wonder she had all those hidden talents –"

Megan turned to glance at Chris as they headed across the car park. "Are you taking the piss? After what you said about the S4C programme?"

He waved the comment away. "Ah, that was television fodder. I am quite prepared to believe in Druid rites and second sight. You'd be surprised how broad-minded I am as a matter of fact."

Megan raised her eyebrows. "Really?"

"Absolutely."

"Well, have to say I am itching to speak to Matthew Barrington-Brown again and find out why he chose not to mention his true relationship with Iris Mahoney when I last interviewed him."

"I'd have thought that was blatantly obvious. If it got out she was undermining his Druid connections and this treasure hoard malarkey, and in so doing cutting off his financial income, he knew he'd be catapulted right to the top of the suspect list." Chris broke stride as his mobile phone rang and he dug it from his jacket pocket.

Megan stopped beside the passenger door of Chris's car. Her mind was buzzing with fresh questions and new ideas. This conversation opened up a whole new line of enquiry that had to be followed up without delay. If Barrington-Brown hadn't physically carried out the murder, she knew contract killers were two-a-penny nowadays, even out here in deepest Wales.

Chris caught up with her and she sensed the urgency in his voice. "Okay, no problem, pal. We'll head straight there, we're minutes away."

Chris ended the call and exhaled loudly, closing his eyes and propping one hand against his Volvo.

"What's the matter?" said Megan.

"I think this case has just blown apart."

She frowned. "Sorry?"

"That was Parry. Another body has been found. According to the First Attending Officer it's the same MO as Iris Mahoney's murder."

"No way?"

Chris nodded. "Way."

Chapter Seven

Gareth raised a hand in acknowledgement to the fresh-faced constable on duty at the farm gate, and squeezed the car down a narrow drive bordered with high, wild hedgerows. Focused on keeping the vehicle in a straight line, he ignored the scrape of branches against the side windows. He parked between a lone squad car and an aged red Ford van in the yard and, in his interior mirror, saw WPC Hewines approaching. As he climbed out, Sue Connolly's Audi appeared behind him.

The WPC looked pale-faced and tired. "Sir, I've secured the scene. The victim is in the kitchen, round the back of the property."

"Who found her?"

"One of the caravanners –"

"Caravanners?"

"Yes, sir. We've not checked it out yet, but apparently there's a mobile home site next door."

"Oh, okay."

"The chap says the place is owned by the deceased, Bronwen Evans. Her husband died a few months back and the caravanners have been rallying round to try and help her keep the farm going. They seem a close bunch."

"Where's this chap now?"

"Sid Fielding. He's gone back to his caravan to have a cup of tea. He's in shock."

Sue Connolly arrived at his side, already kitted out in a pale blue protective suit. She held a spare out to him. "Virgin crime scene. Sorry, but you'll have to suffer the indignity with me today."

Gareth grimaced and balanced against his car as he tugged the thin plastic up over his trousers and shrugged his arms into the material. He finished the ensemble with plastic over-shoes, latex gloves and pulled the hood up to cover his hair.

He caught up with Sue and the WPC at the front door of the farmhouse.

Sue bit back a smile. "Sexy." She reached forward and tugged a rogue flap of material from behind his ear and attached it with Velcro beneath his chin.

"Thanks," he muttered, before taking the lead and easing open the door with his foot. He turned and addressed the WPC. "Can you wait out here? Make sure no one else comes in without a suit and give me a call when SOCO arrive."

WPC Hewines nodded eagerly, relief clear in her eyes.

He paused on the top step, making out a flash of blue water, and in the distance rows of multi-coloured houses that signified the town of Beaumaris across on Anglesey.

"I didn't realise we're so near the Menai Straits here."

The WPC nodded. "Yes, just across these fields. Apparently the farm land stretches right down to the edge of the water."

Sue cleared her throat. "I lived near here when I first moved to the hospital. It's very flat, called Traeth Lafan or Lavan Sands. Goes right across to Beaumaris. I still see folks collecting cockles or mussels or something at low tide when I'm driving to and from work."

"So, where is Penmon from here? As the crow flies, I mean?" asked Gareth, lifting himself onto his tiptoes to see over the tall hedges.

Sue followed his gaze. "Directly across the Straits, on a slight diagonal."

"Could you see it from here?"

Sue nodded. "Definitely. Why ... are you thinking there's a connection?"

Gareth shrugged. "I don't know what I'm thinking to tell the truth. I suppose I'm hoping there's a connection between this death and Iris Mahoney's and they're not random killings. Because if there is a link it might make our job a bit easier. If there's not then it could be nigh-on impossible. Especially if there's as little forensics here as Penmon."

"Well, only one way to find out," said Sue, seeming to sense his reticence.

He nodded and turned his attention back to the building, noting a second door, to something like a corrugated shed, on his right.

"*Ymholiadau*," He pronounced slowly as he read a home-made sign in the window. "Name of the house?"

"No, it means *Enquiries*, sir," replied WPC Hewines. "I think it's a closed-up farm shop or something. I looked through the window, but I couldn't see much apart from cobwebs and dirt."

"Okay." He sighed and held his face to the sun for a moment. "Come on, then, can't put it off any longer."

The contrast between the warm sunshine and the closed-up, musty darkness of the cottage was marked. Gareth shivered. All the curtains were closed; dusty blue velvet affairs that shut out every trace of sunlight. And the smell. Remnants of some last meal mixed with a copper-metallic stench that was unmistakeably blood, and topped off by the indescribable tang of death and decay.

Gareth pushed open each door in turn. A narrow, old-fashioned bathroom, pale blue ceramic bath, stained brown with water marks; a tiny dining room, jam-packed with china figurines; a living room containing a worn emerald green sofa and a television that looked antique. Sue Connolly squeezed past him, flicked on the hall light, and headed for the open door at the end of the narrow passageway. Gareth let her go; he was in no hurry to view the corpse. Upstairs, two small bedrooms yielded few clues; eventually, he ran out of options and joined Sue in the kitchen.

She had opened the curtains, allowing sunlight to add a little warmth and light to the room. It did nothing to improve the atmosphere. The scene was a mirror-image of Penmon cottage. A single chair, positioned as pride of place in the centre of the room. Three other chairs and a matching pine table had been pushed against the sink unit to make room.

Bronwen Evans was a large lady. Navy blue skirt, pale blue jumper and a floral pinafore dress – all stained a muddy, dark brown. Her slippered feet and swollen ankles were secured tightly to the legs of the chair, and a small pond of dried blood surrounded her body. Gareth could never remember seeing so much blood. How could the human body hold so much? Her chin had fallen forward, and both arms were twisted behind her back, secured with the same black plastic cable ties as the previous victim.

Sue moved around the body, finally concentrating on the gaping wound that ran from ear to ear. She probed the rolls of flesh, exposing the wound, and twisted the neck to one side. Gareth swallowed, looked away. The kitchen table was set for afternoon tea for two. Fragile rose-patterned bone china tea cups and teapot, matching plates with slices of Battenberg cake and an assortment of shortcake biscuits. The cup on her side of the table was half-empty, congealing milk coating sandy-coloured liquid, with traces of cherry-pink lipstick on the edge. On the opposite side of the table, crumbs signified someone had enjoyed the biscuits, but the teacup was empty, pristine.

Sue stood upright, unsnapped her case and removed a thermometer. "From preliminary measurements you need to be looking for a long blade, an educated guess at this stage would be over 12cm. And fairly wide, I would say at least 3cm at its base. A standard kitchen knife, but larger than the one used at Penmon."

"If it's here, we'll find it. How long has she been dead?"

"A guess would be about twenty-four hours. You know the drill; I can confirm a tighter window at post-mortem. But hours, certainly, not days."

After taking the temperature of the corpse and typing the data into her Blackberry, Sue moved to the rear of the chair, and dropped to her haunches, with a sharp intake of breath.

"What is it?"

"Well, we may have a different murder weapon, but I think we can say with certainty this crime is linked to Iris Mahoney's."

"Why?"

Sue held her hand out, latex-covered palm held fragments of what looked like tree bark.

"Is that what I think it is?"

Sue nodded. "Yes. Two fingernails and a thumbnail from the left hand. The same from her right."

Outside, twenty minutes later, Gareth briefed Chris and Megan, instructing them to carry out a full search of the property, concentrating on any link to Iris Mahoney or Matthew Barrington-Brown. He also filled them in on the pathologist's discovery of the marks on Iris's hip.

Chris whistled and shook his head. "Christ, wait till you hear what we've discovered from the prof this afternoon. The evidence against this Barrington-Brown bloke seems to be stacking up for sure."

"Megan, can you put a call into Macrae for me, ask him if we can arrange a team meeting this evening back at the station? First, let's blitz this place and knock off the door-to-doors. I'm going to talk to the chap who found the body, see what he knows about Bronwen Evans."

Gareth walked the length of the drive, back to the road, then did a sharp left and headed back towards the Menai Straits, the roofs of static caravans guiding him. Heat shimmered off the water; a flotilla of small multi-coloured sailing boats headed out past Beaumaris and Puffin Island, close enough to hear voices from the decks. He imagined hundreds of people all along the coast, enjoying the sunshine on beaches, boats and mountain walks. It was hard to balance the idea of family holidays against the scene he'd faced this afternoon.

Sid Fielding's mobile home was the first on the right as he entered the gate of the mobile home park according to the WPC. He knocked at the door and was hurried inside by a slight woman with dyed red hair, wearing a long green kaftan.

"Sid's on the terrace. He's hardly said a word. Shock, I think."

Through a comfortable lounge, surprisingly spacious and elegant for what was a glorified caravan, back out into the sunshine. A white-haired man in his sixties, red-faced with a large pot-belly straining a red t-shirt to its limits, sat awkwardly balancing his rotund frame on a patio stool. He turned as Gareth approached.

"Mr Fielding?"

"Call me Sid. Everyone does."

"Sid. My name is Detective Sergeant Parry. I'm in charge of the investigation at the moment. I understand you were unfortunate enough to find the victim?"

Gareth pulled another stool across to the table and sat down.

The man sniffed and nodded. His eyes were swollen and watery.

"Can I get you a drink before I leave you?" asked the woman, who Gareth assumed was Mrs Fielding.

"I'm fine, but thank you."

With a smile, the woman reversed back into the dimness of the caravan and slid the patio door across. The man had still failed to speak. He nursed an almost-empty mug of tea and stared off into the distance.

"Can you tell me what happened, Sid?"

He nodded, looked down, pushed the tea away across the

table. "Yeah. Just before lunch, it were. I thought I'd take Betty – that's our dog – out for her run before the antiques programme that Hettie likes. Thought I'd head as far as the Spar, see if my fishing magazine had come in, so I called in on Bronwen to see if she needed anything."

"Right. So, you walked up the lane from here?" Sid nodded. "Did you see anyone leaving? Any suspicious cars?"

Sid frowned, shook his head. "No, not right then. But I'm fairly sure I saw a taxi last night. I thought that were odd. I'd never known Bronwen use a taxi; she went everywhere in that battered old van."

Gareth nodded encouragingly. "What time was this?"

"Early-ish, 'bout eight, I'd say."

"Can you remember the name of the cab firm?"

"I didn't see for sure, but I think it were Bangor Cabs."

"Why?"

"It were a white Merc. They only run old Mercedes, a trademark thing; you see 'em all over town."

Gareth typed a note of the cab company in his phone. "What did you do when you arrived at the farmhouse?"

"I tried the back door but it were locked, which is unusual. Open house usually, that's what Bronwen likes. Although recent, since she lost her hubbie, I thought she'd gone a bit reclusive. Grief I suppose, but still I had it in the back of my head she might be ill. I don't know why, not really, she could just as easy have been out somewhere. But anyway, I went round to the front, though they never used the front door, dunno when I last saw it open. But I recall Dewi, her late husband, telling me if there was ever an emergency, that he kept a spare key in the hanging basket."

He paused, reached out for the mug, then, realising it was empty, slid his hands away. "I went straight through to the kitchen; it's where she always was. It was dark inside, smelled musty. Smelled like something wasn't right. I put the light on, saw the blood first, all over the floor, thought she'd spilled something, still convincing myself she was poorly." He shook his head. "Then I saw her. All trussed up like a chicken. Throat sliced open. I don't think I'll ever forget it. I mean, how do you forget something like that?"

"It's not easy, sir. Time's a healer." Gareth patted his arm. "And you called the police and ambulance from the farm?"

"Yeah, from me mobile. I called everybody I could think of, didn't know what to do to be honest. I was going to come back here, wait it out. But then I thought what if someone else went in, saw the body by mistake, it'd have a hell of an effect on them. So, I stayed put till the ambulance arrived, nothing they could do, of course. Then you lot turned up and I had to get away, felt like my legs were going to give out, so I came back here."

"And how long have you known the deceased? Is there anything you can tell us about her that might help our enquiries?"

Sid straightened his back. "I'll do anything I can, of course. But I've got no idea what kind of sick-minded bastard could do such a thing. I mean, enemies is one thing – not that I've any reason to think Bronwen would have had enemies – but what went on there ... well, that's beyond comprehension. She was a nice, normal elderly woman. They both were lovely people, well respected, spent their whole lives round here. They've been good to me, Dewi and Bronwen, always have. Since my retirement, I sold up and moved here, ooh, must be nearly twenty years now so Hettie could be closer to her folks – and they've always been good neighbours, could never do enough. Even got me a little part-time job on the farm, was talk of re-opening the farm shop before Dewi died, putting me in charge. But of course, it all went to pot once he passed. I was sad to hear Bronwen was thinking of selling up, though it's understandable, I couldn't see how she'd cope without Dewi."

"Selling up?"

Sid nodded. "Yes, she told us a few weeks ago. Had an offer for the land she couldn't refuse from some property big-wig. Three times the normal value, so she reckoned. Last I heard she was in talks to buy a bungalow in town."

"Do you know any more information about this sale? Names of the developer or anything?"

Sid shook his head. "Bronwen was always private, and right proud, you know. Only tell you what she wanted you to know. All I know is it must've been a hell of an offer to uproot her from her family home. Three generations farmed the land, so she said to me once." Sid stopped, shook his head and blinked. "I'll miss them both. That's fer sure. And I'll miss the old farm too. Truth be told, I enjoyed helping out, it kept me active." He tapped his head. "Up here, you know. Dewi was well-liked; you should have seen how many came to his funeral. Bronwen, she's more on the quiet side, keeps herself to herself, you know." He stopped, looked up, white-faced. "Oh, no, I never thought. Mairwen. She won't know, will she?" He turned towards the patio window. "Hettie … Hettie!"

Gareth cleared his throat. "Sorry, who's …?"

The patio window slid open. Mrs Fielding appeared. "What's the matter?"

"Has anyone told Mair?" said Sid. "I never thought …"

Mrs Fielding put a hand to her mouth, shook her head. "Me neither. I bet no one has called in on her this morning either." She turned away. "I should go …"

Gareth stood up. "Sorry. Hang on. Who's Mairwen?"

Sid shook his head. "Mair is Bronwen's sister. She lives in a tiny little place, right down on the water's edge. Bronwen looks after her, well, I mean she used to. Someone has to tell her … see if she's okay."

"Don't worry. I'll see to it. It's probably better it comes from us."

"She don't take to strangers," said Sid. "You'd do well to take Hettie."

"Okay, and thank you. Go and rest. I'll have someone take a statement from you later."

Gareth retrieved his mobile from his pocket. "Megan. Can

you come down to the mobile home site, straight away? I need your charms; we've got a next-of-kin to notify."

Chapter Eight

Megan shielded her eyes with her hand as they followed a narrow track along the edge of a long field. Gradual undulations sloped right down to the shoreline. The sun was warm on the back of her neck, and she took off her suit jacket, and slung it across the straps of her handbag.

In a small cluster of trees, a white cottage with a purple slate roof nestled in a cut out of rock. The shelf of limestone seemed to cradle the cottage as if carrying it in its palm, protecting it from the elements. A narrow strip of pebbled beach separated the copse from the ocean. Seagulls circled the shoreline, swooping down into the water in noisy, cackling flashes of white; the strong stench of seaweed heavy in the hot air.

Sid Fielding's wife hurried ahead, flip-flops slap-slapping on the cobbled track.

"So, she's no idea," said Megan, "that her sister's dead, I mean?"

Gareth shook his head. "Not unless one of the other caravanners has been down and told her. And Mrs Fielding is worried because Bronwen called on her every morning. I'm not sure if she's disabled or something from the way Sid spoke, but she is a fair bit older than Bronwen apparently."

"Either way, it's going to be an upheaval for her. I can't see she'll be able to carry on living out here without her sister's help. God knows why you'd want to chose such a remote spot."

"The land's been in the family for generations according to Sid Fielding. And it was Bronwen's family. Not Dewi's. So, I suppose Mairwen has an association with the place, probably a share of the ownership too."

"Poor thing. Double whammy. I wonder if we should contact social services, see if there's anywhere local that can take her?"

"Let's meet her first. We might be jumping to all the wrong conclusions. Besides, Bronwen has been looking to sell the farm since her hubbie died, according to Sid. She may have already made alternative plans for her sister."

Mrs Fielding waited at the top of stone steps that led down onto a tiny square of lawn and the front door of the cottage. In the shade of the trees, the air was cool and sour, thick with the tang of rotting wood, fungi and moss. Megan rubbed her arms, blinked to clear her vision, and slipped her arms back into her jacket, fastening two buttons.

When they joined her on the lawn, the woman rapped on the door three times. "Hello. Mairwen? It's Hettie Fielding. Are you there, my love? Can we come in?"

Silence.

Gareth twisted the old-fashioned round handle. It was locked.

"Mairwen?" Mrs Fielding raised her voice. "Are you there?"

Gareth rattled the door. "Is there another entrance round the back we can try?"

Hettie shook her head. "No. But give her a minute, don't startle her, she's not that fast nowadays." She leaned closer to the door jamb. "Mairwen! Can you hear me, my love?"

There was low distant thud inside the house. Hettie turned and gave a thumbs-up.

"It's Hettie Fielding. Are you okay, Mair?"

A shuffling noise, the scrape of metal, and the door swung inward.

"What's with all the yelling? Can't a woman get an afternoon nap without all this fuss?"

Megan adjusted her line of sight. Mairwen was in a wheelchair, crooked and hunched-back, wearing a navy blue dress and a necklace of delicate pearls. She wore tights or stockings and patent ballet pumps that matched the colour of her dress. Although she was smartly dressed, her head dropped permanently forward, pink scalp visible through thinning strands of white hair. She stared at the floor as it was too much effort to lift her head. Megan frowned at Gareth, who shrugged.

"Sorry, my love. It's Hettie. Can we come in?"

"We? Who's we? You've a man with you … and it's not your Sid either."

Mairwen gripped the wheels of her chair, and manoeuvred herself backwards. Looking up for the first time, Megan saw her eyes, coloured like the brightest blue marbles. But empty and sightless.

"Has something happened? Bronwen hasn't been in yet and I've lost track of time. I had breakfast but I think I've missed dinner." She paused, one wrinkled hand reaching up to touch the pearls. "It's Bronwen. It is, isn't it? Tell me."

Hettie waved them through into a cosy sitting room, with two small sofas facing each other across an open fire, now dark, cold and sooty. She closed the door behind her, then dropped to her haunches beside the wheelchair.

"It's the police, Mairwen. They need to talk to you, my love." Hettie stroked the old woman's hand that gripped the arm of her chair like an eagle's talon.

"What's happened to my sister?"

Megan scowled as she took a seat on the edge of the furthest sofa. No one had mentioned Bronwen yet. Yes, okay, she was later than usual with her daily visit, but the certainty in this old woman's voice didn't seem consistent with the facts.

Gareth cleared his throat and took a step forward. "Mairwen, I'm sorry, I don't know your last name, so forgive my presumptiveness. I'm DS Parry and I'm with my colleague, DC Jones. I'm afraid we do have some bad news about your sister."

The head slumped again. "She's dead?"

"I'm afraid so," said Gareth. "I understand it will be a shock to you ..."

Mairwen shook her head. "No, it's no shock."

Gareth paused, then when she offered nothing else, added. "We're very sorry for your loss. Do you have any friends or family we could contact? You'll need someone to stay with you, I'm sure."

Mairwen remained silent, her left hand continued to worry away at the pearls, twisting them between her thumb and first finger, finding comfort as if it were a rosary.

Hettie spoke up. "Mairwen, who should I call –?"

The elderly woman shook her head. "No one, you hear, I don't want no-one," she snapped. "It was always just me and Bronwen."

Hettie glanced up at Gareth. "Well, I can stay for now. And I can get Sid to bring you down a bit of dinner later, how's that sound? There's no rush, we can sort something out."

Mairwen nodded, seemed to acknowledge the words, but didn't reply.

"Would we be able to ask you a few questions, Mairwen? Would that be possible?" Gareth took a seat on the nearest sofa, and Hettie rolled the wheelchair nearer. "It's important for us, but if you don't feel ready to talk, we understand of course –"

Mairwen spoke into her lap. "Talk? What's the use of talking? It won't bring Bronwen back, will it?"

Megan listened to the low voice and wondered why she'd not asked for any details about her sister's death. It was almost like she already knew.

"No," Gareth agreed. "But in any death where there are suspicious circumstances, it's our duty to investigate. And if we find someone was responsible for your sister's death, then I'm sure you'd want justice done, wouldn't you?"

"She was killed then?"

The statement was issued in such a matter-of-fact voice that it silenced the room.

Gareth nodded, then quickly realised. "Yes, I'm afraid she was."

"It was murder? I always knew our Bronwen would meet a tragic end. It was written."

"Written?" Gareth glanced from the old woman to Hettie, who replied with a shrug.

"Yes, written. While I'm left to fade away. Bronwen was always down to be taken."

Megan frowned, deciding there was more than a touch of dementia in evidence here. Mairwen looked well into her seventies, and it was clear, that even despite her blindness, there was no way she would be able to look after herself. It was a wonder she was washed, dressed and in her chair without assistance.

Mairwen lifted her head, turned her face towards Gareth. "I've just remembered my manners. Shock, I think. But can I get anyone refreshments? It feels like another hot one out there."

Hettie put one hand on her arm. "I'm sure the officers don't want anything, my love, don't you fret. If they do, I can see to it, don't worry."

Pacified, the chin dropped again, the hand slipped from the pearls.

"Thank you, Mairwen," said Gareth. "We're both fine, honestly. Are you up for talking about Bronwen?"

The elderly woman nodded.

"Good. So, can you tell me when you last saw her, I mean, I'm sorry, when you last spoke to her, here, I mean, when she last visited ..."

"Young man, I know I'm sightless and I'm sure it's not escaped your notice either, so there's really no need to pussy-foot around the subject. It's hardly news." She took a deep breath. "Bronwen was here yesterday. Twice in fact. She helped me with a bath first thing, about 6.30am. And then we shared a lunch together in the garden, like a picnic, she said. Sandwiches and cake and cider under the shade of the oaks. If I had to have a final memory of her, what a blessing it was that one."

"And how did Bronwen seem to you? She didn't tell you of any worries? Or seem different in any way?"

Mairwen shook her head. "She was fine. Absolutely fine." She paused. "I got the impression she was expecting a visitor when she left. She didn't say so as such. But she seemed to be clock-watching, though I could be wrong. I'm probably the worst eye witness ever." She paused. "I assumed it was something to do with the sale of the farm, an estate agent or the like. She knew I disapproved, so it was the one thing we rarely discussed. I think she felt she was doing right by protecting me from the details until I had to know."

Megan made a few notes, while Gareth pushed on with the questions.

"Okay, but she didn't say anything that gave you a hint who it might have been?"

Mairwen shook her head. "I can't think of anything. And I can't think of anything that had been troubling her either. To be honest, Bronwen had been in a low place since Dewi's death. I actually thought to myself yesterday that she seemed happy for the first time. The first time since he died, I mean. When Dewi was alive, my sister was permanently happy, they were a couple very much in love for over forty years."

"You say you disapproved of Bronwen's decision to sell the farm, why was that?"

Mairwen licked her lips. "Hettie, do you think I could have a glass of water?" When Mrs Fielding disappeared into an adjoining room, she continued. "Why do you think? It was my family's land, had been for hundreds of years, if not more. Oh, I understood Bronwen couldn't carry on alone, and had no one to help and no one to inherit, but I urged her to think about getting someone in to run the place rather than sell, but she was adamant and there was no shifting my sister once she'd made her mind up." She sighed. "But it's all irrelevant now anyway."

Hettie returned and fixed the glass into Mairwen's grip.

"There's a bit of tidying I can be doing in the kitchen. Call me if you need me."

Mairwen sipped the water, then lifted a hand, touched Gareth's knee. "How was she killed?"

Gareth flashed Megan a look. She nodded.

"Are you sure you want to know?"

She drained the glass. "No. But I need to know. I fear it may be important."

Once again, her words brought a temporary silence to the room.

"She was murdered, I'm afraid, in the kitchen of her cottage."

"How?"

"Mairwen, I don't –"

"How, DS Parry?"

Gareth pursed his lips. "With a knife ..."

"She was stabbed?"

"No, her throat was cut."

Mairwen removed her hand, sat back in her chair. "As was Iris Mahoney."

Megan returned Gareth's wide-eyed expression. "You knew Mrs Mahoney?" he said.

"Of course. We heard what happened. First Iris. Now Bronwen." The old woman dropped her chin, but her hands returned to her pearls. "I fear there may be a connection, detective ... it might be time to tell the others before it's too late."

Gareth frowned, matching Megan's own puzzlement. "Others?"

Mairwen drew in a deep breath. "I think it's time you learned about the Servants of Truth."

Chapter IV

MONA INSULIS, BRITAIN - AD 60

"Eyes forward, men. Steady now. Hold your line!"

Marcus flashed a glance along the row of men, stilling the unrest with a raised fist. His legion stood at the edge of the narrow stretch of water that separated the mainland from the island of Mona Insulis. The air hummed with the tension of a hundred men. Every splash of a fish set Marcus's heart pounding. Each invisible cough caused hands to tighten on the solid pommel of a hundred swords. He couldn't see the enemy through the creeping sea mist, but he could smell them – terror mixed with blood, sweat and grime.

As a cool dawn broke, the milky mist rolled off the ocean like a gossamer veil. The pale sun rose above the mountains behind them, casting the first hint of shadow across his feet. Marcus could not help but think of the battle to come; how it would destroy the beauty and peace of the place. His breath caught in his throat as he imagined the sight facing their enemy. Rows of men, four deep, lined the sloping shingle beach. A rippling sea of glistening bronze helmets and gleaming javelin tips seemed to herald the dawn.

At that moment, as if in celebration of the new day, the

piercing cry of Roman war trumpets shattered the tranquility of the scene, answered almost immediately by the defiant blast of war horns from the opposite bank. It seemed the decoy had not been wholly effective. The mist lifted to reveal a healthy band of men, beating swords against their shields in a synchronised rhythm. A scream echoed across the water and Marcus caught a glimpse of a group of naked women, long, wild, black hair and blue-painted bodies, whirling between the groups of men, waving burning branches.

"Listen to them," said Titus, his voice tight. "Like bloody wild beasts. They're no more than savages."

"Yes, very different to the tribes of Britons we have encountered so far, even the language," said Marcus. "But as steadfast and fearless as Caratacus ever was. They fear nothing. Not even us."

"Well, they should," said Titus. "We are the most respected army in the world, defending the best Empire. They should welcome the organisation and prosperity we offer." He spat into the dust at their feet. "Who are they, this tribe that dare think they can oppose us?"

"The Ordovices. This island is their sacred place. The seat of the Druids."

All Romans knew stories of Druids that had terrified children for generations.

Marcus continued, "But it's also a fertile land; rich in minerals and precious metals, like copper, and a trade route for gold from across the sea. Suetonius Paullinus has given very clear orders of the need to crush this tribe."

"It will be a bloody massacre," said Titus. "We must pray Fortuna smiles down on us; we shall need all the gods' favour."

A rumble of agreement rippled through the men.

Marcus turned sharply. "Titus, sometimes you speak less like a Roman than any man I know. You shame me. You see our standard?" He pointed to their flag bearer, then took Titus's arm and twisted him towards it. "The bird is an eagle. A bird of prey, understand, not a chicken. It is meant to inspire men to bravery, not turn tail and save their own skin at the first sign of trouble."

Titus straightened as his cheeks coloured. "I apologise, sir."

"I am a centurion in the most elite army in the world. I do not show fear. Whatever I feel in my heart and my mind stays hidden. You are my second in command; therefore I expect the same from you. We have to set an example for our men. These people are savages, true, but we show no fear in the face of adversity. Never."

Titus bowed his head. "Yes, sir."

Marcus nodded his reply, released the grip on Titus's arm, and faced forward as the echoing call of war horns started up again. Titus infuriated him at times, yet he was by far the best optio Marcus had commanded. He was loyal and intelligent. If only he could learn to hide his feelings, and engage his brain before his mouth.

The fog swirled and clung to the surrounding trees, heavy leaves dripped rain onto their heads in a constant patter. The leaden skies darkened even more as storm clouds mingled overhead.

"Light the braziers, men!" Marcus called.

As he walked the line of men, the wind blew his cloak around his legs. His fingers gripped his javelin like iced claws and he shivered with chills that penetrated his tunic. It would, he feared, be a long, hard battle. This tribe would not roll over as easily as many gone before. This confrontation could be as hard fought as the legendary battles against the Catuvellauni, when Rome first landed on these shores almost two decades ago, and Marcus worried for the loss of men.

But he would never admit any of this to Titus.

He slipped his hand beneath his chain mail, pulling free the leather thong he wore around his neck. Frozen fingers touched the comforting warmth of the tiny amulet of Hercules he carried next to his heart; a gift from his father before leaving Rome. Lifting the figure to his mouth, he pressed his lips against the smoothness of the bronze, repeating a prayer of his father's as he closed his eyes.

'*Divinus vox quod humanus res opus in consensio.*'

'The divine powers and human beings shall work in harmony.'

As Marcus looked across the water with the prayer still on his lips, he got his first glimpse of a Druid priest. His fingers clenched around his javelin, and a shudder ran the length of his spine. While a single Druid lived there would be a constant threat to the Roman Empire. Since their persecution at the hands of Julius Caesar, all Druids regarded Rome, and all things Roman, with a burning and persistent hatred. These poor savages did not realise they were caught up in a battle between two unstoppable forces.

The priest lifted his arms, white robes swayed in the breeze. Chanting, he stamped in circles on top of a grassy mound. A few men turned to watch in awe as his words increased in vigour and volume as he lifted his face to the sun. The painted women matched his steps, whirling and twisting their bodies, caught up in a religious ecstasy. As the drumbeats reached fever pitch, the Druid looked up, long white hair billowing around his face. For a brief moment, his eyes locked on Marcus. One arm fell and the Druid pointed, forefinger outstretched, directly at Marcus's heart.

Marcus looked away, swallowed down a tide of fear that rose from his belly. The bowl of porridge he ate earlier lodged like a boulder in his gut. A squall of wind rippled down the narrow channel, gusting tunics and cloaks. Heavy thunder rolled above them, and huge rain drops splashed into the water.

"You think it's an omen?" Titus asked; his voice strained. "A sign from the gods? Can they really conjure up forces of nature to assist them?"

"Maybe," said Marcus, shaking away the memory of the Druid's dark eyes. "Or perhaps a sign it's going to piss down and we should get a move on before we get soaked."

Titus's frown lifted and his face creased into a grin; the tension easing as a few men chuckled.

A movement to their left; the snort of horses as the men fell back, parting like a tide of scarlet. Marcus recognised the white stallion of Suetonius Paullinus. The horse slithered down the bank, hooves crunching across shingle as he followed the high tide mark, inspecting the neat lines of soldiers.

He paused, arms wide. The men stilled, attention fixed on their leader.

"Gentlemen, the tide is almost at its lowest, time for us to launch our invasion. The decoy has been successful, there are far fewer men here than predicted, and we must move with speed before reinforcements arrive. Each man is to leave non-essential kit here. The boats are sturdy but if for any reason you are forced to swim, no one must be carrying more than they need. As soon as you are in the boats, the artillery crew are primed, ready to mount a protective attack. Everyone clear?"

A positive response rose from the men. Suetonius held up a hand, urging quiet once more.

"You have achieved much. Today, all of Rome looks on you to do more. May the gods preserve each and every one of you. To the boats then, gentlemen!"

Suetonius waited as the men dispersed in ordered rows towards the creek. He leaned down, squeezed Marcus's shoulder.

"And you too, Marcus. The luck of Fortuna and the love of your family keep you safe, my boy."

Chapter Nine

"So, let me recap if you will. All of you – that is a team of above-average-intelligence detectives – are really coming round to the idea that both the deaths of Iris Mahoney and Bronwen Evans are connected with some two thousand-year-old organisation that no one has ever heard of, whose membership is a closely-guarded secret, and who all believe themselves to be descendants of some powerful Druidic lineage?"

DI Macrae looked from one face to the next and tapped the marker pen he held against the white board. "Do you honestly want me to add that to a double-murder investigation in 2013?"

Gareth flashed a glance at Megan and Chris who both nodded, then replied. "I think so, sir. There are way too many coincidences involved for us not to at least consider it."

Macrae sighed. "Okay, so I can take what Professor Bolton told us, and I admit the hunt for hidden treasure could be a motive. I can believe that Barrington-Brown, for all the wrong reasons, has jumped on the back of this legend. But what I'm struggling to accept is that after dismissing his 'Derwydd cult' as a sham and him as nothing more than a charlatan, why are we now ready to accept another, even shadier, organisation are actually the true embodiment of what Barrington-Brown is trying to prove exists?"

"The way I see it, sir," said Gareth. "Is that somehow, at some time, Barrington-Brown found out about the Servants of Truth and the rumours of treasure, and he's jumped on the bandwagon to exploit it. Yes, there's little documentary evidence, Mairwen Thomas told us that, but there will be written word somewhere. The Servants of Truth were created to protect the dwindling lineage of the Druids, because they believe, one day, their time will come again. Who's to say they weren't also put in place to protect this treasure?"

Chris cleared his throat. "Like the Knights Templar or something."

Macrae pointed at Chris. "You ... come on, man, back me up. You're the most grounded bloke I know, surely you aren't falling for this Druid rubbish? Give me a break!"

Chris studied the backs of his hands for a quiet moment, then shrugged. "I don't think we can discount anything, sir. This job used to make me cynical. But remember little Jake West."

Macrae stood motionless. Gareth noticed a nerve twitch above his right eye. Just the mention of the child's name brought powerful images of Edwina's corpse flooding into his head with the speed and force of a spring high tide. He let out a long breath.

Megan looked up from her typing. "Who's Jake West?"

Gareth smiled. "I'll tell you one day. Not now though."

She shrugged and returned her attention to her computer screen.

Macrae sighed and walked back to the front of the room. "Okay. So, I take off the blinkers you guys clearly think I wear ... and this is my problem. This story, told by a little old lady who you admit shows signs of dementia, is the first mention of this secret society for over two thousand years? Really? In an Internet age, where multi-media is available to everyone at the press of the button, the only way we discover its existence is when someone starts killing off its members one by one? Sorry, I don't buy it."

"Both victims exhibited signs of torture, sir," said Megan. "Someone wanted to extract information from them pretty badly."

Macrae rubbed his chin. "But what information?"

Megan shrugged. "I've tried *Googling* 'Servants of Truth' and nothing comes up apart from some references to this being a name for ancient Druids. No mention of any secret society, no mention of modern-day members or rumours of treasure. I don't think we've heard of it because we aren't meant to. Simple as that." Megan opened her notebook. "One other point. Gareth said Sid Fielding mentioned seeing a white taxi at the farm on the night of the murder. I contacted Bangor Cabs, and as many local cab firms as I could find, and none of them had a call out to an address in Tal-y-bont that night. So, Sid could be lying? Is that worth a follow up?"

Gareth wrinkled his nose. "It could be a genuine mistake. The car could have been turning in the drive, pulled over to answer a mobile – or had a wrong address. I don't see him as a suspect. But truth is, I don't see anyone else as a suspect either."

"It all comes back to this treasure if you ask me," said Chris. "Professor Bolton told us there's so little in the archives; he reiterated the oral traditions of the Druids. As an expert, he's spent years hunting its existence and got nowhere. If knowledge got into the wrong hands, I can see someone going to any length, including torture, to access the information."

"So, the Servants of Truth, these guardians … they're a band of little old lady vigilantes?" said Macrae. "I'm not being sarcastic now, it's a genuine question. Who are they?"

"We don't know, sir," admitted Gareth. "Mairwen Thomas refused to name any of the other members before she'd called a meeting to discuss what has happened and ask their permission. She said someone would contact us shortly. I didn't see any other way I could handle it – she'd just lost her sister, I couldn't get heavy. She also refused, point blank, to leave her cottage, which isn't a huge help in the circumstances."

"You think she could be next?" said Macrae.

"I've no idea. But I'm not comfortable about leaving her out there in the wilds."

Macrae frowned. "Okay. So, we give her a day – two tops. If she doesn't talk, then we have no choice but to get heavy and start demanding answers. I don't want to have to haul this woman in for questioning, but if this sisterhood are being wiped out one by one, we will have to insist on names of the rest of them. If only for their own protection."

Gareth nodded. "Understood, sir. And I agree."

"Not exactly the best guardians in the world then, are they?" Macrae shook his head. "They're dropping like flies, taking their secrets with them, what good is that to anyone?"

"I rather think that's the point, isn't it, sir?" said Megan. "They're going to their graves without passing on any information. Little old ladies or not, I think they're doing one hell of a job."

Macrae grunted but remained silent. He crossed his arms and focused on the writing on the white board. "So, regardless of the authenticity of this secret organisation, as I see it we still only have one suspect at the moment, this Barrington-Brown chap. Did you find anything at Bronwen Evans's place to connect to him?"

Gareth shook his head. "No, sir. And the sister had never heard of him either. But that's not unusual, I've a feeling Bronwen protected her sister from a lot of stuff. She's a decade older and totally blind, if there was any unpleasantness she wouldn't have wanted her involved. Mairwen admitted they didn't talk about the decision to sell the farm as she found it too distressing."

"Is there any mileage in that line of enquiry?"

Chris spoke up. "I'm following it up, sir. I've found a planning application, lodged a few days ago, for change of use of the land contained within Sacred Oaks Farm – but there's no developer's details listed online, and obviously the council offices are closed until Monday."

"Good work, Chris. It may lead nowhere, but it needs a follow up."

Megan raised her hand. "Did you say the farm was called Sacred Oaks?"

Chris nodded. "According to this. Why?"

Megan began to turn over the pages of her notebook. "It's a phrase that seems familiar to me, like I've heard it recently. Give me a minute ..."

Macrae added the name to the board. "Any forensics at the crime scene?"

Gareth shook his head. "Clean as a whistle, sir. It would seem the killer was known to the victim. They'd shared afternoon tea by all accounts. But the place was wiped clean, cups washed, and SOCO think gloves were worn during the actual murder. It was a professional job again, like Iris Mahoney's –"

"Yes!" Megan looked up, cheeks flushed. "Sorry to interrupt. Professor Bolton mentioned sacred oaks as being one of the most important Druidic symbols. It was a throwaway comment about Barrington-Brown having stolen the image to adapt into what the professor called a 'tacky family crest'."

Gareth jotted notes onto his pad. "So, if the land had been owned by generations of the same family, and if they were Druidic descendants, I guess it would make sense that's what they'd call the farm."

Macrae sighed. "If ... if ... if. This still all sounds more like fiction than fact to me. I'm not going to discount it, I can see by your scowls that wouldn't go down well, but we can't focus the whole investigation around it. I'm not comfortable with it."

Gareth shrugged. "But I don't see it affects how we proceed anyway. Surely we should pull in Barrington-Brown for questioning? Find out why he lied about Iris and see if he knows the second victim? He's involved somehow, I'm certain."

Macrae nodded. "And Megan, if we leave the boys to sort out Barrington-Brown, I'll let you run with the Druidic connection. Do some research, maybe speak to the professor again, see if he knew Bronwen Evans and if, as an expert, he knows about these Servants of Truth?" Macrae checked his watch. "Sorry to spoil your weekend plans, boys and girls, but you know what this job can be like."

Gareth got to his feet. "Coming, Chris? I'm quite looking forward to wrecking Matthew Barrington-Brown's Saturday evening."

The gleaming white and gold of Barrington-Brown's outfit looked oddly out of place among the muted greys of Interview Room 4. The red fury of his face added to the effect. He'd not yet stopped ranting and raving; the plastic vending machine cup of tea he'd been given on arrival was now dripping in dirty brown rivulets down the far wall.

A thirty-five minute car ride back to the station had done little to lessen his wrath, and although he'd now fallen silent because the room was empty, it was clear he was in the process of winding himself up into another furious explosion on whoever was unlucky enough to open the door next.

Chris leaned against the door frame and glanced through the two-way mirror. "Toss you for it. He's going to go ape-shit. And I'm too tired and cranky to be my usual placid self."

Gareth grinned, added a couple of kisses to the text he was composing, pressed send and then turned his phone off. He gave a deep sigh. "My heart bleeds. I've just cancelled on a delicious blonde Russian with legs up to her ears. He thinks we want to be stuck in there with him anymore than he wants to be here?"

Chris gave a quizzical glance. "You still up to your old tricks, then?"

"What do you mean?"

"With the lasses? I'd have thought you'd be on your best behaviour at the moment. Trying to make a good impression on the delicious Dr Connolly now she's free and single again."

Gareth swallowed hard, hoping to keep his face blank. So, he'd been right then about the hints last time they'd spoken.

"No idea what you're on about, pal."

Chris smirked. "Pull the other one. It's all round the station."

"No joke. Perhaps I'm deliberately out of the loop. I thought she was well loved-up with her Dr Javier and the wedding plans were in full swing?"

"Apparently not since she caught him *in flagrante delicto* with the best man's sister … over from Argentina for a bit of R&R by all accounts."

"You are joking?" Gareth couldn't hide the genuine shock from his face. "I'd no idea."

"Connolly kicked him into touch on the spot apparently – minus his keks. Gavin Hughes lives a few doors down, hell of a do, so he said. I can't believe you'd not heard. I'd say she's ripe for a bit consoling if you know what I mean."

Gareth shook his head. "We're better off as mates. She's too good for me."

Chris shrugged. "Your choice, pal. But I've seen how you look at her. And vice versa. Don't cut your nose off to spoil your face, that's all I'm saying. Hell, your face needs all the help it can get. And if she needs a friend at a time of need, better she turns to you than anyone else, eh?"

Gareth reached out and punched Chris's arm. "Sometimes, mate, you do speak remarkable common sense for a dickhead."

"Why thank you." Chris gave a mock bow. "Talking of dickheads … what we going to do with him?" He gestured to the mirror. "He's going to rip our heads off first chance he gets. We have to go by the book with him, you do realise?"

"What choice did he give us?" said Gareth. "We've done nothing wrong. He couldn't let us step inside Derwydd Hall during a 'ceremony' and he didn't want to speak to us without his 'legal representative'. What options did he leave us with?"

"I worry we're going to lock horns with some fancy-arsed solicitor and get nothing out of him. But you're right to say it's his arrogance that got him stuck in here."

"Exactly. How far has his solicitor got to come?"

Chris pulled a crumpled business card from his pocket.

"Chester … according to this. I must call him in a minute."

Gareth laughed aloud. "Ooh, you are rotten, DS Coleman, but I do love you."

"Ah, he's only himself to blame. Bloody knob. Who does he think he is?"

"That's the million-dollar question, pal. He seems to think he's up there with the second coming of Christ."

"Did you hear him ranting about how we were breaking every rule by dragging him away from the ceremony of the elders? It's like he's living in a parallel universe. And you know, that concerns me, these extremist nutters who think they're above the law. I reckon we should get social services involved when his daughter comes home. There's been no mention of a current Mrs Barrington-Brown, and I don't like the thought of her being raised in these conditions, even if a lot of it is just bluster for our behalf."

"Yeah, you could have a point. He'd benefit from some anger management therapy that's for sure." Gareth checked his watch. "It won't hurt to leave him in there and cool his boots for a while. Meantime, we should make our presence known in the canteen before Marlene shuts up shop."

"Sounds like a plan. Couple of mugs of tea and a bacon sandwich and I'll be about ready to wake Mr Simon Wright, QC, from his kip."

Chapter Ten

A hand squeezed Megan's shoulder. She grunted, drool dribbled down her chin. Pulling herself upright, she blinked and stretched; her neck clicked and she wiped her face with the back of her hand. A steaming mug of tea slid into her vision across her desk.

"Sorry to wake you. You look like you need a cuppa?" WPC Kim Hewines smiled down at her. "Been here all night?"

Megan glanced at her watch. "Seems like it. You just come on duty?"

Kim nodded. "Yeah, holiday cover … the wonderful six-to-two shift to face now. Fabulous. Especially on a Sunday."

Megan yawned and rubbed her eyes, then took a long drink of the hot tea – splash of skimmed milk and no sugar, just the way she liked it. "God knows how long my shift will have been by the time I get to my bed." She shook her head. "No matter. I wouldn't have settled at home. I might as well be here."

"Any developments while I've been away?"

"Nothing yet."

"I can't get it out of my head … that old woman cable-tied to the chair … and the blood." Kim shook her head and shivered. "Not something I want to repeat too often, going in there on my own that first time, I tell you. No amount of training prepares you, does it?"

Megan warmed her hands around the mug of tea. "I know.

There's one sick bastard out there and he's not making any mistakes at the moment. He's certainly not making our life easier. We can't even find a concrete motive but we are following a new line of enquiry. Seems both women had involvement with a society connected with ancient Druids. So, I've spent the last six hours researching them."

"Nice job." Kim wrinkled her nose. "I guess someone has to do it. Tell you what, if I'm in the station when the canteen opens, I'll bring you some cereal. I'm guessing you don't go for a Full English with that fitness regime of yours."

Megan smiled. "Ugh, no. Brown toast and muesli would be fab though, thanks."

Kim headed out of the office; Megan smiled as she blew her a kiss at the door. Megan finished her tea and jiggled her mouse, waiting for the screen to come to life. Her overnight reading had been fascinating. She'd had no idea, for example, that the island of Mona, now modern-day Anglesey, had once been the capital of learning – the 'Oxford' in fact – of Druidic society. Every important Druid in the land came to Anglesey to study with leaders and elders, and during the Roman occupation, when Druids were the arch enemy of the invading army, Mona was the stronghold every Druid in the land rallied to protect.

It amused her that she'd spent years plotting her escape, and had only recently been bemoaning how tedious her life was – born and bred on the island. But now, after reading the wealth of information about Romans and Celts and Druids – a relatively small window in the whole of the past – she couldn't help but look at Anglesey in a different light. Megan had never had much of an interest in history or archaeology. She'd never been a studious type at all and exams filled her with a cold, sick dread, but this was different.

She was aware, of course, of the legends and mystery surrounding the island. The numerous shipwrecks around the coast made it infamous, and the burial mounds and Stone Age burial chambers and standing stones that dotted the landscape were difficult to miss. But it was only in the early hours of the morning as sleep had increased its persistent tug on her consciousness that she'd really thought about how special the place must have been for so many thousands of years. And it was a revelation for her to get so turned on by such a boring subject as history. But the point that seemed to fascinate her was that this was *her* history. And *her* ancestors. It was real and here in *her* place of birth.

And when she finally submitted and closed her eyes, she dreamt of burning pyres and human sacrifice and hoards of screaming Celt warriors covered in battle paint.

Megan remembered a trip once to the copper mines of Amlwch, how she'd been unable to comprehend that people had first burrowed down into Parys Mountain before the birth of Christ, just to try and find a seam of elusive copper ore. But still it had seemed dull and distant, irrelevant to her life. And she remembered a school trip to the Roman Fort in Caernarvon, but she'd been unmoved by the rows of stone foundations that seemed to thrill and enthral her tutors.

But since she'd started her research, she'd already opened an Excel spread sheet and was busy compiling a list of places to visit.

The office door opened and DI Macrae strode into the room, heading towards his office. A scent of soapy freshness and cologne followed him into the room, and Megan at once felt grubby, with an urgent need to clean her teeth to eradicate layers of caffeine.

Macrae did a double-take when he saw her and changed direction. "Blimey, you look rough."

Megan ran a hand through her flattened hair. "Thanks, sir."

He grinned and his face lost at least a decade. He really ought to smile more often, Megan decided.

"Sorry, mouth activated before my brain responded. What I meant to say was you look like you've gone above and beyond the call of duty and have been at your desk all night?"

Megan returned the smile. "Very observant of you, sir. Yes, I got lost in Anglesey's Druidic past."

"And what did you learn about the elusive Servants of Truth?"

"In a word. Nothing."

Macrae raised his eyebrows. "Really?"

Megan nodded. "If it's a secret society – it certainly does what it says on the tin."

"And treasure hoards?"

"Hmmm." Megan clicked her mouse. "A few references, nothing at all concrete. The earliest mention was by a Roman writer, Tacitus, but that seemed to be dismissed as propaganda. He said that an elite tribe of Celt warriors stole Roman gold to appease their masters – the Druids – and the gold was never recovered. Other than one detailed thesis, from a student in the seventies, about the likelihood of its existence, there are no written accounts at all. Professor Bolton was right about oral traditions that's for sure."

"I don't suppose you've spoken to him yet?"

"No, not yet. I thought I'd grab a shower and a change of clothes and then put a call in. Seems a bit rude to call him pre-dawn on a Sunday."

"I would have, but yes, you're probably right." He rubbed his brow. "Megan, do you think we're on the right lines? I know I was dismissive last night, in hindsight, I think I felt the need to play devil's advocate. But is your instinct telling you the connection between these women and their deaths is this Servants of Truth?"

Megan thought for a moment. "Unless we find some other connection, then yes, I'm prepared to believe it is that."

"Damn. I thought you'd say that."

Megan smiled. "How did the guys get on with Barrington-Brown?"

"There's been a delay; we're still waiting for his solicitor, so they should be talking to him very soon."

The door creaked open and Kim Hewines backed into the office balancing a plastic tray. "I must be mental waiting on you hand and foot, I remember you were much the same back at the flat –" She turned, face frozen. "Oh, sorry, sir, I didn't realise. I'll take it back –" She turned and headed back to the door.

"I don't think that's necessary, Officer," said Macrae in his most formal voice. He slid off the edge of her desk and winked at Megan. "I think DC Jones deserves sustenance just now."

Kim nodded. "Yes, sir."

He paused at his office door. "And tea, four slices of toast and some of that lime marmalade would tick all my boxes too, if I may be so cheeky?"

Kim smiled with relief and deposited the tray on Megan's desk. "No problem, sir. I'll be right back."

Kim paused and mouthed 'Sorry' before digging a slip of paper from her pocket. "Front desk asked me to pass this on to you when they heard you were in the building. Had several calls for you last night from a young girl, said she sounded distressed and wanted to speak to you urgently."

Megan frowned and reached for the note. "Who …?"

"Anna Brown. Any connection?"

Megan nodded. "Yes. Damn. I'll deal with it. Thanks, Kim."

She switched her phone on, waited for the cheery intro, then scrolled through to the keypad. Before she could enter Anna's mobile number, a rush of text messages beeped one after the other. The persistent ping of incoming voicemail calls followed, four in total. Megan's stomach contracted, imagining emergencies at home, but when she opened the first of the messages she relaxed slightly but groaned aloud.

Adrian Bolton.

Goddamn it. Their date last night. She'd completely forgotten in the melee of activity, but unforgivably she'd not even thought to call and let him know. And, from the sound of the text messages, which she read and deleted in chronological order, this resulted in him waiting for her for over an hour in The Antelope and getting progressively more pissed off with each passing minute.

She couldn't blame him. She would have responded exactly the same to similar treatment, probably worse. She could only hope he'd understand and forgive her. As she composed a grovelling text apology, she questioned how he could have slipped her mind so totally. Was she so driven, or only able to focus her attention on one thing at a time? She'd been thrilled when he'd asked her out, ready to take the plunge and trust someone for the first time in an age. Now, she could have blown the opportunity before even giving it a chance.

Oh, well. She finished her toast and took a sip of strong tea. No use crying over spilt milk. She couldn't stress over what she couldn't change. Adrian either understood or he didn't. The choice was his.

Surprised, and pleased, with her decision, Megan keyed Anna Brown's mobile number into her phone and pressed call. If it were too early, she'd leave a voicemail, and at least the girl would know she was eager to speak to her.

The call answered on the second ring. Megan had a brief thought that the ring tone sounded English rather than European, but then a breathy whisper filled her ear.

"Hello. Hello?"

"Anna?"

"Yes."

"It's DC Jones. Megan Jones. You called me …"

"You went to the Hall. You shouldn't have gone to the Hall." The voice was still a whisper, but urgent and angry. "He's sent me away. I told you what would happen."

"I'm sorry. I didn't know it would cause a problem –"

"Well, it did. I can't talk there –"

The voice rose, a high pitch. Megan sensed fear and the thickness of tears.

"Anna, I'm really sorry. But the thing is we needed to speak to your father, not just you. And I can't stop my colleagues from asking him questions, I'm afraid –"

"But my aunt says you've arrested him. He's going to kick off big style; you don't know what he's like. He says it's all my fault for getting involved with Iris –"

Megan frowned, tried to concentrate. Her phone beeped. Another incoming call. She pulled it from her ear and glanced at the display. *Adrian B* flashed. Damn it. She sighed and ignored the call.

"Hang on, Anna. Your aunt? I thought you were away with a friend at their family villa?"

Anna sighed. "No. I'm in Essex with my aunt Lucy, my father's sister. I hate it here. It's like living an episode of TOWIE. All my cousins think about is boys and fake tans and hair extensions. I'm going mad here. I need to get home. I've told them I'm on a hunger strike so with any luck she'll send me packing soon. Is it true you've arrested my father then?"

Megan blinked, trying to follow the youngster's train of thought, trying to reason why Anna's father had chosen to lie to them about his daughter being out of the country.

"No, Anna. He's helping with our enquiries. I could really do with speaking to you soon."

A deep sigh. "Okay."

"Your dad can't just send you away, you know that, don't you? We need to question you; you may be a potential witness. And I'd like to learn more about Iris. You mentioned you'd told her something ..."

Silence.

"Anna?"

"Yes."

"Can we meet up?"

The mobile signal faltered for a moment. "I dunno."

"In confidence. You can trust me."

"I don't want to cause trouble. You understand? I can't risk more problems at home."

"I don't understand, Anna. Why could it cause trouble?" A pause. "Anna?"

"Someone's moving about ... I've got to go."

"Anna, please, you have my mobile now, promise me you'll call as soon as you're back in Anglesey."

"If I ever get back ..."

"Well, if not, I'll get a train down to Essex."

Another loud sigh. "Okay. But please, don't get heavy with my dad, don't tell him we've had this conversation."

"I need you back here, if he obstructs –"

"I'll be back. Give me twenty-four hours. Please don't tell him."

Megan sighed, torn. "If my boss finds out ..."

"I'll be there. I'll call."

"Okay. One day or I'm coming to fetch you."

A long sigh. "Thanks."

Megan considered for a moment, then took the opportunity before it passed. "Anna, did Iris ever mention anyone called Bronwen Evans?"

Silence.

Megan checked her phone; the call was still connected.

"Anna?"

"Bronwen from Sacred Oaks?"

"Yes, that's right. Do you know her?"

"Why?"

Megan tried to read the tone of the girl's voice. Maybe this hadn't been such a good idea.

Anna persisted. "I said ... why?"

"How about I tell you when I see you?"

Megan's heart began to thump; something felt very wrong here.

"How about you tell me now?"

Megan swallowed. "First tell me how you know Bronwen Evans. You must realise I can't give details of a case –"

"A case? What case? I thought I was supposed to trust you?"

"It's not about that, Anna, and you know it –"

"Bronwen was my grandmother. Estranged, I suppose you'd

say, in that I was forbidden from seeing her. Through Iris I got to know her again. There, is that a good enough reason?"

Megan closed her eyes. No way. This wasn't going to go down well.

"Now, answer me. You promised ..."

Megan felt trapped, desperate to keep Anna onside. "Anna, if I tell you, this goes no further at the moment. You hear?"

"Has something happened? Is that why you've arrested my father?"

"We haven't arrested him –"

"She's dead, isn't she? Like Iris. She's dead."

Megan couldn't speak. Suddenly forming three small letters – Y.E.S. – was impossible.

Anna hiccupped.

"I'm sorry." Megan struggled for more words. None came. "I'm sorry."

"I could have stopped all this. I knew and I did nothing. This is my fault."

"What do you mean?"

A thump on the other end of the line, the scurry of movement. "I've got to go."

"No, wait –"

"I'll be back tomorrow."

"Please, Anna!"

The call disconnected.

Chapter Eleven

Dark patches under the man's eyes, and the shadow of overnight growth blurring the edges of his normally pristine beard, had done little to eradicate the effect of Barrington-Brown's fury. If anything he looked worse, almost sick with concealed rage. Gareth folded his hands on the table in front of him and waited for Macrae to take a seat. The DI had announced he wanted to sit in on the interview, get a feel for the suspect, and probably – in his usual diplomatic manner – put as much distance between Barrington-Brown and a cranky, early-morning Chris Coleman as possible.

Gareth smiled. "Sorry we had to keep you waiting. Trouble contacting your brief, but I take it the accommodation was acceptable?"

Barrington-Brown flashed a look of disgust at the man next to him, who coloured and adjusted his spectacles.

"It was a cell, detective. I'll leave it to your imagination."

"Unavoidable though in the circumstances, I'm sure you'll agree."

"No." The man bit down on the word, when he next spoke his voice was lower and controlled. "I don't agree. However, I'm aware, legally I have no recourse. So, can we please get this over with, so I can get back to my guests on what is one of the most important events of the year."

Gareth nodded, took his time opening his notes, then scanned through the telephone records he'd received moments earlier. Macrae crossed to the water cooler, drew off a plastic cup, and returned to his seat. No words were spoken, but every gesture had meaning. A way of saying to the man on the other side of the table that despite his fancy words and expensive solicitor, this was their domain, they knew the law too, and this would be done at their speed, in their own time. If a night in the cells wasn't a lesson learned, there were plenty more lessons still up their sleeves they could call on if required.

"We'd like to record the interview, sir, I'm assuming that won't be an issue?" Gareth looked up from his papers. "Purely for our own benefit ... at this stage."

The two men opposite traded glances.

"Yes, okay, whatever." Barrington-Brown dismissed the gesture with a wave of his hand. "Please, can we just get a move on? I'm not sure what else I can tell you that I've not already told you."

Gareth raised his eyebrows. "Really? One minute, please, sir."

He activated the hard drive recorder and read out a list of those present.

"Now, to recap, sir, you were saying you'd told us everything you know about Iris Mahoney?"

Another sideways glance. He nodded.

"You're certain of that?"

A second terse nod.

"For the benefit of the tape Mr Barrington-Brown nodded. Twice." Gareth cleared his throat, flicked through his notes. "As I recall from our last conversation you told us the only involvement you had with the deceased was a brief meeting when she purchased her cottage from your estate. And in recent months, you'd been concerned at the amount of time your daughter was spending with the deceased. You said you had no clear recollection of the last time you'd seen or spoken to the deceased but from memory you would say it was several weeks earlier." Gareth looked up. "Would that be a correct summary of what you told us?"

Dark eyes flashed with pure anger, but Barrington-Brown managed a slight smile. "Take out the police speak, and I'd say it's fairly accurate, yes."

Gareth nodded. "Good. I'd hate to think I'd come away from our last meeting with false details." He paused, turned over a page. "The thing is, sir, during the course of our investigation, we've had information that your involvement with Iris Mahoney was a lot more … well, shall we say on a personal level."

Barrington-Brown checked his Rolex, then crossed his arms. "You'll need to be more specific, I'm afraid. I don't have time for mind games, so let's keep it simple and to the point for both our sakes, eh?"

"Sounds good to me, sir. So, we have information that Iris Mahoney had spent the best part of a year trying to prove you were a con-artist who was exploiting innocent people, extorting money under false pretences. What do you have to say to that?"

The snort of laughter was loud and sardonic; the round of applause patronising. Hackles rose on the back of Gareth's neck, but he kept his face calm, and held the man's gaze; trying hard not to recall the image of self-inflicted scratch marks on Iris Mahoney's skin.

Barrington-Brown turned to his solicitor. "Is that it? Is that all they have? The reason I've been locked up against my will overnight. Are they allowed to do this, surely it can't be legal?"

The solicitor leaned in close to his client and muttered words into his ear. Barrington-Brown sighed, checked his watch again, then gripped the edge of the table.

"Your information is false, detective, as well as being highly defamatory. I think you should be very careful what kind of accusations you go throwing around."

Macrae coughed. "For the record, sir, my officer has made no kind of accusation; he has merely repeated information that has come into our possession during our investigation. I'd welcome your recognition of that fact. We're completely within our rights to question you in this regard; there is no need for any defensive responses or pointless threats here."

Barrington-Brown studied Macrae for a moment, like a man observing a tramp on the street – equal amounts of pity and disgust. But he remained silent.

Gareth looked at Macrae, who gave the slightest of nods.

"So, you dispute the allegations, I take it, sir?" said Gareth. "There was no campaign, instigated by Mrs Mahoney and other historians –"

"Historians!" Barrington-Brown interrupted. "Is that what they told you?"

"Who?"

"Wherever you got your false information from, detective, I assure you none of that merry band are historians."

Gareth frowned. "I'm not sure I'm with you, sir?"

"Iris Mahoney and her cronies. That's my name for them, although I'm sure they have much more appropriate titles. They're a bunch of white witches – at least that's what the locals reckon – that run around Anglesey telling people what they can and can't believe in. What religions they can or can't practise. Who or what they should listen to. And generally disregarding anyone who opposes anything they say with a complete hypocrisy any politician would be proud of. Historians!" He laughed again. "Really? A bunch of old women who'd be better served spending their afternoons down the W.I. baking cakes or knitting baby clothes."

Barrington-Brown eventually fell silent, glancing at his solicitor, who surreptitiously tapped a pen across his lips.

"Well, you seem to have pretty strong objections to someone you barely knew, sir?" said Gareth, with an air of innocence.

Barrington-Brown sighed. "I may have played down what I knew about Iris when we spoke, I admit that. But I would have done myself no favours by repeating the scandalous gossip she wasted her time spreading. I'd hoped it had gone with her to her grave." He paused, studied the back of his hands for a moment. "The only deception I will admit to is not revealing the true reason why I objected so strongly to Anna spending time with the woman. She was, without doubt, turning my own daughter against me, and I felt powerless to stop it."

"So, how did you handle the allegations Mrs Mahoney made over the past year?"

"I employ a competent team of lawyers." He gave another sullen glance to the man on his left. "Well, I say competent. Usually competent anyway."

Gareth shifted his attention to the solicitor. "You'd come into contact with Mrs Mahoney?"

The solicitor, Simon Wright, shook his head, repositioned his spectacles again. "No, my colleague. But if I could remind you it is my client answering questions today, not myself …"

"And if I could remind you, the wording of the charge for 'obstructing police in their enquiries?" snapped Macrae.

The DI held the solicitors' gaze.

"I'm well aware of the charge, detective, as I'm sure you're equally aware of the client confidentiality act?" Simon Wright paused, waiting for a reply that didn't come. "However, in the interests of co-operation, my client has given permission to inform you that I have checked the file containing Iris Mahoney's correspondence with my firm. Letters and more letters. Nothing more than unsubstantiated rumours, as my client concurs. We were about to issue proceedings for libel against her and a request for a retraction of an article in a local newspaper."

Gareth jotted down the information and turned back to 'the client'. "So, she was making your life miserable, sir, you will admit to that?"

Barrington-Brown shook his head. "There's nothing to admit to. Iris Mahoney had no bearing on myself or Derwydd in any shape or form. Yes, she tried, but she failed. She was totally irrelevant to my life, so if this is a desperate attempt at finding a motive, then you are way off the mark." He tugged his sleeve up and glanced at his watch again. "Nothing has changed, detective. I have no motive. I have an alibi for my whereabouts on the night she died, and quite frankly, I feel my time has been wasted enough. I've been more than co-operative and if you don't want me to seek legal redress, I'd suggest it's about time we parted company. So, if you've no further questions …?"

Barrington-Brown pushed back his chair but Macrae stopped him with a raised hand. "Not just yet, sir. We'll say when you can go. Give us a few more moments of your time."

The man dropped back into his chair with a dramatic sigh. "What now?"

Gareth turned over a new sheet of paper. "Do you know of a woman called Bronwen Evans?"

Barrington-Brown shut his mouth; a smart retort seemed to die on his lips.

"Sir?"

"Why?"

"If you'd answer the question, sir," said Macrae.

Barrington-Brown gave the DI a scowl. "Where does she live? I mean, it's a common name in these parts."

"Sacred Oaks Farm, Tal-y-bont."

Barrington-Brown closed his eyes for a second, then gestured with a nod for his solicitor to lean in closer. He spoke into the lawyer's ear, then turned his head to receive the response. The two men made eye contact and the solicitor gave a firm nod.

"I used to know her, yes, a long time ago. She was my mother-in-law. But my late wife passed away about ten years ago, almost to the day, and I've not seen Bronwen Evans since the funeral. That is the truth. Can I ask why?"

"Firstly, can you tell us where you were on Friday evening between six pm and midnight?"

"Not again!"

"Sir, if you could …"

"Yes. Friday evening I was meeting important guests at Derwydd. I'm sure you know, detective, you were there part of the time." He looked from one detective to the other. "Is this woman dead, too, is that the point of all this?"

"Mrs Evans was found yesterday morning."

Barrington-Brown sat back and exhaled. "I don't know what to say. Is she connected in some way to Iris Mahoney?" When he got no reply, he nodded. "Yes, that would make sense. It would even explain some of Iris's animosity towards me; you must be able to see that?"

Macrae leaned forward. "I'm not sure I do, sir. Are you saying Bronwen Evans had reason to hate you and passed that onto Iris Mahoney for some reason?"

The solicitor nudged his client's arm and spoke into his ear.

Barrington-Brown took a moment to consider, then looked up with a smile. "I'm sure you're both very aware how relationships usually work between husbands and mother-in-laws. Ours was no different. I got on with Dewi far better than Bronwen, but then that all stopped when Caitlin died. Bronwen saw to that." He trailed off. "How is Dewi coping?"

"Mr Evans passed away a while ago," said Gareth. "Mrs Evans lived alone."

"What about her sister? Is she still alive? That was a strange set up if ever there was one."

Gareth ignored the question. "So, you've had no contact with Mrs Evans –"

"I told you. The funeral. I've not seen or spoke to her since. Had no desire to. I understand the pain she must have been in, losing her only daughter, but the way she treated me was unforgivable."

"How did your wife die?" asked Macrae.

"Car crash. Anna was only five. Caitlin dropped her off at nursery; hit a tractor head on down the lanes on the way home." His shoulders slumped.

Silence settled across the room.

"And Mrs Evans is not in contact with her grandchild?" said Gareth. "Anna, I mean?"

"No."

"That seems a little cruel, given the circumstances."

"Sorry, I fail to see what the hell that has got to do with you, detective. If I want your advice on parental skills, I'll be sure to ask." Barrington-Brown face twisted with fury. "But as you seem so interested, I'll tell you that I had no desire for my child to be involved with such narrow-minded, bitter individuals. And let's be honest, I still live on Anglesey, not a million miles away from them. If they were that interested, surely they'd have tried to contact Anna before now? But no, they just cut her off entirely."

"Some would suggest that takes two, sir?" said Macrae.

Barrington-Brown got to his feet. "Would they? Well, I'd tell those people to mind their own business and keep well out of mine." He pushed his chair away. "I'm sorry, detectives, but this is straying into details of my personal life that have no bearing whatsoever on your enquiries. I've been completely truthful with you, when to be honest, it would have been easier to lie and not drag up such painful memories. But unless you are going to arrest me, then I'm walking out of here now. I have a life to think about, I can't live in the past. I'm sorry about what's happened, but whatever lunatic is going round murdering OAPs it has nothing to do with me."

DI Macrae got to his feet too. "You can go, for now. But we may need to speak to you again. One last thing … what did you call it? Iris Mahoney and her cronies? Do you know if Mrs Evans was involved in this group?"

Barrington-Brown shook his head. "Genuinely, no, I don't. But it wouldn't surprise me, like I said."

At the door, he turned back. "I hope we don't have to speak again, detectives, for your sakes as well as mine. There's no benefit to asking me the same questions, over and over, because whoever you're looking for, it's not me. I haven't killed anyone and so you can't possibly have any proof of my involvement. Next time, if there is a next time, I promise you I won't be so accommodating. All I ask is that I'm left to continue with my work at Derwydd undisturbed. Understood?"

Gareth remained silent.

Macrae nodded. "But understand this, Mr Barrington-Brown; while I appreciate your honesty, if I find out that you've misled or lied to me, or any of my officers, next time I will be far less accommodating. Understood?"

Chapter Twelve

"This is a joke, right?"

Gareth Parry swung his head from Chris Coleman and then back to Megan. Eyes blazing, close enough to smell coffee on his breath, she took a step back and shook her head.

Gareth shook his head. "No, no, no … this has to be a joke."

Chris cleared his throat. "Calm down, pal. No sense in –"

"Calm down?" Gareth spun on his heel to face his partner.

Megan shrunk further into the corner of the room until the backs of her thighs hit her desk and she could go no further.

"Calm down?" repeated Gareth. "Are you for real?"

"All I'm saying is what's done is done. It's just a bit of cross-wires is all."

Gareth spread his arms wide. "Well that's fine then. A breakdown in communication, you say? Ah, I get it now." He turned towards his desk, stopped and spun round. "Actually, no, that's a lie. I totally fucking don't get it at all. Megan, you want to explain to me why I've spent two hours questioning an arsehole – and worse I've just released said arsehole – while all the time you held proof he was a liar … and chose not to tell me?"

Megan shook her head, cheeks burning under the combined hard stares of both men. She was grateful of Chris's attempts at chivalry, but she could see in his eyes he was as angry as his colleague but doing his best not to show it.

"Come on," Gareth growled. "You must have a reason? What is it? You're so promotion hungry you're determined to get every break in the case and shaft everyone else in the process?"

Megan looked up, shocked at the malice in Gareth's voice, more shocked to feel the pressure of tears. She looked across the room. DI Macrae was on the telephone in his office. The door was closed and he was talking to someone on the other end of the phone, but his attention was fixed on the scene unfolding around her.

Chris stepped forward, put a hand on Gareth's shoulder. "That's enough, pal. Megan meant no harm –"

Gareth shook the hand off. "Like hell she didn't. You know her reputation. You've heard the rumours and laughed about it as much as me. Don't play the innocent now. She's a ball breaker and we all have to watch our backs. This is typical, like the stunt she played with Barrington-Brown in the first place, like the 'coincidental meeting' with the son of Professor Bolton." He took a deep breath. "Well, you might be suckered in, Chris, but I'm not. And I sure as hell ain't letting her make me look like an idiot!"

Megan swallowed back tears as hot anger bubbled inside her. "You're way off the mark, Gareth. I didn't compromise you or the investigation on purpose. I'd never do that, never, whatever you think of me."

"Of course you wouldn't," said Chris. "He's pissed off is all. Words. That's all it is, don't let's break up a solid team over this."

Gareth shoved his hands in his pocket and stamped back to his desk.

Digging deep for courage, Megan followed. "I made a promise to the girl; she begged me not to tell him. She seems in genuine fear of her father, and I thought if you told him we knew he'd lied about Anna's whereabouts, he'd take it out on her and she'd run a mile – when I'm so close to getting her trust. Besides, he told the truth about Bronwen Evans, didn't he? It backs up what Anna told me, although clearly he doesn't know they'd had contact recently. I thought I was doing the right thing."

"By withholding information from a senior member of the investigation team?" Gareth's voice was still tight with anger, but at least he'd stopped shouting. "How can that ever be the right thing?"

Megan shook her head. "I'm sorry."

"Besides, what experience do you have in making those decisions? You're not a child psychologist. You've no idea of the relationship between Anna and her father –"

"I'm sure the girl is terrified of her father and using a typical cocky teenager persona to cover up the fact. I don't need a degree after my name to be certain of the fact." Megan felt her confidence grow. "We could not risk him stopping her coming home. And one sniff of her involvement with us and that would have been the case."

"You can't know that," said Chris. "His reasons for lying about Anna could have been down to some misguided parental instinct to protect his daughter."

Megan shook her head. "No way. He told us she was out of the country when she was with his sister in Epping. That's not a slip of the tongue, that's a deliberate deception."

Gareth banged his desk with a fist. Megan jumped. "Exactly! And you let me release the guy without using that on him. Why the hell didn't you trust me to make the judgement, that's the real issue here. You knew about the marks Iris Mahoney carved out on her own skin, did that not mean anything? Do you not think I needed every bit of ammunition possible to crack the arrogant son-of-a-bitch? Even if the answer to all of that is no, it wasn't your decision to make, do you not get that? I could have tried to keep him in custody until after we'd spoken to Anna –"

"Unlikely, mate," said Chris. "With his attitude and that brief, he'd have laughed in your face."

"Maybe. But we'll never know, will we? Thanks to Miss Eager-Beaver and her self-importance!"

Megan clenched her fists at her side. "I think that's enough, don't you. If you want an apology you have a funny way of going about it."

Gareth's chair clattered to the floor as he snorted with laughter. "You what? You cheeky, sodding, little –"

A sharp hand clap shattered the tension. DI Macrae stood less than a metre from Gareth's desk.

"This stops now. You all know I have an aversion to shouting," said Macrae, looking around the faces. Megan's breathing was laboured, but she closed her mouth, looked at the floor. "Does someone want to tell me what the hell is going on here just now, or am I going to send you all home to calm the hell down?"

Megan slung her handbag over her shoulder and marched through reception without raising a glance to see who was behind the desk. She covered the front steps and car park in a similar manner, and had reached the end of St Pauls before pausing for breath. A decision now. Retrace her steps back to her car and head home to try and get a few hours rest, or take a left down the hill towards the dark water of the Menai Straits. She lifted her face to the warm sunshine and breathed in the salty breeze. She needed to clear her head. A long walk could be the answer. As drained as she felt emotionally, sleep seemed unlikely with her brain full to bursting.

Heading left, her cheeks burned as recalled the clash between Macrae and Parry. Gareth was so furious he'd been unable to come down from his high horse fast enough for the DI's liking and had been sent home to cool down. She'd breathed a sigh of relief and headed towards her desk, before Macrae's gentle voice in her ear had suggested she do the same. Chris's face had been sympathetic as she'd left the office, but she knew serious damage had been done today. She saw it in Macrae's face too. Gareth had been right; it was a trust issue, but not only that, she'd broken an important rule about chain of command. She could kick herself. She was usually so careful to rein in her emotions and enthusiasm, knowing she had to keep within the strict boundaries. But something about Anna Brown made her throw caution to wind, and if Macrae's mood hadn't improved by morning, it might also see her thrown off the case.

Damn it. She quickened her pace, feeling a trickle of perspiration down her spine. She tugged off her jacket and looped it inside the handles of her handbag, unfastening the top button of her blouse as she walked. Maybe the DI was right, perhaps tiredness had affected her decision making, and maybe she shouldn't be so bloody stubborn and just go home to bed. But she felt she needed to get her head straight first, even punish herself in some way. And if marching around the leafy streets of Bangor was the way to do it, then so be it. She slowed for a moment, groped for a tissue in the side pocket of her handbag, and blew her nose. She blinked. No tears. Not going down that route.

Her phone buzzed against her thigh and she leaned against a garden wall to retrieve it from the pocket of her jacket. She looked up as a red car passed, and answered the call without checking the screen.

A male voice. "Megan?"

"Yes, who's this?"

"It's Adrian."

A pause. Damn. She brushed her fringe from her eyes. She'd forgotten all about him.

"Adrian Bolton."

"Sorry, yes, I know. I'm sorry. I meant to call. Sorry."

"Are you okay?"

His voice sounded warm, full of concern, when in truth he should be angry as hell.

She sniffed, throat tightening. "Why shouldn't I be okay?"

Another pause. "Oh, I don't know. Perhaps because you sound like you've swallowed a ton of helium."

She laughed, couldn't help herself. He was so perceptive. Her voice always rose to a tight squeak when she was teary.

"I'm okay," she said. "Bad day at the office. I meant to call. I am *so* sorry about last night. I won't lie, I totally forgot about it. I worked through ... we had another murder."

"Really? God. Nightmare. I was a bit put out but I kind of guessed there was a crisis of some kind, that's why I've been calling. I was worried. I mean, what girl in her right mind would stand *me* up on purpose."

Megan smiled, sat back on the wall and balanced her bag beside her. "Well, when you put it like that ..."

"So, why the tears?"

"I'm not crying."

"Of course not, you're talking to me now, but you're upset. I can tell. Want to talk about it?"

She shook her head, then realised he couldn't see her, although his voice was so warm and comforting in her ear, she could imagine his presence right beside her.

"No. Nothing to talk about. A clash of personalities and I came off worse."

"But you're okay?"

"Fine."

"So ... are you at work now?"

She looked around, imposing red brick Victorian facades and a row of beech trees lined the avenue as far as the eye could see.

"No, I've been sent home to cool off and get some rest. But I can't sleep, I'm too hyped, so instead I took myself a walk round Bangor and to be honest I've not a clue where I am at the moment."

"Whereabouts?"

"Back of some of the Uni buildings. No idea really. Hang on." Megan got to her feet, brushed her trousers and headed to the end of the road. "Fford Moel-y-don apparently."

"No way. That's about half a mile from our house! Listen, Dad's cooking a roast, I'm lazing in the garden with a cold beer ... why don't you come and join me?"

Megan smiled. "I don't drink."

"Ah yes, I forgot. Weirdo. But you eat, right? Or do you not do that either?" He paused; she could imagine his grin and a warm feeling surged through her body. "Dad's a cracking cook. Rib of beef, Yorkshire pud, all the trimmings. Tempted?"

Her stomach growled as if responding of its own accord. In the back of her mind she knew she had to speak to the professor about Bronwen Evans. It might impress Macrae if she were able to kill two birds with one stone. Thank God Gareth or Chris couldn't hear her now.

"Megan?" The warm voice was back. "Say yes."

She sighed and nodded, coming to a decision. "Yes."

"Great. I'll tell Dad another one for lunch. Shall I come and rescue you?"

"I'm lost in suburbia not the Serengeti. Your post code will suffice; me and my trusty sidekick Google Maps will work it out between us."

A snort of laughter filled her ear, raised her spirits, and she found herself already imagining the smell of meaty gravy and the warmth of Adrian Bolton's crooked smile.

"Bronwen Evans, you say?" Professor Bolton drained the last dregs of wine from his glass and furrowed his brow. "Bronwen Evans. I have to say I thought the name seemed to ring a bell, but that could be down to familiarity. It's a common enough name in these parts." He sat back in his chair and shook his head. "No, I don't know her, sorry. It's definitely not a name I remember Iris ever mentioning either."

Sunday lunch had gone well. By the time Megan found herself tucking into tender slices of roast beef and the best honey-roasted parsnips she'd ever tasted, the stresses of the day and the clash with Gareth Parry were a distant memory. She surprised herself by relaxing into the conversation almost immediately, something she found difficult under most circumstances. Both men had an effortless charm and warmth that put her at ease.

Even Professor Bolton's natural curiosity and gentle digging had no negative effect on the atmosphere. She'd appreciated his interest in her life and her work.

Ten minutes earlier, after helping clear the plates, Adrian announced he was in charge of dessert and disappeared, leaving Megan an opportunity she couldn't pass up on. A chance to talk about all things Druid with an expert on the subject.

"We're led to believe there's a connection between the women. They were in regular contact." Megan paused, took a sip of her water. "Professor, have you ever heard of the Servants of Truth?"

"Well, yes, it was an old Celt name for Druids, came over from Ireland originally. The Servants of Truth. People looked on the Druids in much the same way as devotees regard the Catholic Church today. So, in a historical context, I've heard the name, but I have a feeling that's not what you mean?"

Megan shook her head. "No. Modern day is what I'm interested in. Have you heard it used to describe some kind of society that is trying to preserve and protect what little we know of the Anglesey Druids?"

The professor studied Megan for a moment. "Iris Mahoney? I knew she was a bit obsessed because of this family connection she believed in so strongly. But no, I'd no idea there was more to it than that. I had it in mind she did community work – caring for the elderly and W.I. type things. Putting something back into society. I'm shocked if there was more to it than a natural resentment of people like Barrington-Brown who are, as she saw it, exploiting her ancestors."

"Well, it does seem as if there was more, and it's not the easiest subject to research. I spent most of last night trying to find some mention of the Servants of Truth and drew a complete blank. In fact, what I managed to learn about Druids you could write on the back of a postage stamp."

"I did warn you." The professor glanced towards the door. "Sorry for the delay with dessert. Ade's only got to warm through the custard. I don't know why he volunteers, he's no Gordon Ramsay."

"Which is a bad thing?" said Megan, wrinkling her nose in distaste.

The professor smiled. "A point well made. Ah, well. No excuse not to have a top up. I always find the wine loses its depth if it's left to stand anyway, don't you?"

"You're asking the wrong person, I'm afraid."

"Ah, yes. We have a teetotaller among us." He poured another glass of deep red wine, which glinted in the rays of afternoon sunshine. The dining table was in a small room at the back of the Victorian detached house; tall, sash windows, white walls and a marbled black fireplace gave it a sophisticated, yet airy, feel. "You've been given a tough task. Researching anything about Druids requires the patience of several saints. I've spent decades piecing together fragments of historical fact and still find the whole thing can only hang together with large amount of imaginative fiction."

"Because they had an oral tradition?"

He sipped his wine and nodded. "Partly. Pre-Roman little was written down. Laws, rules, traditions, gods … even currency in some areas … they all existed but were passed from generation to generation by word of mouth alone. That's why the elders and priests were so revered. They literally held the word of truth."

Megan topped up her glass from the water jug. "I see."

"But there is a secondary, darker, reason nothing exists today. Beginning in the first century AD, the Roman Empire and the Christian Church took it upon themselves to suppress the Druid teachings. Later still, the Saxon invasion of Celtic lands all but eliminated the memory of the Druids. So, to preserve their knowledge they went underground and swore solemn oaths of secrecy and I believe it true that their descendants remain there to this day." He looked up. "That's why I decided to base myself in Bangor all those years ago. I thought I had more chance of cracking the secrets of the Druids if I was near Anglesey."

"It was that important to the Druids? Anglesey? I mean, Mona?"

"Oh, yes, indeed. As important as the Vatican City to the Catholic Church today. Or as Oxford is to the British education system. And the local Celts would have welcomed the Druid incomers, more than likely originally via boats from Ireland, with open arms, ready to bask in their wealth and importance. It is known Druids were widely respected within the community, no doubt due to the fact there was a preparatory period of twenty years before one was a genuine Druid. And Mona Insulis was an important – if not *the* most important – site where this preparation occurred. The location of a Druidic college."

Megan nodded. "I saw several mentions of that in the research. How the island was important as a place of learning."

"Very much so. And talking of hidden depths, we don't even know what Anglesey was called in Pre-Roman times … even that is a closely guarded secret, or one that has died out with the faith."

Megan frowned. "I thought it was Mona. In everything I've read that's what it's referred to as."

The door opened and Adrian carried a large tray into the room containing three steaming bowls of yellow custard.

"Ah, at last." The professor smiled. "We were beginning to think dessert had been cancelled."

Adrian slid the tray onto the dining table. "I burnt the custard, okay, don't make a big deal. I had to open a tin."

Professor Bolton rolled his eyes at Megan and accepted the dish from his son. "Well, no matter, it is the rhubarb and ginger crumble I'm looking forward to. It's my absolute favourite." He stared into the dish. "I take it the crumble is in there, somewhere? I wonder if you've not overdone it a tad with the custard …"

"Dad …" Adrian warned as he took his seat opposite Megan and flashed a look in her direction. "I did my best. You never complain about the size of pudding normally so don't make it an issue today. Okay?"

The professor looked from his son to Megan and back again. "Ah, very well."

Megan picked up her spoon and dipped it into the mountain of custard. Not having finished all the vegetables in the main course, there was no chance she'd be able to consume what had to be a thousand calories worth of sugar. But she had to at least be seen to make an effort. She swallowed a mouthful of creamy custard and licked her lips. Heaven.

"That okay?" asked Adrian.

She nodded. "Divine. Not sure I'll be able to finish but I'll give it my best shot."

"Leftover puds are usually sent my way," said the professor between mouthfuls. "Don't be shy."

Megan smiled. Professor Bolton had the same warm, confident manner as his son. And he certainly loved his food; it was a wonder he wasn't a man mountain. But at around six feet tall, solid build, muscles visible beneath a black V-necked pullover, he moved with grace and fluidity. A man comfortable in his own skin, even with the approaching years showing in the silver flecks of hair above each ear. Attractive. Adrian had his eyes and prominent nose. The lips belonged to someone else. Luscious they'd be called on a woman. She wondered briefly about Adrian's mum, there must have been a Mrs Bolton …

Megan realised the professor was talking again.

"You know some people believe the Druid name for Anglesey was Avalon."

Megan licked her spoon. "Really? Isn't that tied up with the holy grail legend?"

Professor Bolton shook his head. "Not to be confused. The word 'Avalon' itself is derived from the ancient Welsh name, *Afallach*, which means 'rich in apples' and back then the island was known for its apple production." He took another mouthful and swallowed. "In fact, Geoffrey of Monmouth, one of the best-known chroniclers of Britain's history, called the island *Insule Ponorum*, 'the island of apples' suggesting, according to some historians, it does qualify for the name, Avalon."

"Dad … do you think Megan really wants a history lesson from you today?"

Megan took a bite out of a piece of crumble, winced slightly at the tartness of rhubarb. "Actually, I do. I asked. I'm getting a new-found respect for my home."

"Well, if you're sure," said Adrian. "Dad does go on a bit."

Professor Bolton scraped around his dish. "Don't mind me, just make like I'm not here."

Megan smiled. "One thing I didn't get from the research is why the Romans had such a problem with the Druids. I mean, the invasion of Britain as a whole wasn't a light-hearted affair for sure, but it wasn't a blood bath either. They were willing to compromise as long as people lived by their rules and laws. What was different here? Why did they wipe out the Druids? Were they scared of them?"

The professor slid his dish away and averted his eyes from Megan's barely-touched pudding. She removed the spoon and slid the dish towards him; his eyes lit up in delight as he recovered his spoon and dug straight in.

"Dad!"

"Waste not, want not, son. I'm always telling you." He scooped up a large mouthful, chewed then swallowed. "Partly they were scared, yes. The propaganda machine worked both ways, and Romans arrived on our shores hearing tales of Druidic sacrifice – often human – and other-worldly powers. But there was another reason, equally as pressing."

"What?" said Megan.

"The Druids controlled the trade in gold that passed through Wales, on its way from Wicklow Hills in Ireland, away to the east and then over the North Sea to Europe. And the Druids took their position seriously. Being in charge of this key economic trade route made them a natural target. Even after the Roman Emperor, Suetonius Paullinus managed to get his army across the Menai Straits and massacre the Druids and burn all their sacred groves, it was still thought these 'druid terrorists' might rise again and continue to cause a problem. Hence the reason they constructed a fortress at Segontium, the place you went on your school visit, to ensure what little remained of an intact Celtic culture stayed on Mona and did not try to seed on the mainland."

Adrian pushed back his chair. "Coffee?"

Megan shook her head. "Not for me, I try to avoid caffeine; I'll stick to my water, thanks."

"Ooh, I wouldn't say no to a pot of Earl Grey if you'd be so kind." Professor Bolton scraped the last tiny smears of custard from Megan's dish and sat back with a satisfied smile. "That would be just the ticket."

Adrian rolled his eyes at Megan, collected the dishes, and disappeared back into the kitchen.

"I found a fair bit of information about the Roman invasion of Anglesey," said Megan, "but even that contained little mention of any Druids waiting on the other side."

"Yes, there were numerous accounts. In fact …" The professor got to his feet and disappeared out of the door, returning moments later holding a small book with a plain black cover and gold leaf lettering. "Yes, here we are, we have an eye-witness account of the invasion of Mona from a Roman writer who was allegedly present at the time."

"No way!"

Professor Bolton rifled through several pages. "His name is Tacitus and he paints a very dramatic, though rather biased, view of the event. There's a sample of his work translated into English." He cleared his throat. "Tacitus wrote how the battle occurred on the coastline of the Menai Straits. 'On the beach stood the adverse array (of Britons), a serried mass of arms and men with women flitting between the ranks. In the style of Furies, in robes of deathly black and with disheveled hair, they brandished their torches; while a circle of Druids, lifting their hands to heaven and showering imprecations, struck the troops with such an awe at the extraordinary spectacle that, as though their limbs were paralysed, they exposed their bodies to wounds without an attempt at movement. Then, reassured by their general, and inciting each other never to flinch before a brand of females and fanatics, they charged behind the standards, cut down all who met them, and enveloped the enemy in his own flames. The next step was to install a garrison among the conquered population and to demolish the groves consecrated to their savage cults; for they considered it a pious duty to slake the altars with captive blood and to consult the deities by means of human entrails.'"

He looked up as Adrian came back into the room carrying a tea tray.

"You still going, Dad?"

"No, it's me," said Megan. "I find it all fascinating. Besides, it's not often you have to go back two millennia to try to find clues to solve a case." She waited while the professor poured his tea. "So, with Tacitus producing pretty much the only written accounts of the time, and acting as some kind of propaganda machine for the Roman army, it's no wonder people were terrified of Druids. Were they really involved with human sacrifice and all the other stuff?"

The professor stirred in three sugars and a splash of milk. "Conflicting reports, I'm afraid, no one really knows for sure. But personally, I admit, I can't see it. Their beliefs, it is widely assumed, were of a nature religion – that is they worshipped the sun, the moon and nature. They held lakes to be especially sacred and many offerings have been retrieved from lake beds, especially on Anglesey. As they worshipped nature deities, most sites were natural, which is why so little evidence remains – like sacred groves, caves and particular lakes. It is known they had some temples constructed, but none have ever been found. My point, I suppose, is that if we believe that nature and the sanctity of all life was so fundamental to them – why would they use human sacrifice in their religion?"

Megan took a sip of water. "To appease the gods? In all of

the writing it seems to be the priests who were most revered. Perhaps they used it as a kind of control mechanism to keep their followers in fear and awe. It happens today in religion; it could have happened back then."

"Wow, Megan," said Adrian. "This has really got to you, hasn't it?"

Megan felt her cheeks redden. "I don't know as it's got to me. It's like any case I'm working on, I try to put myself into a point of view – be it the killer or the victim. That's how I work. I'm trying to see through the eyes of one of these Druids because getting to grips with their beliefs could be the key to this case."

"You believe that?" said Professor Bolton.

"I don't know. I think the connection between both victims has to be the Servants of Truth. And now we also have a link between the latest victim and Barrington-Brown –" Megan closed her mouth. "Sorry, ignore that. Classified."

The professor drained his cup. "Well, for what it's worth if you have any connection between a murder victim and that man – you're halfway to getting the crime solved. Iris saw something in him that others did not, and I feel she would have harried him about it to her death. Or maybe she did." He paused. "She would never have given up, I know that. She wanted him stopped."

Chapter V

MONA INSULIS, BRITAIN - AD 60

Marcus watched Suetonius canter away to oversee loading of the boats, then turned to his century. "Right, men. It's our turn. Ten to a boat, fast as you like. Let's show these savages the true power of the Roman Empire. Agreed!"

"Yes, sir!"

He flashed a smile of reassurance at Titus as they led their men to the water's edge. Marcus jumped aboard the first craft and signaled Titus to take the second. As the boats pushed off, a loud crack split the air and the ballistae launched a volley of fireballs above their heads. Seconds later, a dull thud as the first assault hit target. Marcus turned in time to see sparks shoot into the sky, catching fire to trees and illuminating the Celts' defensive line. Another crack, another flaming fireball catapulted across the sky like a comet. It crossed the earthen ditch, and this time the impact was accompanied by screams and shouts as body parts exploded in all directions.

The response from the Ordovices was swift and lethal. Arrows rained down, bouncing off the boats, skimming the surface of the water. Marcus turned at a cry from behind him as one of his men took a hit. A sudden feeling of panic and disorientation overwhelmed him as it became clear the currents were much stronger than anticipated. The flat-bottomed boat began to list, then turn, one way then the other, in the swirling eddies. From the corner of his eye, he saw Titus in the same precarious position.

"Row men, three aside," Marcus yelled. "Get some order, some rhythm, or we shall all drown. Careful now!"

Slowly, the men manoeuvred the craft into a forward position, and followed the lead boats toward the shore. Titus jumped to his feet, gesturing for his men to row harder. Marcus opened his mouth to scream at him to take cover, and at that same moment he saw an arrow heading straight for his optio's back. Marcus's eye trained on the point as if he knew exactly where it would land.

"Titus!" he screamed, the words carried on the breeze.

Titus turned, registered Marcus's face, then dropped to his knees as the arrow struck his side, burying deep in his right shoulder.

"No!" Marcus leapt to his feet. "Titus!"

Titus lifted his hand, acknowledging a reply, but the white pallor of pain on his face was obvious. He waved his boat forward. Marcus's attention was distracted by a huge splash on the far side of his boat. An armed cavalryman swimming alongside took a direct hit. The horse collapsed, peppered with arrows, thrashing in the water as the current dragged both it and the rider away.

Within minutes the scrape of gravel shuddered below their feet. Marcus launched himself out of the boat, boots sinking into soft silt. Javelin raised, he raced towards the surging battle on the foreshore, screaming above the metallic din of clashing weapons for his men to follow. The fireballs continued to pound the makeshift defences and the air was heavy with cloying black smoke. His eyes stung and streamed as he dragged himself through clinging mud.

In the chaos, Marcus lost sight of his men, lost sight of Titus, and found himself confronted by a snarling Celt, naked to the waist, his skin painted in vivid blue patterns. Knees bent, he swung a heavy pike from side to side, goading with an evil grin. Marcus dodged to one side, raised his sword and brought it down across both wrists. The man dropped the pike, squealing as he fell to his knees. Marcus took one step forward, pierced the man's belly and dragged the blade up to his chin.

Panting, he surveyed the scene. Celt reinforcements poured in from every direction. He sensed movement behind him and spun round, coming face to face with the grey eyes of the Druid he'd seen earlier. The priest spat and cursed, stabbing a short sword, all the time muttering foreign incantations. He looked awkward and ungainly, increasing terror etched his features, no longer the ominous threat Marcus imagined – just an old man in a white robe. Marcus laughed in the priest's face as he swung his sword with all his strength across the man's neck, slicing from ear to ear, stepping back as a gush of crimson splattered his boots.

The Druid toppled to the ground, landing on his back, eyes wide, searching the sky.

"N-no ... Awen ...Aw ..."

The attempt at words turned into a gargle that sprayed a fine crimson mist into the air.

Marcus stood above the prone figure, panting as adrenaline coursed through him. Grabbing a handful of long white hair, he cheered long and loud, feeling the rise of battle hysteria. He yanked back the Druid's head, exposing a pale, veined neck, and hacked through sinew and bone, not stopping until the skull came free from the devil priest's body.

Screaming, Marcus held the head high in the air, waving it before the horrified tribesmen. They reacted slowly, in shock, fear visible on every face as the blood of their priest poured down Marcus's arm. He knew the kill would have more impact on their enemy than a thousand Roman lives lost.

The following minutes, hours were lost to Marcus in a crimson fog of fear and pain. He lost count of the amount of lives he took, blocking out the looks on the faces of each victim, concentrating solely on the task in hand and his role as a Roman Centurion. He didn't feel more than the sharp sting of a bee, when a stubby blade pierced his left arm, slicing his bicep and dragging its tip against the bone. His adrenaline was so high, he could have fought on for days, thrashing and stabbing each figure he crossed, slipping and sliding in piles of steaming entrails with the smell of shit heavy in the air.

Finally, numbers began to dwindle, and as one, the Roman army pushed through the defensive line. With a blast of horns, the remaining Celts fell away. The mass of legionnaires swarmed forward and Marcus at last paused for breath. He stumbled in a daze back down to the boats, deafened by the screams and shouts of the injured. Traces of the vicious battle littered the beach – spent arrows, dead horses, destroyed boats. The bodies of the dead floated face down in swirling eddies of muddy red water. He turned bodies over, one after another, searching each face for his optio.

Standing in the middle of the beach, he cupped his hands to his mouth. "Titus!"

A voice, weak and heavy with pain, answered. "Sir!"

It was a young legionnaire, Prius. He kneeled above a prone body, grasping a bleeding wound in his own shoulder. Marcus's legs trembled as he stepped over the injured and dead, struggling to keep his footing in the slick mud. The expression on Prius's face told him all he needed to know.

When he reached the legionnaire's side, Marcus fell to his knees. Titus's eyes rolled backwards as Marcus pulled him into his arms. Titus twitched and shivered while Marcus quickly examined the extent of his injuries. The armour was so covered in mud, he could not make out where the worst of the blood came from, but it had already pooled in a sludgy red puddle around him. Marcus knew in an instant, there was little point trying to get back to a boat, and when he opened his eyes, focused on Marcus's face, it was clear Titus understood.

He licked his lips. "A bad omen, Marcus," he whispered.

Marcus nodded, biting down on his bottom lip hard enough to draw blood. "But a battle won, Optio Titus, by a brave and honourable man."

Titus gulped. "In my tent ... my chest. Letters ... see they are sent home?"

"Of course. Now, rest, Optio. That's an order."

In the chaos of the scene, amidst choking smoke and the smell of death, Marcus held Titus until his breathing grew shallow; until, with a soft sigh, his body fell limp.

Marcus dropped his head, leaned in close to his optio's mud-streaked face. "May the gods protect you on your final journey, brave Titus."

Digging beneath his armour, Marcus retrieved a gold coin from his inner pocket, and slipped it into Titus's still moist palm.

"There, dear lad," he said in a choked whisper. "Your fare for Charon."

Marcus dragged himself to his feet, turned to the skies and screamed his anger at the gods. Then, along with Prius, he carefully carried Titus's body back to one of the boats, and gave orders for the body to be taken back to Segontium for a proper burial.

With a heavy heart and aching body, Marcus turned his back on the ocean, unable to bear the sight of Titus leaving his side for the final time.

Chapter Thirteen

I t wasn't really a window seat. An extra-wide sill reinforced by the back of the sofa worked for him though, and comfortably accommodated his skinny ass. Gareth leaned back against the wall and stretched his legs along the top of the cushions, taking a sip of whiskey and rolling the fiery liquid around his mouth. The view from his lounge window was one of the reasons he couldn't force himself to move out of this cramped apartment, even though he could probably afford a decent mortgage and would save a small fortune in rent. While it was no Manhattan skyline, the lights from the university buildings on the hill above, leading down in glowing rows of dotted streetlights to the reflection of the moon off the ocean, never ceased to warm his heart. And usually improve his mood. Tonight, however, even his favourite view seemed to fail him.

It had been a big mistake locking horns with Macrae. Huge. Like Bambi taking on the biggest stag in the herd. It was a stupid idea at the best of times, but in the middle of a major investigation, it was plain suicidal. Macrae would see Gareth's spat with Jones and his subsequent explosion of temper as unforgivable and unprofessional. People had been booted from the team for less, and that's what worried him more than anything. He'd be gutted. The look Macrae gave him as he'd left the office, a mix of pity and disappointment, chilled him. Legendary for not taking sides, Macrae had done what he always did – refused to be drawn into the rights or wrongs of what Gareth saw as a completely legitimate argument. And that's what had really drawn his temper. Megan Jones had it coming as far as he was concerned. And if Macrae couldn't see that, surely he could see she'd knowingly withheld important information which could have resulted in more success questioning Barrington-Brown. That man still had secrets. Gareth would swear on it.

Ice chinked as Gareth took another sip of whiskey and laid his head against the cooling window pane. The town looked as if it was bathed in a golden glow; the streetlights reflected off the ocean, giving an aura to the usually shabby buildings and shops away to his right. He was sure it was a sign of aging. Things like that would never have entered his consciousness a few years ago. The only views that had any effect on him usually involved a particularly deep cleavage or the thrill of an extra-short mini skirt. And with Bangor Uni a stone's-throw away, he'd never been short of displays of the flesh during summer months. In fact, a few short years back the only way he could have come down from his rage tonight would be a quick shower, shave, several bottles of larger, a session at the rowdiest student nightclub in town … and hopefully conclude with a long night of sweaty sex. Now, he'd settled for three glasses of single Irish malt so far, and the furthest he intended to move was to the kitchen to reheat last night's left-over pizza. Yes, an age thing for sure.

What annoyed him more than ever about this imposed break of service was how it had broken his chain of thought. He had a trip to Cardiff scheduled for tomorrow; the train was booked for 7.30am. He'd intended discussing with Macrae whether it was still necessary. Clearly Bronwen Evans hadn't been a television celebrity – the psychic detective connection was looking more and more tenuous. Whilst Mairwen Thomas and her Servants of Truth were becoming central to the motive. That's where he was needed. Gareth was sure the answers were to be found close to home, rather than any criminal retribution. He drained his glass, sucked an ice cube into his mouth and rolled it round until his tongue became numb. Damn and blast sodding Megan Jones and her sodding ambition …

His mobile beeped and he pulled it from his pocket, breath catching as he read the name. He cleared his throat and quickly accepted the call.

"Sue. Hiya. To what do we own the pleasure?"

"It's owe. Not own. Are you drunk?"

Gareth grinned. "Sober as a judge, your honour."

"And how many alcoholic judges do we know?"

"Hmm. Point taken. Anyway, if you're ringing me with any exciting discoveries from the post-mortem you may as well know I'll probably be suspended from the case from tomorrow, so you'd best save it for Macrae."

A pause, the hiss of static. "Is that why you're drinking alone?"

Gareth frowned, blinking back the haze of whiskey. "Who says I'm drinking alone?"

"You're under observation, detective."

Gareth's heart jumped. "I am?"

Sue Connolly's laugh was as warm as melting chocolate. "Chill. I'm joking. Look down. I'm in the car park."

His chest tightened but he couldn't stop the smile spreading across his face as he spotted Sue's car. "I think at this point I should advise you of the legal definition of stalking."

"Quit being the smart-arse. I have chips. And wine. You going to let me in?"

Gareth slid from the window sill and cleared the sofa in one fluid leap. "You having a laugh. Get a move on … I hate cold chips."

Gareth screwed the fish and chip paper into a ball and lobbed it through the open doorway, aiming for the general direction of the kitchen bin. It hit the door frame and ricocheted into the sink.

"My aim is as bad as my luck at the minute."

Sue stretched out on the opposite sofa, crossed her ankles in front of her. "And your self-pity is as tiresome as your pessimism at times."

Gareth reached for his wine glass. "Point taken."

"Oh, come on. I wasn't trying to hurt you. But you need to learn not to take things so personally."

"Yeah, yeah. Tell me something I don't know." He took a sip of the rich, fruity Merlot. "Anyway … not that I ever turn away gorgeous women bearing wine and chips, but was this a spontaneous mission or a pre-planned action? Because you know I'm a cheap shag; the chips would have been enough …"

Sue smiled, rolled the stem of her glass through her fingers. "I spoke to Coleman."

"Ah, makes sense. Ganging up on me?"

"I'd say friends who cared is closer to the mark. I delivered Bronwen Evans's post-mortem report to your office. Macrae had a face like thunder and grunted at me. Chris filled me in. I thought you might need company."

Gareth looked up, horrified to feel the sting of tears. He sniffed hard, rubbed a hand across his face. "You were right. As usual."

"Like I said, you shouldn't take it so personal."

"I bawled him out, Sue. I bawled out Macrae. I will be walking for sure."

"Chris thinks not. And I agree. You're too important to the case. What you need to do now … after you apologise, of course … is work your bollocks off to show Macrae how intrinsic you are to the team." Sue sipped her wine. "That's why I'm here. Plan A is to find some detail in the case that's been missed so far, so when you roll back up at the office with an apple for the teacher, you'll also have a brand new lead Macrae will be unable to ignore. Make yourself invaluable. Comprende?"

"I think Megan Jones has beaten me to that title."

Sue held her glass aloft. "See! So bloody pessimistic. More

wine before I retune my violin to accompany the misery of it all."

Gareth smiled and reached for the wine bottle. "Sarcy cow."

Sue leaned forward to position the glass as Gareth poured the wine. The heaviness of her breasts filled the front of her black blouse, tightening the material, clearly outlining a black lace bra beneath. Gareth slammed the bottle down on the coffee table and crossed his legs. Sue slid back onto the sofa, apparently oblivious to the effect she had on him. Thank God.

"We need to be serious," she said. "Can we access the case files on your home computer?"

"Yeah, I can log in remotely if they've not already deleted me from the system –"

Sue got to her feet. "Christ's sake, Parry. I'm out of here before I slash my wrists …"

Gareth reached out and caught hold of her wrist, pulling her backwards with more force than he'd intended. Her leg caught on corner of the coffee table and she toppled into his lap. Shit. Let's hope she couldn't feel …

Sue got to her feet with a laugh. "I think at this point I should warn you of the legal term for molestation, detective."

Gareth's sarcastic response, as well as his face, seemed to freeze; the smile he'd intended vanished and he felt the urgent breathlessness of tears.

"What's the matter?" Sue asked, still standing, looking down at him with a bemused expression.

Gareth shook his head, unable to find the words, knowing the alcohol was making him maudlin, and embarrassed where it may lead but equally unable to prevent the journey.

He reached out. "Come and sit with me."

Sue hesitated.

"Please …"

With a nod, she settled on the two-seater sofa, feet tucked beneath her, knees grazing his thighs. The heat of her seemed to melt his skin. This was ridiculous. Just ridiculous. But did she feel it too … or was he pissed and being more stupid than usual?

Sue crossed her arms. "We should concentrate on work, Parry. That's the general idea."

"Is it?"

"Yeah. Getting you out of the latest pile of poo and smelling of roses."

"You always get me out of the shit, babe. Maybe it's your turn to need help?"

Sue frowned. "I'm not the one who bawled out his boss …"

"I've heard about Dr Zhivago."

"Javier." Sue corrected automatically. "And there's really no point discussing it."

"Okay."

The silence lengthened. Gareth kept his gaze on Sue's face, while she kept hers firmly on her lap. The click of the wall clock seemed to deafen him as he waited. But something told him to wait.

"How did you hear?" she asked eventually.

"Chris."

She gave an ironic laugh. "Ah, ganging up on me."

Gareth reached forward, ran the back of his fingers up her arm to where the material ended at the crook of her elbow. He was pleased to see her shiver at his touch.

"I'd prefer to say friends who care about you. Really care."

"Touché."

The silence settled across them again. If Gareth was to be the one to break it, he wanted to break it well. Despite her reticence, he sensed she wanted to talk, but what if he'd got it wrong?

"What happened?" he asked in a whisper.

Sue shrugged. "The usual. He cheated. I never learn."

"I'm sorry."

"He didn't shag you too, did he?" she snapped.

Gareth laughed. "No. But I am sorry."

"It wasn't your fault."

"Maybe it was."

Sue looked up with a frown. "Where's that coming from?"

Gareth reached for his glass, swallowed the last of the Merlot, then took a deep breath. "If I hadn't let you go ... if I'd treated you better ... you would never have got involved with Dr Zhivago."

Sue snorted. "Christ, Parry, your ego takes some beating!"

Gareth shook his head. "It's true. You know it."

"For your information I did not get together with Luca on the rebound or out of any kind of sympathy shag. I fell for him. I really fell for him. He was passionate and intelligent and fascinating ... and everything most men in this god forsaken town are not!"

Gareth swallowed, looked down, cheeks burning.

Her hand slid across the sofa, fingers tightened around his wrist. "Not you. That wasn't a dig. Just don't get so wound up that everything in my life revolves around any feelings I may ... or may not ... have had for you at one time. Luca was the real thing, Parry. Sorry, if that offends you but it's true. You think I would seriously have got engaged if I hadn't been in love with the guy? You know me better than that."

"Then I'm sorry. You must be hurting. You don't deserve that."

"No, I don't. I've moved on from being hurt. I can't even cry, you know, I've not shed a single tear. I'm just so angry, it's eating me up. Angry but thankful we didn't commit to anything more than a shared rental agreement for the flat. And grateful I found out before the wedding. That's what's getting me through." She paused, reached for her empty glass. "Have you got more wine?"

"I thought you were driving."

"I can call a cab."

Gareth untangled his legs and got to his feet. "Then I have more wine. But I want you to open up to me and get it off your chest. You need to ... I can hear it's choking you. I'm right, aren't I?"

Sue looked up, eyes shining. Her voice when she spoke was high and tight. "I could kill him. I swear I could stab his eyes out for humiliating me like that in my own home. I had a mate with me that night. Can you imagine … getting home after a twelve hour shift, with a slightly drunk pal who'd missed the last bus … and facing that. In my bed …" She broke off, hiccupped. "Can … you … imagine?"

"No, babe. I can't. I'm so sorry."

Gareth leaned forward, pulled her into his arms and held her tight as the sobs exploded into his shoulder in an uncontrolled torrent.

"Better?"

Gareth collected the damp tissues into a pile. After ten minutes or so, her tears had finally dried. His shoulder was soaked and Sue's face was crimson, streaked with mascara, but she looked more relaxed than he'd seen her for an age. Some pressure valve had been released tonight. If only Gareth could release his own. But now wasn't the time for those kind of thoughts. Yes, that was definitely an age thing too.

Sue exhaled. "Much. Shit. Where did that come from?"

Gareth tapped his chest. "In here. You had to get it out. You'll start to heal properly now."

Sue regarded him with her head on a sideways tilt. "Quite a little philosopher, aren't you?"

"Tell me I'm wrong."

Sue shook her head, stayed silent.

"Still want more wine?"

"No, bad idea, probably best I go." She wiped a hand down her thighs and inched towards the edge of the sofa. "I'll make a move."

"I'd prefer you stay," said Gareth. He grinned at Sue's raised eyebrows. "For all the right reasons. I can sleep on the sofa. We can work on the case. And you can lose the blotchy, plague-infested look before braving the streets of Bangor."

Sue snorted. "Well, when you put it like that. How can a girl resist?"

Gareth grinned and jumped to his feet as Sue aimed a kick towards his crotch. "I'll open the wine and get the computer warmed up. How about you go and freshen up, there's fresh towels on the rail. You'll feel better."

Sue nodded and left the room. Gareth watched her go; there was an ache in his chest, like an actual hand had gripped hold of his heart and was squeezing, cutting off his blood supply. As he heard the click of the lock on the bathroom door, he'd no doubt who the hand belonged to.

Chapter Fourteen

The neon-green Post-It note was stuck to the top of her telephone when Megan arrived back at her desk at 7.30am on Monday morning. She was hoping for an early start, a clean break, and a bit of peace and quiet. Gareth was supposed to be in Cardiff for most of the day interviewing production staff on Iris Mahoney's S4C television programme. She knew she'd have to apologise at some point, but not yet, it was too soon. His unnecessary nastiness still rankled and she wasn't ready to back down without an apology from both sides. She hoped Chris would understand; she needed him on side. Something she'd discussed over a quick orange juice in the pub with Adrian the night before, after Professor Bolton had insisted his son take her back to her car at the police station.

She pushed the comforting thoughts of Adrian Bolton to the back of her mind, and ignored the feel of his lips on her cheek, even though the skin still seemed to be glowing some twelve hours later. She'd slept the best part of ten hours. Her dreams filled with dramatic adventures – battle lines of Roman infantry facing white-robed priests and howling women, hair billowing in the wind. She was there on that shoreline. The smells, sounds … the fear … alive inside her. And beside her throughout, gripping her hand in his, and affording her his widest smile, was Adrian Bolton. What bizarre things dreams could be.

The note was succinct. 'Anna Brown. Train arrives 9.30am.

Please meet her at Bangor Station.'

The girl was already in the car park when Megan arrived. Leaning against a vending machine: bored expression, blonde hair piled on top of her head in the latest Edwardian trendy bun style, iPod cord looped between her ears, blue rucksack wedged between Doc Martens. Dark jeans and a grey hoodie with vivid pink lettering, she looked like any typical teenager. Yet something told Megan, Anna was anything but that.

Megan tooted her horn and waited while Anna threw her rucksack on the rear seat.

"Train was early," she said by way of introduction.

"Have you eaten?" asked Megan.

"No. I left in the middle of the night so no one could make a fuss. Walked to the village, got a cab into Epping, got the train to Euston, changed at Chester and here I am. Doubt they even know I've gone yet."

"You didn't tell anyone you were leaving?"

Anna turned as she tugged at the seat belt. "Like, you think they'd have let me go?" She rolled her eyes. "Don't worry. I left a note."

"We have to tell your father."

"Later. I'll text him."

"I'm taking you home."

"No!"

"Anna ..."

"I said no. Not yet. If you want me to help you ... back off."

Megan shook her head and started the engine. "Let's go and get breakfast."

"I'm not hungry. I'd rather walk. Will you take me to Sacred Oaks Farm?"

Megan glanced sideways as she maneuvered the car round the narrow lanes of the station car park. "What for?"

"I want to see it. The crime scene. I want to see where my

grandmother died."

Megan shook her head. "I don't think that's a good idea, Anna, honestly."

Anna touched Megan's left hand as she changed gear. A spark of electricity passed between them and seemed to shoot up her arm, into her shoulder, neck and upwards. She shivered.

Anna spoke, and it seemed an end to the matter. "I need to go there."

The track leading from the farm down to the shoreline was a sun trap. Megan paused beside a gate that opened into a long, lush green field, feeling the warmth of the stone pillar against her arm. The sun was bright, shimmering like blue diamonds off a flat calm ocean.

"Will I be able to go inside?" asked Anna, looking back at the farm cottage.

Megan shook her head. "It's still a crime scene. We may need to send forensics in again. Sorry."

Anna closed her eyes for a moment. "I'd only just got to know her. That's what's so sad. I think we would have been friends, you know?"

Megan nodded. "I know. Iris introduced you?"

"Yeah. I don't know how they made the connection, probably through her boycotting Derwydd Hall. Maybe she told my grandmother or something ..." Anna stepped away. "Let's go down to the shore. I need to be near the water. It's where I do my best thinking."

"You go there to be alone? So do I."

Anna turned, fixing Megan with her deep blue gaze. "I'm never alone. Never."

Megan rubbed her arms through the thin cotton of her blouse. Despite the increasing heat as the sun burned off the morning mist, she was suddenly chilled. She lengthened her stride to keep pace with Anna's long limbs and loping gait.

"I have to ask you some questions, Anna. You understand that? It doesn't mean you're a suspect or anything like that, and anything you tell me will be in the strictest confidence. But you may have witnessed something important and not even know it. By rights I should take you to the station; I could get in trouble just speaking to you without an adult here. But I'll risk anything if it helps you open up to me."

Silence.

Megan reached out and touched Anna's sleeve. "Okay?"

Anna moved her arm away, dragged the cuffs of her sweatshirt over her hands, then nodded.

"When we met first, out at Iris's cottage, you said it was all your fault. That Iris was dead and it was because you'd told her what you'd seen. Or words to that effect." Megan dropped her voice, softened the tone. "What did you mean?"

Anna lengthened her stride, twisting the toggles of her sweatshirt into knots. Megan hurried to keep pace, following side-footed as they reached the grassy bank that led down to the shoreline. At the bottom, Anna waited, searching out a seat among the tumble of rocks on the water's edge. Finding one, she stretched her legs out in front of her, crossing them at the ankles, facing the wide expanse of water and the Anglesey coast beyond. A heron stood, statue-like in the shallows, stick-thin legs balancing in the retreating tide. Moments passed, the bird darted its beak beneath the surface, bringing up a tiny silver fish.

"Can I tell you what I told Iris?" Anna's voice was low and serious; her gaze still far off towards Puffin Island and Liverpool Bay beyond. "Can I trust you … like I trusted Iris?"

"Of course you can. You can tell me anything … in complete confidence."

"See, I want to tell you. I need to tell someone. But …"

"But … what?"

"I'm scared." Anna's voice cracked. "Really scared."

"Scared about what?"

"Scared that if I tell you ... you might end up dead. Just like Iris and my grandmother. Something bad is going on here, something bad that I can't stop!"

Anna put a hand to her face and took deep gulping breaths, fighting, Megan presumed against the threat of tears.

Megan waited. She had all the time in the world.

Eventually, Anna gave a deep sigh. "Sorry."

"It's okay. Totally okay. But how about we start from the beginning and you tell me exactly what it is you've been trying to face alone?"

Anna rubbed a hand across her face. "I've tried so hard not to cry, you know. See, I could have saved Iris. Saved my own grandmother too, I'm sure." Megan shook her head, but Anna reached out, gripped her arm. "No, I could. I know I could. No matter what you say!"

"Okay, okay. I'm not going to argue. But it would help if you explained it to me."

"Promise my father won't find out?"

Megan paused. "You know I'd love to promise that, especially if it helped you open up to me. But I won't lie to you. I can't promise, not until I know what you're hiding."

"My father has nothing to do with this. I know it."

"Until we can be sure of that too, we have to keep an open mind, and I know you understand that." Megan crossed her legs, settled back as the sun warmed her face. "In your own time."

Anna sucked in a long breath. Megan waited, snapped off the head of a bobbing sea daisy peeking from the mossy crevices between the rocks, and began to pluck the white petals, one by one.

"I remember doing that with my mum," said Anna. "One of the very few memories I have of her was walking the Straits." She paused, looked out across the water. "That's where I met Iris the first time, over there on the other side, out on the dunes, couple of months after she moved in. She was on her way to a cottage that sold eggs right on the beachfront. I never even knew it existed. A little shack made of corrugated iron sheets and by the front gate a little wobbly table with a platter milk jug for the money, and piled high with egg boxes. It was like another world to me. You didn't do that kind of thing in North London … I was still going to boarding school down there then."

"Your mum died when you were five, didn't she? How old were you when you moved to Anglesey?"

"It was on the cards before she died, although I don't remember it, of course. We lived in Highgate. I just about remember the house and my dad working all the time – he was a financial advisor in the city back then. I think my mum wanted to move back closer to her roots, and her family, I guess. Not sure how my dad agreed to it, but after she died, he admits he went to pieces a bit … said being up here made him feel closer to her. Makes sense, I suppose."

"So, you met Iris … what three years ago?"

"About that, yeah. I met her in the summer holidays and refused to go back to boarding school in the September. It caused a bit of a rumpus." Anna shrugged. "You can probably imagine. But I wanted to be here, I hated London. Dad couldn't stand me being under his feet all the time, but it's not a problem now as I prefer my own space. We muddle along, you know. He rubs a lot of people up the wrong way, I get that. But his heart's in the right place; he really believes in what he's doing at Derwydd."

"So, you have a good relationship with your father?" asked Megan, hoping to keep the surprise from her voice.

"It's okay. We keep out of each other's way. I don't interfere in his business and he keeps out of mine. Suits us both."

"And Iris? You've not answered the first question I asked …"

"I know. I know … it's just difficult."

"Why?"

Anna sighed, uncrossed her legs and poked at the sand around the rocks with the toe of her Doc Marten, building a pile of broken limpet and periwinkle shells into a mound.

"I have a secret," Anna whispered, as if she feared someone

may be listening. "I have these things, like dreams. But sometimes, most times, the things I see in the dreams … they come true."

Megan frowned, bit down on her lip, summoned up the willpower not to interrupt. She needed to listen, not ask questions. Whatever it was she'd been expecting – and the list was long – she hadn't seen that one coming.

"I told Iris about the dreams. She said that they weren't normal dreams, not like what everyone else has. She called them portents. She said I was a special girl, and because I was approaching adolescence, these special gifts would develop more and more. Have to admit, I thought she was a bit bonkers to start with. But she really seemed to understand. She said I had the ability to see into the future. She said I was born a Seer, though I don't really know what that means."

Megan started. Seer. Where had she heard that word recently?

"What kind of things do you see?" Megan asked.

"All sorts. One Christmas, my uncle Luke came. He was my dad's brother, we only saw him once a year because he worked abroad somewhere. While he was staying with us, I saw him die. I never told anyone. I was a bit scared of him and I thought it was my mind playing tricks. But a month later his motorbike crashed into a tree. Dad was gutted, said he'd hit a patch of black ice. But I knew different. I'd seen him racing a car. It drove away and left him in a ditch to die."

Megan's heart began to flutter. "Did you tell your father?"

"No! Can you imagine what he'd have said?"

"But you told Iris, didn't you?"

Anna nodded. "Met her there, in the dunes, just after Uncle Luke died. And you know, it was almost like I didn't need to tell her, like she already knew. She said she could see it in me. I can't put it any other way than that she really understood me."

The words choked up. Megan waited for the emotion to pass.

"I told her about Uncle Luke, about the car and the number

plate thingy the driver picked up off the road. I saw the number, remembered it. She had the case re-opened and a man confessed. He got charged with death by dangerous driving. Dad said he got sent down for four years."

A light bulb went on over Megan's head. "Iris did it through the researchers and her television programme, didn't she?"

Anna bit her lip, then nodded. "Yeah, but I did nothing wrong. The bloke was guilty."

Megan held up a hand. "I'm not saying you did. I'm just trying to get a picture of the relationship you had with Iris. You couldn't really have gone to the police, not with only your dream as evidence, so Iris probably did the right thing. She never involved you, did she, or gave your name?"

Anna shook her head. "She'd never do that. She knew Dad would've killed me for getting involved in that kind of stuff. He used to joke my mother was a witch ..."

Megan raised her eyebrows. "Really?"

"Yeah. He won't admit it but I think that's the real reason he stopped contact with my grandparents. Despite his weird beliefs, he detests anything to do with what he calls 'hocus-pocus'. I think it terrifies him, to be honest." Anna paused. "I suppose it's because of these portents that I know he had nothing to do with Iris's death. Even though I really should suspect him."

"Why's that?"

The girl cleared her throat. "He had this big row with Iris. About a week before she died. I heard them screaming at each other on her doorstep. I'd never heard her raise her voice before."

"Does he know you overheard the argument?"

"No. I was the other side of the hedge, in the field. He'd already banned me from seeing Iris by then, so I had to sneak round there in secret."

"Did you hear what was said?"

"Not all of it. I got the feeling ... I dunno ... he was trying to bribe Iris or something. Maybe threaten her. But she *really* bit back. Said she'd expose him, especially if he tried to stop me seeing her. She had no family of her own you see, I was everything to her –"

"Expose him? Do you know what she meant?"

Megan heard Anna's voice catch. In the heat of the moment, the girl had revealed more than she intended.

"Anna?"

"Trust you ... you said I could. Remember?"

Megan nodded. "Go on."

"Well, the reason my dad hates people coming to Derwydd, or prying into his affairs, is because he has two wives."

"Eh?" Megan shook her head, perplexed.

"When he started Derwydd, he followed these old Celtic laws and he married two women, Fiona, and her sister, Elsa. They had some ceremony, so he says, so he's married to both of them. That was the reason he kept me as far away as possible at boarding school, because of course, I don't fit in here now. Not that I have a problem with Fiona or Elsa. I feel sorry for them to be honest, from what I've seen, he treats them like rubbish and they're mad to put up with it. But still, I can't forget my mum, you know ...

"He says he can't be arrested for polygamy because the marriage wasn't blessed by a church, under the law, it was some kind of Druid ritual. I don't understand a lot about it, something to do with the men being allowed more than one wife. He likes to gloat about it, but then he's paranoid about anyone finding out, so I don't how much truth's in it."

Megan paused, thinking over the confession, trying to tie it up with his clash with Iris. Knowing the ego of the man, wouldn't he have brushed off Iris's threats if he knew no real harm could come to him? He must have known it wasn't a legal marriage. Why would he have got so angry? Surely he was more likely to pass it off with a dose of sarcasm.

Anna continued, echoing Megan's thoughts. "It wasn't just that. I'd seen him around Iris's cottage a few times but she wasn't giving anything away. She was the most private person I'd ever met. I suppose that's why I was snooping around that day, trying to find out. I'd got myself so wound up; worried I couldn't trust Iris, that she might tell my dad about the dreams."

"But she didn't?"

"No. Least he's never said anything."

"So, that first day we met, that's what you meant – about telling Iris what you saw, and that's why she died?"

Anna nodded. "That's what I was coming round to telling you. We made a list of every one of the dreams, and we talked them through. Analysed them, she said."

"Do you still have that list?"

"No, Iris had it. But I could do another one."

"And when was the last dream?"

"I get them every few weeks. I saw rivers of blood at Iris's cottage. I told her and she laughed it off, said my imagination was playing tricks. I think that was her way, you know, to make me feel better. Then a couple of nights ago, I saw more blood and I knew it was somehow the same as Iris. And to think it was Bronwen, my poor grandmother. I could have stopped it!"

"Not at all, Anna. We have very little evidence at the moment. Unless you could supply me with the name and address of the killer and enough evidence to allow me to arrest him – which I assume you can't?" Anna shook her head. "Then there's nothing you could have done to stop either death. I can imagine how both deaths have shocked you, but trust me, it's not your fault, and you mustn't feel guilty. Understand?"

Anna nodded. "I'll try. But the thing is … I've been having more dreams. Worse ones."

"Worse? How?"

"There's blood and lots of screaming. More women will die. I hear them begging and begging to be let go. I thought if I went away, I might take the dream with me, it might stop altogether. But it's not. It's every night now. I can't see who's there, but I know it's the same person who killed Iris. I know there's a connection. And I don't know what to do about it! If Iris was here, she'd know what to do …" Anna's eyes seem to clear and her voice trailed off; her face drained of colour as she reached out and took Megan's hand. "Oh, God …"

Megan frowned. "What's the matter?"

Anna swallowed, squeezed hard. "You."

"What?"

Anna shook her head, released her grip.

"Me? What?" Megan asked.

"Nothing. But you must be careful."

She smiled. "Of course. Part of the job description."

"I know this sounds bonkers but I want to help. Will you let me?"

"Maybe. My secret advisor sort of thing?"

Anna turned, eyes wide. "I could do that? I mean, you believe me?"

"Why wouldn't I?"

"You're police. And my dad says the police are all morons who can't see further than the end of their own noses."

Megan smiled. "Well, your dad might have a point, with some of my colleagues, that is. But I am very open-minded. Besides, I need all the help I can get with this case. If you promise to talk to your dad and let him know you're safe, then you can help me find this man before he hurts anyone else. What do you say?"

Anna nodded, managing a tiny smile. "I'm so scared what will happen …"

Megan reached out and touched Anna's arm. She didn't pull away this time.

"Nothing will happen. Work with me and we'll put a stop to this. I promise."

Chapter Fifteen

Gareth yawned and rolled over in bed, groping for his alarm and at the same time confused as to why it seemed to have gone so quiet. He stretched his arms above his head and smacked his knuckles into a solid object. A wall.

"Ow, shit. What the ..."

He blinked and realised two things consecutively. He wasn't in his own bed and it wasn't his alarm. He sat up on the sofa and waited for lucidity to join him. He tugged his t-shirt down to meet his boxer shorts and thought about standing. Before he could summon up the motivation, the noise started up again, and he identified it as the front door buzzer.

"Shall I get it?"

He jumped, hand reaching, it appeared, for an invisible gun. Bizarre.

"What?"

Sue Connolly stepped into the room. She was fresh-faced, make-up free, hair scraped back from her face, wearing the black trousers from the night before, but accompanied by one of his grey polo shirts. His pulse started up a peculiar Samba rhythm.

"Get what?"

She studied him. "Christ, you look rough. The door. I didn't know whether to answer the intercom or not, thought you might have been expecting one of your women visitors?"

The buzzer started up again.

Gareth shook his head. "It's Coleman. He does that because he knows how much it pisses me off."

"Oh." She disappeared into the hall. "I'll let him in then."

"Leave him on the step, the noisy sod."

The door release beeped.

"Coffee?" She asked from the kitchen. "Then I'm going to make a move."

"Tea. Strong. Three sugars."

He dropped back onto the sofa and closed his eyes. Christ, his head hurt like a bugger and his mouth tasted like cat litter. How long had they spent drinking and researching into the early hours? He'd no idea what they'd discovered either, but a niggling voice informed him they'd had a plan of action by the end of the night. Or at least Sue had made some important decisions, and after two and a half bottles of wine between them, he figured that was bloody impressive. Shame he couldn't remember what.

Voices from the hallway, footsteps. He opened his eyes.

Chris stared down at him, eye brows raised. He gestured towards the kitchen with a nod. "What's going on ...?"

"Nothing," Gareth whispered.

"Pull the other one ..."

"Seriously. We were working."

"Whatever!"

"Chris!" Gareth's voice was low and urgent. "Do you think she doesn't know exactly what we're talking about at this very minute? And it's the truth. We were working and she drank too much wine. I got the sofa." He rolled his neck until it clicked. "Anyway, who kicked you out of bed?"

Sue walked into the room with a steaming mug of tea.

Chris held out his hand. "Ah, bliss. Thank you ..."

"That was for the patient. No matter, I'll make him another ..."

Chris shook his head. "Sorry. No time. I can manage to get this down me while he's making himself look beautiful."

Gareth frowned. "What's the matter?"

"Another body. Called in within the last hour. As usual your mobile is on silent."

"I don't know where my phone is." Gareth looked around the room, tugged his jeans from the gap under the sofa and recovered his Blackberry from the pocket. "Ah. Sorry."

Chris blew on his tea. "I'm here now, don't worry, and I might have done you a favour. Macrae took the call so he's not in the best of moods. Go and grab a shower and make it quick."

Gareth got to his feet. "It's not Mairwen Thomas, is it?"

He almost didn't want the answer.

"No. Bit of a generation gap this time. It's a student."

"A student?"

Sue groaned and headed for the door. "I'm supposed to be off-duty but I may as well be prepared, they're sure to contact me if it's connected to the other deaths. I'll go and get my stuff together, see you down there."

"Student?" Gareth repeated after Sue disappeared into his bedroom. "But ... that makes no sense. Where's the connection?"

Chris jammed his free hand into his trouser pocket and made a show of rummaging around. "Nope, no good. My crystal balls aren't working today."

"Ha ha."

"Well, stop with the dumb questions. Quicker we get there, quicker we find out. So get your sorry ass in the shower pronto because you look like death's ugly sister. Surely the delicious doc can't have done that much damage?"

Gareth flashed a look to the door and made a zipping motion across his lips.

He got to his feet. "And it's definitely our guy?"

"Apparently so. But we'll see when we get there, won't we?"

College Road Halls of Residence was located in a leafy suburb, with beautiful views across to Anglesey. A line of police cars surrounded a three-story block of student accommodation. Brightly flowered landscaped areas, looped with blue and white police tape, broke up the expanse of grey concrete. But as ever anywhere along the Menai Straits, the views more than made up for the architecture.

A constable waved them through, lifting yet more tape sealing off the approach road.

Gareth wound down the window. "Can I park round the back?"

"Yeah, DI Macrae's waiting, he sent me to look for you. It's chaos at the moment, we're still trying to evacuate the block of flats, and we've got the usual assortment of gawkers too, so we've had to push the cordon right back."

"Cheers." He pressed the button to close the window. "Macrae is here. Great."

"He said he wanted to see this one first hand," said Chris. "You gotta remember his neck is on the line as much as ours. His reputation too."

"I know. But I could have done without facing him just yet."

If only he could remember Sue's inventive plans for making himself look invaluable in front of his DI. But the whole night was a blur ... or possibly an alcohol-induced spell.

"Was me, I'd rather get it over with," said Chris. "Mind you watch your step. You know he's fastidious about 'blurring the focus of an investigation.'"

Gareth turned to Chris as he parked the car. "But I have to offer an apology, don't I? We can't ignore it. What would you do?"

"Panic." Chris pushed open his door. "If that's any help."

"Great."

Gareth climbed out, glancing at the assortment of youngsters behind the cordon, most dressed in nightwear, and all with matching expressions of fear, shock and confusion. Nothing alerted him. No sixth sense that someone there who shouldn't be. It wouldn't have been the first time a sick bastard had returned to the scene of his crime, desperate to bathe in what he saw as his own personal attention and glory. But as he skimmed his eyes over the area, there was nothing to alert him. Poor kids. Not pleasant to face something like this right in their midst, away from home and without family support.

He recognised a reporter from the local rag, clean-shaven and eager, like a puppy, clutching a notebook to his chest. He couldn't remember the guy's name, had seen him at a couple of press conferences, but knowing they had a history, Gareth kept his eyes fixed to the ground as he passed the crowd. If Macrae wanted to issue a general comment, he could do it himself. Gareth's resolution for the remainder of the day was not to tread on his DI's toes.

They headed towards the main entrance of the block of flats in silence. Gareth already predicting the scene they had to face and trying to prepare himself. As they neared, Macrae appeared on the doorstep, face lined with anger and frustration.

Chris broke the tension. "Bad in there, sir?"

"Aye, not great. But you've seen the other crime scenes first hand, you know what to expect."

"Change of tactic, sir," Chris suggested. "A student this time?"

Macrae shrugged. "There has to be a link. That's your job. Feeling better this morning, DS Parry?"

Gareth jumped, lifting his gaze for the first time. "Yes, sir, if I could just –"

Macrae raised a hand. "No. Let's move on. We don't have time at the moment for histrionics. I want you focused and in control, that's all I want to say on the matter. For now. Do you understand?"

"There'll be no repeat of yesterday, sir."

Macrae stared at him. "No. There will not."

The meaning was crystal. Gareth flashed a grateful glance at Chris who replied with a nod and the hint of a smile.

"DC Jones is inside. I called her in. We need to identify the deceased as a priority. I thought Megan would connect with the students, being nearer their age, and most of the ones I've seen in this block appear to be female. We need to do this with a degree of subtlety."

Gareth nodded. "Fine. And there's no doubting it's the same killer?"

"One hundred percent, I'm afraid. By coincidence a uniform who'd worked out at Tal-y-bont was here when the corpse was discovered and picked up on the detail. It's pretty conclusive although again, no murder weapon. It strikes me he may be collecting the knives as some kind of trophy hoard." Macrae descended the steps and turned back at the bottom. "I'm away back to the office to open a report. We need to reconvene later, let's say 4pm. For now, Gareth, forget Cardiff, I'm increasingly certain the answer is local. But do the door-to-doors and searches on this one and we'll pool resources later. I've asked for the post-mortem by tomorrow at latest, but we don't need to guess the cause of death for sure. Let's get to work guys; I hope you find a lead, best of luck."

Gareth gave what he hoped his DI recognised as his most grateful expression and headed towards the front door of the building.

From Gareth's experience of uni life, usually via girls he'd dated, this flat was quite a step above usual student accommodation. The kitchen was modern and expensive-looking, all white and chrome. A matching brushed-chrome fridge, microwave, washing machine and dishwasher with a name he'd never even heard of – was not what he'd expect to find in uni digs. In the bedroom, not only were the sheets cream silk, there was an abundance of electrical items – plasma screen television, Blu-Ray, games console, and an iPad still plugged in at the wall. The lounge was at the furthest end of a long central corridor, voices drifted towards him as he finished a search of the other rooms.

He knew he was using delaying tactics, part of him not ready to face death head-on again so soon. Chris had made straight for the crime scene, picking his way carefully along the Common Approach Path already in place. Gareth signed and followed in his partner's footsteps, heading to the lounge.

Without a word, Chris gestured towards a circular staircase that led up to what looked like a mezzanine floor. At the bottom was a sight that was becoming familiar; the twisted remnants of a human form. Secured to a chair, head slumped down to the knees, face hidden by long black hair. Hands and feet fastened to the frame by the all too familiar restraints. And what looked like once pink pyjamas now soaked through, from chin to thighs, with copper-coloured blood.

"It's a girl? Another female." Gareth drew in a deep breath. "Christ, what a mess."

"Looks like the place has been extensively searched." A familiar voice spoke behind him. "I would love to know what he's hunting for."

Gareth turned to face Megan Jones. She gave him a weak smile and a hopeful stare.

"Yeah," he said. "Hell of a mess."

Her cheeks were flushed but her face was a mask of calm professionalism. "I'm going to speak to the neighbours. Uniform have got them all together in the basement flat. I should get an ID pretty quick so I'll let you know."

"Cheers, Megan," said Chris.

Gareth couldn't seem to find the right words, so made do with a sharp nod. Megan left the room and Gareth relaxed his guard, glad to see her gone.

Chris put a hand on his shoulder. "Let it go, mate. You only have to work with her – you don't have to date her. You know what Macrae said. He means it, you've had a second chance, don't go blowing it."

"She could have apologised though, you have to admit that?"

"Maybe she thought wrong time, wrong place. Give her a break, eh? She's not a bad kid once you get to know her."

"That's what I thought too … look where that got me. I'd rather keep my distance, if it's all the same, until she learns a bit of humility." Gareth tugged up his trousers and squatted beside the corpse. "Nice looking girl. Bloody hell. Such a shame." He pulled a pair of latex gloves from his pocket and slipped them on. Moving round the back of the chair, he lifted her right hand, then the left and groaned.

"What is it?" asked Chris.

"What I expected, this sick bastard's trademark."

"Fingernails?"

"Yeah, two fingers and a thumb on each hand. I guess that's what Macrae meant about there being no doubt. Jesus." He stood and kicked out at the red leather sofa in frustration, stomach tensing as he saw the discarded, bloodied nails beneath the chair.

"Easy," warned Chris. "Don't risk destroying evidence. You don't want to piss off Doc Connolly or the forensic bods." He closed the drawer he was searching, part of a modern smoked-glass-fronted cabinet. "Some nice kit here; this is no IKEA special."

Gareth nodded. "I noted as much. Rich kid, I bet."

"So, if you had to hazard a guess … what's the link between this student and our little old ladies?"

Gareth ran a hand through his hair. "Well, up to half seven this morning, I was convinced everything was linked via the mysterious Servants of Truth. And I'd decided to close in on Mairwen Thomas, start demanding names and addresses." He finally remembered one of Sue's suggestions. "But now … who knows. For all we know, this girl could belong to Barrington-Brown's Derwydd crowd. We can't lose sight of his possible involvement. I still don't trust him." He sighed. "What the hell are we missing, mate?"

"I don't think we're missing anything. I think we're up against someone who is astute and intelligent ... not to mention bloody thorough. And these attacks, they seem so random, but I know they're not ... you know they're not. He wouldn't take all these risks for nothing. The key to cracking this is finding the motive, I'm sure of it."

Gareth looked around the high ceilings, noting four pieces of modern red artwork, one on each wall. "Are you picking up the same vibe here as me? The running theme?"

"Torture? It's the only thing that works for me. He's getting information from these people – using them for whatever he needs. And then, in my opinion at least, he's getting some perverted kick out of killing them."

"But what information? We have to find out. Have to." Gareth brushed his hands together. "I've seen enough. Nothing more we can do here until forensics have finished."

Outside, Gareth dug a packet of cigarettes from his jacket. He was sick of trying to give up. Sick of failing. He ignored the shake of his hand as he lit up and inhaled, tossing the pack across to Chris who did the same.

They smoked in silence for several minutes.

Chris waved smoke from his face. "Better?"

"Not really."

"If it's any consolation, I'm feeling exactly the same. The bastard has the edge on us. And it's killing me too, mate, trust me ... I know how you feel."

Gareth took another drag and stamped the butt out with vigour before pocketing the stub. "Do you? Well, I feel like a failure. I'm angry and frustrated and out of my depth. This is clearly too much for me. While I'm faffing around, people are dying."

"Macrae clearly thinks you're the man for the job."

"Doesn't mean he's right. What if I'm not?"

"You are ..."

Gareth turned as Megan Jones approached.

"I shadowed you last year, while I was still in uniform, that serial date rape case, remember? I never forgot what you told me. You said, he'll make a mistake, it's only a matter of time. That time's getting nearer and we've got to be ready. We can't crack now. No way can we let this bastard break us," Megan paused, took a deep breath. "And I'm sorry if I've caused another load of unnecessary shit. I've learned my lesson." Megan squeezed the bridge of her nose and sniffed. "I shouldn't be laying this on you, not now, but I overstepped the line. I hope we can get over it."

Gareth nodded, reached out and touched Megan's shoulder. "Maybe you did a bit. I did over-react though." He looked up, saw Chris's encouraging smile. "I lashed out so ignore what I said. I'm sorry too. But it doesn't change how I feel. I'm so bloody drained by this case ... so scared I may be missing the obvious."

"You're not, I know it. Chris does too," said Megan.

"Yup," said Chris. "We're a team, and a bloody good one. I'm not prepared to let this bastard beat us."

"Well said, that man." Megan opened her notebook. "I've got a probable name for the deceased, well, the occupier of the flat. Melanie Wright, known as Mel. A media student apparently, and part-time club DJ. Seems pretty popular, especially with the male contingent. Daughter of some rich local builder apparently. Hence, the fancy student digs."

"Whoa, Wright Brothers?" said Chris. "If so, I think the jigsaw pieces may just have started to fit."

"What's that?" Gareth's heartbeat picked up a beat, drumming in his temple, gnawing away at the headache.

"I was going through my internet searches last night. Remember my first job today, prior to all this happening, was supposed to be contacting the local planning department at the council offices about the sale of Sacred Oaks Farm?"

Gareth nodded. "So ...?"

"I remember the details on the planning application, it's on my desk. I printed it out this morning before I left the office. The name of the developer was Wright Brothers. I recognised it because they built the new block of apartments at the end of my road."

Megan looked up with a smile. "There, see. What did I say? This could be the break we've all been praying for. Immediately there's a connection between with murder and Bronwen Evans. Brilliant work, Chris."

Gareth smiled and clasped his colleague's hand. "Absolutely. Top marks. Let's leave this place to the experts and go do what we're good at."

Chapter Sixteen

Megan pushed open the door to the main CID office and was greeted with the humming noise of an active beehive. Every member of CID, apart from Gareth, was on the phone, voices mixed in a weird maelstrom. Gareth was busy updating the white-board with the latest murder details, jotting notes with a black marker alongside the photograph of Melanie Wright downloaded from the student's Facebook page.

Megan sighed and rolled her shoulders. Thank God they'd buried the hatchet; this job was hard enough without a bad atmosphere. Even though it was easy to blame the stress each new day seemed to bring. What didn't kill you though …

As she crossed the room, she glanced at the copy of the initial post-mortem report she'd collected. It made for depressing reading. At Macrae's door, she knocked. He looked up, gestured her inside.

"Post-mortem prelim report, sir." She handed the file across and turned to leave.

"Before you go …"

Megan tensed. "Sir?"

"I'd like you to handle the next-of-kin for this one. Are you okay with that?"

She swallowed. "Of course, sir. Do we have the details yet?"

"We do. But we have a problem." He glanced down at the laboratory findings. "Look, I can't concentrate on two things at once, I'm a man." He smiled. "Let me scan through these notes, then I'll come and brief you all."

"Sure, sir."

Ten minutes later, Megan closed down her computer screen; the chatter of the office died down and conversations ceased one-by-one as Macrae waited at the front of the room.

He cleared his throat. "First off, dental records prove the identity of the victim was the occupier of the flat, Melanie Wright. So, we do not need to force next-of-kin to attend an identification unless they want to. I'd like you to go easy on the family, there's no hint of suspicion involved … and losing a child … well, I for one can't imagine how you get over that. Especially in such circumstances. As such, I'm going to ask Megan to work as family liaison officer until further notice; I think she's the best skilled amongst us."

Megan shot a glance across the room. Chris seemed absorbed in Macrae's speech, while Gareth's face was a blank canvas as he surreptitiously glanced at his computer screen. Family liaison. Her face burned. Usually she'd be chuffed at her DI's compliment, eager to get her teeth into any new role. Pleased to be chosen as a central player in the case. But now, she wondered, was this his idea of a sideways move? A demotion? Was this all a set up to keep her from under Parry's feet? If so, what had Gareth really said about their argument …

Macrae's voice pushed her spiraling thoughts aside. "Rest of the report pretty much backs up our findings at the crime scene. Cause of death was a large wound to the throat, made by a serrated blade, which sliced the trachea and both common carotid arteries. Death would not have been instantaneous. Meaning he may well have hung around and watched the deceased bleed to death."

A few muted comments circled the room.

"Also on this victim was the killer's trademark sign – the removal, by force, of numerous fingernails. Doctor Connolly thinks some kind of grips or pliers were used, and details in the report that it would have required considerable force." Macrae looked up. "Also, the deceased was found to have a missing tooth, right at the front. It was a recent injury. In fact, forensics found part of the broken tooth in the rug in front of the fire. So it's pretty clear she was struck forcibly, and again the findings are quite positive this was caused by a punch from the clenched fist of a human hand. Doctor Connolly says it's impossible to say how often, because of internal bleeding, but certainly more than a single blow. There are no fractures to the skull. I think our man used his fists on the victim this time, got what he wanted, then killed her anyway."

"Shite alive," whispered Chris. "The sick fuck."

Megan fixed her gaze on a point at the front of the room and tried her hardest not to look at the pretty dark-haired student smiling back at her from the white board. Focusing on the terrible details of the crime at least kept her paranoia in check.

Macrae tapped the board with a marker pen. "One more thing, we've another change of tack this time round. There was a high content of a benzodiazepine drug used in anaesthesia found in her blood. Rohypnol."

"Date rape drug," said Megan.

Gareth looked up for the first time. "Really? She was drugged. Any sign of …" He rubbed his face. "Any sign of sexual abuse?"

Megan prayed the answer was negative.

Macrae shook his head.

"Well, that's something at least," said Megan. "She was probably a fighter. Well, I hope she was. I hope she gave him hell."

"My thoughts exactly," said Macrae. "Cowardice is typical psychopathic behaviour. However, according to this, there were no defensive wounds on the body or any trace elements at all under the deceased's fingernails."

Chris scratched his two-day old beard. "Give me half hour in a room with him and I'll show him the real meaning of cowardice." He exhaled, sat upright. "And no sign of forced entry. So, she let him in, apparently in her pyjamas, which means it had to be someone she knew. Somehow, probably in a drink which he cleared away, he slipped her the drug to knock her out … and when she came round she was trussed up like a chicken. And we can only guess what she went through then."

Megan rubbed her arms, shivering under the air-conditioning vent.

"The drug was probably administered in alcohol," said Macrae. "There were traces of alcohol in the gut and blood stream. Oh, and she was a marijuana user too."

"Jesus, what you can tell from post-mortems nowadays, pretty damn amazing," said Chris, shaking his head.

"Actually, SOCO found a tin box full of unsmoked joints in a kitchen drawer."

Megan smiled as muted laughter broke the tension in the room.

"So, that's the post-mortem out of the way," said Macrae. "I don't know that it helps us very much. How are you lot getting on? Chris, what did you find out at the administration office at the university?"

"Quite a lot, sir. Rumours must spread like wildfire as they knew before I got there this morning, place is buzzing with the news. They'd already pulled Melanie Wright's file, eager to pass on her family contact details. I think the secretaries were worried they might get the job of contacting them."

Macrae took a seat on the edge of Megan's desk. "I already know, but for the benefit of the rest of the team, reiterate how you got on."

"Not great. Her local address is in Conwy, but when I rang I got the butler –"

"Butler?" said Megan.

Chris nodded in her direction. "A very classic English butler, too. I felt like I was in an episode of Jeeves and Wooster. Not even sure how much of my Scouse accent he understood."

Megan smiled.

"Anyway, *Cartwright* informs me Mr Wright and his private secretary are currently mid-Atlantic on their way to a business trip in New York. There's no Mrs Wright apparently – although he was vague about the details. Best I could do was ask him to get an emergency message to his boss. Hopefully he'll call when he lands."

"Not the sort of news you want to get on an airport pay phone," said Megan.

"I can't see this guy using an airport pay phone, can you?" said Gareth. "He probably travels first class, and don't they have in-flight telephones? Hard to believe old Cartwright couldn't have got in contact if he'd wanted too." Gareth scratched his head with the tip of his pen. "Did you tell him why you wanted his boss?"

Chris shook his head. "Not protocol, I thought. And to be honest, the butler rubbed me up the wrong way. Snotty git. *Evasive* isn't the word. Once I told him I was from North Wales Police he clammed up like an oyster."

"Interesting." Macrae frowned. "Wonder why?"

"It's the way of these servants to the rich and famous, isn't it?" asked Chris. "Seem to have this philosophy whereby they'd fall on their own sword if their paymaster asked 'em to. Truth of the matter, half the time, they're filching behind the bosses' backs."

Macrae rolled his eyes at Megan and she smiled. "Another of your amazing generalisations, I'm sure. But I know what you mean. So, just now, we have to wait for the father to contact us, and as we think the murder could be linked via this property deal, we're at a bit of a loose end." He checked his notes. "How did you get on with the students and neighbours, Megan? Anything of note?"

Megan shook her head. "Nothing much, sir. One thing, though, I think Melanie may have been gay."

"Really?"

"Nothing concrete," said Megan, trying to put into words what had felt wrong about one particular girl's reaction. "That's the thing. None of the lads said a word, but a couple of the girls dropped a few cryptic remarks. When I pushed them, they backed off."

"Cryptic ... how?"

"Like her having a gang of male groupies who followed her round to the DJ gigs, but one said they should have known they were wasting their time. And another," Megan flipped the pages of her notebook, "Steph Wlodarski, a stunning Polish girl who lived in the opposite block, seemed to clam up at this point. Made me think their relationship may have been closer than she was letting on. She seemed overly upset about Melanie's death, more like you'd expect from a lover than a friend."

"Did you get her phone number?" said Chris. "Sounds like it might be one to follow up. You know, she might respond better to a male."

"You are a creep at times, you know that," said Megan, trying not to smile.

"What?" said Chris, his face a mask of innocence. "Eye witness. It's obvious we'll need to take a full statement."

"Whatever," said Megan. "Sorry to disappoint, I've already taken one."

Gareth cleared his throat. "One thing, sir. I've had a call from a Bryn Edwards, a journo with The Daily Post. I saw him out at Melanie's flat, could see he was after my attention, but I managed to avoid him. Anyway, he caught me on the phone, said he had information about the Tal-y-bont place, Sacred Oaks Farm, and wanted to speak to the S.I.O. He's clearly already put two-and-two together and connected Melanie Wright's murder with Bronwen Evans. So, I came down a bit hard, told him if he printed anything at this stage without our full permission he'd be spending some quality time in our cells."

Macrae nodded. "And?"

"He acted all innocent, of course, said he had a story he'd picked up recently. I had a feeling he wanted to trade information, when I made it clear I didn't do deals with journalists, he got a bit huffy. But I did manage to find out what he knew ... apparently a planning injunction has been lodged by the National Museum of Wales and seconded by Bangor University against the company who recently purchased the farm."

Macrae crossed his arms. "Go on."

Megan pulled her notebook from her bag, senses alert. Under normal circumstances, she had no time for the press or their clever tactics for getting exclusives. But this felt important. From Gareth's face, he clearly thought the same.

"Said it had been listed for his regular day reporting at the Magistrates Court couple of weeks back. He made a note of the name of the company, Wright Brothers Holdings. The court granted a ninety day stay of execution which prevents the new owner proceeding with any building projects until after a second review on that date."

Macrae nodded. "Right. And were details of the reason for the injunction provided by the university?"

"Not a great deal, he said, at least not released by the Court. Apparently there was a co-funded excavation in its preliminary planning stages and the new owner put the block on it. Bryn said it must be a big concern, this property developer, as he was represented by some fancy London barrister – and they still lost. But it seems the opposition had some pretty strong backup, representatives from the local authority planning department, Department of National Heritage and the Council for British Archaeology."

"That's interesting," said Megan as she made notes, trying to visualise the lay-out of the farm and surrounding area. "Did he have any more information about this proposed excavation?"

"No. And he said it wasn't for want of trying. He'd tried all his sources." Gareth tapped his keyboard. "So, this afternoon, I've spoken to the museum, the university, even CADW. No one knows anything, and those what do aren't spilling. Whatever it is, it's majorly hush-hush, which makes me think it's something pretty big."

Chris looked up with a frown. "So, where's this leading?"

Gareth shrugged. "I'm not sure. But it's not unheard of, is it? You know, some property tycoon unhappy his plans have been put on hold, not used to not getting his own way. Time is money in big business. It's got to be a line of enquiry, hasn't it?"

Chris shook his head. "And so he killed his own daughter? No way."

"I think you might be looking at it the wrong way round," said Megan. "This could be a warning. Stop the development or you're next. But I don't get how that links to the first two deaths. Unless ... we come back to sacred oaks being a potent Druid symbol. Maybe this excavation is key, maybe there's something on the land ..."

"I like your thinking," said Macrae.

"I've made some notes from online." Gareth cleared his throat. "It refers to the 'Planning (Listed Building & Conservation Areas) Act 1990', specifically Sections sixteen and sixty-six. And the local authority referred the Court to Planning Policy Statement 5 : Planning for Historic Environment (PPS5): – which sets out Government planning policies on the conservation of areas of intrinsic archaeological interest. All double Dutch to me."

"I think we need to know everything we can," said Macrae. "Good work, Gareth, stick with this one. Get onto the Magistrates Court, will you? I think it may be the first link in the chain. Chris ... see if you can find anything that connects Melanie Wright to Iris Mahoney other than the sale of the farm. It's remote but I don't want anything missed."

Megan raised a hand. "My contact. Professor Bolton. The first time we interviewed him about Iris and her opposition to Derwydd Hall ... he mentioned something about rumours of missing treasure along the Menai Straits. I wonder if it's worth talking to him about this planning issue; he's in the right department at the university, he may have more details or may be able to point us in the right direction."

Megan gave a nervous glance in Gareth's direction, but he acknowledged with an encouraging smile, which did not seem to be missed by the DI.

Macrae nodded. "Absolutely." He got to his feet. "So, you've all got plenty to get on with. Megan, I'll let you know when we hear from Melanie's father. For now … I'll leave you to it. And I'm pleased to see you working again as a team."

Megan gave a frustrated sigh. Professor Bolton's phone went straight to voicemail for the fifth time. She pulled her mobile from her pocket. She could text Adrian. Would be a reason to get in touch in fact, though she wasn't sure why she needed a reason. He'd made it clear enough the night before he was keen to see her again. A warm tide of excitement rose inside her, and her fingers brushed the spot on her cheek where the feel of his lips still lingered.

"Megan!"

Macrae's voice, louder than usual. She turned in her seat.

"There's a call from New York on Line One. Trevor Wright. Ready?"

Megan nodded, took a deep breath, and pressed the flashing red button on her phone.

"DC Megan Jones. Good afternoon, Mr Wright?"

"Yes, it is. What the hell is the meaning of this? If it has anything to do with Bangor build project, I'm afraid it will have to wait –"

Megan was aware of Macrae's presence behind her. "Can I ask where you are, sir? If you are alone?"

"Is that relevant? What is this?"

Megan sighed, she had no option. "I have some very bad news for you, Mr Wright, and I'd rather you weren't alone."

"I've just got into my car. My driver and secretary are with me. Can you please tell me what this is about? I am a busy man, I'm sure you appreciate."

"Of course. Sir, there's no easy way to say this, but your daughter has been involved in an incident at her student accommodation."

The crackle of static carried across the line. "Melanie? How involved? What kind of incident? I'm not sure I understand what you're saying."

"I'm terribly sorry to inform you, sir, your daughter is dead."

There was a pause.

"Really? Is this some sort of sick joke? Some kidnap attempt gone wrong? I spoke to Mel on Saturday, she was fine. Absolutely fine. You have the wrong person."

"Sir, your daughter has been identified by dental records. I'm afraid there's no doubt. I'm very sorry to have to break it to you in this way, Mr Wright, and you have my deepest sympathies."

Silence.

"Mr Wright?"

"This is bullshit."

"I'm sorry, sir, I understand –"

"You understand sweet FA. How did she die?"

"Sir, at this stage, I'm not sure you should unnecessarily distress yourself –"

"Distress myself? You've just told me my only daughter is dead. Do you not think I might already be a tiny bit distressed?"

"Of course, sir."

"So, how did she die? Was she … raped?"

"No. Her throat was cut. I'm sorry."

"Oh, God. Murder, that's what you're saying?"

"Yes, that's correct. We believe she was drugged, restrained and then killed. I know this is no way ideal, but at such an early stage, I really need to ask a few initial questions, it will only take a few minutes of your time."

The man clearly had his hand across the phone as a rapid fire conversation could be heard in muted tones.

"Detective, I am going to head back to the airport. If this is the truth, I must get back to my family. Can your questions wait until tomorrow?"

"Not really, sir. I know this is a bad time, but the first forty-eight hours are vital. I'll try not to take up too much of your time."

"I just can't believe it. Melanie. Christ, this is too cruel."

Megan heard the wobble in his voice, and knew the ice man was beginning to thaw; the shock beginning to penetrate.

"Mr Wright, you have my full sympathies. We are doing everything in our power to ensure this person doesn't strike again –"

"You mean ... this isn't the first death? What are you telling me?" The voice was taut as steel wire again, no trace of the earlier emotion. "That my daughter's death could have been prevented by efficient policing?"

"There have been other murders and we believe there is a connection. We suspect that connection may be you –"

"Me? What are you talking about? Me? I know nothing about any murders. You think I'm some madman who kills his own flesh and blood?"

"Sir, please, calm yourself. I understand how difficult this must be for you. May I ask you a few questions about your property deals here in Bangor?"

"My ... my property deals? My daughter is dead and you want to talk about property deals? Are you mad?" His voice rose, higher and louder. "I demand you put me onto your superior right now, this is ridiculous –"

"Sir, please listen. One of the previous victims, who we believe was also killed by the same person, was Bronwen Evans." Megan waited to see if the penny dropped. It didn't. "The owner of the Tal-y-bont farm, Sacred Oaks."

"Yes, okay, I have purchased the land. But it has all been very amicable. I can't see how this can possibly be connected. It's madness. I don't understand what you're trying to say, detective."

"We believe there is a link, Mr Wright. What involvement did your daughter have in your business deals?"

"Melanie has nothing to do with my company. She's not

interested in following the family business. She's totally a free spirit." A pause. "I mean … was. Christ."

"I know this is hard, but can you think of anyone who may have wanted your daughter dead? Do you know of any enemies she had?"

"No enemies, no. For certain. Melanie was so well liked."

"Did she know you were buying the land at Tal-y-bont?"

"We discussed it briefly. She knew I had plans for a hotel and leisure complex, but to be honest she wasn't interested. Music was all she really cared about. I can assure you there is nothing, *nothing* in my business dealings that would have got my daughter in any kind of trouble. If you're thinking big business espionage or contract killing, forget it. It's not my style. I make my money legitimately – or I don't make it at all."

The phone broke up and Megan waited to see if the signal would settle.

"Look, we're almost back at JFK, I must make arrangements."

"Could I ask you at some point to call in to our police station to complete a witness statement? If you think of anything at all, please let us know. Thank you for your time, Mr Wright, and again my most sincere condolences."

"I shall have my own reasons for calling in to your station. I shall expect to speak to a more senior figure. I want explanations."

With little more than a grunt; the line went dead.

Chapter VI

MONA INSULIS, BRITAIN - AD 60

"Grant, O Spirits, Thy protection
And in protection, strength
And in strength, understanding
And in understanding, knowledge
And in knowledge, the knowledge of justice
And in the knowledge of justice, the love of it
And in the love of it, the love of all existences
And in the love of all existences, the love of Spirit
and all Creation."

Awen stepped away from the altar, and lifted the wooden bowl, still warm to her fingertips, holding it up to the heavens, then tipping it gently, allowing the tepid blood to pour in a steady stream across the surface of the altar. At the same time her father's servant, a noviate by the name of Luis, stepped forward and held a flaming branch to the small pyre. It ignited with a whooshing noise and in minutes the body of her father's trusty stallion, Ura, along with his favourite goat and chickens, began to sizzle and spit while their combined blood continued to drip from the sides of the altar, soaking into the fertile forest floor.

Awen cleared her throat and lifted the bunch of meadowsweet to her nose. She forced a smile, knowing what was expected of her at such occasions. Druidic funerals were a time of rejoicing; much laughter and celebration of the rebirth of the soul into The Otherworld. She knew all this. She accepted her beliefs, as did generations of her family who came before her. But still she could not shake the vision that haunted her – her father's headless body carried home, strapped across the back of Ura. Bloodied sinews dripping scarlet raindrops down the side of the dappled grey stallion, where her father's flowing locks should have been.

She had known. By the power of all the gods she had seen it. And despite his words, she was sure her father had believed her omens. Still she never expected such horror. It had hit her like a lightning bolt, knocked her off her feet. The next thing she remembered was Ked's cool hands, fingers working their magic as she dabbed lavender oil on Awen's forehead and held a small vial of essence of vervain beneath her nose. She had woke sweating and screaming, cursing her father in the most foul language she knew for ignoring her warnings.

And now … now, he was gone. She was alone in the world. And she hated him for his selfishness.

Days passed in a blur of fogged confusion, where she had gone about her business in an almost drugged state, greeting visitors with blank smiles, and accepting tributes for her father with deadened reactions. And now, somehow, she found herself standing before the altar at her father's funeral.

Awen looked up at rows of pale faces, all facing her, waiting for her to deliver the '*nuall-guba*' or eulogy. She recognised many among the crowd. Fathan and Caratacus among the most esteemed. She needed to do her father proud. Ked had helped prepare the words, as she'd helped her assemble her father's most cherished possessions to accompany him on his journey to The Otherworld. She hoped he would be happy with her choices – his hand-carved wine warmer and divining rods; his favourite flax robe pinned with jet and amber brooches; his beloved board game, the blue and white glass counters still laid out as they were when they'd postponed their final game; and finally a collection of his surgical instruments – copper alloy scalpel and surgical saw, hooks and needles.

Now, the prepared words vanished from her head and she floundered. She couldn't do this, she couldn't celebrate and laugh and sing as if her heart wasn't shattered into a thousand pieces. She looked for a way out of the wooded copse, somewhere to flee where no one would follow or ever find her again. But strong hands pinned her down, heavy on her shoulders. Her father's manservant slipped his arm around her.

"I know your feelings, Awen," he muttered. "I see it in your eyes, my lady, and it is also my pain. Your father was everything to me – my master and my guide. My very life I would have given to save him. But today is a celebration of your father's life. We must put aside our own pains, just as your father did when he buried your mother, and just as he would have had you been taken before him."

"Luis, I cannot celebrate his loss. Not when inside I too am dying –"

"To the outside world, we must. We owe it to your father and his memory. Inside, you and I, we can continue to grieve. We will bear the burden of each other's pain until it passes. Agreed?"

Awen looked around the small clearing, listening to the call of birds and the steady hum of insects. Shafts of sunlight danced between branches of oak leaves, and she remembered times her father preached here; his voice carrying clear across the fields to the commune. She met Ked's eyes and saw such love in her servant's face and tear-filled eyes, it gave Awen strength. She squeezed Luis's hand and stepped forward.

"We're here to celebrate the rebirth of my father. These are difficult times for every man, woman and child on Mona, and so I thank each and every one of you for making the perilous journey here today. My father died in his duty as a leader of men. I know he would not have wanted to pass in any other way. My father may have been the most peaceful of men, the wisest of the wise, the healer of the sick – but when called upon to fight for what he believed in, and the people he cared for, he was a warrior through and through. A true Chieftain."

Awen held up the bunch of meadowsweet and mistletoe and took a step forward, her toes stopping at the very edge of the rectangular hole in the ground. She looked down at her father's corpse, arranged now so his head sat on his shoulders, bound by a scarf of flax and wool. A jug of his favourite mead sat beside his right hand, and a wooden bowl of hazelnuts near his left. His face had been washed, his hair combed through. Eyes closed, with a gentle smile, he looked at peace – ready to move onto his next life. Awen's heart lifted and a sob escaped her lips.

"My father did not fear death. He saw it as the natural progression of the Universe and the start of his next life – a thing to be cherished and celebrated. And he cared not where his soul landed. Be it a woman, a snail, a fish out at sea or the green moss beneath our feet. In his eyes all were equal. Wherever you are, my beloved, we wish you wisdom, creativity and love. To Chief Druid Cadadius. My father!"

Awen let the flowers fall from her fingers, one at a time, slowly covering her father in petals and leaves. Luis stepped forward, repeated the ritual. Then the front row of friends and family did the same, moving in a single, ordered procession. A drumbeat started and people began to clap along with the rhythm. A local bard took his position aside his harp and performed the requiem, the 'cerdd farwnad'.

The gentle music lifted her, carrying her on a cloud of warm oblivion. She closed her eyes. When the usual wailing accompanied the drumbeat as the song drew to a close, she barely heard the haunting cries which accompanied the interment and provided the only sombre moment of the ritual, and a much needed release for the pent-up grief.

Awen let her memories take her away from the temple of

sacred oaks, transporting her back to happy times with her father. Sunlight warmed her cheeks as she closed her eyes, and recalled flashes of special moments, happy memories, cherished times that no one could ever take from her.

The drumbeats grew louder, resonating through her feet, shaking the ground. The wailing turned to screams; terrified shrieks sending the birds from their roosts.

"What's happening?"

Voices whirled around her. Footsteps hurried back and forth.

She opened her eyes as a hand grabbed her arm.

It was Ked.

"Move, my lady!" Ked panted. "Move. Follow Luis. Quick, now."

"What is it? My father …"

"Luis will come back and attend to the final touches. There's nothing more we can do here now, and we must make haste."

"Why? I don't understand –"

Her cheek stung as Ked slapped her across the face. "Forgive me, my lady. Please … wake up. Look around you. Invaders!" Her voice wobbled.

Awen allowed herself to be dragged along, looking back over her shoulder in time to see a flood of Roman soldiers pour into the clearing. The metallic song of swords broke out as the soldiers clashed with Celt leaders and tribesman there to attend her father's funeral. Cries and screams carried on the air as she fled, stumbling on upturned roots and springy grass as Luis half-dragged, half-carried her towards the sunlight that heralded the edge of the forest.

"We should stay and fight," gasped Awen, pulling back against Luis's grip. "My father would not have run away from a battle."

"And your father would never forgive me if I let you get killed. A battleground is no place for a lady. You may have the courage of a lion, but you've no more battle skills than my kitten. We need you now, Awen. Every Druid on Mona needs your lion heart now your father is gone. We have to get you to safety. Please ..."

She gave a curt nod, knowing Luis was right. She could be more help from behind the scenes than behind the blade of a sword.

In a daze she hurried away from the oak copse, away from her father's side for the last time.

Chapter Seventeen

"This is stunning, don't you think?"

Susan Connolly stood, hands on hips, at the top of a gentle bank that sloped down to a shingle beach. Beyond silky mudflats exposed by the falling tide, the fast-flowing waters of the Menai Straits exploded into the Irish Sea. Gareth's stomach flip-flopped – but not at the view. Sue looked like a warrior queen. The closing scene from a Hollywood movie, with the sun behind her, and hair swirling in the sea breeze. He shook his head, being with her was almost like being under a spell, he couldn't think straight.

She turned, face alive, eyes shining. "Can you not feel it? Have you no soul, Parry!"

Gareth laughed. "Probably not. It is lovely."

"Lovely? It's more than that. This little cottage, it's almost like a look-out post, standing guard over the farm, looking out across the water, ready to face any sign of the enemy from foreign shores."

"Have you been on the gin again?"

Sue shook her head. "There's no hope for you."

"I don't have your fertile imagination, that's all. Can't shoot me for being a realist. Doesn't mean I can't see it's a pretty spot."

"I give up." She slid down the bank, back into the shade of the trees. "Come on, let's go talk to this lady."

"I think we should wait for Hettie Fielding. She said she'd be here. From what I hear, Mairwen can be a prickly one if she puts her mind to it."

Sue shook her head. "With your charm, I doubt it."

"No, really. You've not met her … I'd rather wait. I've no idea how to handle her alone."

Sue gave his shoulder a squeeze as she headed towards the tiny cottage. "Have faith, it will be fine. Come on …"

Gareth shrugged. "Don't say I didn't warn you. If she kicks off …"

As they approached, the front door opened. Mairwen Thomas rolled herself onto the step, sniffing the breeze like a hound on the hunt. Gareth came to a stop at the gate, tugged Sue's arm.

"Do you think she can smell us?" he hissed into her ear.

"I think it's more likely she heard me yelling at you from up there." Sue nodded to the bank. "But if you want to believe she can sniff out our blood like a troll, you go right ahead, Parry."

He felt his cheeks tingle. "Oh, yeah."

Sue shook her head and opened the gate. "Mrs Thomas?"

The old woman lifted her head to one side. "Who's asking?"

Sue approached, touching the arm of the wheelchair. "My name is Susan Connolly. I'm a pathologist working with the police on your sister's case. May we speak to you?"

Mairwen tilted her head the other way, patted her lap until she found Sue's fingers, then clasped the hand between her own. "Pathologist, eh? You one of them types that chop up dead bodies?"

"I do. But today I'm here with Detective Parry, who you met before, to try and find out more about Bronwen."

Mairwen continued to stroke Sue's hand. She tugged at her wrist, forcing Sue to lower her head so she could speak into her ear. "You're …"

"Detective! Sorry I'm late …" Hettie Fielding appeared in a chink of bracelets and a flash of silvery turquoise, like a glimpse of an elusive, colourful kingfisher against the greyness of the woodland. Her face was shiny red, sweaty strands of hair curled from beneath her headscarf. "Missed the bus back from town and waited an age for a taxi. I'm sorry."

Gareth turned, nodded. "No worries, we seem to be doing okay."

"Lucky you caught her. She's finally been persuaded to move out. Her daughter will be along to collect her later."

"Daughter? I didn't know she had children?"

"Yes, just the one. Delwyn. Lives in Menai Bridge. She's tried for God knows how many years to get her mother to move. And it's only now she has no choice she's submitted. Stubborn's not a strong enough word for Mairwen Thomas."

"I kind of gathered that." Gareth watched as Mairwen reversed her wheelchair back into the cottage. Sue followed, gesturing with a nod for Gareth to hurry up.

"You'd best go," said Hettie. "Do you need me to stay? No problem if you do, if not I'll be off and put the shopping away before it melts in this heat."

"I think we've got it covered, but thanks for all the effort."

"Mairwen seems to have taken to your colleague. She's always on edge with men." Hettie pushed up her sleeves. "How are you getting on? With the case, I mean, any closer to an arrest? Sid was asking ... it's playing on his mind more than he'd like to admit."

"Not yet, I'm afraid."

"They're saying that lassie from the university ... well, that her death is involved with Bronwen's somehow. It's just too terrible to think about, isn't it? I mean, there's none of us safe in our beds while there's a murderer on the loose."

"I don't think you have too much to worry about, honestly."

"No?" She stared at him with pale grey eyes that clearly didn't believe his words of reassurance. "Me and Sid are going to be looking after the farm on our own once Mairwen goes. From what I hear it could be a while before the estate is settled. If there's something here this madman wants, I don't like the thought of me and Sid left here as sitting ducks. But I mean, I've said yes to Delwyn now, I can't exactly change my mind."

"Well, we hope to make an arrest very soon. Until then, all I can do is advise you to be vigilant and report anything unusual to me straight away. And if you're in any way concerned just dial 999. But I really don't think you should worry too much."

Gareth watched as the woman retraced her steps through the oak trees. He hoped he hadn't given her false promises. But if they were right about the deaths being connected to the missing treasure or the members of the Servants of Truth – surely Hettie Fielding would be of no interest to their killer?

Inside Mairwen's cottage, the air was cool and still. Mairwen sat alone, a knitting basket on her lap, carefully sorting balls of wool into differing sizes before storing them in the side pockets.

"Your woman is making tea."

"Ah, right." Gareth waited in the doorway, unsure whether to join Sue in the kitchen.

"She says you've come wanting answers."

"Ah, well, yes. That is …"

"Why don't you come and sit down and quit hovering like a vicar at a brothel."

"Ah, right. Sorry." He lowered himself onto the sofa opposite, not quite sure why he felt like a naughty schoolboy about to get caned. "Last time we spoke, you mentioned an organisation both Iris Mahoney and your sister were involved with. You were going to get advice from other members. The case is moving on and I need answers, I'm afraid. My boss is leaning on me. I'm getting heat because you're potentially withholding evidence so we need to get that sorted today, okay?"

The words came out in a nervous rush and Gareth was embarrassed at the whining tone. What was it about women that made him feel so inadequate? First Susan, now this blind old woman who'd barely ever spoken more than a dozen words to him before today.

"Tea time!"

Sue appeared, breaking the tension.

Mairwen put the bag on the floor. "I think your fella was waiting for an answer. He'll be cross you've supplied a diversion."

"Oops, sorry." Sue smiled. "But I think we all cope better with a nice cup of tea, don't we?" She stirred a spoon round inside a pretty pink bone china mug, with a picture of a very young-looking Queen Elizabeth II on the side, then handed it to Gareth. "There. Three sugars. Strong."

He accepted the cup, blew on his fingers and waited until both women were settled.

Mairwen took a small sip and balanced the mug on her knee. "I've spoken to some of the others, they're obviously distressed and realise you're working on our side. So, I can answer your questions … up to a point at least." She took another sip. "Anything I can't, or won't tell you, you're welcome to speak to Delwyn, my daughter. She'll be along later. Or Hettie, of course."

Gareth looked up. "Hettie Fielding? She's a member … or whatever you call them?"

"Yes, of course."

Gareth let it drop, remembering the woman's cool grey gaze. No point enquiring why he hadn't been told. He already knew the answer. The sisterhood and their secrets. He had a sudden urge to stomp back up to Hettie Fielding's caravan and start yelling for someone to start talking common sense and quit talking in riddles. He'd just told her she had nothing to worry about, when, in fact, she could potentially be the next victim. If he didn't get answers from Mairwen; he was tempted to haul Hettie in for questioning and insist she give them the names of every single member of this sisterhood. But that was for later. He blew out a long breath and relaxed his shoulders. Yelling would have little effect on the woman in front of him now; he was certain of that.

"So, I want to know what you can tell us about the Servants of Truth?" he said.

Mairwen groped for the coffee table, used both hands to settle the mug down. "It's not what I *can* tell you, it's what I *will* tell you. I know how it works today with computers, not that I've ever used one, but I'm sure you've been trawling or surfing, or whatever it is you do, to find out what you can about our sisterhood."

"Well, yes, not that it's got us very far …"

"No, it wouldn't. Wouldn't be much of a secret society if it didn't have its share of secrets, now would it?" Mairwen lifted her head a little. "We have been active for many hundreds of years and our role is to preserve the intelligence and knowledge of our ancestors. Knowledge that is passed down mainly orally, from mother to daughter, and onwards through the generations. We keep our convictions close to our chest because in our hearts we know one day, our beliefs will be called upon to appease a troubled world. Our ancestors lived by the laws of nature; their customs, traditions, rules and faith have been left to us to carry into the future. It's no small task, and no one in the sisterhood takes it lightly. I can't really go into anything more specific, but I hope that gives you a picture of what we are about."

Gareth typed a few notes into his Blackberry, not wanting to upset anything by asking if he could record the interview.

He cleared his throat. "I read somewhere that Servants of Truth was an old Celtic title for Druids. Can you confirm there's a connection?"

"I won't confirm anything other than what I've told you."

Gareth leaned forward, rested his hands on his knees. "But …"

"I think what we really need to know, Mrs Thomas," Susan interrupted, "is if there is anything in your beliefs and the knowledge that could be used today for personal gain if it were to get into the wrong hands. We're thinking specifically of stories of lost treasure rumoured to belong to the ancient Druid tribes of Anglesey." Susan gave him a bright smile and took a sip of tea. "That's what you meant, isn't it, detective?"

"I ... yeah ..."

"We cannot divulge the knowledge. We can only say that we protect all things connected with our ancestry."

"I'd take that as a yes," whispered Susan into his right ear. "No point pushing it. She won't have a treasure map and if she did you'd never get to see it."

"And in terms of membership ..." said Gareth.

"I am not allowed to reveal details ..."

"So you said. You may be forced to change your mind if your members keep getting themselves murdered." Gareth tried to keep the irritation from his voice. "We already know Iris and Bronwen were members. Is there any kind of hierarchy? I am wondering why they may have been chosen in particular."

Mairwen reached for the mug, arthritic fingers tapped the table, seeking out its heat. "Iris was one of the higher order. Bronwen and myself, we had our roles, but we were nothing special."

"Can you tell me what your roles were?"

Mairwen shook her head, sipped her tea.

"But that's not a huge help, is it, really?"

Susan squeezed his arm. "Mairwen, do you think Bronwen was killed because of her role within the Servants of Truth?"

Mairwen frowned. "I don't know and that's the truth. We have lived here in peace all our lives. I cannot see what might have changed or why Bronwen didn't know she was in danger. Her death was written. It came as no shock to me, but then, I don't understand why she didn't foresee it. I can only assume she was double-crossed, someone she trusted as a friend turned into her enemy."

"Any idea who that might be?" said Gareth. "Could it be anyone within the Servants of Truth?"

Mairwen snorted on a mouthful of tea. "You clearly know nothing about the sisterhood."

"Agreed. I know nothing because you won't tell me."

"*Can't* tell you."

"Okay, can't tell me. But I find it a little odd that you're being so evasive when, as you point out, we are working on the same side. Do you not want the person who murdered your sister, in cold blood in her own home, locked up behind bars for life?"

"Gareth …" Sue put a finger to her lips but his temper was fired up now.

"I won't go to the trouble of reminding you that there are penalties imposed for obstructing police in their investigations – but I will remind you that my interest is in the here and now, protecting innocent people from a killer who seems obsessed with either your sisterhood or something your sisterhood is intent on hiding."

"We are protecting the present as well, detective," said Mairwen. "The only difference is we're protecting the past and the future too."

"And while you're busy protecting yourselves, there's been another murder. I don't know if that news has reached you. This was a student, nineteen-years-old. She was drugged and tortured prior to having her throat cut … so if you can't tell me to help me … can't you tell me to help her family?"

Mairwen's hand shook as she put her mug back on the table with the same slow procedure as before. "I know of Melanie Wright. It's a tragedy."

Gareth glanced at Sue. She shook her head. He took a deep breath.

"Then you know what we're up against. Was Melanie a member?"

"She would have been. Her mother and grandmother were before her."

"And her father …"

Mairwen frowned, rubbed her palms along her grey, pleated skirt. "Of course not …"

"No, I mean, you know about her father? That he has bought the land here at the farm?"

"No!"

"Yes, I'm afraid so. The planning department have confirmed it. He plans a hotel, marina and leisure complex on the site."

"No! I won't let him."

"I'm afraid the deal has already been signed. I believe Bronwen hurried it through because she knew there was an archaeological dig planned somewhere along the Menai Straits and she wanted to sell up before anything got in the way of the sale."

"Bronwen wouldn't do that. She must have made alternative arrangements ..."

"For you ...?"

"No. Not for me."

Susan leaned forward. "Mairwen, it would really help us if you could think of any enemies Bronwen had, either connected to the society or in the outside world?"

Mairwen shook her head. "I told the police woman last time, Bronwen protected me from the outside world in much the same way she protected the knowledge of our people. Had done ever since I lost my sight and lost my husband within a year. She's been like my right arm. I can't believe anyone would want to harm her. And if they did torture her to try and discover any of our secrets, then they were wasting their time. We are taught from an early age the importance of conserving our knowledge for the future – a gift bestowed on us we would never give away."

"Did she ever talk about Matthew Barrington-Brown?" said Susan. "Or Derwydd Hall?"

"We all knew about Derwydd Hall. We all knew Iris would have fought until her dying day to see it closed down. Of course, Bronwen wanted nothing to do with the man, too many old wounds would have been opened, too many painful memories of her daughter, Caitlin. She wasn't surprised he'd chosen to demean Caitlin's memory but she wouldn't have gone out of her way to make an enemy of him, if you know what I mean. In fact, as soon as we knew of Iris's death, Bronwen was sure there was a connection to that man and his evil cult. But I can't see why he'd have an axe to grind with Bronwen personally … and then there's young Anna to consider. Would he put her through that?"

"And there's seriously nothing else in your arsenal of secrets that you can see could have caused these deaths? I'll be honest, I need a motive. Badly need a motive," said Gareth. "So be honest with me please."

The old woman sighed, her head bobbed. "Nothing. I have tried to imagine such evil but I cannot. I know there are rumours locally about our ancestors being involved in witchcraft and black magic and the like … but it's all utter nonsense. Our beliefs are at one with nature. We would never advocate harming another human being, so why anyone would want to harm any of the sisterhood, I really have no understanding. I wasn't lying to you last time, detective, I just didn't have anything to say. Your killer may have a different view, a very twisted logic, but whatever he believes … it has no bearing on reality. All of us in the Servants of Truth simply want to avoid publicity, hone our skills, share our troubles, protect our knowledge … and be left to lead normal lives until the day we – or most likely our descendants – are called upon. We cause no one any harm at all and without this kind of adverse publicity, no one would be aware of our existence, as it has been for many hundreds of years."

Gareth nodded, accepting the woman's words. "And you've no idea when this day will be?"

Mairwen shook her head. "No. But I do know this day is not it."

Chapter Eighteen

The coffee shop overlooking Bangor Pier bustled with activity. Megan was lucky to grab a small table in the bay window. Professor Bolton had responded to her messages at the end of morning classes and arranged to meet her here. She'd heard nothing back from Adrian, and was annoyed at herself for making that fact even a small issue in her life with everything she had going on at the moment. She breathed in the smell of freshly-roasted coffee as the professor weaved his way carefully through the lunch crowd, tray held high.

"Didn't think it would be this busy," he said, distributing the drinks and pastries. "Sad indictment of the state of food in the Uni canteen, I fear. Right. Tea and an oatmeal flapjack for you. And a double cream Mocha and a blueberry muffin for moi. Splendid."

"It is lovely here," said Megan, helping to unload the tray. "Food and the view. It's a rare treat for me though. I usually grab something at my desk when I'm on a case. And I'm so grateful for all the assistance ... really, it's been a huge help."

"Of course, not a problem."

Megan watched as he added three sachets of sugar to his already sugar-loaded Mocha and took a long gulp, eyes closed.

"Ah. Bliss." He wiped his lips with his napkin, removing a chocolatey moustache. "Thing is, I was rather shocked when you mentioned the project at Tal-y-bont and anything I tell you has to be in confidence at the moment. The project is very hush-hush. There's only about three of us at the Uni who know about it, most of the work is being carried out by the National Museum of Wales."

Megan shrugged, added a splash of milk to her tea. "Of course. Whatever you tell me, at this stage anyway, is off record. However, I can't make guarantees if my leads come to anything important –"

"No, no … I understand that. Catching a killer is a tad more vital than finding buried treasure."

"Buried treasure? So this is connected to the digs you mentioned before?"

"Yes, as I told you, there have been rumours and counter-rumours right back into the Dark Ages. I was involved at the last dig at Moel-y-don that drew a blank, and since then, there have been all sorts of sites mentioned around Caernarfon. And then out of the blue, about six months ago, a colleague of mine got an anonymous phone call. Very mysterious. Saying they'd come into information about a Roman gold hoard around the Menai, and wanting information about its existence. Well, what could we say? Very little. I suppose we were both shocked and excited because, although the rumours were known throughout academia, it had been an unspoken rule to keep it from Joe Public. No one wants to see armies of metal detectorists invading, especially as we're talking such a large area, and we've no idea where to narrow the search." Professor Bolton paused, took a sip of his coffee. "At least we hadn't."

"So what happened, what did this caller say?"

"Well, I got involved as Professor Giles Kendall needed a sounding board. He was head of department then and we'd worked together at Moel-y-don. This person rang a few times, built up a rapport with Giles, I suppose, and then suggested a meet. The week before the arrangement, Giles suffered another stroke – he was already wheelchair bound, you see. And to be honest, with the stress and extra work load, it went completely out of my mind. Obviously, Giles failed to turn up on the planned date. I suppose the person thought Giles was a fraud, and everything went quiet."

"And was that an end to the matter?" said Megan.

"For a time. I got made temporary head of the department, while Giles was recuperating. It became clear he wasn't going to be fit to return, and things were quite manic for a couple of months. And then, about three months ago, I got another call. This time from Iris Mahoney and she clearly knew about this earlier communication between the stranger and Giles, and was asking the same questions."

Megan stared at the professor, trying to read his expression. Her mind was at once focused, suspicious. He was busy peeling a thin layer of paper from the base of his muffin, but Megan could see, above his shirt collar, his neck was turning a deep scarlet.

"And yet, when I asked about her death, you didn't think to tell me about it?"

"I … no. I suppose not. Look, I won't lie, I suppose I couldn't see how there could be a connection and I was desperate to keep my findings secret. We were just about to go to court with the injunction you see, I couldn't risk …" He put the muffin down. "This all sounds very lame, even to my ears. I am sorry if I've led you astray or withheld evidence, but believe me, I thought you were focusing on Barrington-Brown, you seemed quite determined he was your man. All I did, I suppose, was go along with that. But honestly, I still don't see how this treasure can have anything to do with your investigation."

"With due respect, sir, that's not your decision to make."

The professor bowed his head. "Point taken."

"And even when I came to you asking about Bronwen Evans, you still chose not to mention her land was at the centre of a dispute between your department and a property developer. In fact, you blatantly lied about knowing her."

"I'm embarrassed to admit that my selfish pride was the only reason. There was, nor is, anything sinister in my actions. Will I get into trouble?"

Megan stirred her tea, trying to keep her anger in check. She might want to promise the professor there would be no incriminations, but she couldn't. Macrae would be furious, while Gareth would no doubt be utterly delighted her key expert had ulterior motives for keeping their investigation at bay. Scatter-brained professor or not, it wouldn't look good on him – or her – that he'd admitted to lying. What a mess.

She sighed. "I don't know. I hope not. But you should have told the truth, you must see how this could look? I can't help you unless I have your word you'll tell me everything you know."

"But of course. Lesson learned." He gave her a relieved look and bit into his cake, chewed and swallowed. "You see, when you came to me, it was such a shock. I don't read newspapers as a general rule. And the only television in the house is in Adrian's room. I apologise, it must seem remiss of me. It's been troubling me; the fact I could have withheld information, without ever realising it, for all the wrong reasons."

He held her gaze as if willing his honesty across to her. She thought she could believe him, but in the course of her short career she'd been fed so many stories, by people who begged her to believe the lies as truths – it left her feeling numb, cynical, and unable to shake off the cloak of suspicion. She had to treat the professor the same way; he'd taken the decision out of her hands. Guilty until proven innocent.

"Okay, I can buy that, just about. So, Iris contacted you after your colleague retired … can you continue with the story?"

"This is where it could sound even more lame. You see, I don't have your investigative gene, and I'm afraid I took everything Iris told me as gospel, and got so bloody excited by the whole thing, I never pushed for more information."

"No matter. Just tell it like it is."

"Iris had information, she never said from whom, but I took it to be the person who contacted Giles –"

"Was the original caller a man or a woman?" said Megan,

pulling her notebook and pen from her handbag.

"It was a man, so Giles said. Of course, I never spoke to him. But Giles had no reason to lie, not that I can see anyway."

"And Giles's full name was Professor Kendall? Where can I get hold of him?"

He shook his head. "You can't, I'm afraid. He passed away on the twenty-eighth of March."

Megan looked up with a frown. "Did he know about Iris?"

"No, he was too ill, alas. The second stroke about finished him. It was a sad end to his life." He paused. "Anyway, I carried on, thinking I was doing it for Giles in some way."

"So, Iris had information. What exactly was it?"

"She had part of an inscription in Latin. What we call *Old Latin*, Romano period. She knew Latin, had studied it. She'd come up with a rough translation of legible words, not one hundred percent accurate, but enough to realise its significance."

"And she came to you – why?"

"She came to the university for help and I was head of the Welsh History Department by then. We are well known for our Romano British studies. She'd made the mistake of telling this third person the translation, and at that point their relationship soured. She feared the other person was going to try and recover the hoard himself and sell the gold for as much as he could get. The last time I met her she was in a terrible state. They'd had a major argument, she'd tried to make him see sense, but he was having none of it."

Megan made hurried notes. The pieces were stacking up nicely, and her gut was screaming one name. *Barrington-Brown.* B.B. Hadn't Iris done her best to name her killer all along by scratching his initials on her skin? She had known he was lying, and now she could see why. She looked up; Professor Bolton was clearly expecting some kind of response.

"So …" Megan tapped her pen against her bottom lip. "Iris wanted to go through the proper channels. I assume that would be declaring the hoard to the local authorities, having a full excavation, and getting the valuation via the treasury committee or whatever is the correct procedure?"

He nodded. "I think she realised the massive significance of this find. It has the potential to fill in so many gaps about the Roman invasion of Anglesey. It could be of international importance, not only Welsh."

"She wanted to do the right thing. The third party didn't want to accept a share of the treasure trove valuation; they wanted to off-load the goods to the highest bidder. Am I right?"

"Exactly."

"Which is a pretty good motive for murder. Get her out of the way and he – or she, I guess – is free to carry on with their plans. But then, we hit another complication because by now you're involved, and presumably you've told other people –"

"Very few. The National Museum, as I said, and the local authority. Oh, and CADW."

"So, quite a lot, in fact. Which makes me wonder if it doesn't negate the motive for killing Iris?"

"I got the impression she never told the other person she'd gone behind his back. Had the feeling she would have been scared to."

"Did you ever get any inkling who the third person might have been?"

Professor Bolton shrugged. "No. But in the back of my mind I guessed it was Barrington-Brown or someone at Derwydd Hall because Iris hated the place so much."

"But you never asked her?"

"I did. She point blank refused to answer."

"Okay."

"I think she was torn between her allegiance to the past and her dreams of the future. That's certainly the impression I got. I told her she'd done the right thing, but try as I might, I couldn't get a name or location –"

"Location?"

"Ah, sorry, waffling again. The Latin was found on a stone.

Like a headstone or memorial stone. I assumed it was around Penmon. I'd actually got another meeting arranged with Iris, but she failed to turn up, and I thought she'd gone cold on me."

"When in actual fact, she was dead?"

He looked down. "Yes."

Megan took a sip of tea, taking time out to calm her frustration. In an interview room, she would be having a serious time biting her tongue right now. She was so annoyed at the evidence the professor had withheld. For what? All in the name of professional pride and one-up-man-ship. But she sensed bullying or anger wouldn't work. She could only lead him gently by the nose, hope he'd follow, and not miss out too much vital information on the way.

"You didn't try to persuade her?"

"I called her a few times. Decided she was ignoring my calls, and by then the project had moved up a gear."

"How come?"

"Ah, well you see, that's when I began to put two and two together. The part of the inscription we had from Iris detailed the hoard was possibly buried in a grove of sacred oaks, near rushing waters. Oak trees are rare right near the sea, but on all the old maps going back thousands of years, there'd been a large wood of oak trees right on the edge of the Menai Straits –"

"And it was on the farm at Tal-y-bont? Bronwen Evans's place?"

The professor nodded.

Megan waited for Professor Bolton to return with a fresh coffee. She'd scrawled pages and pages of notes, her handwriting deteriorating as her excitement built. At last, they were closing in. At last, the edge of the jigsaw was almost complete; it was now a matter of twisting and turning the middle pieces until she got them all to fit. Anna Brown's face kept popping up in Megan's mind and she had no idea why. Was it the girl's warnings of danger? Or was Anna the missing connection? Was it she who discovered this marker stone, took Iris to see it? And then, what, her father found out, took control …

A chair squeaked as the professor returned.

"Right. I don't suppose you have a transcript of the Latin bits?"

"Not here. But I can get it to you, of course."

"Can you email it to me, later today?"

"It's on my home computer. I'll ask Adrian."

"So, Sacred Oaks Farm. You knew the site, or suspected you did. What did you do about it?"

"Iris beat me to it, actually. I'd told her about the research, that we had a location in mind. I was trying to get her to take me to the stone so I could have it expertly analysed, and I suppose I bragged a little too much. I went out to visit the farm, ask for permission to do some preliminary tests on the land, and they already knew. No doubt in awe of the famous Iris Mahoney."

"That's a point. Did you know who Iris was? I mean, that she was a television personality?"

He shook his head. "Not a clue. I've never seen the programme, although I did Google her name. Adrian got very excited when I told him. But that kind of thing is really not my scene, quite surprised at Adrian actually, but there you are. Youth of today are a minefield of oxymorons."

"Iris never told you her identity? I'm wondering, you see, if her programme may have had something to do with her discovery. Or maybe her gift?"

Megan mused, as Anna's face insisted on filling her mind. Her quietly-spoken assurance she could read other people's thoughts, could predict future events, maybe even speak to the dead. Was Iris of the same lineage? Was she genuine, not the fraud she had always dismissed her as being?

"Never. She was very private. No chitchat. Not rude as such, but she never gave herself up to questions or anything personal."

"Mmmm, she would be private," said Megan, imagining the list of things Iris must have been forced to hide. "But ... we're digressing. The farm at Tal-y-bont?"

"Right, yes. Lovely couple of sisters, grieving the recent loss of the farmer, I recall, and struggling to make the right decision about the future. I was shocked Bronwen was killed. Again, it's no justifiable reason for not telling you everything, but I couldn't believe it might be because of something I'd led them into. I still can't ..."

"We don't know that. Did they give you permission to work on the land?"

"Absolutely. They were excited at the prospect, not least because of Iris's involvement. We'd got them to sign a confidentiality agreement, and I'd booked archaeologists ready to start the dig ... and then they dropped the bombshell."

"What bombshell?"

"A few weeks later they told me they'd sold the farm. And apparently their solicitor had been in touch with the buyer and because contracts had been signed, but the money hadn't yet been transferred, he threatened to pull out of the deal if they allowed an excavation on the site."

"So you went to the courts ..."

Professor Bolton looked up, eyebrows raised. "Well, yes. The developer wouldn't speak to me directly, nor any of my contacts, so we got a protection order on the land. Extreme, possibly, but we weren't dealing with a reasonable man. We had enough evidence to buy us some time, so we used it. It gives us three months to excavate, makes the developer put his plans on hold. And he's not a man who likes his plans thwarted."

"We're talking Mr Trevor Wright?"

"Yes. Wright Brothers Holdings. He tried everything he could to get the injunction lifted. Screamed, shouted, threatened ... and if I'd gone along with it, bribery."

"I think you should know, professor, his daughter was found murdered this morning."

Colour drained from the professor's face. "No. You can't mean that?"

"I wouldn't joke. We think it's connected to Iris and Bronwen's murders too. Did you know Melanie Wright?"

He shook his head, apparently struck dumb.

"As far as you're aware she had nothing to do with either of the women or the Servants of Truth?"

"What?" He shook his head, pushed his second Mocha aside. "Not to my knowledge, but it's a secret society, I could be wrong. I just … I can't take this in. What's happening here? This cannot be connected to archaeology, it makes no sense whatsoever. I mean, what do you think? Am I a blithering idiot or do you think the treasure hoard could be important in all this?"

Megan blew out a long stream of pent up air; she felt like she'd been holding her breath forever. "I hope, professor, you've just handed me the key – the vital missing piece I've been searching for."

"So I did the right thing?"

"A bit late, but yes. I'm going to have to ask you to do it all again at the station. I need a signed statement from you."

"No problem, here's my card, all my contact details."

Megan slipped the business card into her bag, along with her notebook and pen.

"I should make a move, brief the team. Just work with me and help me find this killer, tell me everything at all times, and I'll do my very best to prevent repercussions. Okay?"

The professor nodded, held out his hand and squeezed hers. "I see now the fascination. Adrian is a lucky lad."

Heat flooded Megan's face and she pulled away. With a final wave, she pushed open the café door, hurrying towards her car. She needed to call Gareth, fill him in on the new detail immediately; no way was she making the same mistake again. He'd want to get back to Derwydd Hall, talk to Barrington-Brown again and she wanted to be with him when he did. As she reached her car and unlocked the door, another thought struck her. She fished the business card from her handbag, and dialled Professor Bolton's mobile.

He answered on the first ring, sounding slightly breathless. "Hullo."

"Hi. Sorry to bother you again so soon, I've had another thought."

"What can I help you with?"

He sounded as if he was walking, slightly out of breath and muffled, probably on his way back up the hill to the Uni although he'd not passed her.

"One last question," she said. "Did Iris ever mention an Anna Brown?"

Silence.

"Professor?"

"Just thinking. No, no, I don't think so. Who's Anna Brown?"

"If I'm right, I think she was behind the first call to Giles Kendall."

"But I'm certain it was a man. Ah … I see … her father?"

"Yes. Anna, I think, is the key to this mystery and she was very close to Iris." Megan shook her head. "I'm waffling, sorry. It could be nothing, I just wondered if Iris had ever talked about a young girl at all?"

"No. Not at all. Sorry I can't help."

"That's okay. Thanks again for the tea, and the info. Bye."

Megan hung up, switched the phone onto hands-free and selected Gareth's number.

Time to revisit Mr Matthew Barrington-Brown.

Chapter Nineteen

"Jesus, can you not slow down a little?" Gareth lurched forward, restraining himself against the dashboard as Megan sped down the winding lanes between Beaumaris and Penmon. Trees and hedgerows flew past his window like a speeding express train, shadows creeping the full width of the lane as evening approached. "I'm going to be visiting the chorizo I thought I'd last seen at lunchtime at this rate."

"Do you hear me bleating when you're on the blues?"

"With respect, Megan, I don't drive like Schumacher's dog on heat."

Megan snorted, eyes bright and wide.

He recognised the pent-up emotion making her almost euphoric. He loved that feeling, getting the first break, the first sniff of something huge. Having listened to her transcript of the interview with her professor pal, he was of the same opinion as Megan. This was the key. He was even optimistic enough not to have the scatter-brained oaf locked up for wasting police time. But he had bigger things to worry about – and a prospective fortune in buried treasure was more than enough justification for the tally of murders they had so far. And he was in no doubt the person wouldn't stop until he was either successful in his mission – or stopped.

"So, we accuse him, do we, Barrington-Brown?" asked Megan,

He opened his mouth to reply but a low groan broke free as she shot across a Give Way sign.

"Or play our hand?" she added, selecting gear and accelerating hard, "tell him what we know, and expect him to fill the gaps?"

"I've been thinking the same," said Gareth once his stomach had settled back into position. "Much as I want to go in there all guns blazing, I don't want to lose him now, not at this stage. I think we let him lead us to his own downfall. Clever and cautious, reveal what we know – a little at a time."

"And what if he's innocent, Gareth? You've considered that, I assume? That he might be a con-artist or a delusional weirdo, but we might be wrong and he may not be our killer."

"Of course. He's guilty of *something* though. You must feel it too. I don't know what at this point, but we're not leaving until I do. He's lied to me for the last time." Gareth gripped hold of the interior door handle and leaned to the left as ballast. As they straightened, he continued. "See, I've been trying to work this thing through. Much of what your prof told you stacks up. I found the contract with Wright Brothers Holdings today in the safe out at Sacred Oaks, and it's all signed and sealed so far as I can see. I found a copy of the Court protection notice too. So, what worries me is if Barrington-Brown knew where the hoard was, why not just go and dig it. So, whereas I get Iris's murder – the need to shut her up, why kill Bronwen and the developer's daughter? What's with the torture?"

Megan gripped the steering wheel, brow furrowed in concentration, but remained silent.

"I mean, this inscription he sent you." Gareth held aloft the email. "It's not exactly your normal treasure map, is it? There's lots of ifs, buts and maybes, if you ask me. And let's say our man, Barrington-Brown … well, he knew everything Iris knew, why go to the trouble of killing all these other people? If all he really wanted was a few extra readies on the black market instead of going legit?"

Megan sighed. "I don't know. You're asking much the same

questions I've been asking myself. But you agree, I hope, that Barrington-Brown is withholding information?"

Gareth nodded. "There's something wrong there."

"Right, let's go and extract it, shall we? We're here."

"Thank God," Gareth muttered.

Gareth stood at the farm gate, looking over the wide expanse of furrowed earth that led right up to the rear boundary of Iris Mahoney's garden. He hadn't realised the two properties were so closely bordered. New green shoots penetrated the earth in ordered rows, leading his eyes to the roof of Iris's cottage just visible above the hedgerow. It had been a less stressful exercise getting into Derwydd today, predominately because the boss was not at home – working away on the farm, one of the tenanted areas of the estate where Barrington-Brown liked to spend much of his time according to the security guard at the main gate. A scribbled route, a further five minutes of even narrower lanes at even higher g-force, and they'd arrived here, at a neat farmyard, with hens scratching in the dust, and two beautiful black and tan border collies secured to a kennel by the back door. There had been no answer at the farmhouse, so as the sun began to slide down towards the horizon, Gareth had decided to wait. And he didn't have long to do so.

His stomach tensed as he heard the rumble of a tractor pull into the yard, and turned to see the furious scowl of Barrington-Brown, navy blue overalls and cap, in the driver's seat. He looked less the religious guru today and more the regular farm-hand. A slim blonde girl, who he first thought may be Anna, stood beside him, swaying as the tractor cleared the rutted yard. The tractor disappeared into a barn and the engine fell silent.

Megan climbed out of her car. "Ready as you are," she said. "I take it that wasn't Anna in the cab?"

"No. Might be the reason for his apparent interest in farming, though. Ready?"

"Oh, yes," she said, rubbing her palms together. "Raring to go."

There was no pretense of civility this time. Barrington-Brown stormed straight past them, heading for the house, apparently leaving his companion somewhere in the depths of the gloomy barn.

"Out of my way. I'm onto my solicitor. This is police harassment."

Gareth hurried to keep up. "Actually, it isn't. New information has come to light. And it's urgent we speak to you about it."

Barrington-Brown reached the small porch and tugged off his boots. "Bullshit. You want another intimidation session. Well, you can do one. You hear!" Spittle flew and his face was full-on crimson. He slid a key into the lock and pushed open the door.

"Please … five minutes of your time," said Megan. "We are trying to be reasonable, help us out. We can do this here or at the station, your choice entirely."

Barrington-Brown turned on the door step, rage making him shake. "This better be good. I warn you."

Gareth stepped forward. "We're not on tape now, sir, but I'd still suggest, for your own sake, not to be bandying unnecessary threats around."

The man took a step forward. "Or what?"

"Or we throw you back in your favourite cell and go home." Gareth sighed. "Sir, why do we have to do this every time? Look, I know stuff. I know you know the same stuff – but have withheld it up to now. If you can convince me why you'd do this, then fine, I'll be on my way."

"You're talking crap," said Barrington-Brown. "And wasting my time. I've still not decided what action I'm going to take against your colleague, here –" He stabbed a finger in Megan's direction, "for demanding my daughter travel home alone in the middle of the night, putting her welfare at considerable risk. And then, to compound it, refusing to let her contact me and interviewing her without the presence of parent or guardian. You do realise the kind of trouble I could make?"

"That's not –" Megan began but Gareth stopped her with a raised hand.

"Funnily enough," he said. "I have a similar problem. Two in fact. Firstly, I'm unsure who to go to with a confirmed report of polygamy. And second, I've not yet decided what action to take with regard to the fact you told lied about the whereabouts of your daughter, knowing she was potentially a key witness in a murder enquiry. You'll be amazed how many boxes that ticks on our charge sheet."

There was a deadlock of silence.

"I did it to protect my daughter; any father would do the same."

"Then if I were you, I'd hope the judge on the day has a particularly strong paternal streak." Gareth sighed. "I'm bored and frankly have better things to do than make pointless banter with you. Let me come inside, refuse your kind hospitality, and spell out what I need. Or, as Megan said, you can come down to the station and get all huffy, same as last time. Your choice."

With a growl, he flung open the door, crashing it against the wall. Gareth followed, pulled out a chair for Megan, then took the seat beside her. Barrington-Brown strode across to the sink and scrubbed his hands, sending clouds of steam across the room. Gareth waited, fingers drumming on the table.

Finally, he took his seat at the head of the table. "Make it quick."

Gareth took his time. "I believe in the course of my investigations, I've come across the real reason for your involvement with Iris Mahoney."

Barrington-Brown smirked, but Gareth would swear he saw a flash of fear in his eye.

He pushed on. "At the moment, I can only base it on conjecture. But my conjecturing is second to none. Isn't that right, Megan?"

Megan nodded. "'Absolutely right, I'll say.'"

"Cut the comedy routine, get to the point, or I'm out of here," snapped Barrington-Brown.

Gareth leaned forward, elbows on the table. "Okay. You set up Derwydd on the back of local legend regarding ancient treasure and Druidic rites. Amazingly, people brought into it and spent fortunes on the mumbo-jumbo you preached. So, you had to up the ante, give them more of what they craved. You heard a rumour locally about an ancient landmark that was, in effect, some kind of treasure map. And you made it your business to find it, or most likely, if you hadn't you'd have gone and purchased one and planted it." He paused, studied the other man's expression. "Now, I may be a bit hazy. But at this point, I think you got lucky. I think you found an ancient standing stone on your land." Gareth watched his eyes. Nothing. "I don't know where, but you discovered odd markings on the stone that intrigued you. I'm not sure how, probably from digging around on the Internet or perhaps had someone research it for you, but anyway, you realised it matched the historical document that detailed the enigma of a stone very like the one you'd found. Hinted at Romano period, possible Latin inscription. How am I doing?"

Barrington-Brown crossed his arms, but his face was slowly draining of colour. "Keep talking. I'm listening."

"Appetite whetted, you look up local Roman experts, and lucky for you, Bangor University has some of the very best. So, you speak to the head honcho, Professor Giles Kendall, and although I'm not sure exactly what he tells you, he certainly says enough to get you excited. He tells you the inscription probably is Latin, maybe translates the odd word. And then, what happens? He goes and dies. Very inconvenient for you, I bet?"

"Glad to see you're so sympathetic." Barrington-Brown stretched, rolled his neck from side to side. "Let me guess what's coming next. In my anger, I go on a murderous rampage, killing my neighbours –"

"No, you go to Iris for help. She's into all the historical guff – you told me as much yourself. Maybe you've heard about her Druidic lineage. Perhaps it was a chance meeting, or perhaps I don't know, through your daughter you discover Iris can read Latin. I think either you show her the stone or make a rough copy and ask her to translate it. And this is where your plan starts to unravel."

The man glared. "Lots of perhaps's so far. But do go on. I'm intrigued."

"Well, she stitches you up, doesn't she? She realises the significance of what you've found. Remember, she was a bit of an expert of local history, you realised too late she was never going to keep this quiet. You had your eye on wads of cash and an early retirement, while she wanted to go to the authorities and tell the world. Really blew your plans out of the water."

"So I killed her." Barrington-Brown smiled, small even white teeth more like a snarl. "Well done, Sherlock. That really is what you think, isn't it?"

Gareth shrugged. "Unless you can convince me otherwise. I know you've been lying through your teeth. I want to know why."

Barrington-Brown looked at him; his stare direct and cold. He looked down, studied his knuckles and sighed. "Give me strength."

Gareth jumped out of his chair as the other man scraped his own back and stood.

"Calm down. I'm not making a run for it." He nodded toward the door. "You best come with me."

Chapter Twenty

They trooped single-file across the farmyard. Barrington-Brown seemed less tense, humming as he locked the door. He brushed off the dogs, who were yelping madly and performing acrobatic feats around him.

"*Taw!* Tess. Nell. *Lawr!* Now then."

Both dogs trooped off toward their kennel.

Megan's eyes adjusted as she stepped into the gloom of the barn, and she saw, with horror, that Barrington-Brown was mounting a huge red quad bike. The space echoed with the roar of an engine as he reversed it round to the entrance and stopped in front of her.

Megan waved away the fumes. "What are you doing?"

"What's it look like?" shouted Barrington-Brown, above the engine noise. "If you want to see the evidence, I suggest you clamber aboard."

Megan pointed. "On that. With you? You have to be kidding. What about Gareth?"

"One on the front, one on the back. It's easy, come on."

Megan shook her head. "I'll follow you, in the car."

"We're going cross country; the car's no use to you. It's this or nothing. I'm not waiting for you to tramp across my fields in those shoes."

Megan glanced down at her patent high heels, then flashed a look of desperation at Gareth. He shrugged. It seemed their choices were limited. Megan scowled and cocked her leg over the leather seat. She glared at Gareth again and looked around for something to grip onto that didn't include a piece of the man in front of her, managing to wedge her fingernails under the edge of the seat. She gestured for him to climb aboard and tried not to think of the state of her trousers as Gareth balanced on the carrier above the front wheels.

The engine revved and the bike shot forward. Megan squealed and grabbed for the rail behind her as she slid backwards, trying to find purchase with her heels.

Barrington-Brown shouted over his shoulder; his face bright with amusement. "It's going to get bumpy any minute. You'd do as well to hold onto me. Grab my waist." He laughed at Megan's horrified expression. "You're safe. I've no wish to add manslaughter of a policewoman to my list of crimes."

Megan was scared, but she'd be damned if she'd show it. They accelerated along the track and Barrington-Brown dismounted as they reached a gate, shoved it open, then jumped back onboard.

"Ready?"

She nodded, trying to keep her trousers away from the muddy sides of the bike.

Barrington-Brown laughed again, annoying her at the pleasure he was so obviously getting from their discomfort. "You won't be worrying about your clothes in a minute. I hope you've got strong thighs, detective!"

He revved the bike, this time shifting through the gears in a rapid succession as they flew across the centre of the field. Megan moaned aloud, shuffled forward, and had no option but to hold onto the belt loops on Barrington-Brown's jeans, while gravity did its best to throw her off, like a cowboy in a rodeo. She scowled again at Gareth although she knew the predicament wasn't his fault. She closed her eyes, bowed her head, and began to enjoy the experience. Adrenaline soothed her nerves as the speed built steadily. Cool air streamed around her and she relaxed a little. Her eyes opened in a shot when rough fingers tugged on her hand.

"Hold tight, we're going through a ditch, and lift your legs a bit if you don't want your shoes ruined."

Megan did as she was told, letting go with her feet, as Barrington-Brown stood to manoeuvre the bike down a steep ditch, then straight back up the other side. Seconds later, they were flying again. This time, Megan opened her eyes, held her head back and watched the white clouds scudding past as the roar of speed filled her ears.

All too soon, they were slowing down.

"This is the boundary of my place, this embankment, some kind of old flood defense." Megan flicked her hair away from her face. "Are we there yet?"

"Yes, you can let go now," said Barrington-Brown, waiting for Megan to unhook herself and clamber off the bike, before jumping down beside her. "Enjoyed that, didn't you?"

Megan shrugged. "A bit of a speed demon, yeah. Where now?"

"Up to the top."

Gareth brushed his trousers as they trudged to the top of the embankment. Megan followed. As ever, the view from the top across to the mainland forced her to stop and stare. A small fishing boat following the deeper channel, way out, crossed in front of them, accompanied by a flock of screaming gulls. Minutes later, they stopped at a dip in the bank, almost like a break in the defensive wall.

Barrington-Brown pointed out a jumble of fallen walls. "There was a fisherman's cottage here. Way before my time. You can make out the ruins in the grass. Anyway, follow me, it's through here."

Megan picked her way through the long grass, feeling the soft shift of sand beneath her feet, hurrying to keep up with Gareth. When they reached a small clearing, Barrington-Brown had taken a seat, on what she assumed were foundations of the old cottage. He pulled off a blade of grass and began to chew, then nodded to where a standing stone dominated the small clearing. It was about five-foot high, and on the side facing the sea seemed to be engraved with some kind of concentric central design with grooves along both edges.

"The writing's on the far side, less wind damage and that away from the sea, I suppose, but it's not that clear."

Gareth and Megan trod carefully around the stone. She shielded her eyes, stared at the rough stonework, and eventually began to make out lines and curves, which, because she knew what to expect from the email, she could form into letters. What looked like a backwards, E and a K, were clear in the centre of the stone; there was one word with a clear T as its first letter, and another with a V in the middle. No way of reading the words, even if she'd known any Latin; it would take considerable work to translate this into the verse in the email. Gareth pulled the folded paper from his pocket and held it up between them, examining the stone and the verse:

> *Take a boat* ----------------
> ----------- *grove of sacred oaks,* ------ *rushing water*
> *On the highest* ---------------------
> *Turn* --
> ... *and there you'll find* -------------------
> *In* ------------------------ *of my father.*

Megan looked across the sparkling water; a few yachts zoomed across, multi-coloured sails flapping in the breeze. Her thoughts were tinged with the memories of so many deaths that may have resulted from this very find. In the distance, she could make out the far shore. While she couldn't quite distinguish Sacred Oaks Farm, she could see the white gleam of caravan roofs leading down to the water's edge. It *was* a marker, and it certainly seemed to point the way. Perhaps whoever wrote it couldn't get back to the other side, so left this as permanent pointer to show the way. And then never got the chance to go back again. But why …

"Bullseye," whispered Gareth, breaking her trance. "We found it."

Megan nodded, at a loss for the right words.

"Do we have any idea who wrote this?" asked Gareth, trailing his fingers across the engraving. "In …………of my father …"

"Not that I'm aware," said Barrington-Brown, from the other side of the clearing. "I think Iris did her best to find out. That's the bit you got wrong, you see. Your conjecturing isn't as hot as you think. Though I've no real proof either way now Iris is dead … which is another reason, I guess, why she was more use to me alive."

"Care to explain?" said Megan.

"Iris found this stone. Not me. Well, technically it was Anna. I told you she's fascinated with history. Anna spent hours digging round this old cottage, here, finding shells and bits of pottery, playing at being an archaeologist. I think she saw something on this stone, told Iris about it, and once the old woman saw it, she knew it was something special." Barrington-Brown shook his head. "Do you really think I'm the type of guy who has the time or inclination to go wandering round the place staring at old bits of rock?"

Probably not, Megan thought, with various wives and a cult to run. Whereas she could easily imagine Anna would revel in the solitude of the place. Megan rubbed her arms as the sea breeze rolled off the ocean, rustling the grasses – an eerie sound, like sandpaper on wood. Yes, there was something in Barrington-Brown's words. Something that felt immediately right. Of course, she'd check with Anna, but she didn't feel she really needed to. Anna would know the significance of her find and Megan doubted she would have needed Iris's validation. Maybe a second opinion, sure, but this whole place carried Anna's presence as if she'd spent much of her life here, living among the echoes of people long gone. But if she believed Barrington-Brown's story, where did that leave the investigation?

"So, you want us to believe you're innocent in all this?" said Gareth. "Excuse me if that seems a tad unbelievable."

"I didn't say I was innocent." Barrington-Brown flashed a fierce glare at him. "If you'd not put words in my mouth, I'd carry on with the story."

"Okay, so Anna found the stone," said Megan. "What? Iris came to you?"

Barrington-Brown kicked out at a loose piece of rubble. "Yes. After she'd been poking around – I mean *researching*, she came up with this document from some Roman expert about missing treasure, war loot. The old witch was buzzing, wanted to go public, call in museums, treasure hunters, the lot."

"But you had other plans?" said Megan.

"I had to think about Derwydd, what the discovery would mean to the group. You see, Derwydd means the world to me. I set it up for Alice, Anna's mother. Anna has inherited her mother's gifts and her connection with nature. Alice was attached to the land here in a way I'd never seen before. I know what you think of me, and that's fine, but I am passionate about keeping Alice's ambitions alive. And that takes money." He spread his arms wide. "So, I didn't have any plans to start with. But I did my own form of research, and realised I'd probably get a pittance through these treasury valuations. I knew, if the treasure did exist and it was gold, and I could find it and sell it, I'd pay off all our debts and set Derwydd up for life. Of course, that was before we got the full translation. At that time we all thought the treasure was on my land, somewhere round here, and that was the marker."

"So, how did you stop Iris blabbing to the authorities in the first place then?" asked Gareth, leaning a shoulder against the stone. "I mean, you contacted Professor Kendall, didn't you?"

Barrington-Brown nodded. "I got Anna to talk to her. Convince her I'd play merry hell if she told anyone. The old woman was soft on Anna, if she thought I'd make Anna suffer, by sending her away again, she'd have done anything. Not that

I would, of course, the threat was enough. Plus, I said once she went and broke the news, the place would be swarming with blokes with metal detectors, not to mention the media. She liked her privacy did Iris Mahoney. I think she had her own skeletons she wanted to keep closeted, if you know what I mean."

"So, you bought her silence?" asked Gareth.

"If you want to put it like that. I wanted to find out everything I could myself. It's my land, my rights. I don't see I did anything wrong. Time over, I'd do the same."

"So, what happened? Why did Iris go behind your back to the University?"

"I think you can put that down to Anna again, though she's not admitting it. I'd been put in touch with some – associates – who were willing to take the treasure off my hands if I was successful. Anna stuck her nose in. I even caught her outside the pub listening in on conversations. Told you Iris managed to turn my own daughter against me, didn't I? Mind, she probably saved me a ton of work. I'd gone out and bought a metal detector, had done a few bits and pieces, when Anna had one of her tantrums one night. Told me I was too late, Iris had already gone to the university; they reckoned they knew where the treasure was, and that it was miles away from here."

"So, that's what the row was about? With Iris not long before she died?" said Megan.

He nodded. "Old witch wouldn't tell me where they reckoned the treasure was, but said some professor believed it was genuine. They wanted to see the stone, excavate it. I told her if she let them onto my land, I'd sue her."

"No one has ever been here, from the Uni, I mean?" said Gareth.

"Nope. And I've no intention of letting them set foot on my land –"

At that moment, a short yelp sounded from the other side of the hedgerow, and Nell came hurrying out with her tail between her legs. She ran straight to her master.

"*Tyrd yma!* What is it, girl?" Barrington-Brown asked, stroking her ears. "What's the matter? You hurt?"

He mumbled a few low words and soon the dog was circling his legs, tail wagging in delight. His scowl cleared. He put a finger to his lips and stepped quietly across the clearing, jumping through the gateway with a yell.

"Gotcha! You little sod. Have you not learned your lesson about listening where you don't belong?"

Barrington-Brown appeared, gripping a squirming Anna.

"Don't!" Anna squealed, trying to tug herself out of her jumper. "Let me go!"

Megan stepped forward. "Leave her be, sir. I know you're cross, but don't hurt her."

"You've no jurisdiction here to tell me how to treat my own kids, lady –"

"Can we not drag that attitude up again, please?" asked Gareth. "If you don't want me to embarrass you in front of your daughter, how about you let Anna go, eh? I'd like to hear her side of the story, even if you don't."

For a moment both men remained motionless, gazes locked. Barrington-Brown looked down first, pushing Anna away.

"She's all yours. See if she'll tell you the same lies she told me." Her father rubbed his hands together. "Anyway, if I'm free to go now, I've got work to be getting on with back at Derwydd."

"We'll need a signed statement from you," said Gareth.

He nodded as he reached the quad bike. "As long as I'm no murder suspect, I've no problem with that."

"How will we get back?" yelled Megan as the quad rattled into life.

"I'll take you," said Anna. "We can follow the beach, along the bank, till we get to Iris's house, then out onto the lane."

Megan took hold of Anna's outstretched hand.

"Am I in trouble?" asked Anna as the three of them followed the embankment round the curve of the beach.

Megan shrugged. "It's not my decision. This is my boss. You'll have to convince him."

"You should have told us the truth," said Gareth.

Anna plucked a sprig of sea clover, and rolled the stem of the delicate flower between her fingers.

"I didn't think it was important. I couldn't see how it was linked to the murders, or why anyone would want to kill Iris because of something so ancient. It's stupid."

Megan smiled at the girl's naivety. Greed wasn't something Anna understood. Yet.

Anna sighed, rubbed her eyes. "I wanted to keep the cottage private. It's my special place. And I don't want other people coming, walking all over it, damaging it. I remember my mum here; this was one of her favourite places too. When I told Iris, she said it was important to keep it a secret."

"But as I see it, if no one excavates the site properly, you may never know who wrote that message," said Gareth. "Surely that's important. There could be all kinds of important discoveries, and you can say you were the person who found it. The archaeologists might even let you help out with the dig. How cool would that be?"

"Really?" Anna's blue eyes opened wide. "You think so?"

Megan nodded, making a mental note to speak to Professor Bolton. "I'm certain."

"Wow, that would be cool. If only Iris were here ..."

Megan nodded as Anna picked the pink petals and tossed them individually into the wind, turning to watch them soar out to sea.

"I'm sorry I didn't tell you about the stone. I told you about the argument I overheard, because I wanted you to get the story from my dad, there was loads I didn't know, see. But he didn't kill Iris, he wasn't there in the dream ... I told you that, didn't I?"

Megan knew Gareth was watching the interaction with a

completely bewildered expression, no doubt trying to work out what was being left unsaid that seemed to be so important.

"You did. If only you could see who was in the dream."

"I've tried. I had another dream. I tried to call you. I am so worried … so scared. I saw a man yelling, some twisty stairs …" Anna looked up. "Is it going to stop soon?"

Megan stopped and took hold of Anna's hand. "Yes. I promise you. It's going to stop *very* soon."

Megan said a silent prayer that she was right.

Chapter Twenty One

"Gareth? ... Gareth!"

He looked up from his computer screen, the blurred background clearing as he blinked. "Huh? What's that?"

Chris sighed. "I said I'm off then. Mrs Mahoney's funeral? See if I can spot anything interesting. Anna will be there with her father for one thing, and I want a chance to see who else they might get chatting to. Anything else you want me to focus on?"

"Nothing specific. Just keep 'em peeled, look for any guilty faces in the crowd and any odd pairings – people connecting who shouldn't be connecting unless there's a reason. Funerals are good places for reading signs that aren't usually visible. And I must admit I'm intrigued that none of Iris's family has come forward. If anyone is there, grab hold of them. Otherwise, there's going to be a very rich cats' home on Anglesey, I reckon."

"Shame I didn't meet her earlier. I've always fancied being a toy boy."

Gareth scratched his scalp with the tip of his pen. A persistent itch to accompany the constant throb above his right eye.

Chris paused at the office door. "Are you okay? Only you seem a bit distracted. You ignored one of the WPCs a while ago when she knocked."

Gareth stared. "Did I?"

Chris nodded.

"Sorry. Lots on my plate, mate. Trying to make these murders link to this treasure hoard … and pissed off I seem to have lost my number one suspect. Trying to make sense of the torture aspect, the randomness … and I've got Macrae on my case on the hour, every hour. Seems he now feels the urge to pass on any pressure he's getting from above, straight down the line to me. In the back of my mind I'm worrying about Anna Brown and her portents, and what to do about this Servants of Truth brigade." He sighed, rubbed his temple. "And I if I'm brutally honest, I've no idea what to do about a certain female pathologist who seems to be taking up far too much of my thought processes at the moment."

Chris took a step into the office. "Ah. I thought I was right."

"There's nothing to be right about. That's the problem. Nothing has happened."

"But you want something to happen. Don't bullshit me."

"I don't know. She confuses me. Last time we were together it was a total disaster. She's far too intelligent for me, doesn't trust me, and deserves to meet a better bloke who will change her life and make her happy. But the thing is … and I don't want to sound gay … I can't stop thinking about her. I can't stop wanting to be with her. I can't stop feeling happier than I have ever felt in my life when I'm with her. My head's a mess, I will admit that. And it's the last thing I need at the moment."

"Sounds like you've got it bad, mate."

Gareth shrugged. "And if she doesn't feel the same?"

"What does she have to say about it?"

"She hasn't said a word. It's not a conversation we've had."

"Then perhaps you should."

"I'm not sure I want to hear it. She's been honest enough to tell me it was the real thing with Luca Javier. She loved him."

"So?"

"I dunno really."

"Then let me try and translate. I think you're saying because she's been engaged to another man since you two were together,

her feelings for you could never have been that strong ... or she would have spent the following, oh, I don't know, however many years you deem appropriate ... in mourning for you and your doomed relationship."

"That's not what I'm saying –"

"Pal, that's exactly what you're saying. You want to take a listen to yourself. How many women have you bedded over the past three years?"

"That's different."

"Of course it is."

Both men smiled.

Chris shrugged. "Hey, I'm no expert when it comes to women, the last Mrs Coleman will testify to that ... but seems to me the worst thing you can do in these circumstances is bottle it up. Don't leave it till it's too late."

"And if she doesn't feel the same? I mean, she finished it last time."

"Then at least you'll know, hey? Surely that's better than screwing your head up indefinitely?"

Gareth sighed. "Maybe. We'll see." He looked out into the main office. "Where's Miss Eager-Beaver this morning?"

"Thought you had her off on one of her expeditions?"

"No. Probably using her initiative as usual. Well, she's welcome to it. With any luck she'll have the whole case in the bag by lunchtime and we can sod off home." He pushed his chair back. "Argh. It's me. I need caffeine. Or nicotine. Or both. Come on, I'll follow you down and sneak a quick ciggie in the car park."

He trailed Chris down the stairs, through the corridor and out into the blustery morning. Both men lit up and stood beneath the canopy of the smoking shelter, backs hunched against the mild wind.

"Megan talked your man round ... Barrington-Brown, I mean," said Chris. "He's agreed to let two Latin experts take a look at the stone. See if they can produce an accurate translation, and depending on what they find, I think he'll see sense and let the archaeologists in. All he cares about is how it might benefit Derwydd and this could be a real coup for him. Seems his defences are coming down, one by one, and you've Megan to thank for getting through to him."

Gareth grunted. "Excuse me if I don't flip somersaults of delight."

"What's the matter now?"

"Well, exactly how does the state of Barrington-Brown's happiness help me to solve this sodding case? As far as I'm concerned, this could all be another pack of lies designed to keep us from the truth. He's a guy I wouldn't trust so far as I could throw him, so like I said, excuse me if I don't give a shit."

Chris groaned. "Are you being deliberately obtuse about everything today? No? Well, look at the bigger picture then. I've no idea if the guy is telling the truth. But if he is, sorting out the meaning of the message on that standing stone is vital. You can be sure of that."

"But the experts already know, surely, it's across the water. Sacred Oaks Farm. Otherwise, what was the point of Melanie Wright's death?"

"From where I'm standing, we still don't know the reason for her death. We don't know the reason for a lot of things."

Gareth dropped the cigarette and ground it into the tarmac. "So, what are you saying?"

"I suppose I'm saying give Megan Jones a break. She's got skills. Let her use them."

With that Chris squeezed Gareth's shoulder and walked to his car.

Gareth turned the car into the narrow driveway, keeping Sacred Oaks farmhouse on his left. Blue and white police tape buffeted in the wind, broken ends snapping at the side of the car as he followed the track as far as he could go and turned off the engine. On the furthest edge of the property, before the rolling green landscape became choppy blue water, there were two separate thickets of trees. One on a low mound, the other in a small hollow. Could this be the sacred oaks that gave the farm its name, and by association the place mentioned in the inscription? He'd barely given them a second glance on his last visit, but now he studied the area in detail, trying to decide the quickest route down to the beach.

Gareth got out of the car, untied another crime scene tape from across the gate, drove through and parked next to the old red van. Nothing had changed here since his last visit that he could see. *Fferm Derw Fendigaid*. It was ingrained in his mind now. Sacred Oaks Farm. Although they were still awaiting the full Latin translation, he knew they were right. His instincts screamed at him that this place was the connection. Ergo the answer must lie here too. Today, he was determined to open his eyes and see it.

Securing the car, he set off along the track leading down through the caravan site towards the wooded hill. Sid's car was missing; his caravan locked and in darkness. Gareth thought of Hettie Fielding and resisted the urge to march up to her door and start demanding answers. Once in the shadows, under the canopy of thick oaks, he shivered in the chill. There was something quite eerie, almost other-worldly, about the atmosphere, making his way through a caravan park that time seemed to have forgotten. A magpie cawed on the branch above his head; he jumped and stood stock still, one hand ready to grab a loose branch if required.

When he reached the last row of caravans, he pushed open a gate and began to climb the incline. Something caught his eye in the tall nettles edging the path, and he used his foot to flatten them down, bending to pick up a blue label. It was some kind of guarantee card; the name caught his eye. *Tesoro. Twelve Months Manufacturer's Warranty.* Dropped recently as it was yet to be damaged by rain. Whatever it was, the person would be losing a warranty if they failed to send this card back. He slipped it inside his pocket to ask Sid about later.

The air grew more salty, with the unpleasant smell of muddy foreshore drying out at low tide. His leg muscles burned as the bank grew steeper, and he followed a pathway through the brambles. *Tesoro.* Why couldn't he relate the name with anything? Electrical? Sporting? Stupid as it was, it was beginning to bug him. Pausing to catch his breath, he pulled out his phone, glanced to make certain he'd missed no calls or texts, and typed the name into the search engine.

His breath caught in his throat as it returned the result. *Tesoro. Lightweight metal detector models for treasure hunting, coins, relics, gold, silver, artefacts, diving, beach combing ...*

A large bird broke through the canopy, startling him; tremors rippled along his spine. It was dim now, and cool in the shade. Dense foliage and an uneven track made it tough going, and twice he slipped, paused to regain his balance and composure. But the discomfort was worth it. Someone had been here, very recently. If the broken down nettles and trampled gorse weren't enough of a clue, this tag certainly was. And if archaeologists hadn't yet put a foot on the land with their equipment, there was a good chance whoever had been here had done so without permission ...

Squinting through the gloom, grateful for the occasional flashes of sunlight through the trees, he approached the summit of the mound. It was still densely covered, but there was something unusual about the ground. There was less undergrowth, and more of a russet colour to the forest floor, almost like a pile of sand. What was it?

Gareth stepped over a fallen log, heading for the disturbed earth. His phone rang, shattering the peace, sending more birds crashing from the branches above. Heart hammering, he checked the display. *Number withheld.*

"Hello?"

"Parry!"

"Sue? What's the matter?"

Susan Connolly screamed. "No, don't …"

"Sue?" Gareth checked the display, shook the phone, pulse drumming in his ears. "Sue! What is it? Please … for God's sake talk to me!"

Sue squealed and hiccupped, then spoke in a flat voice. "Someone has taken me. I'm safe and well, but I'm scared. The man holding me says he hopes you've appreciated his handiwork so far, and says he'll enjoy refining his hobby on me. He says I don't need to explain, you will understand. He also wants me to tell you this call will not be long enough to trace, short by at least nineteen seconds." Sue gulped and sobbed. "Th-the message. He wants to trade me, in exchange for Anna Brown. He will contact you again this evening with further details. If you do not bring Anna, or you tell anyone else about this phone call, he says he will kill me at midnight."

Sue panted. "Gareth … Help! Please, get –"

The phone went dead.

Gareth stared at the blank screen. This wasn't happening, couldn't be happening. A dull pressure seemed to be filling his head like a balloon, blurring the edges of reality and slowing down time.

He turned and began to slide his way back down the slope, staggering at first, then breaking into a run, ignoring anything in his way, arms wind-milling, slipping, skidding, trying to breathe, trying to think. Trying to … what? What was he going to do? Anna was at Iris Mahoney's funeral. What did he intend doing? Marching into the crematorium, snatching the girl, and making a run for it? Don't be stupid, man. Think!

He had to be logical. He needed to speak to Chris, Macrae. Megan even. He couldn't do it alone. Could he? Gareth sucked in long lungfuls of air. What had the message said? If he told anyone else, Sue would be killed. Killed? His Susan? How had he let this happen? No, no, no, no. He couldn't do it, couldn't risk it. He had to do what this psychopath wanted.

But how could he?

Chapter VII

MONA INSULIS, BRITAIN - AD 60

A twig snapped, echoing off the surrounding trees like a slingshot off a shield. Marcus flashed a glare at the guilty man, pressed a finger across his lips. The chanting was clearer now. The distant strains of music that had first alerted them to human presence in the centre of this copse ceased, replaced with rhythmic clapping and the sounds of animals in pain. He'd never heard such a noise – howling like the great wolves mating at night – but something told him it was human. The small hairs on the back of his neck rose as chills rushed through his body.

He'd heard stories of such cruelty among Druids – blood-thirsty rituals and tales of dark magic – but he'd long been certain they could be nothing more than tall tales to scare the enemy. Now, with these echoing moans reverberating all around him, he could well believe every single one of the horror stories he'd heard.

The flicker of flames caught his eye, and he recognised at the same time the crackle of burning wood and smell of cooking meat. This had to be some kind of feasting. Rings of people filled the small clearing, marching in circles around a central slab of stone. Some clapped and chanted; several threw back their heads and howled, while others cast plants into a large hole in the ground. As he studied the scene, he saw that the table, although decorated with intertwined flowers of every colour under the rainbow, was also slick with crimson puddles of what looked like blood.

Marcus swallowed down his repulsion. He'd heard stories of human sacrifice. Now, here was the evidence; a fair-haired, slender woman writhing in a kind of trance in front of this makeshift temple. He looked around, expecting to see bloodied corpses littering the forest floor. Instead, his eyes were drawn to the burning pyre, where twisted remains spat and sizzled, ignored by the crowd as if it were nothing more innocent than the preparation of the evening meal. As his eyes followed the smoke, up through the ring of ancient trees, arthritic fingers pushing to the sky, he saw human skulls hanging from the branches, like grotesque decorations.

Bile rose in Marcus's stomach, and he turned to address his men, flinching as he brushed his injured arm against the rough bark of an oak tree.

"Druids," he hissed. "Dozens of them. Some kind of feasting. Human sacrifice. This is one of the groves they talk of, consecrated to their savage cults."

A rumble of groans ran through his men.

"Hush, now. We outnumber them at least three to one. We need to wipe the evil from this island or none of us shall sleep easy in our beds tonight."

His men nodded, but their eyes were scared. And he could not blame them. The scene had turned his stomach. Especially the girl, eyes closed, swaying on the spot, hands bloodied …

"Split into three groups, normal procedure. Do not become undisciplined or surrender to the blood lust, men," he whispered, raising his voice a little as the wailing reached its peak. "Cover each side and wait for my signal. Go now."

Marcus squatted behind a thick gorse bush; his eyes trained

on the snaking procession of robed Druids. There were as many women and children as men; it was likely there would be innocent casualties. But he couldn't worry about that now. They had to go in hard. And fast.

Waiting till he calculated his men would have surrounded the clearing, he gave the signal to ready for attack. He sensed his men moving behind him, poised, ready for battle. He reached inside his pocket and fingered the small figure of Hercules for luck.

"Now!" he screamed.

Faces turned, slowly at first, pushing back their hoods to reveal expressions of confusion before the fear took hold. Then, as the first slash of blade struck home, the first gush of blood splattered the face of a child, panic swept through the clearing like fire through the driest forest.

"Forward!" Marcus ordered. "Avoid the children if you can …"

His words were drowned out by the stampede of feet, clash of swords and thud of bodies hitting shields. Then the screaming began as knives and spears found their targets. The ground echoed with the dull thump of bodies hitting the floor, faster and faster until it felt like the gods were shaking the Earth.

Marcus lunged forward, pushing women and children aside, searching out the men. He grabbed hold of the hair of a man who was about to yank his sword out of the bloodied belly of a legionnaire. With a growl, Marcus spun the man towards him, raising his gladius ready to slice his head from his body. But the man was too quick, and as he turned, Marcus realised he carried a knife in each hand, and was as deft with his left as his right. Marcus parried each stab; his weakened arm throbbing from the pressure of the blows.

There was something about the passion in the man's eyes. The face, creased in intense concentration, seemed familiar. As Marcus drew back, he heard the Celt muttering under his breath and realised where he'd encountered the man before.

"Caratacus?" Marcus panted.

The man grinned, brown teeth splitting the silver beard. "Aye. We've met before I take it?"

Marcus swung his sword but the man dodged to one side.

"As your father before you," hissed Marcus. "Why are you here? With these … savages? I thought you were dead?"

"Hidden. Watching …" The Celt thrust forward, the tip of his blade grazing Marcus's shoulder, shooting white pain along his arm into his chest.

He was weakening. He could feel it. And up against the toughest opponent he could have faced.

"Waiting!" Caratacus leapt forward, all his weight behind the blow.

Marcus felt the slice of skin on his neck. A hot gush of blood followed and when he opened his mouth to speak, more covered his tongue. He spat and tried to balance himself. It was no good, the world was spinning. This couldn't be it. It couldn't be the end, here in this wood, in this outpost no one had ever heard of. He *wouldn't* die here.

He blinked to clear the blurriness. The smoke from the pyre seemed to be choking him, cutting off his air supply.

A heavy blow landed on his stomach. For a heartbeat he feared he'd pissed himself, then realised the hot liquid running down his thighs was his own blood.

Caratacus's face filled his vision. "Waiting … for justice for my father, for the humiliation he suffered at your people's hands!"

Marcus staggered and spun, arms outstretched as if someone would save him. He toppled backwards and the earth seemed to melt away as he fell lower and lower into the bowels of the earth.

He landed on a soft bed of sweet-smelling flowers. Was this the River Styx? He breathed in the delicate aroma of the pale petals. With a grunt of pain, he turned over, tried to push himself to his knees. He shrieked as he came face to face with a sleeping Druid, white hair fanned out around his face, lips curled up in a vile sneer. This must be a dream. Or he was dead.

He was hit by a sudden moment of lucidity. He'd seen the face before. Like Caratacus the Junior, this image too had imprinted onto his memory as he'd hacked the Druid priest's head from his body. Held it up high as blood from the severed arteries flowed down his arms. He'd laughed at the fear and panic on the Celts' faces.

And now, the priest had returned to follow him into the next life. Was this to be his penance?

"No!" he cried, thrashing around, slipping and sliding in his own blood as it continued to flow from his body.

Exhausted, he lay on his back, panting. Above the swirling smoke and canopy of thick branches, clear sky was visible. Bobbing human skulls danced in front of his eyes, mocking him as he swirled in and out of consciousness. He blinked, focused on the blueness, waiting for Charon to come for him. There was no point fighting. It was over.

Marcus closed his eyes, the darkness was total.

Chapter Twenty Two

"Penny for them?"

Megan looked up, one hand still holding a spoonful of soup. "Sorry!"

Adrian Bolton took a drink of his beer and smiled back at her. "It's okay. I usually get to at least the third or fourth date before I actually put a girl into a coma, so I might be on for a bit of a record with you."

Megan felt her face redden. "It's not you. It's me."

Adrian grabbed his chest in mock horror. "Not that line, not yet. It's only our second date, you can't dump me. I won't let you!"

She glanced around the quiet public bar and hushed him. A few grey heads turned, elderly folk enjoying the mid-week two-meals-for-a-fiver offer.

"Sorry," he said, keeping his voice to a whisper. "We don't want to shock the clientele too much and have a heart attack on our hands."

Megan sipped her soup and shook her head, laughing.

"That's better." Adrian slid his hand across the table, gave her left thumb a squeeze. "I like to make you laugh. You have a beautiful smile."

"Okay, okay. Enough already. You'll make me choke on my tomato and basil."

His eyes stayed calm. Serious. "It's true, isn't it? My dad said the same. You really don't know how to handle a compliment, do you? I was being serious."

Megan broke off a chunk of wholemeal bread. "Then, thank you. What can I say?"

"Nothing. Just believe me."

She nodded. "Today was a lovely idea. It's ages since I've been out for a proper lunch – and as I've been interviewing students since seven am, I figured I deserved a break."

"My dad told me … about the student. I didn't know her but it's still terrible. I can imagine the shock waves going round the campus." He paused. "Dad's concerned he's let you down, not telling you about the planning injunction and Iris Mahoney's marker and all that. But honestly, if you knew him, that's what he's like. He doesn't see life like you or I. He lives in his own little world where what happened two thousand years ago has far more impression on him than what happened last week. All he would think about was protecting a site of national importance. He doesn't think rationally sometimes and it's bloody frustrating. But it's just the way he is, I'm used to it, but I can see how it may look to you. Believe me though, he's gutted, it wasn't intentional and he never meant to mislead you."

Megan nodded. "Okay. But I really shouldn't talk about it with you. Sorry."

"But he won't get in trouble, will he? I mean it's obvious there was no intent."

"Like I say, I can't discuss your father with you. It would be more than my job's worth and I'm already avoiding the wrath of my DI at every opportunity. Sorry."

A cloud passed across Adrian's face. "Of course. I didn't think. I don't want to put you in an awkward position. It's just … it's my dad. I wanted you to understand."

Megan nodded, remained silent.

"Is that what's on your mind … work, I mean?" said Adrian.

Megan shrugged. "I guess. It seems more real when it's someone closer to your own age. And talking to her friends this morning, no one could believe it's happened." She paused, reached for her glass. "I had to tell her father. That was tough."

Adrian nodded. "I can imagine. Perhaps we should talk about something else. Give your mind a bit of free time."

Megan sipped her water. "Perhaps we should. Go on then."

"So …" Adrian took a long pull of his beer. "I was plucking up courage to ask if you liked boats?"

"Boats? Erm. I don't think I really have an opinion. Why?"

"Me and my dad share a boat. We keep it at Beaumaris. I wondered if you fancied a trip out on Saturday if the weather's good?"

Megan raised her eyebrows. "I didn't know you were a nautical family."

"Ah, there's lots you don't know about me. Yet." He gave her a cheeky wink. "She's an old lady, all striped cushions, polished brass and rosewood. Very 1930s. It's been my dad's project for about twenty years; he's done her up from a virtual wreck. In fact, my mum and dad did their courting on her, many moons ago, so it seems quite appropriate." He stopped. "Did I actually just say that aloud?"

Megan grinned. "Yeah, you did. And I bet you say that to all the ladies."

"No. You're the first. Dad looked shocked when I said I wanted to take you out on her. There's so much about her that reminds me of my mum, you see. She designed the galley, everything I touch in there … Well, sometimes it's hard. I tend not to 'do' emotions …"

Megan nodded, trying to mentally weigh up if this was the right time to ask about his mother. Only one way to find out …

"Your mum's not around anymore?"

"She died."

"I'm sorry. There's no easy way of asking, is there?"

"No. Don't worry. I tend to prefer not to discuss it. If I do talk about her, it's usually on the boat. Memories, you know." He gave an ironic laugh. "There, that's a bit crazy. If that's not put you off,

I don't know what will."

"No, don't be daft. I'd love to come. I'm seriously impressed you're a sailor. But I warn you, it's years since I've been on a small boat, so I've no idea how my sea legs will hold up."

"Well, as long as you don't chuck up on the paintwork, that's my only worry." He winked. "And you know I'll look after you. I'll have you in that many lifejackets if we capsize you'll fly back to shore like a hovercraft."

Megan burst into laughter, causing a few more heads to turn. "Sorry, shush. I have this vision of me jet-skiing across the water, propelled by over-inflated lifejackets."

"And me holding onto the straps like a water-skier!"

Megan laughed again and wiped her eyes. "You're mental."

"You can talk."

She pushed her plate and dish away. "Well, that was lovely, are you sure we can't do halves?"

"Absolutely not. My treat. I'm sorry you have to go."

"I think two hours for lunch is as much as I can push it. Today, anyway." She folded her napkin. "But I'm looking forward to Saturday. It is my day off luckily. I worked through last weekend so I shall have to take a break. Shall I bring food?"

"No. I'll cook. That's another of my secrets. And don't let my last attempt at dessert put you off. There's something about cooking on the boat that really makes me happy. I love mooring up alongside a little beach where there's no access from the roads, cooking lunch, sunbathing on deck, maybe swimming to shore. It's idyllic."

Megan felt a shiver cool the back of her neck. "It sounds it. I can't wait. I'll even break my own rules and buy a bottle of wine. For you, of course. And a bottle of Elderflower fizz for me. That will be my contribution. So, when and where?"

"Say I pick you up, about eleven. We can drive down to Beaumaris together. I'm sure Dad will let me borrow the Merc for the day, that's another of his vintage projects. He doesn't just teach about the past, he lives in it. But it does mean we can travel in style."

"Wow. Well, how can a girl refuse?" Megan reached for her bag. "Now, however, I have to make a move. Sorry."

In the car park, they paused, awkward again in each other's presence.

"You sure you don't want a lift?" said Megan.

Adrian patted his flat stomach. "I need to work off that burger. Not to mention the beer. No, it's fine. But thanks." He leaned forward, pecked her cheek. "Text me your address and I'll see you on Saturday, okay?"

Megan bit her lip and nodded. Then, on impulse, reached out and tugged the zip of his anorak, urging him towards her. She couldn't look at him, didn't dare meet his gaze, didn't trust her reaction with what she might see there. Their lips met. Warm and dry, slightly salty. His hands reached up her back, slid behind her neck, gripping her tight. She knew her legs were shaking, was amazed he couldn't feel it. Her head spun and her heart raced, and when he finally pulled away, it was seconds before she could open her eyes.

Adrian took a step backwards. "Oh, God."

Megan swallowed. "I couldn't put it better myself."

"I want to do that again, but I don't trust myself."

Megan touched her lips. "Nor me."

"God, don't do that."

"Sorry." She brought her hand down, dug in her pocket for her keys. "I'll go. I'll … see you Saturday."

She held her breath as she started the car, reversed out of the space, braked, changed gear, drove forward towards the exit. Then she allowed herself to look back and breathe. Adrian was standing there, like a statue. She lifted hand, waved, then pulled out into the traffic. Only then did she allow herself to explode. She whooped like a banshee, sang at the top of her voice, and thumped the steering wheel in time with her favourite Stereophonics track all the way back to the police station.

"What the hell!"

At the station car park gate, she slammed on her brakes, avoiding Gareth Parry's Volvo by inches as he pulled across straight in front of her. Her car stalled. She looked over her shoulder, lowering the stereo, checking if it had been her mistake. Her mind certainly wasn't on her driving. But no, it was her right of way. By the time she'd restarted the engine and made it safely to a spot a distance away, Gareth was out of his car and pacing the tarmac, scuffing the toes of his shoes against the floor.

He looked like a caged tiger, prowling. And she couldn't read his expression. Shock? Fear? Guilt? She took a deep breath, focused. Mentally preparing herself for the rollicking she was sure to come. Yes, she'd taken a long lunch, but it was hardly the crime of the century, and she was sure they'd made up after their previous altercation. She'd work over if she had to as long as it prevented another screaming match.

Gareth strode towards her, eyes red and wild. "Who have you told about Anna Brown?"

She took a step back. "Wh-what?"

"Anna. You know *exactly* who I mean. Barrington-Brown's daughter. Who have you told?"

She shook her head. "No one. Why, what's happened?"

"You must have done. Think!"

"Why are you shouting at me?" Megan took another step away. "Have you tried shouting at Chris? Why me?"

"I've spoken to Chris already; he hasn't breathed a word to anyone."

"But I have?"

Gareth punched a clenched fist into this open palm. "Someone has!" he yelled.

Megan gulped, made to a reach out to touch the arm of his sleeve, but pulled back as he whipped away from her.

"Gareth, what's happened? Tell me. Please, calm down, let me help."

"I think you've helped enough. Think. Who have you told? Someone knows about Anna. Probably knows about her gifts. Certainly knows she is the one with information ... the same information that ended up with three innocent victims being tortured and killed!"

"I get that. I get where you're coming from. But I don't understand why you're blaming me. Please ..." This time she caught hold of his sleeve, stopped the pacing. "Tell me."

Gareth stopped, shaking hands dug around in his jacket for a pack of Marlboro Lights. She took the lighter and packet from him, struck the flame and lit the cigarette. He accepted it with a nod and inhaled deeply, holding the smoke for several seconds, then exhaling with a rush.

"I need you to go and fetch Chris. Then we'll talk, but not in there. Go and fetch him while I smoke this. Tell him I need him."

Megan frowned. "Are you sure you're okay –"

"Just do as you're told and go and fetch Coleman now!"

Megan hurried up the steps, legs shaking, terrified of what she'd find out when they returned.

Chapter Twenty Three

The gun was heavy. For something so small, it was deceptively weighty. Gareth fastened it inside the shoulder holster, slipped the spare ammunition into his jacket pocket and zipped it shut. While it was years since he'd completed his firearms training, once he handled the small Glock 17 it was like coming home. God willing, he wouldn't need it, but the weight of it against his chest was comforting.

He stretched out on his makeshift window seat and glanced at his watch. Ten to seven. Getting nearer. Checked his phone for the millionth time. Nothing. He laid his forehead against the window pane, remembering happier times. Down there, in the car park. Susan's smiling face looking up at him, holding a bottle of red wine aloft. The comfortable hours they'd spent together; the warmth that seemed to consume him in her presence. And the way she'd looked the next morning; fresh out of the shower, make-up free, bare breasts straining against the material of his polo shirt. She'd never looked so good. Christ. He shuddered, diverted his attention to the security of his favourite view.

Outside, the day had cooled, shadows reached across from the mountains as the sun disappeared in the west. The rush hour traffic had thinned and a hush settled along his street, rudely broken by a crowd of noisy male students making their way into town on the opposite pavement. A normal day. How could it be? He checked his watch again, then his phone …

"Quit stressing, mate."

Chris's voice made him jump. He'd almost forgotten Chris was there, moulded into the lengthening shadows of Gareth's lounge.

"What's keeping him? I thought he'd have been in touch by now."

"And you're judging that on what?"

Gareth shook his head.

"Exactly. Everything's under control. We wait."

Gareth exhaled. "Anna?"

"Safe as houses with Megan at Derwydd Hall. We've been through this. You worry about what you need to do. Leave the rest to me."

"Do you think Barrington-Brown will go along with this in the end? I mean, I know he says he will … but would he put his only daughter at risk –"

"That's the point. She won't be at risk, not at any time. Megan's armed, so are we. The girl isn't going to put a foot to the floor without one of us at her side. Let's see what this bastard is up to, then we can judge how to play it."

"Megan is fully trained with firearms, isn't she? I know you said –"

"Top of her class, mate. She'd put us both to shame. What did you expect from Eager-Beaver?"

Gareth smiled despite himself. "Of course." He checked his watch again. "Do you think we did the right thing telling Macrae too?"

"Christ, yes. Susan Connolly isn't your property, mate. And I know how cruel that sounds. I don't mean to be. But she's not your kid. You can't go around making those kinds of decisions and going it alone. What if it all back fired and you'd gone in there all guns blazing. Absolutely it was the right thing to do."

Gareth's mouth was dry as dust. "Nothing is going to go wrong though, is it?"

"Not if I have anything to do with it. But it's not a risk anyone can afford to take. Susan wouldn't thank you for being a hero, especially not a dead one."

Gareth snorted. "Thanks, mate."

"You know what I mean. We work as a team."

Gareth nodded, tapped his watch face with his nail. Kept his gaze lowered. "I'm scared."

"So am I. Nothing wrong in that."

"Last time I was this scared … I was facing that nutter on a boat off Llanddwyn Island. I lived the cliché of seeing my whole life flash before my eyes that day. Seriously, I was so sure I would drown. I'd hate to think of Sue having to face those kinds of thoughts."

Chris sat forward, face illuminated, clasped his hands between his thighs. "She's a tough cookie. I don't need to tell you that. And she's got a brain on her. Look at what she does for a job? She faces stuff you and I would chuck our guts up over. She will be fine. You concentrate on doing your bit. Let everyone else do theirs. And trust her."

Gareth rubbed a hand through his hair, blinked. "If I lost her, Chris. I mean … you don't know how strongly you feel till something like this happens. You can't imagine how guilty I am. That she's caught up in all this because of me, just because she stayed over one night and tried to help me do my job properly. But if I lost her, I don't know –"

"Drop it. You don't know any of that, you're surmising. Just concentrate on manning up enough to tell her how you feel next time you see her, okay?" Chris made a show of rubbing his ear. "Give the rest of us a break."

Gareth smiled, despite himself, and checked his wrist again. According to him it was one minute to the hour.

"I should be at work, I feel helpless here –"

Chris shook his head. "And if he is watching you as you suspect, that would go down like a fart in a lift, no? Play the role he expects and let's see where it takes us."

"I know you're right. But every instinct is screaming at me

to –"

His mobile leapt into life. Buzzing and shuffling along the surface of the coffee table.

"Deep breaths," Chris whispered. "You can do this."

Gareth slid onto the sofa, grabbed the phone and pressed speaker. "Hello? Hello. Yes."

"Hello, detective." A pause. "How very nice to speak to you at last."

It was him. *Him.* The voice was distorted. A voice changer. He'd dealt with them before in ransom demands. There was little point trying to get anything from the voice, he knew that, but still his training took over. A good thing – he had to stay in professional mode. *Had to.* Okay, so definitely male, probably twenties or thirties, Caucasian, no discernable accent, but from the phrasing he'd guess educated.

"What do you want?"

"You know what I want. Ms Connolly was very clear. She's a good girl, have to say. Does *exactly* as she's told."

"This makes no sense. What do you want with a child?"

"That's my business. But I think you know. Her father has all kinds of secrets to tell. And I'm sure when he hears his daughter undergoing one of my special manicures, he'll be more than happy to spill."

Yes, definitely educated, but the phrasing jarred. Someone young pretending to be older? Or older trying to speak like a teenager?

"You can't expect me to kidnap a child and leave her in your hands."

"If you don't I shall enjoy a few fun-filled hours, and then put Susan out of her misery." He chuckled. Gareth's skin crawled. "And trust me, she'll be begging to die by the time I've finished with her. Such smooth, tender flesh. Wonderful."

"Enough. When and where?"

"Park on the seafront at Beaumaris. Nice and open. Right at the far end, near the Castle entrance. I'll be watching and waiting. Bring Anna. If I see any of your buddies around, Susan will suffer."

Gareth's fingers traced the outline of the gun through his jacket.

"I know it. Susan will be there?"

"As long as Anna comes too. I know it's a toughie, detective. But it all comes down to choice. And affairs of our heart will always prevail."

"This is crazy, is there no other way? Can't I help you?" He kept his voice steady.

"Don't waste your breath. You know nothing of consequence. I want Anna. She is the key to all this. If you're telling me you don't wish to play –"

"I'm telling you nothing at all. But I warn you, you sick bastard, if you hurt her –"

"Eight o'clock, detective. Let's meet at sunset, nice and romantic."

The call ended.

Chris leaned across, prised Gareth's fingers from the phone.

"We've got forty-five minutes. Let's get moving. We need to get you wired up –"

"No wire. You heard what he said. I'm taking no risks."

Chris hissed through his teeth. "We have to keep you safe, mate."

"And what about Sue? I can't risk him getting spooked. I've got a gun, that's enough. No wire."

Chris stood, brushed off his jeans. "Okay, we'll do it your way. But we have to get a move on. Time's pushing on."

Gareth nodded and jumped to his feet, shaking off the feeling of dread that clung to him like the devil's own cloak.

"Gareth? Everything's in place. We have the area surrounded." Chris's voice crackled through the walkie-talkie slipped inside the dashboard of his car. "Everything okay there?"

Gareth rubbed his nose, shielding his mouth. "Yes. No sign of anything."

"Soon as he pulls into the car park, we'll cut him off. Keep calm. This is under control."

"Thanks."

Gareth looked across at Megan, hunkered down in the passenger seat, a blue hoodie pulled low. "Are you okay?"

"Fine, stop worrying. Hope he gets a move on."

Gareth stared out of his window, scanning the area. About a dozen cars were still parked along the seafront, another few on the grassy field. He knew some contained under-cover officers, but the area looked as beautiful as normal. Shadows lengthened, turning the choppy water from grey to purple. Only the tips of the Snowdonia range were still dappled by golden sunlight; the rest already in shade, various tints of greens and golds.

He checked his watch, was sick of doing it. *Come on.* He'd reversed back against a wall, keeping the passenger door up close to a stone shelter. There was no way he could get to Megan without getting to him first. Hopefully if he got close enough to discover the decoy, the backup would have plenty of time to take over. Gareth tried not to think what Sue was going through. He had to stay focused. He'd taken a risk but they had to flush the guy out.His phone trilled. His heart leapt into his throat.

"Hello?"

"Ready for step two?" The voice was the same robotic drone.

"You said nothing about another step." Gareth's heart began to pound. "Where are you?"

"Watching. Clever idea parking right up against that wall. I can see little Anna though. But it's not my scene to be so public and there's lots of activity this evening. Hope you've not double-crossed me, detective. The consequences could be quite disastrous."

"No. No." Gareth swallowed, searching every car. "I've done what you asked. Where's Susan?"

"Just behind where you're parked there's a path that leads

through the woods to the church. I have the path covered, so I suggest you and Anna take the walk alone. It's a pleasant evening after all. I'm not a religious man, but I'll see you in church, detective."

The line went dead.

He slammed his hand against the steering wheel. "Shit!"

"What is it?" asked Megan.

Before he could respond, a frantic hammering shattered the silence of the car. Gareth jumped and turned to see a white face pressed up against his window. Heart thumping, he pulled open the door and dragged the girl across his lap, slamming it behind her.

"Anna! What the hell ...?"

The walkie-talkie buzzed into life. "Gareth! Mate! Have you got her?"

Megan bundled Anna into the back, squeezing her between the seats with hissed warnings to stay down low.

Gareth grabbed the walkie-talkie. "What the hell's happening, Chris?"

"She turned up saying she had to speak to you, urgent. I was trying to keep her quiet, get her and Barrington-Brown inside the hotel, and she sodding bolted. God knows how she knew where to find you ..."

Gareth turned, met the wide blue stare boring into his eyes. He knew.

"Okay. Give me a minute. Let me think." Gareth paused the transmission, ran a hand through his hair. "Christ, let's pray he didn't see that."

"If he's gone into the woods, he wouldn't have," said Megan. "What do we do now?"

Gareth turned in his seat. "What's going on, Anna? Do you know how dangerous this is? How are we going to get you back to your father without being seen –"

"I'm coming with you. I know what he wants. I've seen it. I have to be there."

Gareth shook his head. "No way."

Anna stared, defiant, shrugged. "Then I go alone." She reached for the door handle.

Gareth yelled. "No!"

Megan lunged her arm through the gap, grabbed the girl's wrist.

"Please." Anna's voice cracked. "He wants me. I know it. Please. I can do this."

She yanked her arm out of Megan's grasp and was out of the door before Gareth could formulate a reply. She raced across the green and disappeared into the shadows of the trees.

Megan screamed. "Anna!"

"Christ … no!"

"Gareth?" Chris's voice hissed, tinny and distant. "What's happening?"

Gareth closed his eyes for a moment, then muted the volume. His fingers brushed the Glock as he grabbed the door handle and pushed.

"Wait here," he said. Megan's face was pale, shocked. "If I'm not back in ten minutes, take the car and fetch Chris."

"But …"

"Just do it!"

The woods were cool and shadowy; the setting sun long since disappeared over the hill to his right as he followed the path down into the gorge that carved out the Menai Straits millions of years before. Gareth shuddered as a gust of wind whipped the trees, adding to the whirling mess in his brain. Every step felt like another towards hell. His lungs were two solid cannon balls in his chest, and stitch cramped his side, but he didn't drop his pace as he pounded along the track deeper into the darkness.

It seemed an age before he caught sight of the girl, standing in the middle of the track, hands on knees, breathing hard. Waiting for him. He reached out and grabbed her, ready to rant at her for her stupidity. But the words died on his lips. Her hand was small and fragile in his own. As cold fingers gripped his with the trust of an innocent, the feeling of guilt piled on top of him, like soil on the coffin lid of someone buried alive. He was that person, trapped between the world's biggest rock and its hardest place. Silently terrified.

He tugged on Anna's hand, focusing her attention. "What the hell are you doing? Where are you going?"

Anna's breathing was ragged. "Don't know. This way. Had to come this way."

Gareth shook his head. "We have to get you back to your father … this could jeopardise everything …"

"I don't care! You don't understand. I have to be here. It's the only thing that will stop it happening again and again. It's not your decision. Or mine."

Gareth frowned, not totally sure what to make of her words, but there was no real fear or defiance in her voice. Just a simple relaying of the truth.

He sighed, glanced around the woodland. They appeared to be the only two people there, but the shadows were getting longer, evening chill permeating the air. He had to get the girl out of there.

"Look. I have to do my job. I've no choice and neither do you. From this point on, you're to do exactly as I say. Understand?"

"I'm not going back."

"We'll see …"

She pulled away from him, tensed, ready to run.

He held up a hand. "No! Don't, please. Think about this. It's too dangerous. I know what I'm doing. Come with me." She shook her head. "Anna, I don't have time for this right now. People's lives are at risk. I'm begging you. Come back with me; wait in the car with Megan. If I need you, I'll call for you, I promise."

"I have to be here …"

"Fine. In the car. That's the deal. Take it or leave it."

Her head dropped. Reluctantly, she nodded.

He reached for her sleeve. "Good, come on. Let's go. Walk with me and stay close at all times. If I tell you to run, you run. If I tell you to stay, you do it. Got it?"

"Yes." Anna met his eyes, frowning, searching. "If you say so. It's a waste of time though ..."

The Glock felt snug and warm under his arm as they hurriedly retraced his steps. Things were happening so fast. He couldn't even take a moment to consider what Macrae would make of this mess. Besides, he didn't really care. Getting Susan back alive was far more important to him than a demotion, losing his job, or anything a fancy disciplinary committee chose to throw at him. Anna turning up was the last thing he'd expected or needed. But fate seemed determined to play its hand.

Gareth had thought about it long and hard over the past hours; he'd decided if he got Susan free, he'd shoot to kill if it meant escaping with her uninjured. There would be time for a question and answer session later. Time for IPCC investigations. Truth told, he didn't give a shit. All of that was child's play compared to what he was going through now.

A thin stream of russet-coloured evening sun broke through the trees. A twig cracked somewhere close. He scanned the area, turning a full rotation, heart thumping. Not here, surely? But there was nothing. No movement. No sounds, except the gentle whoosh of the tide as it swirled around the headland below. The air was heavy with the smell of seaweed. He jumped as a gull swooped and squawked, and tapped his foot, buoyed with adrenaline, eyes moving back and forth. He hadn't wanted to risk a wire, had kicked off against Chris's suggestion, but now he was beginning to regret the decision.

"Come on, quickly," he said with more confidence than he felt.

Anna pulled against him, still scowling, but she quickened her step.

He turned as he heard a noise; a distant hum like traffic on the wind. Anna stopped, cold fingers tightening her grip on his hand.

"What is it?" whispered Anna.

"Nothing. Thought I heard voices, that's all."

They walked another few paces.

"I don't like it." Anna turned her head sharply. "I don't –"

There was a loud bang and at the same time a branch toppled, crashing on top of his head. Pain exploded like fireworks. He staggered forwards, reaching out towards the dancing lights.

The world went black.

Chapter Twenty Four

Megan blasted the horn again. Where the hell was he? She revved the engine. If he wasn't here in two minutes, she was going. No way was she losing the trail. She held her hand on the horn, pressing down hard. She was starting to attract attention from the families on the green, dog-walkers staring with interest. No doubt putting it down to her boy-racer image in a sporty car.

Chris appeared and hurdled the hotel steps, one arm in his denim jacket, one out. Face flushed and sweating, pursued by a furious-looking Barrington-Brown.

He yanked open the passenger door.

"Get in," yelled Megan. "Hurry up. For God's sake."

"Lock the doors," Chris panted as he slid into the seat.

Just in time. Barrington-Brown yanked at the back door handle and banged on the window, before rushing round the car, towards the driver's side. Megan checked her own door was locked.

"What the hell is happening?" he yelled. "Where's my daughter? I demand answers!"

Chris lowered the window an inch. "Sir, I'm sorry, I don't have time right now. Please wait in the hotel with one of the other officers. We'll be back shortly and update you then." Chris turned to Megan. "Just fucking drive!" he hissed.

Megan spun away from the kerb, gravel spraying the

underside of the car.

She checked the rear view mirror. Barrington-Brown stood, looking broken and helpless in the middle of the road.

"I almost feel sorry for him. Almost."

"So, what happened?" said Chris, clicking his seat belt into place. "I've been ignoring calls from Macrae but it's obviously already got back to the office that the sting has gone tits up."

"There was a second entrance, funeral access for the church. We've got a partial registration and he's taken the coast road back towards Menai Bridge. Hopefully cameras should track him so far, and we've called in the traffic 'copter, but I need to catch up."

"Great."

"I've got my advanced certificate you know. Just hold on tight. Thank God we were allowed to use the Evo."

Megan waited until she was clear of Beaumaris High Street and then opened up the super-charged Mitsubishi. Via the main control room, Chris kept constant contact with the helicopter which was on scene within minutes. Soon they'd cleared Britannia Bridge and were flying along the dual-carriage way towards Caernarfon.

Chris replaced the receiver. "We've got him, picked him up turning inland off the main road towards Llanrug – about three miles away. I've told Uniform to keep the squad cars well away and wait for us to arrive."

The squad car was blocking the drive down to what looked like an abandoned farm.

Megan pulled alongside and lowered her window.

The traffic cop in the driver's seat did the same. "He's down there in an old white Mercedes, parked behind one of the barns. Odd thing, since we've been here he's not got out, has he, Dave?"

The officer in the passenger seat lowered a pair of industrial-strength binoculars. "No. He's still in the car. Shame we couldn't have got here a bit quicker."

"We've stood the 'copter down," said the first cop. "Thought it would alert him, with the noise. They said there was definite movement in the yard when they first spotted his vehicle, but they don't report seeing any of the hostages."

Hostages. Megan shivered. How odd to think of Gareth caught up in something so chilling. It seemed wrong he was on the other side of the fence; he should be here, with them, leading the troops. And Anna. How on earth would she be coping?

"What's he doing in there?" said Chris, leaning across Megan's lap.

"Can't see," said the second cop. "I think he's talking to someone. Hands free phone, maybe?"

"Do we know anything about this place?" said Megan.

The cop shrugged. "We got called in from Llandudno. I don't know the area. I'll radio in and ask the local base for info, if you like."

Megan nodded. "I'd like to know who it belongs to."

"Movement. We've got movement." The second cop spoke, voice alert.

"Is he getting out?" said Chris. "What's he doing?"

"No. He's moving the car. Shit! He's heading in this direction. I think he's coming back out."

"Damn it." Megan gripped the wheel. "We can't let him go."

"No, but we don't want him to see the squad car," said Chris. "Can you guys go and block off the lane at the junction? Stop him if he does make a run for it. Get any other vehicles that attend to do the same. I want you out of sight for now. We'll take your place with the Evo. He won't get past that and he might not associate with cops. I don't want any hassle until we've found Gareth and others. We can pretend it's a breakdown. Go on, move."

Without a word, the traffic officer started the engine and drove the car quietly out of sight, around the bend.

Megan unclipped her belt, coming to a decision.

"What're you doing?" said Chris.

"You stay with the car. I'm going down the drive on foot."

"What!" Chris gripped her wrist. "No way. You stay here."

Megan shook his hand off. "Think about it. If Gareth is down there, and the killer has got called away for some reason, this is the perfect opportunity. You're doing the dangerous part."

Chris sighed. "I don't know …"

"Well, while you're making your mind up, I'm out of here."

Megan opened the door and jumped out, heading for the adjacent field and the cover of a high hedgerow. The last thing she saw as the white Mercedes closed the gap between them, was Chris grunting and cursing as he climbed over into the drivers' seat.

The engine roared and then the door slammed. She jumped as Chris spoke right behind her.

"Keep down," he said.

"What are you doing?" Megan whispered.

"I've blocked off the drive. No need to sit there and face a confrontation. Let's see what he does."

The rumble of the Mercedes engine grew louder; she could hear the creak of the suspension as the driver negotiated the pot-holed drive. Soon the rapid tick of the engine was just the other side of the hedgerow.

Chris leaned forward, hissed. "He's getting out. We should make a move down to the house now. We can get Uniform to pick him up."

"Wait. Let's see if we know him."

A figure slid out of the car, keeping to the hedgerow, hood pulled down tight around his face, dark trousers and trainers blending into the shadows. He approached the Evo carefully, checking each door, before standing back and kicking the front wheel.

"Easy," hissed Chris.

"He's well pissed off. Let's get moving, he's going nowhere."

Keeping low, Megan followed Chris along the edge of the field, over a rusted gate and into the farmyard. Every window and door of the house was boarded-up with plywood sheets, decorated with faded security firm surveillance notices and warnings for trespassers. Weeds as high as Megan surrounded the outbuildings, and the only visible tyre tracks seemed to belong to the Mercedes.

"Can you see anyway in?" said Chris.

"No. I can't even see a door with a lock, everything's covered."

"But he has to get in somewhere, if they're in there, how the hell …"

"Let's try the garage. He'd got the car backed up against it."

Crunching through broken roof tile, rusted tin cans and negotiating clinging brambles, they squinted through the fading light and picked their way round to the back of the garage. Megan nodded. A door. Plywood sheet smashed, lock broken. Her breathing quickened. This had to be the way.

"Through here, I reckon," she said. "I bet this was some kind of back way into the kitchen for the farm workers."

"Bloody stinks," grumbled Chris. "Dread to think what state the sewers must be in. Here." He eased his way past Megan. "Let me go first, just in case. You keep a lookout."

Megan gave him a solid shunt in the back as they crossed from dusk light into a musty gloom. "No way. I'm coming with you. There's a mad man on the loose out there, in here I only have you to contend with."

She heard Chris chuckle and bent low, following his denim-covered back, down a narrow, twisting stairwell that led … to who knew what.

Chapter Twenty Five

"Wake up!"

Gareth rolled over in bed. Surely it wasn't time to get up yet? He groaned and opened his eyes. It was still dark. He'd had the most god-awful dream and now had a hangover to die for. Like a whole brass band was marching through his head.

"Parry!"

He tried to sit up. Was that who he thought it was? Had they slept together? And he couldn't remember! What the hell …

"Sue?"

"Yeah … are you okay?"

"Course I am. Where are you?" He lifted his head. "Put the light on, what's the matter?"

Sue sighed. "Wake up. Can you hear me?"

Gareth shook his head. It was an odd sensation, almost like he was swimming under water. He *could* hear, but the sounds were distorted, echoey. He swung his legs out of bed; heart racing as he suddenly connected there must be a problem. Susan in trouble. His weight travelled forward and he crashed to the ground, banging his chin hard on the floor. Blood seeped from his bottom lip and tears sprung to his eyes. Christ, that hurt! He struggled to free his arms from the tight blankets. No. He was tied. What was this? Why was it all black?

"Calm down, Gareth, please." Sue's voice broke off into a sob.

"Please, you'll hurt yourself. Stop struggling!"

"Detective?"

Another voice, over to his right.

"Yes, who is it?"

"Anna."

Gareth tried to get to his feet and staggered sideways. The heavy weight bruised and bit into his flesh as he twisted. It was such a weird sensation, as if his feet were pinned to the floor. He could sway back and forth, side to side, but couldn't take one step forward. And why couldn't he see? A pain exploded in his head. He dropped back into the most comfortable position he could find, one that didn't feel as if his arms were being stretched out of their sockets. He took deep breaths and licked his lips; if he didn't slow down he'd start hyperventilating. What the hell was this?

"Parry? Can you hear me? I think he's drugged you. You have to stay calm. Please don't hurt yourself. I need you!"

It was the sharp edge of pain in Sue's voice that seemed to make his own pain fade into the furthest recesses of his mind. Sue needed him. And it explained everything. He'd been drugged. He swallowed away the acrid taste. It would pass; he had to sit it out. The headache would fade, it was all to do with the fact he'd been drugged. His chin dropped and his eyes began to close. Drugs he could cope with, no problem.

Who?

How had they drugged him?

A flood of memories hit. Susan. Him. Anna. Him. The woods. Him. Blackness. Oh, God. Him. *Him!*

He let out a low moan. The pain in his head was real, not imaginary. This was no hangover. He'd been whacked over the head with something solid enough to knock him into next week. He flexed his hands, using his fingertips behind his back. He could make out thick plastic straps binding him to something wooden, heavy. A chair. Handcuffs. But not the police regulation ones, homemade specials, something he'd seen a lot of in recent weeks.

"Parry." Sue again. "You're blindfolded. We all are."

"I'm not," Anna said.

"Are you okay?" said Gareth. "Are you hurt?"

"No. I mean, yes, I'm okay. No, I'm not hurt. I'm tied to something on the floor in the corner of the room, but I'm not blindfolded."

Gareth twisted his head, ignoring the shooting pain. Rough cloth covered his face, making his breathing laboured.

"What can you see, Anna? Where are we?"

"It's dark. I can see a little bit of light, like a door frame or something. And the floor is cold. Very cold."

"I think it's a cellar or something," said Sue.

The fog cleared. "You're not hurt, are you, Sue? Do you know where we are? Who he is?"

"Not a clue. I assumed it was some kind of ransom demand. And then I heard all these noises, and Anna crying. It's to do with the case, isn't it? The murders?"

Gareth's throat constricted. This was his fault. His own stupid stubborn fault. Why hadn't he agreed to a wire? Where were Chris and the rest of the team now?

"Anna, if he's not blindfolded you, you're going to have to be our eyes, okay? Do you know what happened back in the woods?"

"He hit you with a branch, then he grabbed me, put this cold cloth over my face. And I woke up here."

Gareth's stomach rolled. "Did you see the man? Can you describe him?"

"He had a blue cap and a blue coat. I saw the sleeve, oh, and a big, shiny watch. And I heard him laughing."

Gareth forced herself to think, ignore the throb in his head. "And you, Sue? What happened?"

"I was walking to my car, in the hospital car park. Didn't see or hear a thing. Something pushed me forward, then a hand grabbed my face. Nothing else till I woke up here. I thought he was going to kill me. He comes and goes, brings water and a b-bucket." Sue coughed. "He never speaks, that makes it worse. Even when I beg, he ignores me."

"You're tied to a chair, detective." It was Anna. "I can see the legs sticking out. And I think it's held down or something."

"Same as me," said Sue. "My arms and back are numb. I can't feel my fingers anymore." She broke off and quiet sobs echoed around the room.

Before Gareth could speak, Anna's voice filled the air. "I know you don't know me but we're going to get out of here. I can't see it all, not yet ..."

Gareth turned to the direction of Anna's voice.

"You've seen it, Anna?"

"Yes."

"How? Can you tell me how?"

"No. But it's going to be alright. At least I think so."

Gareth exhaled, feeling a trickle of hope. "Sue, love, try not to cry. You'll only feel worse. We need to stay strong. I promise I'm going to get us out of here. I swear to you, okay?"

"I've screamed," said Sue. "God, I screamed the place down. We must be in the middle of nowhere or someone would have heard me."

"Any idea of the time?" Gareth asked. "How long we've been here?"

"No idea. What are we going to do, Parry?" Sue sniffed.

Gareth pulled himself to his knees, rocked the chair until it was in an upright position, then sat down. Right now, he had no idea what they were up against. Who *he* was. What his next move would be. All Gareth knew was what he was capable of. And that was the thing that truly scared him.

But Chris was out there. The whole of North Wales police would be searching for them. This bastard may have got one over on them, but Gareth knew his team would never give up.

"It's going to be all right," he told them. "I'll think of something. I promise."

Chapter VIII

MONA INSULIS, BRITAIN - AD 60

"My lady, we cannot!"

She had never seen such fury and resolve in Ked's gentle, brown eyes.

Awen sighed. "I'm not asking you to come with me, Ked. I'm prepared to go alone. But for my peace of mind, I must ensure my father's funeral rites are complete."

"Luis promised –"

"Luis is missing," said Awen. "I don't want to be harsh, Ked, but you know there's a chance he didn't survive the battle. No, I must go alone and I shall be back before nightfall."

Awen got to her feet and took her woollen cloak down from the hook near the door. When she turned, Ked was at her side.

"What?"

"If you go, I come too," replied Ked, her jaw set in determination. "And if my children wake up in the morning as orphans, I hope you will tell them their mother begged you to listen but you refused!"

Awen hid a smile. She couldn't help but be heartened by Ked's apparently unwilling servitude. Not to mention her melodrama.

"I wouldn't ask such a thing of you –"

"Let's not waste time with pointless squabbles."

Ked wrapped her cloak around her, tightened her hood, and pushed open the door, heading out into the swirling mist that seemed to have settled over the island since the invasion of the Roman army the day before. It was as if the sunshine had been sucked from the land, and this dense clinging fog heralded a new beginning under Roman rule. Morale in the commune was low, and Awen knew she could do nothing to lift her people until she could settle her own nerves and convince herself her father's final resting place was intact.

She hurried to catch up with Ked as her servant's footsteps disappeared into the sea of mist.

"Silence!"

Awen stopped still, hand clutching her throat as they approached the temple site.

"What?" she whispered.

"I thought I heard something." Ked's voice was low and eerie, coming through the white layer of fog that separated them. "Voices … or moaning?"

"I can hear nothing," Awen replied, hoping the chatter of her teeth wasn't evident in her words. "Let us just organise the funeral rites as quickly as possible, and then get away from here. I sense danger. Can you collect the ashes from the pyre, Ked? I'll check the grave is ready to seal."

Ked disappeared in the direction of the pyre, and Awen headed towards the stone slab which she knew marked the edge of the grave cut. Dropping to her knees, not wanting to pitch into the grave, she crept forward, running her hands back and forth, trying to pick out the start of the burial chamber.

"Yurr … hmmmm."

Awen stopped, head on one side, ears straining, senses alert. She had heard something this time. A moan? Or perhaps it was some injured forest creature? She listened for the tread of feet. Nothing. The snap of a rogue twig. Silence. Just the sound of Ked dismantling the outer slats of the pyre in order to collect the ashes of her father's animals for his funeral urn.

At last her hands slipped down into an opening; a flurry of dirt fell in from the side of the grave cut. Leaning forward, she closed her eyes, bracing herself for another viewing of her father's corpse. She held her breath, opened her eyes and let out a loud shriek, pulling back from the edge, heart pounding.

"My lady? Where are you?"

"It's okay, Ked. I am well, no cause to panic. There ... there's someone else in father's grave."

"What? Stay there, I'm coming."

"Take care. Follow my voice. No need to hurry, I think he's dead. He looks dead."

"Is it Luis?"

Awen drew breath, sneaked another look over the edge. "No. It's a Roman."

* * *

Her name was Awen. He'd heard visitors call her. She'd saved his life, tended him for days, and he knew it hadn't made her popular. He wanted to thank her, to make those eyes crinkle into laughter lines and see her pale neck stretched tight as she threw back her head and laughed. Marcus knew she could laugh, had seen it in his dreams. In his waking hours, she was mute and stern, ignoring his attempts at any form of connection through eye contact or body language. It was like she could not bear to look at him.

Today, he would thank Awen for tending him to health. And today, she would acknowledge him as a man first, Roman second.

It took him four attempts to make it to the door, but he succeeded by inching along the wattled walls, pausing when pain and exertion overcame him. When he reached the opening, he drew long breaths of sweet air into his lungs, and took in the scene of huts, smoking fires, braying goats and giggling children. The place was alive with activity, and he realised how near death he must have come.

He gave no thought to his future, whether these people would deal with him with compassion, or slaughter him on their altar like a fowl. He was glad to be alive, and he blessed a thousand gods for his good fortune. His hand was drawn to his chest, fingers finding the warm bump of Hercules beneath the flax gown.

As he watched two children chasing geese around the nearest hut, Awen approached. She carried a covered basket, and her concentration was on her servant who walked beside her. Awen smiled as she listened to the woman's words, but the smile failed to reach her eyes. Her hair was loose this evening, strands blowing across her face. He imagined smoothing back the blonde tresses, burying his nose in the heather-scented hair he remembered from his darkest nights when she grappled with his dead weight.

Marcus shook his head. The captivity was playing on his mind; he was hot and feverish again. Awen looked up, met his eyes, and her cheeks flushed. Her gaze was at once alert and guarded. A slim, blond-haired Druid, dressed in brown robes, followed her into the hut.

The man clasped his hands before him and spoke in halting Latin. "My name is Oibhne. I come from the lands of the South and have been tutored in your language. My lady, Awen, brings you food and asks how you are feeling this eve?"

Awen frowned, muttered a few low words.

"And she asks why you are out of your bed?"

"Tell her I wished to surprise her."

The man relayed his words back to Awen. She responded;

eyes averted from Marcus's gaze although she must have known how much he wished to make eye contact. Her voice was clipped and flat.

"My lady says then you are to surprise her again – get back to your bed and take your meal."

Awen laid the covered basket at the foot of the bed.

"Ah." Marcus gripped tight onto the door. "I didn't think about that. I do not think I can."

He wobbled a step forward as Oibhne translated and Awen responded.

"My lady says then you will go hungry." Awen straightened the cotton sheets, keeping her back to him, and removed a tray of food from the wicker basket. "She says ... there is nothing to be gained by being a hero. Besides, if you try and escape, she cannot promise you free passage. Some of the men, they are still angry, fearful –"

Marcus frowned, turned to Awen. "Who said I wanted to escape?"

Her eyes flicked upwards, grazing his face. Brief words passed between the Druids.

"You are a Roman," said Oibhne.

Her reply was final, and she brushed past him, leaving him propped against the door frame, with a trace of honey blossom in the air.

He called her name but she didn't turn. Her strides were purposeful as she headed towards the centre of the camp; the man trailed some way behind, glancing back with an apologetic smile. Marcus sighed and began to retrace his steps, annoyed at his lack of success. There had to be a way to get through to her. Why did he clam up like a juvenile legionnaire on his first visit to a whore house? In his frustration, he let go of the wall, determined he could make it in a straight line to the bed. His stomach growled and led him forward. Halfway across the room, his knees buckled and he hit the ground hard, rolling over in agony as the wound in his shoulder split open.

"Argh! Awen. Help!"

Footsteps approached as he curled into a tight ball, trying not to pass out as waves of pain seared his body. Droplets of blood dripped onto the floor in a steady patter of rain.

"Awen!"

Sandaled-feet appeared before him. "No, it is Oibhne. Look at the mess of you, my lady will be furious."

"I'm sorry. I thought I could manage. I'm bleeding ..."

"You don't say. Wait. Let me get help."

Oibhne lifted him back onto the bed, shouting in their strange tongue until faces appeared at the doorway, none seemingly eager to set foot inside his hut. Awen's servant, Ked, arrived a short time later and did a competent job, changing his dressing and sealing the wound with camomile cream. But she lacked the healing touch of Awen he so craved. Nausea gripped him and he began to shake.

"You must eat," Oibhne said, translating Ked's words as she held out a honey-smeared pancake. "At least take a little milk or Ked shall tell my lady you have been a poor patient."

Marcus nodded and lifted the wooden bowl. The milk was warm and sweet. He swallowed most of the contents and wiped a hand across his lips.

"I don't think Awen would care. She despises me."

Ked scowled as Oibhne translated; she pulled the dish from his grasp.

Oibhne blushed as he followed the servant's words. "Ked says there is no place for self-pity here. If Awen hears you talking like that; she most probably will despise you."

Ked stood, hands on hips, waiting for Oibhne to catch up.

"She saved your life. You do realise?" said Oibhne, trying to keep up with Ked's outburst. "When most others here would have happily hung you from the nearest oak and let the crows finish you off."

Marcus swallowed; his throat tightening with fear.

"It has not made her popular," said Oibhne; his flat tones not matching the red-faced fury of Ked's hurried dialogue. "My lady is out there now, defending you, asking for clemency. Would she bother doing all this if she hated you?"

Marcus looked down, horrified to feel the burn of tears.

"Ked says … she told my lady that she was mad, said only bad things could come of tending you, but would she listen?" Oibhne continued, pausing to let Ked speak. Ked tutted and shook her head as he translated her words. "And so soon after losing her beloved father, this was the very last thing she needed."

Marcus looked up. "She lost her father?"

Oibhne nodded. "Yes. Your men destroyed his funeral."

Ked snarled a torrent of words, which Oibhne relayed. "Not enough, you took his life when all he was doing was trying to protect the land and the people he loved." Ked spat on the floor. "Ked asks that may Hu forgive her, but if she had been Awen, she would have left you in that pit to rot."

Ked turned to leave, motioning for Oibhne to follow.

"Don't, please," Marcus called out. "I'm sorry. Don't go."

Ked hovered at the doorway; her face still creased into a frown, trembling hands gripped the folds of her skirt. Then she turned and disappeared into the twilight.

"Wait. I need to know … was Awen's father a priest?" whispered Marcus.

Oibhne nodded, clasped his hands. "He was a Chief Druid. Cadadius. A king among men. A god among mortals."

Marcus shivered. It was fate at its cruellest, he was certain of it. He recalled the dark eyes and pointing finger of the Druid. Although the image was blurred in the heat and tension of battle, he knew he'd slain that same man.

The enormity hit him, robbing him of breath as sweat broke out all over his body.

Chapter Twenty Six

Chris had a torch. Why hadn't she thought of that? Megan cursed as she stumbled into his back for the umpteenth time on the worn stone steps. The walls either side were slimy and damp, and the whole place smelled of mould and decay.

"Mind your step, we're coming to the bottom of the stairs."

"A cold store?"

"Looks like it was, many moons ago."

Three sides of the cellar had brick walls. Chris flashed the narrow beam of light from floor to ceiling. On their right, there was a door. Chris took a step forward, leaned his head towards the edge of the frame.

"Anything?"

Megan's teeth rattled and she could hardly speak with the mix of adrenaline and cold.

"Nothing." He shook his head. "Silence."

The torch beam settled on the lock. The key.

"Go on," urged Megan, nudging his arm. "Hurry!"

"What if it's a trap?"

"How can it be? Besides … Uniform will have picked him up by now. Let me do it …"

Chris held up a sturdy arm, blocked her way. "Just wait."

Carefully, he gripped the key and turned it. The door swung open.

"Gareth?"

Chris stepped forward, swallowed by the shadows.

"Anna?" said Megan, one step behind.

"Who's that?"

Gareth's voice, distant in the darkness.

Chris spun round. "Bloody hell, mate, thank God …"

The shot sounded like a bomb in the small room. The room illuminated for a brief second. Images flashed in front of Megan's eyes. Anna's white face caught in a photographer's flash. Chris, half-turned, half-crouched, hands raised to his ears.

Megan stepped forward, away from the noise. Someone was screaming. She wanted to tell them to stop but for some reason she was dumb and deafened by the blast. The resonance of the shot continued to echo around inside her skull.

Torchlight settled on her face. Chris pushing her backwards.

"Megan, are you okay?"

She wanted to nod, but she couldn't do that either.

Chris shook her shoulders as her legs went limp.

"Megan, talk to me. What happened?"

She needed to sit down. Had to sit down. Her legs didn't work anymore.

Something sticky flooded her mouth, like she was being sick without the retching.

"Shit! No!" Chris's face hovered about hers.

"What is it?" Gareth's voice cut the darkness.

It was like she could pick up every single tiny detail, but it was all happening around her, not to her. Like she was on a different level. A different planet. Another explosion of noise and light. Chris dropped to the floor beside her; he landed with a groan and a thud. She felt his hands on her body, squeezing, burrowing. She wanted to slap him away … but couldn't do that either.

"Big mistake, detective."

The voice came from the darkness.

"Shit, where's my torch." Chris moved against her. Megan

moaned. "Keep still. Keep quiet. Megan, can you hear me?"

She nodded.

Chris cleared his throat; spoke out to the blackness of the room. "Who the hell are you? What do you want? What is all this about?"

Silence.

"Look … we have an officer down. If you don't want another death on your hands, you best start talking." Chris's voice was high and tight.

Megan struggled to keep up. An officer down? Who? Parry?

"Do you hear me?" he yelled.

"I'd prefer to speak to the organ grinder, I don't deal with monkeys."

"What!"

"DS Parry. Permission to speak … but first I want your mobile phones. You and the woman. Throw them into the centre of the room."

No one moved.

"Now!"

The shot fired down low. Megan screamed. Her left arm leapt with pain.

"Okay!" Chris panted. "Okay. Wait."

A thud as he tossed his phone towards the shadow of a man. "Get hers."

Chris shuffled forward; she felt his panic as he patted her clothing. "God, I'm sorry," he whispered. "Just keep still, try not to panic. We'll get out of this. Okay?"

"Okay."

His fingers found her phone in the pocket of her jeans and he threw it hard against the floor.

"Right. That wasn't so hard, was it? Now, Parry, tell your friends here that we're all one big happy family."

Gareth coughed. "We're okay, Chris. Sue is here. Anna too. Just do what he says. He's not messing around."

Chris groaned. "Are you injured?"

"Not much. We're tied up, have hoods on. The girls are okay, that's the main thing."

"Enough!"

Another shot exploded above Megan's head. Her ears were numb and everything felt blurred, like she was moving underwater, not quite connecting with reality.

"This is all very pleasant but we need to move this on before anyone else gets hurt."

A stranger's voice. In control. She concentrated, not wanting to miss a word, aware somehow that everything was important. Every snippet was vital.

Chris's voice was warm next to her ear. "Don't move. Don't try to do anything. I think he's shot you in the back. Can you feel anything?"

Megan blinked. Shot her? What did he mean? Wasn't there supposed to be pain and blood if someone was shot? It was the darkness that was disorientating. She was fine, just confused …

"No … pain." The words took an age. Bloody hell. What was wrong with her?

"Good. That's good. I don't dare take a shot at him, he's moving around too much –"

"Enough! Get against the wall. Hold onto that pipe, I'm going to put restraints on your wrists. Try anything and I will kill you."

The room fell quiet, ragged breathing the only noise.

"So, the plan changes, but no matter," the bodiless voice said after a few minutes. "We swap one for another, quite simple. Dr Connolly get to your feet. Try anything and the next shot will be in your face. Understand?"

Shuffling noise. "I can't move until you untie my feet.

More scraping. Megan tilted her head towards the sounds.

"Nothing changes. I want information. The same information Anna told Iris Mahoney. I know about the farm. I just want to know where the gold is. Then I can be on my way, leave you all in peace."

"What do you want me to do?" said Sue Connolly. "I don't know anything about this."

"Of course you don't, doctor, whatever you say. But no matter, Anna knows everything, she's the key. I need you to get your boyfriend to leave us alone until this is over. I want him to call off the police that have probably surrounded this place by now. He's more likely to do that if he knows I have a gun to the side of your head and that I am more than happy to use it ... don't you think?"

"And what about Parry?"

"I need collateral. He will have to stay here with his heroic pals. But if you do as I say and survive our little trip, then you can be back within a few hours to free them. That's my deal."

"Don't listen." Gareth's voice. "Ignore him. We don't do deals ..."

"Gareth!" Chris raised himself on one elbow; Megan felt his movement beside her. "Do it. Please. We need help for Megan."

There was a growl of anger. "Fine. Get on with it, but I warn you ... hurt anyone else and I will find you and rip you to pieces with my bare hands. That's a promise."

"I have to say I don't appreciate your tone, detective."

"And I have to say I don't give a shit. Just get on with whatever you're going to do."

"No. I want an apology from you."

Gareth snorted. "Do what?"

"You heard. Apologise."

"No way. Never."

Megan groaned. She wanted this to stop. The noise, the shouting it was making her nauseous.

"Gareth!" Chris said. "Leave it ..."

"I can't!"

The killer laughed. Megan frowned, something ... something about that laugh. What was it?

"Not even if it stopped me putting a bullet through your girlfriend's skull with your own gun?"

"No!" Gareth shrieked.

A gun clicked, trigger cocked.

The sound seemed so loud in the confines of the darkness.

"No!" A girl screamed. "No! Don't hurt her. Leave her. It's me you want."

"Anna, shush," Gareth cried.

"Now, now. Let Anna speak."

That voice again, familiar, yet strange. Annoying that she was so tired, it meant something, but it was too far for her to reach out and grab.

Anna's voice was tight, on the edge of tears. "It's me you want. Take me. I know where the gold is. Iris knew, she told me, showed me on a map. I'm the only one can help you. If you let these people go, I'll show you the way."

"Anna, no!"

"I was going to ask how I knew you were telling the truth. But those reactions kind of give it away. So, I was right, you are the key." A pause, hands clapped. "Good girl, Anna. Let's go dig ourselves some treasure. Parry, here's a mobile. Make the call. Call off your men. No tails, no helicopters. I want free passage. Any sniff you've gone back on your word and I'll kill both of them. Understand?"

Megan listened to the brief phone conversation. Gareth sounded choked, angry and scared. Message relayed, there were more sounds, scuffles, footsteps … the occasional muted sob.

Everything began to drift out of focus. She was tired, weak. Voices faded.

Megan closed her eyes and let an icy wave engulf her.

Chapter Twenty Seven

"**N**o …Anna!" Gareth kicked out against the ties, flailing with his legs like a drowning man trapped in seaweed. "Don't listen to her, whoever you are. Listen to me! She's lying. Take me!"

His last desperate plea died on his lips as somewhere close, a door slammed.

Gareth panted with the stranglehold of pain; the heat inside the hood was making him nauseous.

A wet cough came from low down on the floor.

Chris's voice. "Megan? Christ …"

"Is it bad?"

Chris exhaled a long breath. "I think so."

"Christ!"

Gareth kicked out again, closed his eyes for a moment, leaned his head back and tried to focus. Not that it made much difference, eyes open or closed. Unless he could get out of this chair, he was making more promises he couldn't keep. And the longer that madman was out there, without anyone on his tail, the more he feared for Susan and Anna.

The sound of rattling breaths. Megan sounded in a bad way.

"Chris are you tied up?"

"Yeah. Handcuffed to something on the wall. I've ripped my skin to bits, but no way I can get free."

"What about Megan?"

"She's shot, mate. What do you expect her to do?"

"But is she free?"

Chris paused. "I think so, yeah, I can't see anything. I think she's asleep. Megan!"

"You need to try and keep her awake."

"Get away. Megan!"

A grunt.

"Megan?"

"Yeah." Little more than a whisper.

"Are you okay?" said Gareth.

Chris snorted. "If ever there was a stupid question!"

Megan sighed. "I can move ... a bit ... but ... ooooh, it hurts." She drew breath. "A lot."

Gareth's heart raced. "Can you move towards me? I need help to get out of these restraints. Can we try?"

A shuffling noise, interspersed with moans, filled the room. The odd hissed swear word penetrated his thick hood. Gareth could only imagine the pain and discomfort she was going through, and prayed it wouldn't kill her.

Gareth bent as low as he could, pulling tight against the cuffs. "That's great, Megan. I have a knife. In my inside coat pocket. He took my gun but I'm sure my knife is still there. Just keep going. If you can help get me free, I'll get us all out of here somehow."

"Give me ... minute. Hurts."

"Are you sure this is a good idea?" Chris's voice was heavy with tension. "What if it's doing more damage?"

"I don't know. Start praying. But she's our only hope."

The room fell into a silence, heavy with tension. When he could stand it no longer, Gareth cleared his throat.

"Megan, are you okay? Nearly here yet? I can't tell."

Silence.

"Megan?" Gareth strained his ears. "Chris, can you hear anything?"

"No. Shit you don't think –"

"I'm here ... here." The wet breathing started up again. "I

need to sleep, just for a minute … my strength back. Just … five minutes."

"No!" Gareth shrieked as loud as he could. "Don't go to sleep. You have to keep awake. Stay focused. Please, keep moving towards me. Please. We need you, Megan."

Gareth tried to block out the groaning that accompanied the dragging noises. He concentrated on issuing words of encouragement. After an age, he sensed body heat next to his left leg, then a weight on his thigh; a hand sliding round his waist, up into his coat.

"I've got the knife. Dunno if … strength. He's taped your … wrists and ankles."

"Fine. Do whatever you need. Just tell me what I can do to help."

Slippery fingers probed at his ankles. "Part your feet."

He stretched his feet as wide apart as possible, feeling his skin burn as the knife dragged back and forth like a saw on splintered wood. Megan's breathing was shallow, her movements jerky. Gareth willed himself to keep still, stay calm, ignore the shakes gripping his body. After what seemed like hours, the knife clattered to the floor and his feet were free.

"Thank you. Thank you." He twisted his ankles. "I know this is hard for you. Can you try my wrists now? Please, we're so close."

"I dunno." Megan coughed, spat. "Dunno … if I can reach. Hurts …"

"Tell me what to do. Anything. Let me help."

"Twist yourself. Round … to me."

"Okay, okay. Like this, yes?" Gareth scraped his feet on the floor, feeling the bands tighten on his wrists. "These feel thicker or something. Tighter."

"That'll do. Keep still."

He sensed the effort involved in lifting the knife and cursed with Megan as it rattled on the floor. She tried again, patient and methodical, muttering to herself in Welsh. Gareth inhaled and winced as the point of the blade punctured his skin.

"I cut you?" Megan coughed again. "Sorry."

"It's okay. No problem. You're doing fine."

Something hot dripped onto his arms. He knew it was blood and it wasn't his own. Megan was bleeding so badly it was running down her hands onto his. Darkness swam and vomit flooded his mouth.

"Can you ... can you get this hood off? I think I might be sick."

Another moan as Megan yanked his head forward, just as his mouth filled with bile. He turned to the side, managed to avoid splattering Megan.

"Nerves. Sorry."

"S'okay. Just keep still."

"Yeah. Still. Sorry."

Gareth knew he was teetering close to the edge. The darkness was almost as impenetrable without the hood, but at least he could breathe, get cooler, less fetid air into his lungs. Lots of long, deep breaths, focus on the next step of the plan, ignore the throb in his hands and arms.

"Are you badly hurt?" Gareth asked as Megan gave out a loud yell.

"Arm's bad. Back too ... I think."

"As soon as I'm free, I'll help you. I promise."

"Help me ...?"

"Yeah, of course, anything. What?"

"Shut up ... keep still."

Under different circumstances, Gareth would have smiled. Megan had lost none of her charm. The weight of her torso against his legs was stopping the circulation, cramp tightened in his hip, and he could feel the hot spread of her blood through his clothes, seeping onto his skin like sweat. He forced herself to remain motionless. Minutes past, more and more time seemed to be slipping away. Megan slumped backwards twice, paused in the sawing motion, then from somewhere seemed to drag another ounce of strength and started up again.

When Gareth's hands finally flew apart, the momentum pulled him off the seat. Megan collapsed with a groan; her eyes half-closed, the whites just visible in the darkness. Her chest rose and fell, but her breathing was shallow, hardly there at all.

"Are you free?" In the tension, Gareth had almost forgotten Chris, waiting in the shadows.

"Yeah."

"Thank God, come and see if you can get me out of these …"

Megan touched his ankle. He looked down.

"Here." He leaned over her face; the words were barely audible now over the rattle from her chest. "Car keys … back pocket."

"Megan Jones, you are amazing." Gareth whispered as he tugged the bunch of keys free of her clothing.

Megan licked her lips, rolling on her back as blood seeped from her mouth. "Go … save Anna."

Gareth got to his knees, pushed two fingers against the blood-slicked neck, searching for a pulse. It was there, barely, the tiniest of flutters.

"I'll get help, Megan. As soon as I can."

"Too late." More blood bubbled between her lips and dripped down her chin. "Please … save Anna."

"I will, I promise. But we'll come back for you –"

Her hand was rough on his chest, pushing him away. "No. Go. Anna."

With a sob, Gareth took the knife, dashed across to Chris, and hacked through the cable tie restraints.

"You should stay," whispered Gareth as Chris rubbed his wrists. "She shouldn't be moved. I'll radio an ambulance but one of us should stay with her."

Chris looked across the floor, tears flooded his eyes. "Oh, Christ, what a nightmare. I'll stay. You go. Just hurry … for God's sake, hurry!"

Gareth yanked open the door and scrambled up a flight of

stone steps. He turned right at the top, heading towards pale threads of light, rather than a long, dark corridor to the left. He shielded his eyes as he entered a high-ceilinged kitchen. A single bare bulb illuminated a cavernous room, furnished with outdated fittings; it clearly hadn't been occupied for years. Cobwebs clung across the beams, and dust coated every surface. Gareth ran to the outside door, praying it would be unlocked. It was but on the far side he found himself in a small veranda, the door of which was covered in a plywood sheet. Four solid kicks loosened the wood enough for him to squeeze through the gap. Moonlight bathed the yard in silvery light. The outside areas were as abandoned as the interior of the house. It was some kind of small-holding. Abandoned chicken coops and an empty pigsty led to a row of boarded-up stables.

Minutes later, he reached the end of the drive, and saw the unmarked police car. The passenger front wing was damaged, headlight smashed and white scratches grooved into the silver paint. Someone had wanted to get away fast, and wasn't going to be prevented by this obstacle.

Gareth jumped inside and grabbed the radio receiver issuing a list of urgent instructions to control, forcing himself to breathe and speak, not choke up and scream. Then he started the engine and spun the wheels as he accelerated hard along the narrow lane. He grabbed the seat belt and strapped himself in, finally allowing himself to inhale and re-focus.

Next stop Sacred Oaks Farm.

A white Mercedes blocked the drive, reversed in tight, ready for a speedy getaway. He drove the Evo toward it, yanking on the handbrake only when the front bumpers were touching. That would stop him in his tracks. He jumped out, leaving the door open, and crept around the car. Other than a dented wing and damaged bumper, the Mercedes was pristine. One of these vintage models people spent a fortune restoring. It was locked and empty. He recalled Sid Fielding mentioning a white taxi. Shame he'd jumped to the wrong conclusion.

The yard was deserted, but Gareth knew where to head. God, he wished he still had his gun. Knowing *he* had it made it worse. Knowing he had Anna and Sue was almost unbearable. He scanned the yard, eyes adjusting to the moonlight, rested on a pile of rusting farm equipment. There were discarded iron links with banjo-shaped ends, some kind of tractor parts, on top of a pile of junk. He lifted one. It was heavy, solid enough to do serious damage to a human skull. It wasn't ideal, but better than nothing.

He followed the same track as on his last visit, keeping tight to the high hedges. As he approached the wooded hill, he recalled finding the label from the metal detector in the bashed-down nettles. He remembered the disturbed ground on the top of the mound, evidence someone had recently been there. From the moment Sue had rung, he'd diverted all his energies, blinded by the thought of rescuing her. No doubt exactly as this manipulative killer intended. This had all been planned out to the minutest degree, and even when something went wrong – like Megan and Chris turning up out of the blue – nothing fazed him. It was the sign of a confident madman and it chilled Gareth to the core.

But something called him back to that spot on the mound now.

He began to climb, slowly at first, until he got more accustomed to the steep ground. Soon, he was pulling himself up on hands and knees. The temperature dropped as the trees grew thicker. As he reached the rise, he heard the roar of an engine and the crunch of gravel; he turned to see an unmarked police car swerve into the drive and jolt to a halt behind the Evo. Damn it. Who was it and why were they ignoring his orders?

The door opened. Macrae climbed out, keeping to the shadows he jogged towards the rear of the house. Gareth held his breath, then whistled, once. Low. A call sign they used on surveillance ops. He waited for Macrae to turn, as he knew he would, then waved one arm above his head, at the same time pressing a finger across his lips.

Minutes later, Macrae was at his side, face pale in the darkness. "It was a long shot, but when I heard about the call to stand down, I felt this had to be where he was heading. I thought I could beat you here."

"I was in the Evo. We've got to be careful, sir. He's got Anna Brown and Susan Connolly. Somewhere round here. Anna told him she knew where the gold was buried. Sue is his collateral. He's got my gun ... and he's already used it." Gareth took a deep breath. "Megan's injured. Shot. It looks bad. Chris is with her. I've radioed for an ambulance."

"Shit. You okay?"

"Fine. But we need to find him. Stop him. He'll kill them once he gets what he wants. He's a psycho – a cold-blooded killer in every sense of the word."

"You've seen him?"

"Spoke to him. Not an ounce of remorse. He's dangerous, sir."

Macrae nodded to the improvised weapon at Gareth's feet. "And you think some rusty old spare part is going to be a match for him? We should wait for backup. You know the routine. We'll be hung up by the bollocks if anything happens to them –"

"Due respect, you think I give a shit about protocol right now, sir?" hissed Gareth. "I want to save this girl. And Susan. I'll do whatever I have to. I need you with me?"

Macrae sighed. "Against my better judgment." He dug around in his jacket pocket. "You'll want to see this. The full translation of the inscription on the stone after those boffins went out to Barrington-Browns' place."

Macrae held a small torch steady as Gareth took the creased sheet of paper and studied the words.

Take a boat to the rising moon
To our grove of sacred oaks, beside the rushing water.
On the highest ground …
Turn towards the sun before the valley grove …
and there you'll find blood stains mark the gold.
In loving memory of my father, Cadadius.

Macrae was watching him. "Are you thinking what I'm thinking?"

"If you're thinking it's down there." Gareth pointed to the far grove that dropped into a hollow in the centre of big field. "Then yeah, I am. That must be the valley grove. But …" He stood and looked back up the hill behind him; positive he hadn't imagined the piled earth he saw yesterday. "I was sure there was something up here, certainly been lots of activity."

"Well, I'd say it's pretty clear. Perhaps there's been a lot of guesswork. And there's no sign of anyone in these woods just now. If you're sure they're here somewhere, I'd hazard a guess we need to be looking down there."

Gareth got to his feet, brushed off his knees. "Okay. But how the hell we going to get down there without him seeing us? It's in the middle of an open field."

Macrae bit down on his lip as he peered down the slope. "I've an idea. Two minutes."

He pulled out his mobile phone, scrolled and held it to his ear.

"Keep a look out. Any movement, yell."

Gareth kept his eyes forward, but couldn't help but listen.

"Listen we have ourselves a situation here. Where are you?" A pause. "Right, well, be careful, you hear? He's armed and dangerous." Another pause. "Yeah, he's here with me. I need you to cause a diversion. This is my plan."

Macrae turned away and the words were lost.

Gareth's heart banged like a drum. He wanted to sprint across the field, rush into the woods, whooping like a wild man and take that nutter out. But he couldn't. He had to trust Macrae. They were close, closer than close. One way or another, this would finish here and now in a field at Sacred Oaks Farm. And if history were to be believed, things had come full circle, back to where the whole story started with bloodshed and murder.

Gareth closed his eyes and prayed it didn't end the same way.

Chapter IX

MONA INSULIS, BRITAIN - AD 60

Awen looked down at the waxen face; rivulets of sweat ran in a steady stream from his hairline.

"Any improvement, my lady?" Ked's soft voice asked.

Awen shook her head. "I cannot see he will make it through the night. The infection and fever have spread. I have failed him."

Failed my father too, she thought.

Ked's fingers squeezed her shoulder. "You did all you could. More than most would under the circumstances. You have nothing to chide yourself over. Let him go."

"My father –"

"Would have been proud of you today. As he always was. Let him go, my lady."

Awen nodded; her throat tight. "Leave me now, Ked. I'll stay the night in case he wakes."

Ked sighed but remained silent, closing the door as she left.

Awen tucked her feet up under her bottom, balanced her chin on her knees. She was exhausted. Her head dropped and she yawned.

My father's face.

'Cadadius?'

He smiles. 'You honour me, Awen, my fawn.'

My father stands on a grassy mound, next to rushing water, arms held high as he chants. His druid staff lifts to the sun and clouds block out the sunshine.

Then an explosion of noise. Arrows rain down like hail. Flaming bolts flash across the sky like shooting stars. Smoke chokes me; the smell of death squeezes my throat like the tightest of hands.

Men rush back and forth, screams fill my ears.

'Awen?'

'Father?'

'Show courage, child. Show strength. Remain true to your principles no matter what life presents you. You will be called to account many times over. Be loyal to your heart and the beliefs of our people. Even if you must sacrifice your own needs.'

"What do you mean? Father, I miss you so much!'

His face dissolves, swirling away from me like water through my fingers.

'No! Please! Help me …'

And then, I see my father again, caught in combat, facing the enemy with a look of terror in his eyes. With one deft move, a soldier slashes my father's throat. Laughing, as my father's blood splatters his legs and feet. The Roman turns to me, his face alight with blood-lust, eyes wild and glassy.

'Cadadius!' I scream but the words are silent.

And then darkness.

"No!"

Awen screamed, sat upright as her feet slipped from the edge of her chair. She took gulps of air, waiting for her head to stop spinning and her heart to slow its furious pounding.

The Roman's eyes were wide open, staring straight at her, blank and glassy.

Awen looked away, sickness tearing at her gut, unable to face the dead gaze of the man she'd watched slaughter her father.

Awen checked to see if there was any sign of life. There was none. His eyes were closed; skin the colour and consistency of candle wax. The faces of the stretcher-bearers made it clear they thought the journey was a waste of their time and energy. Not to mention the ever-present edge of danger lurking, crossing half the island while it was still in the grip of the Romans. Distant sounds of ongoing battles reached her ears. The sight of burning hamlets on every hill worsened Awen's stress.

This trip would be fruitless. She hadn't seen it. But in her heart, she knew. He had not woken once since the latest fever took hold. The wound had taken one lung and damaged his heart. If the holy waters of Llyn Cerrig Bach could not cure him, then at least he would be anointed before he made the journey to wherever Roman souls travelled after death.

Soon the ground turned soft beneath their feet, the grasses grew long and thick. And as they rounded a jutting outcrop, the lake came into view. Awen shivered, the same familiar tug of wonder she got every time she saw the glistening waters of this ancient lake, where Bacchus himself was said to reside. His home, the island that rose out of the depths, was covered with trees and gorse. Bacchus never showed himself, but his power extended to the very edge of the lake. All who immersed themselves in his water would be blessed or cured.

Awen unfolded her father's favourite robe, holding it to her nose and breathing in the scent of the man that still lingered on the rough cloth, before shrugging her arms into the folds and taking her position at the head of the group, ankle deep in the bloody red sludge. She unwrapped her father's most ancient possession, his sceptre made of rowan wood, and closing one eye she called out in a strong voice towards the island.

"A ELFYNTODD DWYR SINDDYN DUW
CERRIG YR FFERLLURIG NWYN;
OS SYRIAETH ECH SAFFAER TU
FEWR ECHLYN MOR, NECROMBOR LLUN."

Wind rustled the swaying grasses and bullrushes, whipping

the cloak against her legs. Bacchus was home; he was listening. Now, she had to pay her fare.

She was handed a leather sack containing some of the artefacts collected after the battle at her father's burial site. A Roman sword, war trumpet and bronze helmet. Bacchus liked any precious metals, and while these were foreign objects to her people, she hoped they would appease the God. She flung each object high into the air, one by one, watching them splash down into the water. The sword clattered against the rocks on the island, before slipping below the rippling water. Next, she removed a handful of quartz pebbles, scattering them across the water as she would feed for her birds. And finally, she closed her eyes and began to sway, chanting her prayer to Bacchus over and over as the women marched in a circle, matching her voice.

When the wind dropped, the two men lifted the stretcher from the circle and carried the Roman into the lake until they were waist deep. On Awen's instructions, they dipped the stretcher under the water, holding it for ten seconds, and then bringing it back out into the cool air. There was no reaction from the Roman. Awen waited, praying for some movement. Anything. While she didn't imagine he would sit up in shock, or leap from the stretcher, she hoped for something, some sign Bacchus was listening.

The ritual was repeated, this time Awen added an *Imbas Forosnai*, a prayer for illumination. Hoping Bacchus could at least give her guidance on her future path. But even after a second immersing, the Roman remained a waxen shell of his former self. What little colour remained, now began to drain from his face. She gripped his hand; it was ice cold. And his eyes, when she lifted the lids, were dull and blank. She pushed her fingers into the cool skin of his neck; the pulse was still.

Awen headed back to the shore.

"You did all you could," said Ked. "At least his soul is purged, ready for its journey."

"I thought he might find more strength here. I thought

Bacchus might help."

"Perhaps Bacchus doesn't help Romans," said Ked, a bitter edge to her voice.

"He is still a human being," snapped Awen. "You of all should know that."

Ked bowed her head. "Shall we bury him here?"

Awen wrapped her father's cloak around her as she dried the crimson droplets from her legs.

"No. I want to bury him beside my father. "

Awen ignored the looks of anger and incredulity among the group. She oversaw the dressing of the body, binding it to the stretcher ready for the return journey. Then without a word or backward glance, she began to march in the direction of the commune, turning away from the group before they saw the stream of tears that poured down her face.

Chapter Twenty Eight

A police siren carried on the air. Flashes of blue illuminated the lane.

Gareth looked up. "What's going on? He said no police; if he thinks I've gone back on my word he'll kill them! I left specific instructions –"

Macrae appeared at his side. "Calm down. Change of plan. Trust me on this. We want his attention focused. Let him think we're looking for him down there." Macrae nodded. "At the farm. We can sneak round the field the back way. Armed police will be arriving with backup anytime soon. Once the marksmen are in place, we can make a move."

Gareth dropped down onto an old tree stump. His legs were shaking and he knew guilt was most of the problem. This was routine. Any other time, he'd be out front, leading the troops, issuing orders, making decisions. But now, he couldn't. He was so scared of making another wrong move in this dangerous game of chess. The thought of letting Macrae take charge was appealing. He was too close, and being too close could mean making the wrong decisions. There had been no discussion on the subject, there didn't need to be. Macrae was his backup. No words needed. He tried not to think about Chris. Or Megan. Tried not to imagine them back in that cellar …

Macrae's mobile buzzed. "Yeah?" he whispered. "Okay, where?" He turned to his left. "Right, gotcha. It's the wood in the middle of the big field. We think he's in there. Make as much commotion as you can at the house, I want his attention focused. I'm going in round the back. Ask one of the men to head up here, follow the track from the caravan site, I'm sending DS Parry down to meet him …"

Gareth got to his feet. "No, you're not. I'm coming with you."

"With respect, Parry. You're in shock. You've had a hell of an ordeal. Leave it to the rest of us, it's time to delegate."

Macrae was right on so many counts. In his position, he'd be advising the exact same thing. But Anna Brown's face wouldn't clear from his mind, and his promise to Susan weighed heavy on his heart.

Macrae sighed. "Parry, don't make me pull rank …"

"Sir, I have to do this. I'm coming with you."

More police cars sped along the narrow lane, sirens shattering the peace. The sound of slamming doors, barking dogs. The show was in full swing.

Macrae studied him for a moment, then held his mobile back to his ear. "Change of plan. Stay on the far side of the field, make sure all exits are covered. When I give the signal, head towards the woods. Speak soon."

Macrae slid the phone into his coat, pulled out a walkie-talkie. "All units. Keep the focus of attention in the vicinity of the farmhouse. We do not believe he is in the house, but make a full sweep of the area. Armed units, we're dealing with the wooded copse in the centre of the big field. Make sure all exits are covered. Please note, we believe he is holding two hostages. One is a minor. Do not shoot unless there is an immediate threat, and do not take any chances without a clear line of sight. Understood? Out."

Macrae got to his feet. "Ready to do this, Parry?"

They kept low, glad of the thick cover of swaying grasses as they crossed the field on their hands and knees. The sky was clear; hundreds of stars led the way, aided by the full moon which gave almost perfect visibility. There was no fear now. Adrenaline had kicked in once they stepped out of the shade of the wood and skidded down the steepest part of the embankment. Now, low down, Gareth felt as if he were level with the oak trees in the valley copse; the swaying branches beckoned to him like curling fingers. The thought that the killer was in there, and Susan too, chilled his blood and heightened his senses.

Macrae raised a hand. Gareth stopped, scrambled round to his side.

"Can you hear voices?" Macrae whispered.

Gareth tilted his head. "Not sure."

Macrae nodded. "I'm sure I can. Some sort of chanting." He shook his head. "God, I dunno. Perhaps it's my ears. You ready then, Parry?"

Gareth tightened his grip on the iron rod. "As I'll ever be." He paused. "Sir, let me get Susan and Anna out. Whatever happens, I need to get them to safety."

Macrae nodded. "Everyone's ready. I'll go for the guy, you find the hostages. Soon as it's clear, propel them across the field and an officer will be at the gate ready to grab them. Don't worry, they are our priority, I understand that."

Gareth exhaled. "Good. Thank you, sir."

Macrae's phone buzzed. "Shit. Hang on."

He hissed into the receiver, broken words, inaudible grunts. When he turned back, his face looked pale, eyes full of pain, reflected in the moonlight.

Panic gripped Gareth's gut, twisted. "What is it?"

Macrae shook his head, turned away.

"Sir? What?"

He turned. "That was Chris. Megan ... Megan didn't make it, I'm afraid."

"What?" He looked down at the bloodstains on his sleeves, his jeans. *Megan's blood.* His head whirled. He took deep breaths.

"No. No. No, it can't …"

Macrae's hand gripped his shoulder, holding him tight. "Keep it together, Parry. Keep it together or get out of here. You have no choice right now."

He couldn't hear. His pulse hammered. He bit down on the scream that threatened to burst free. Tears swam in his eyes. Megan. How she'd crawled across the floor to free him. Her face, eyes closed, gripped with pain. Blood. So much blood. How he'd yelled at her, humiliated her. Oh, God …

"Are you going to be able to do this?" Macrae's voice was hot and urgent in his ear. "Nothing to be ashamed about if you can't. But you need to make a decision and you need to make it now."

Gareth blew out a steady stream of pent-up air and anger. How could Macrae be so cold, so calm? He'd just lost a member of his team. Training. This is why Macrae was top of his field. This is what it meant to enter the world of the elite. This was real pressure. Gareth nodded once, then took the lead, aware of Macrae's heavy breathing behind. Once they reached the cover of trees, Gareth got to his feet and trod with care across the forest floor, heading down into the copse of oak trees. The floor was spongy and damp, moonlight hardly managing to penetrate the thick branches. The air was heavy with the smell of moss and buzzed with unseen insects. Gareth shivered, but pushed on, every sense alert and focused.

The sounds got louder, still unidentifiable. Macrae touched his shoulder, then pointed to his ear. Gareth nodded. Yes, he could hear it now. A high-pitched buzz and the low rumble of voices. Then the thud of something heavy and the ground shook. They were close.

As Gareth strained his eyes against the gloom, he became aware of flashes of silver. He blinked. Were his eyes playing tricks? But as he stole a look at his DI, he saw his attention was caught by the same phenomena. They approached a clearing, circled by a ring of huge oak trees. Shafts of moonlight danced between the canopies of leaves, creating elaborate silvery patterns on the forest floor which seemed to dance and twist to a silent drumbeat. In the centre of the clearing was a hollow, like a giant scoop had removed a section of earth.

The noises came from that hollow. Macrae moved in front, holding back any protestations with a raised hand. They crept along the perimeter of the clearing, keeping in the shadows of the trees. Gareth couldn't see anyone, wasn't sure which way *he'd* be facing. Macrae made a rushing gesture with his fingers, and Gareth nodded. Raising the iron bar, he raced forward, shoulder to shoulder with his DI.

Several things happened at once. Gareth spotted Anna, sitting on the twisted branch of a fallen tree. As he headed towards the girl, he was aware of a thud and a grunt, the noise of thrashing bodies. Anna tried to stand as Gareth approached; her eyes were scared but her face was a picture of calmness. Her arms and ankles were bound to the thick branch with coils of black sticky tape. Gareth straddled the branch, taking the shaking girl in his arms, pressing her tight against his body as he tried to unpick the heavy-duty tape. Scuffles continued behind him, but for the moment, he was fixed on freeing Anna, getting her away from danger.

"Are you okay?" Gareth panted. "Are you hurt?"

"I'm okay. I was talking to him, trying to keep him here. I knew you'd come." The words came out fast and furious as Anna continued to shake; her breathing was rapid and tense. "I thought if I could slow him down, scare him a little … didn't want him to get away. I wasn't scared. No, not scared. Just wanted you to come and get me."

Gareth's fingers burned as he tore at the tape in vain. It was hopeless; he needed a knife. As he turned to search the area, a gunshot echoed through the clearing. Instinctively, he covered Anna's ears and pulled her against his chest.

The copse was alive with noise, scurrying rodents in the undergrowth, and fleeing birds, wings beating through the canopy above. Gareth's head spun from the noise, and disorientated, he slipped from the branch, gripping hold of Anna for support. A loud scream added to the chaos. A man's scream.

"Sir?" Gareth picked herself up. "Sir!"

"It's okay, Parry. I'm fine." A hiss of static. "All units. Hold fire. One man down. Send an ambulance. It's clear."

Gareth's legs shook as she looked round. Macrae was standing in the centre of the hollow; a hooded man writhed, face down, at his feet. Macrae kept the Glock centred on the back of his skull.

"I almost got the gun off him, then he turned it on himself. Took a bullet in his shoulder, superficial I think."

"Stay there," Gareth whispered to Anna. "Someone will come and cut you free. Take deep breaths, it's over now."

Anna looked up; her face was grimy and streaked with dried tears. "Susan ..."

Gareth's mouth froze, mid-word. Susan. He'd forgotten about Susan. In the panic, he'd completely ...

"He shot her. Back there ..."

Gareth didn't stop to get directions; he launched himself into the undergrowth. Crashing. Stumbling. Screaming.

"Susan!"

He ran one way, turned, ran another.

"Susan!"

He stumbled, hit the ground hard, chin smacking into a moss-covered tree stump. The pain brought him up short. More lights were beginning to fill the clearing, bobbing between the branches. Voices called out, sirens echoed in the distance. He got to his knees.

"Susan! For Christ's sake!"

He sensed someone beside him, spun round. "Sue?"

Anna Brown's pale face stared up at him. "This way."

She held out a hand and he took it, trembling as he staggered to his feet. He couldn't breathe, couldn't speak, just concentrated on the pressure of the girl's touch, not sure what else could get him through the next few minutes.

Back towards the lights and voices. Macrae's face. Torchlight blinding him.

"Parry, I'm sorry …"

He shook his head. He didn't want to hear. Didn't want to speak. He wanted Sue Connolly in his arms, hugging him hard. Warm, sweet breath on his ear, telling him it was okay, everything was going to be all right.

Anna stopped, tugged his hand, squeezed tight. Warmth, like the tingle of electricity, trickled into his fingers, up into his arm, into his chest. He took a gulp of air and his lungs cleared enough for oxygen to fill his brain.

Then looked down, followed Macrae's torchlight.

Susan was on her side, head resting on the gnarled root of an ancient tree. Eyes closed, hands folded beneath her head like a pillow. Sleeping. A thin trickle of inky looking liquid slid from beneath her right ear, disappearing into the forest floor.

Just sleeping.

Gareth dropped to his knees, grabbed her right hand, and gripped it to his chest. Her skin was still warm, smooth as a marble statue.

"Susan. Wake up. I'm here. I promised you. I'm here."

He shook her hand, reached down to stroke her face.

"Come on, Connolly. That's enough. Please …"

She was so beautiful. His mind couldn't take it in. Memories of the same sleeping face on his pillow beside him, hands like this, cupping her cheek. The gentle sound of her breathing, how her lips twitched in her deepest sleep. If he could wake her, just to tell her. Finally. How much he loved her.

Anna knelt beside him. "She's at peace. I'm sorry. She was so brave. He went berserk when we got here, said I wasn't needed anymore. He aimed the gun at me, but Susan got in the way, pushed me to one side." She broke off with a sob. "I am so sorry."

Tears blurred his eyes, slid down his nose. He continued to squeeze her hand, hoping to manipulate the life back in there.

He shook his head, sniffed. "No, she's not dead. She's a

pathologist you see … she knows about death. She can sort it out. Don't worry."

"She saved my life. I'll never forget that."

Gareth turned on the girl, heart ready to explode. "You think I give a shit about you and your stupid life. I don't care. Do something!" Tears dripped down his face, landing on Susan's coat sleeve. "You're supposed to have all these powers, so use them! Do something. If you're so grateful, bring her back to life! She shouldn't be dead; this is nothing to do with her. This is all my fault. You. Do. Something!"

He yanked Anna's arm, pulling her forward.

She began to weep, shoulders shaking. "I can't. I'm s-sorry. I've tried. I was praying and praying …"

"Well … pray harder!" Gareth shook the girl. "She cannot be dead! Do you hear me? First, Megan. Now …"

A strong hand gripped under his armpit, dragged him away. Macrae's voice. "Enough, now."

"Sir, it's okay. Anna can fix this. She's one of these Druids. Please, just …"

"Come on, now. We need to get out of here. This is a crime scene."

The will to argue left his body. Along with the will to live.

There was a flurry of movement. Voices soothing, sobs echoing. Gareth half-walked, was half-carried, out of the woods. Blue flashing lights filled the sky, howling sirens shattered the silence. Across the moonlit field of swaying grass; the warm gentle breeze dried his tears, hardened his heart, but didn't seem to penetrate his brain.

Nothing was real. It was ridiculous to think in the past few hours he'd lost the two bravest and most capable women he knew. It was just ridiculous. This was no more than a bad dream and when he finally woke up; he could imagine how much Megan and Sue would delight in taking the piss.

It was just a bad dream.

Chapter Twenty Nine

Gareth stared at his reflection in the bathroom mirror and fingered the lump on the back of his head. He grimaced. Showered and changed, he felt cleaner, but no more human. There was still a sensation of static charge running through his body. An adrenaline high that kept him functioning when all he really wanted to do was lie down and cry. Lie down and die even. His life had changed, tilted on its axis in the past few hours, and the future looked like a massive black void he wasn't sure he wanted to face. Nothing would ever be the same again. He held his hands under the cold water tap, trickling water across his wrists until it was numb. Cooling his pulse points, calming his nerves, blocking thoughts of two women whose names he couldn't even bring himself to think about.

He took a deep breath, pulled open the door.

Chris was waiting in the corridor. Also freshly showered, the soap and water could not remove the taint of grief from his features or the air of sadness from his shoulders.

"Are you one hundred percent sure about this, mate?" Chris asked.

"Never been surer." Gareth reached down, tightened his tie, ignoring the shake of his hands. "Come on. Let's finish this."

The man was slumped across the table, head resting on his arms. His left shoulder was heavily bandaged, the padding clear through the regulation blue plastic boilersuit.

Gareth strode straight to the table, and gave a curt nod to the legal representative opposite, recognising the duty solicitor as someone he'd had previous altercations with.

Chris took the seat next to him and organised the tape recorder.

Gareth cleared his throat and recited the date and time. "Present are Mr Clive Pitt, duty solicitor, DS Coleman and DS Parry, and the accused, Professor Brian Bolton."

The man looked up for the first time, lifting his head in slow motion. He grinned, but it contained no humour. It was the not the expression of a sane man; it shifted his whole face, every one of his features into something so strange it barely looked human. This man had tricked Megan Jones, led them to believe he was acting in the role of expert witness, whilst all the time he'd been using it to his advantage, gaining access to the investigation.

And this man had killed Susan Connolly.

He was playing an invisible piano on the edge of the table. Over and over his fingers flew up and down, and he hummed under his breath in accompaniment.

Gareth cleared his throat. "Professor?"

Silence.

"Mr Bolton, sir?"

More humming. More tapping.

Chris slammed his hand down on the table top. Gareth jumped. So did the duty solicitor, who grabbed his papers with a scowl. The piano playing ceased. Bolton raised his head, blinked and smiled. His movements were slow; his whole demeanour disconnected. Drugs. That was the usual thing. That would explain a lot.

"My name is DS Parry. This is my colleague –"

"Get on with it. Get it over."

He nodded. "So you know why you're here today? We wish to question you in connection with the murders of Mrs Iris Mahoney, Mrs Bronwen Evans, Miss Melanie Wright, Miss

Megan Jones and Dr Susan Connolly." He paused, exhaled, focused. "And the abduction and attempted murder of Miss Anna Brown."

Bolton held up a hand. "After prolonged legal advice, I wish to confess."

Gareth flashed a look at Chris, who shrugged.

"You do?" he asked.

"Yes," Bolton continued. "I'd like to confess to the kidnapping of Anna Brown, Susan Connolly and yourself."

"What?"

"You heard my client, detective." Pitt looked up from the paperwork on his knee. "I think his confession was clear enough. In the absence of any evidence to back up your theories about my client's involvement in any one of your suspicious deaths, my client will only be looking to discuss the kidnapping charges."

"You have to be joking?" said Chris. "And you've advised this? You mad?"

"You have no evidence, Detective Coleman, not even circumstantial that I can see." Pitt sneered. "Unless there's something you're not telling me, in which case I shall request further time to discuss said new evidence with my client."

Chris looked down, flexed his fingers on the table.

"I'll take that as a no," said the solicitor. "In which case, my client's confession stands. He is willing to make a statement to that effect."

Gareth hadn't thought it would be easy. It rarely was. He'd hoped to find some flaw he could probe, try to get him to crack or open up to them. Maybe that's what the solicitor was trying to avoid, knowing the man's mental state was fragile, worried he might snap. Well, Gareth knew all about fragile states of mind at the moment … there was one way to find out if he could break this man. He needed to beat him; he needed justice to be done for Susan and all the other victims, and better it be done legally than what he'd really like to do to him if he had chance.

"And Megan Jones? Her murder? You shot her. I was there

_"

"Did you actually see my client shoot Miss Jones?" asked Pitt.

Gareth shook his head.

Pitt cleared his throat. "Exactly. You know what you heard, but alas you weren't a witness to the event."

"Anna Brown saw *your client* murder Megan Jones and Susan Connolly. At this very moment, she is coming to terms with those facts, and I shall be taking a detailed statement to that effect from her later." Gareth pushed back his chair, seeing the solicitor's questioning frown. "We can throw *your client* back in his comfy cell for a few hours until after I've questioned Anna. No problem for me. Conclude the interview, Chris."

"No!"

It was Bolton. His eyes flashed blue bolts of electricity as he glared at him.

"Why? Worried what she'll say?" said Gareth, gripping the back of his chair. "Worried the jury will believe an innocent child up against someone as twisted as you?" He laughed. "You have every right to be worried, *Professor*." He spat the final word. "This is a battle you can't win. It was a big mistake showing off in front of Anna. What was it? Your attempt to show her how hard you were, how in control you were? Or did you want to break her, terrify her to within an inch of her life? Well, she'll have the last laugh when she testifies against you in court, won't she?"

"She's an evil little bitch," Bolton muttered. "Possessed."

"What's that?" Gareth sneered. "A change of heart? Besides, you must crave some kind of notoriety. Surely you want other people to be in awe of your crimes? You need to show the world what a genius you've been to run a whole police force in circles."

Bolton took his time to respond, then uncrossed his arms and began to applaud, slowly at first, then faster and louder.

"Bravo! Bravo, detective. Bravo!"

Gareth shook his head, hating the man with an almost

physical pain. "Your mind games won't work on me. I don't intimidate easily. Trust me; you're wet behind the ears in comparison with some of the criminals I've had the pleasure to meet over the years." He forced a smile but there was no humour in it; he doubted he would ever smile a genuine smile again. "Now, you have ten seconds to decide if you want to do this now or wait until I've taken a statement from Anna Brown."

Silence.

"Ten ..."

"You know," said Chris, "you should have told the whole truth to your solicitor. You've gone and made him look a bit of a knob now. He can't be a happy man."

"Nine ..."

"Eight ..."

"I think perhaps I should take five minutes to discuss things further with my client," said Pitt, glaring at Chris with open hostility.

"Seven ..."

Silence.

"Six ..."

The solicitor leaned across to whisper in Bolton's ear. Bolton held Gareth's gaze and didn't flinch.

"Five ..."

"Four. We're into the final three, Chris."

"Very exciting. I'll go get young Anna settled." Chris rose from his chair.

"Three ..."

Bolton smiled.

"Two."

"Okay. You win, detective."

"It's not a game."

"No, but you're right. I want to talk. There comes a point, don't you find, where you have nothing to lose, no reason to fight? No point in going through all this if no one knows about it. Can't exactly publish a best-seller if I don't confess all, can

I?"

Chris sat back down. "Your solicitor may wish to advise you before you say more."

Bolton shrugged. "What's the difference? I'm going down anyway."

Gareth met the solicitor's eyes. He gave a resigned shrug and continued to make notes.

Gareth tugged off his jacket, rolled up his shirt sleeves. "Okay, we're going to ask you some questions. Whatever you tell us will be used in evidence against you. I understand you've already been read your rights, but you are clear on the purpose of this interview?"

He nodded.

"For the tape …"

"Yes."

"Okay. As you've decided to admit to the murders, you could help yourself by telling us everything you can remember, starting with Iris Mahoney. Can you do that?"

Bolton frowned. "Why are you talking to me like I'm retarded? I'm not. You think I'm insane don't you? Well, I'm not. At least I don't think I am. Have you spoken to my son?"

Gareth shook his head. "No. Not yet."

"I want him kept out of this. This had nothing to do with Adrian. This all started many, many years ago before my son was even born."

"Go on."

"My wife. Alice. She was a seer. A Druid descendant. We met at university and I was in love with her from the moment I saw her. She was perfection. And for some reason she loved me like no one has ever loved me, before or since. After we graduated, I wanted to move away, take a scholarship to teach at Oxford, start a better life for both of us. She wouldn't hear of it. Had to stay close to Mona, that's all she would ever say. So, I went to Oxford alone. I lasted six months, was so broken-hearted, I had to return to Bangor. Looking back, I've never doubted she had me under some kind of spell. A wonderful, breath-taking, life-changing spell … but still a spell. We married within a year and Adrian was born six months later."

"And you knew about this ancestry from when?"

"When her mother died, just a few months after Adrian was born, Alice changed. She had some kind of breakdown – hormones, grief and stress, the doctors said. Too much for her to cope with – the birth and then death. She told me a whole load of responsibilities had passed to her on her mother's death. She told me about the Servants of Truth."

"So, is that where your interest in Druids stemmed from? Did you find out about the treasure back then?"

"No. That came later. Alice deteriorated. She never recovered her strength and the more pressure she got as the head of this secret society, the more she seemed to fracture. It was terrible to see." He paused, rubbed the bridge of his nose. "They as good as killed her. Pushing her, intimidating her, bullying her …"

"Who's this?" said Chris.

Bolton spread his hands wide. "How could I know? These faceless, nameless witches. No one was allowed to know their identities. Alice would have been in so much trouble if they'd known I knew the Servants of Truth existed."

"What happened?" asked Gareth.

"She lasted three years. Tried to juggle life. Tried to love our baby. Tried to cope. But she couldn't. She took her own life, jumped from the Menai Bridge. It took two months before her body was found. My life ended. Quite simple. There's not a night I don't dream about her, not a day I don't cry for her. The loneliness is as painful now as it was two decades ago and I've never looked at another woman since."

"So, this was revenge?" asked Gareth. "After all this time …"

Bolton shrugged. "Maybe. In a way. More an obsession. I felt guilty that I hadn't been able to protect her. I was her husband, that was my job and I failed her. And I found I couldn't live with that guilt. I made it my life's work to study her kind. And then rumours of this treasure started to trickle through, I thought it would make some sort of payback. Adrian deserved something for what the Druids had taken from him."

Gareth frowned. "What do you mean?"

"Love, detective. I couldn't love my son. I blamed him for his mother's death equally as much as I blamed the Servants of Truth. I couldn't love him. I couldn't even hold him. Without my mother's involvement, I'd have lost him to social services, and to be blunt I wouldn't have cared a jot. But he deserves something, I see that. It's remarkable he's turned out so grounded. I can assure you it was nothing to do with his upbringing. He's a remarkable lad … just like his mother."

"I get all this. I understand your motivation to a degree. But why now?"

Bolton sniffed, grimaced. "It started with that old witch. The con artist. *The Psychic Detective*. Bragging she knew where the gold was, that she'd translated some old Latin inscription. I went along with it, realised early on, she was part of the Servants of Truth. And something clicked. I don't know, can't explain it any more than that. I knew she was protecting someone. I didn't know about Anna Brown back then. I just got angrier and angrier that no one had tried to protect Alice in the same way. I decided that if this gold existed, it was going to be mine. And no one was going to stand in my way. If that meant wiping out every single member of the Servants of Truth along the way … well, that was an added bonus I could more than deal with."

Gareth nodded. "I see. And the other deaths? Bronwen Evans and Melanie Wright?"

"Two more of the clan. I had to extract information. I knew if Bronwen was the guardian of Sacred Oaks she had to know where the hoard was buried. And I realised Melanie Wright had to be involved. I've no doubt she used the same kind of spell on her father that Alice used on me. He would develop the land, but she'd still own it, she'd still be the guardian. I had suspicions, didn't take long to get close to her at the university and find out about her lineage. Her mother had died in childbirth, but I could see in her eyes Melanie was a seer. Like Alice. Like Anna Brown.

"And time was running out you see. The dig was scheduled. Once the big guns moved in, I would lose my chance of bagging the treasure for myself. Things seemed to be spiraling out of control; even getting DC Jones on side wasn't getting any results. If I've any regrets, it's that she got in my way. She didn't need to die. It's going to cause Adrian more pain, which was never my intention. But, well …" He shrugged. "I had no choice. Megan handed me Anna Brown's name – which was perfect. I needed the information and fast."

"Is that why you tortured the victims prior to death?"

"Well, yes, partly. I wanted to break them and also I wanted a *Modus Operandi*."

"And did you break them?"

Bolton shook his head. "Not one of them. Whatever they indoctrinate into these gals, it certainly works. They protect their secrets with their lives, simple as that. I've tried both ends of the age scale, makes no odds. And I *really* tried to break them." He smiled, an evil sneer that flashed a real insight into his twisted mind. "Strikes me these gals, most of them end up dying a tragic death, only the really strong ones make it to old age, and they become the most revered of their clan. It's almost like the lineage is cursed. Maybe they know that, maybe it's in their teaching and it makes them resilient. Whatever it is, we will never know, of that you can be sure. Nothing will break these gals."

Gareth shuddered. He'd seen the evidence. A recurring image. The marks on Iris Mahoney's skin. As she was dying, she'd tried to tell them. B.B. Brian Bolton. Not Barrington-Brown. If only he'd not let himself get tunnel vision …

Looking at the man, he looked sane now. Focused. Alert. He'd have to recommend a psychiatric evaluation before he could forward the paperwork to the CPS. There were issues here that needed to be addressed, and despite the havoc this man had caused, Gareth wouldn't be doing his job if he didn't ensure he got all the help he needed. As much as he wanted to inflict the most terrible, painful death on the man sitting opposite him, he had to be a police detective and do his job to the best of his capabilities. Susan would expect no less.

Gareth closed his file.

But there was one more thing he needed to know.

"Why Susan Connolly?"

"Isn't it obvious?"

The throw-away comment sent blood surging through his brain. "Not to me."

"Part of the clan. She had to die."

Chapter X

Awen stood looking out at the rushing waters and the grandeur of the mountains on the mainland opposite. Marcus's body was safely interred in a grave alongside her father's and now she had one final act to complete.

In among the Roman's possessions, she'd found a pack of letters, a bag of gold coins and a bronze statue. She wanted to bury these items in a safe place, somewhere they may be found one day and passed onto relevant friends and family. She'd only read the first letter, her stomach turning as Oibhne's basic Latin interpreted the man's love and references to Titus. These letters were important to someone out there, and although she couldn't exactly march back to Segontium and hand them over to the Roman General, she could transport them across the water to the mainland, where they were more likely to be found by his own people.

She lugged a heavy sack of Roman gold onto her shoulder. Around her person, she carried all of the treasure her father had amassed during his lifetime. Even her mother's precious jewellery, rings of garnet and brooches of pearl, were included. She hoped in their final resting place they would be of great importance, more than any benefit she alone would receive. Only time would tell, but time was one thing she didn't have. Time was running out. Terrible tales of rape and murder reached the commune every day. The Roman army was stretching out across the island, pillaging every farm and hamlet they came upon.

She turned and smiled at Aibhne, Ked's betrothed, brother to Oibhne. She had few friends at the moment among the Druids, but the brothers had remained solid allies; she knew talk was of her mind being affected by the Roman traitor. She could only hope her final deeds helped restore her faith in the eyes of people who meant so much to her.

"You've left your brother instructions at the stone?" asked Awen.

Aibhne nodded. "He will do a fine job. Latin or Ogham. He's the best engraver on Mona."

"Good. I owe you. You and Ked both. Will you tell Ked I've left her something beneath my bed?"

Aibhne dragged the boat down to the water's edge, waiting for Awen to step aboard, before pushing off into the choppy water. "Why? You can tell her yourself when we return, no?"

Awen nodded but remained silent.

The small boat bobbed and turned on the tide, even though Aibhne assured her the water was at its slackest. Solid ground couldn't arrive soon enough, and, as Awen helped pull the boat through the clinging mud to cover between the sand dunes, she realised how different Mona looked from this side of the water.

Keeping low in the long grass, Aibhne scanned the area for any sign of Roman activity. The woods grew almost down to the water's edge, and Awen was pleased to see the first clearing they came to was enclosed by ash and oak. In another life, this would have made a perfect temple site, with uninterrupted views across the water to Mona. If she squinted against the sunlight flashing on the surface of the ocean, she believed she could see the site of the stone that marked the opening to the temple grove, and the final resting place of Marcus and her father.

"You have the pick?" asked Awen, holding out her hand.

"Point out the spot, my lady, I'll do the digging."

Awen shook her head. "You keep watch."

Soon the hole was as deep as her thighs. Awen dropped the sack of Roman gold into the bottom of the hole, then unwrapped the heavy leather packets from around her waist and placed the gold her father had collected over the years - goblets, pendants and her mother's jewellery on top. Over that she added the hessian sack Aibhne had given her, which he said contained the spoils of war Celt tribesmen collected from Roman soldiers cut down in the initial invasion of the island. The battle where her father had lost his life. She wanted none of it. Surely the gods would have more use for it.

On the top of that, she placed the leather satchel that contained Marcus's possessions, letters and gold coins. Finally, she positioned the tiny bronze figure he'd worn around his neck next to her mother's precious amber eagle. Both miniatures stared up at her, gazes unblinking in the sunshine.

She clambered up from her knees and pushed the soil back into the hole until every object was covered. She stamped down on the earth, and from her pocket removed ten precious mistletoe seeds, planting them in a circle in the dark earth. She mumbled an incantation as she sprinkled a final dusting of soil over the seeds. If this didn't appease the Roman gods and keep her island safe, surely nothing would.

Aibhne was still crouched at the perimeter of the trees, almost lost in the long grass.

"All clear?" she asked.

"Eerily so. It's quieter than it's been in a long time. I'd almost think the Romans had turned tail and fled."

Awen laughed, but it was humourless. "I doubt we could be so lucky. My father always said the gold route across to Eire was the main reason the Romans wanted Mona. They won't give up their supply route so easy."

Aibhne shrugged. "Well, there's certainly nothing to be seen this side of Mona. Not a boat has passed along the channel. It's a puzzle."

"Well, let us take advantage and get back across."

"You're all finished?"

Awen nodded, taking a deep breath of salty air as she gazed up at the green mountains for the last time.

Aibhne was right. His brother had done a wonderful job on the standing stone. It stood like a proud marker pointing the way both to her father's final resting place, behind her on his beloved Mona, and in the opposite direction, across the water to the mainland and the offering she'd made to the gods.

Awen sighed. She felt replete. Her job here was done.

Almost.

"Thank you both, so much." She gripped Aibhne's hand, then replicated the gesture with his brother, Oibhne. "Ked has your payment. Safe journey home, both of you."

Aibhne frowned. "You're not coming with us? Ked said nothing about leaving you here, I'm not sure it's safe –"

"You said yourself it was almost as if the Roman army had been wiped clean from Mona." Awen smiled and held up a hand to silence him as objections sprang to his lips. "I'll be fine. I promise you. I wish to spend a few moments alone with Cadadius."

"Then we shall wait –"

"No, please. I wish to watch the stars rise one final time with my father. I was robbed of a funeral. Please, do this for me now."

Eventually, with a vow to return in the morning if she wasn't safe in her bed when Ked arrived to rouse her, the brothers departed. For the first time in a long time, Awen was completely alone. She ran her hand against the rough coldness of the stone. The Ogham markings on the sea-side detailing her father's funeral site, and the Latin inscription on the near side pointing to the offering she'd interred on the far shore.

She walked through the archway of oak branches, sitting on the strip of grass between the two graves; her father on her left and Marcus on her right. Finally, she felt at home. After all the tears and turmoil, now at last, a sense of peace. As the shadows lengthened and the moon and stars rose in front of her, Awen knew the time had come for her final act. The only thing she had left to offer the gods in the hope of a peaceful and prosperous future for her people and their lands.

Awen kissed her fingertips and pressed them into the petals of lavender, bluebells, vervain and fireweed that covered her father's grave. She was pleased to see there was already a small pile of white marble balls and quartz pebbles piling at the foot of the grave, a sign of numerous visitors. She hoped wherever his soul rested now, that he was happy, and a small part of him would remember her forever.

Perhaps in the Otherworld, they may be reunited. That more than any other thought, gave her the motivation to proceed.

She pulled the short sword she'd recovered from Marcus's uniform from the sheath attached to her belt, and marched forward into the moonlight. When she reached the standing stone, she took a deep breath, fixed her eyes on the bright orb of the moon, and plunged the knife into her left breast.

The pain came in stages. Bearable at first, then hot and intense. When her legs began to tremble, she slid to her knees. Staring forward as her breathing shallowed, she recalled the words Cadadius said in her last vision ... *you must sacrifice your own needs.* Sacrifice. Well, this would be her final, ultimate act of sacrifice.

"I pray, Hu the Mighty, take my soul. I give it to you now with honour. And in return, I beg you grant peace to the Druids of *Mona Insulis* so future generations may flourish and prosper."

Awen coughed as pain began to flood her body while warm blood coursed down her stomach, dripping down her legs.

She licked the blood from her lips. "Grant them wisdom,

creativity and love."

With a final smile to the glowing moon, she slumped back against the stone.

Closed her eyes.

And at last felt a true and lasting peace.

Epilogue

It had the feeling of an interment. Grief heavy in the air. To a passer-by this small group of people, arranged in tight bunches around a rectangular hole in the ground, would look exactly like mourners attending the funeral of some distant relative.

There were no tears. But plenty of emotion.

Gareth looked around the chosen few. Hand-picked to preside over today's important proceedings. The academia kept themselves to themselves, positioned in an orderly row along one edge of the coffin-shaped trench. All wellies and shorts, torn jumpers and bad hair, beards and glasses – they buzzed with an almost embarrassed collective excitement, muted by the recognition that tragedy at the hands of one of their own had led them here.

On his side of the trench, the atmosphere was far less charged, far more sombre. Curiosity was evident, but it was combined with layers of confusion. Even now, almost a month after his last visit to Sacred Oaks Farm, grief was still a major factor in many lives. Adrian Bolton had turned up at the farm to everyone's surprise and stood alone in the shade of a gnarled oak tree. He seemed to have retreated into his shell, and ignored all attempts at eye contact. His father's multiple murder charge and Megan's death had been more than he could cope with, resolutely refusing in interviews to discuss his mother. Gareth had spent much time persuading Adrian to get help and speak to a trained professional. An irony that wasn't missed.

Gareth now admitted to himself he'd need to talk in time. But not yet. When he thought of Susan at the moment, it was as much as he could do to hold back his tears. And when he tried to imagine her face or her voice, the images and sounds seemed to twist with memories of Megan – so it had come to the point where he couldn't remember with clarity what either woman looked like. The thought of opening his heart to anyone at the moment would be too much like torture. But he would. He'd promised Susan and that was one promise he'd no intention of breaking.

His attention was drawn as a muddy archaeologist slid a blue tarpaulin to one side. At his side, Chris stifled a yawn and Gareth couldn't help but smile. Chris was bored to tears, but Gareth needed him today. The internal investigation into the case had begun and his involvement was under scrutiny. Even with Macrae's support, things weren't looking bright. But the truth was … he couldn't bring himself to care. His disciplinary hearing was scheduled for the following day, until then, his whole career hung in the balance. He pretended to care. But all he really cared about was his loss.

Susan. The funeral had been one of the hardest days of his life. He couldn't come to terms with Bolton's words. Susan was a Druid descendant. Did that mean *he* was under some kind of spell? It all seemed ridiculous. But then, he'd spent many sleepless nights since her death, analysing things about her. How she had some kind of gut instinct that always seemed spot on. How he trusted her judgment. Yes, she was an incredible pathologist, of that there was no doubt. But was there something more? And if so, what? Did he really believe she was having a conversation with the dead whilst she was chopping up their mortal remains in the lab? Ridiculous. Maybe. But was it any more ridiculous than *The Psychic Detective* who it appeared solved cold-case crimes with the help of victims from beyond the grave.

He shook his head, tried to sweep the thoughts away, remembering what Professor Bolton had said. They'd never know. That knowledge was not for the likes of them. It was something the Servants of Truth would take with them to their graves until the time came again for their powers to be put to use. Gareth hoped that would not be in his lifetime.

He leaned forward to catch a glimpse of Anna Brown at the far end of the trench. She gripped her father's hand. Dressed in ripped black jeans and jumper, she balanced as close to the edge of the hole as Barrington-Brown would allow, concentration focused on its contents. He wondered if she was the guardian now. Who else was left? Mairwen Thomas, of course, and her mysterious daughter. Hettie Fielding. And who knew how many more, keeping to the shadows, watching from the sidelines. He scanned the small crowd. Were there more here?

Somehow this day felt special; like a final meeting of people drawn together in the face of adversity, they were here. Grouped around a hollow in a wood of sacred oak trees, just like the Druids had done thousands of years earlier on the exact same spot.

For Gareth, it was a kind of closure. The pressing need to know the treasure was real. That people hadn't lost their lives on a whim and a fancy of some psychopathic professor. That Susan's death hadn't been completely in vain.

The copse had been a hive of activity since his last visit, police called in within hours of the commencement of the dig. Security immediately tightened. Once the artefacts started to come out of the ground, they ran like liquid gold, no end in sight. And here were the final pieces in situ, ready to be lifted by the experts.

Eager to see the treasures of the past for the first time for over almost two thousand years, the crowd pushed forward as the archaeologist pointed out a huge gold goblet, still half-buried in the sandy soil. A delicate bracelet and matching tiara with inlaid garnets had been semi-excavated, and were now ready to lift. It was fascinating. Gareth was enthralled by the delicate pieces, the precision of the designs, and the beauty of each object.

He walked along the row of white plastic finds trays, where pieces lifted earlier in the day were available to view. He bent to examine a cluster of small gold brackets.

"Sword pommels. From Roman swords called Spathas, by the size and shape. These are part of the decoration that held the blade to the handle. We've had twelve so far, massive amount. It's clear the swords have been dismantled and separated into different components. The blades aren't here; they would have been reused, more than like. Anything of value, like this gold, was collected ready to melt down."

The voice brimmed with excitement. Gareth looked up with a polite smile; one of the head archaeologists, who'd introduced himself earlier, grinned back.

"It's amazing. Not just Roman finds, but strong evidence of Druids too. Dozens of small white marble balls, boar teeth pendants, quartz pebbles – all known Druidic offerings. Here, look at this." The bearded man bent and picked up a perfectly-crafted statue of a bird. "It's amber, one of the Druids' most cherished stones. Look, a tiny eagle. And next to it, this small bronze statue of Hercules which is clearly Roman. Almost like they were placed together for a reason, something symbolic. But these groups were such bitter enemies … I've never heard of such a mix buried together before. I hope one day we can discover the story behind the hoard."

"You seem happy with the dig, Professor?"

"Happy probably isn't the right word, not considering what led us here …"

"I mean the finds. I hope they're everything you'd dreamed of."

"And more. I can't tell you. It will bring a whole new chapter to history in this area. We even found Ogham writing, as well as Latin, on the marker stone. This find is quite literally rewriting history."

Gareth clenched his fingers. There was something in the

man's voice that took him back to that interview room, facing Professor Bolton. The passion. Obsession. *'She was part of the clan. She had to die.'*

He had to get away. He stood, brushed the knees of his trousers.

"I'm glad everything has worked out for you. And the university."

Gareth headed towards the wooden pallets laid out end to end to form a pathway out of the wood.

"Detective Parry?"

A slight, blonde figure blocked his path.

He forced a smile. "Anna. How are you?"

Anna Brown returned the smile, but it didn't brighten her face or eyes. "Okay. Not great, but you know, time's a healer. Being involved in this project is a help, it keeps my mind busy."

"Good."

Anna lowered her head. "I miss Iris. And my grandmother. Sometimes it feels like I'm cursed – all the women I love die too soon. Everyone leaves me."

Gareth swallowed, focused on his shoes. Bolton's voice again. *'It's almost like the lineage is cursed. Maybe they know that, maybe it's in their teaching and it makes them resilient.'*

"Will you come and visit soon?" said Anna. "I'd like us to stay friends."

The question brought him up short. "I don't know, Anna. I'll try. I may not be around much longer, but if I'm still in the area –"

Anna's small hand reached out, gripped his sleeve. "Your hearing?"

He nodded, trying to ignore the surge of warmth feeding into his body from her fingers. "How do you know –?"

She put a black-painted fingernail to her lips. "It will be okay. You've nothing to worry about. In fact, you're going to get a promotion."

Gareth blinked. "What?"

She nodded, smiled. "It's all going to be fine. I promise. You have my word."

With that she released him, and the cold emptiness he'd carried for the past month filled his body again. She turned away, retraced her steps along the makeshift pathway.

"Anna!"

She turned her head, but kept walking.

"How do you know?" he called.

Anna smiled. "Susan told me."

Gareth choked back a sob, rammed his fist to his mouth to stop the scream that threatened to follow.

"And she said to tell you to make sure you come and visit me soon. You will, won't you?"

Gareth stared at the girl, then nodded.

"Good. See you soon, then."

And with a wave of her hand, she was gone.

THE END

Thank you for reading
a Triskele Book.

Enjoyed *Complicit*? Here's what you can do next.

If you loved the book and would like to help other readers find Triskele Books, please write a short review on the website where you bought the book. Your help in spreading the word is much appreciated and reviews make a huge difference to helping new readers find good books.

More novels from Triskele Books coming soon. You can sign up to be notified of the next release and other news here:
www.triskelebooks.co.uk

If you are a writer and would like more information on writing and publishing, visit **www.triskelebooks.blogspot.com** and **www.wordswithjam.co.uk**, which are packed with author and industry professional interviews, links to articles on writing, reading, libraries, the publishing industry and indie-publishing.

Connect with us:
Email admin@triskelebooks.co.uk
Twitter @triskelebooks
Facebook www.facebook.com/triskelebooks

Also from Triskele Books

TREAD SOFTLY

"You don't attract trouble. You go looking for it."

Disheartened by her recent performance, Beatrice Stubbs takes a sabbatical from the Metropolitan Police for a gourmet tour of Northern Spain. In Vitoria, she encounters a distant acquaintance. Beautiful, bloody-minded journalist Ana Herrero is onto a story.

Beatrice, scenting adventure, offers her expertise. The two women are sucked into a mystery of missing persons, violent threats, mutilated bodies and industrial-scale fraud. They are out of their depth. With no official authority and unsure who to trust, they find themselves up to their necks in corruption, blackmail and Rioja.

Beatrice calls for the cavalry. The boys are back, and this time, it's a matter of taste. But when her instincts prove fallible, Beatrice discovers that justice is matter of interpretation.

TRISTAN AND ISEULT

In a land of fog and desperate tribes, Tristan fights to protect western Briton from Saxon invaders. In the wake of battle, he returns to Kernow bearing grave news, and the order of power shifts.

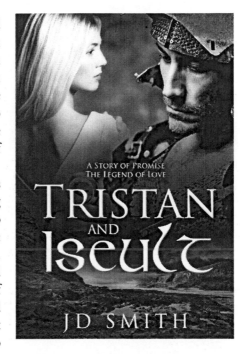

A STORY OF PROMISE
THE LEGEND OF LOVE

As Tristan defends the west, his uncle, King Mark, faces enemies to the east beyond the sea: the Irish Bloodshields. Mark is determined to unite the tribes of Briton and Ireland and forge an alliance that would see an end to war and the beginnings of peace.

Iseult, the daughter of Irish kings and a woman of the blood, resigns herself to her inevitable fate: marriage to Lord Morholt. A bloody duel changes her course, and she finds herself stranded on the coast of Kernow bringing with her the possibility of peace. But when she loses her heart to one man and marries another, her future and that of Briton flutters grey.

Three people and a hope that will never fade, this is a story of promise; the legend of love.

Also from Triskele Books

GIFT OF THE RAVEN

The people of the Haida Gwaii tell the legend of the raven – the trickster who brings the gift of light into the world.

Canada. 1971.

Terry always believed his father would return one day and rescue him from his dark and violent childhood. That's what Indian warriors were supposed to do. But he's thirteen now and doesn't believe in anything much.

Yet his father is alive. Someone has tracked him down. And Terry is about to come face to face with the truth about his own past and about the real nature of the gift of the raven.